The Napoleon Complex

About the Author

E.M. Davey is a 33-year-old journalist specialising in undercover investigative journalism. He is currently working for BBC Radio 4 and has presented on the World Service. When not working he enjoys travel to far-flung and occasionally dangerous spots to inspire his fiction, and just for the heck of it. He has visited forty-seven countries (and counting) and while researching this book he was charged by an enraged hippopotamus. History has been his lifelong passion. This is his second thriller.

ALSO PUBLISHED BY THE AUTHOR

Foretold by Thunder

FORTHCOMING

The Sapien Paradox

@EdDavey1
www.emdavey.com

The Napoleon Complex

E.M. DAVEY

Duckworth Overlook

First published in 2016 by
Duckworth Overlook

LONDON
30 Calvin Street, London E1 6NW
T: 020 7490 7300
E: info@duckworth-publishers.co.uk
www.ducknet.co.uk
For bulk and special sales please contact
sales@duckworth-publishers.co.uk,
or write to us at the above address.

2

978-0-7156-5108-7

A catalogue record for this book is
available from the British Library

Set in Minion by Tetragon, London
Printed and bound in Great Britain

For Anna

Contents

complex – noun.

1. an intricate or complicated association or assemblage of related things, parts, units, etc.
2. *Psychology.* a system of interrelated, emotion-charged ideas, feelings, memories, and impulses that is usually repressed and that gives rise to abnormal or pathological behaviour.
3. a fixed idea; an obsessive notion.

Far-called, our navies melt away;
On dune and headland sinks the fire:
Lo, all our pomp of yesterday
Is one with Nineveh and Tyre!

Rudyard Kipling
for Queen Victoria's Diamond Jubilee

Every quotation attributed to a historical figure in that which follows is genuine.

Part One

Ennui

(JAKE)

Shake your chains how you may, the man is too great for you.
Goethe, on Napoleon

Prologue

The explorer was dying at last. His fever was coming back harder this time, and when he stood the world began rotating: mud huts and reeds, baobab trees and acacia, all of it billowing around him. From the far side of the village he heard a snatch of boisterous song, the blast of an antelope horn. No steam train could get him out of here, no horse – the tsetse flies saw to those. There probably wasn't a horse in a thousand miles. The rasping of the bush seemed to mesh with the heat and humidity to become a single thing. Something like panic hit the explorer then. He was destitute, a prisoner of the wilderness.

It had rained for weeks on end, and the clouds unravelled towards the horizon before becoming entwined once more in a knot of black. As he staggered towards his hut the fever peaked in a spasm of hallucination. He heard clicking in his ears, as if he were deep underwater. There was a rumble of thunder, and at this the explorer emitted a low moan.

He couldn't resist looking back.

As if in reply the lightning broke: a trunk of violet-white streaking from the north-west, spreading its forks instantaneously across the sky, like a nervous system spreading out at immense speed. The boom was maddening – it shook the ground – and the explorer clamped his hands over his ears and howled.

Industry was a known cure for the fever. He had to keep up the pugnacious spirit, set an example for the natives. He fumbled for his field diary, the ink he had made from tree sap and berries. Mosquitoes formed a haze in the candlelight and he swatted them away without interest.

The journal fell open on a recent entry.

*No rain fell today for a wonder, but the lower tier of clouds
still drifts past from N.W. The stratum of clouds is composed
from cottony masses, the edges spread out as if on an elec-
trical machine.*

He turned the page, blinking away the hallucinations, and in a
trembling script wrote what he thought was the date:

23rd January, 1873.

Somewhere out in the darkness came the tortured growl of a
lion. The explorer paused, panting with exertion. He whispered
the next sentence to himself twice before admitting it on paper:
I don't know where we are.
Another crack of thunder echoed across the savanna.

*

Another crack of thunder echoed across the Gulf of Thailand.
"I don't know what I'm doing here," whispered Jake Wolsey.
The journalist was standing alone on the balcony of a beach
hut in Thailand. It was 5 am, and he had been up all night. He
was bare-chested, breathing slowly in and out as if trying to
absorb the hedonism of this place through the skin, by osmosis.
Koh Phan Ngan was the most lawless island in the gulf, but also
the most beautiful. The mountains had a Jurassic quality, ptero-
dactyl wings of jungle unfolding from the sea. He was living in
a playground for adults – wild deeds would be taking place that
very moment. The sand was a sickle of silver and ridges of rock
and jungle flanked the cove, silhouetted against the moonlight.
Candlelit gangplanks connected the huts, perched upon giant
boulders of granite, like something from Tolkien. This was the
most magical spot he had discovered in three decades on the
planet. It was *his* beach, his special place. So he had come back, in
the hope that being here would help him. For Jake Wolsey, who

could have broken the biggest story in the history of journalism but chose not to, was undergoing a personal crisis.

Yet coming back hadn't helped him.

It had made things worse.

"Jake?" Her voice wheedled him from the gloom of their hut. "Are you coming to bed?"

He ran a hand through long blond hair, matted with sea salt. "In a bit."

"Hey, you ..."

"In a bit, baby."

The lightning had moved away: mushrooms of light diffracting over the horizon, like a First World War bombardment.

What's out there?

Bare feet thudded onto wood; planks creaked as she approached. "Storm watching again?"

"Uh-huh."

An arm snaked around Jake's neck; the tip of a tongue brushed his throat. "Come on, Jakey. Bed time."

Her name was Chloë and she had once been a journalist too, based in Hong Kong. She had quit to become a diving instructor and after she'd packed that in too they had met. He had always found the name Chloë sexy. There was something *creamy* about it, like rich latte. Chloës were meant to be unattainable to him, far beyond reach. It would have been daft to resist her – bagging a girl with such weapons-grade sex appeal was near-miraculous. But Chloë was not Jenny. Jenny had left him.

And Jenny was ... Jenny was ...

The arm pulled at him, the pull turned into a tug, and Jake allowed himself to be led into the hut. Empty Coke bottles clinked at his feet, rolling across the balcony which wore the signs of long habitation: salt-curled paperbacks, a washing line, candle stubs melted onto the planks. As Chloë led him into the darkness a bar of moonlight fell sideways across her face at eye level, so she momentarily resembled a ninja. She smiled and closed the door.

Jenny was god knows where by now.

1

Jenny was in a restaurant in Bangkok when she saw the boy who changed everything. This was a woman of unimpeachable self-discipline, and most observers would have noticed no change in her body language. But on spotting him she sat with a frisson of extra poise, like a cat in that half-second before it jumps, unaware of its own body despite the static crackling through it.

Jenny Frobisher looked different. She had brown contact lenses in and her hair was dyed chestnut; she wore fisherman's trousers and a single dreadlock that her mother would have hated. What would Mum have thought of her new life? Jenny had been pondering this question as she dined alone. She worked for a charity, providing advocacy to village girls tricked into entering Bangkok's sex trade. That led briefly to thoughts of Jake: his loathing for the business. She recalled a story he'd told her about being talked into one of the strip clubs as an eighteen-year-old. How upset he had been by it all, almost in tears.

Through the swell of Israeli travellers, elderly Brits and waitresses in miniskirts, she saw the boy.

In his mid-twenties; scruffy brown hair; tall and handsome in that well-bred, Berkshire way. He was playing the gap-year hippy and sported a Glastonbury wristband – nice touch. But at home this breed wore tailored shirts and cashmere jumpers, timeworn in the fashion of families too affluent to care much about appearance. His limbs were bronzed and lean, his teeth very white. An undeniably beautiful boy.

Jenny examined him using her peripheral vision. She had learned the technique at MI6: how to observe with your pupils fixed ahead as the picture is filled in, like a computer downloading detail. Once she was certain, Jenny placed her knife and fork together. She glanced over the road, where a tuk-tuk

driver snoozed in his three-wheeled contraption. She produced
a banknote and tucked it under her glass.

Then she *leaped* out of the restaurant.

The boy was on his feet, but he hadn't paid his bill and waiters
pulled him back. Already Jenny was on the far side of the street.
She planted her left foot on the front wheel of the tuk-tuk. Her
right hit the bonnet with a *prang*, startling the driver awake. Her
third stride took her onto the canopy of the vehicle and in two
more bounds she had propelled herself off the back and over a
six-foot wall.

She landed on grass. The Wat Chana Songkhram lay ahead.
Somehow it felt cooler in the temple grounds, away from the
lights and licentiousness of the street.

The boy was scrabbling over the wall.

Jenny fled, panther-like, through the compound. But he was
a sprinter and the gap between them was closing. She leapt onto
the dais, eliciting a scandalised hand clap from an octogenarian
monk. Orange-robed figures descended on them from all directions, flames converging on a single point. Jenny reached the far
side of the compound, hurtled over another wall and dropped
into an alleyway. Cockroaches scuttled away from her feet and
pools of some noxious liquid glimmered in the streetlight. Two
palms slapped on the wall behind her.

As Jenny ran the alley widened into a street gym. The pair
raced through a press of Muay Thai fighters, brushing limbs and
ducking hands. The boy made a grab for her, grasping a handful
of shirt. Her front buttons pinged off, the sleeves turned inside
out and suddenly Jenny was attached to it only by her wrists,
arms wrenched backward like a sprinter crossing the finishing
line. Jenny strained against the leash; with a ripping noise she
was free again, wearing only a T-shirt. The pair streaked from the
alleyway into the choking beeping melange of Bangkok proper.
Khao San Road, dead ahead.

At 10 pm backpacker central oozed with tourists. Stalls sold
bongs and throwing stars and cocktails were distributed from

an open-top VW Combi; women in the costume of the northern hill tribes palmed off trinkets on the uninitiated. The bedlam was illuminated by a blaze of neon signs: this was a dystopian hive of the future, addled on sex and drugs. The smell was of LPG fumes and cheap pad Thai noodles, greasily sweet. Each pace took them deeper through a babel of tongues. The boy made another grab for her, raking his fingernails down her back and drawing blood.

"What do you think you're playing at, bru?"

He was being surrounded by burly Afrikaners, buffeted from one to the other. The last thing Jenny heard was, *Mistreating a lady?*

As she turned away the first punch went in. A figure emerged before her and she jerked to a halt.

During her years with the British Secret Service, Jenny had encountered thugs and fanatics and wicked individuals. But standing in her path – grinning like a dog grins, his arms outspread – was the person she feared most. A man who was supposed to be dead.

2

As the woman he still loved fought to preserve her liberty, Jake was lying on the beach and reading a book. It was about the Battle of Trafalgar and a quote from Nelson's chaplain brought him up short.

> *Our dear admiral is killed. Chaps that fought like the devil sit down and cry like a wretch. I am become stupid with grief for what I have lost.*

He stared out to sea. He breathed out long into his fist and a shudder went through him.

Stupid with grief for what I have lost.

He picked up a handful of sand and let it bleed away. His twenties had drifted past either going out with girls he didn't love or loving girls he didn't go out with. Then he'd met the love of his life – and let her slip through his fingers. Why had she ended it? He didn't know.

Jake had found this sanctuary aged eighteen. That was the era of Alex Garland, when legions of backpackers were tramping across Thailand after their own slice of *The Beach*. By sheer good fortune he'd found it – a spot discovered only by word of mouth, where the police were paid off and residents dreaded the creep of tarmac towards their corner of the island. Years later he and Jenny would arrive as fugitives on this beach, before one terrible day she had summoned him to sit next to her on the bed.

Pat, pat, pat.

He had not known then that each touch of the mattress was a tremor preceding a devastating earthquake which would reshape his life completely.

I've been thinking about the future. I need to do something more than this with my life. I've fallen out of love with you, Jake. I'm leaving you. I'm sorry.

For their mutual security, Jenny ordered him not to contact her. Their panic button would be an online message board for car enthusiasts: if either was in trouble, they should post a coded message. That done, she left him to his beach. Her last words to him: "Stand tall, Jake. Stand tall."

He set off up the mountain, heading in a straight line through the jungle until he was weeping and staggering and torn to shreds.

That was six months ago, and here he was. In his pre-Chloë life, Jake had slept with two attractive girls and two unattractive ones. That made him an absolute slag by Victorian standards, but by the barometer of twenty-first-century London it wasn't a particularly impressive tally. He was quite good looking, but when it came to seduction he was an absolute duffer. For some reason he was incapable of flirtation: not for him the mystic arts of the forearm touch, nor the look that simmered with meaning. Of the two attractive girls, one was a fluke and the other was Jenny. Heartbreak clichés Jake had ticked off so far included: crying, long walks, a risky telephone call to his mother. Jesus, he'd written *poetry*.

After a few months, Jake decided a new lover might help him. With history as a guide, he was braced for the long haul. But strangely enough, this time it was easy. For along came Chloë Fleming.

Jake was playing Grandmaster Flash's *The Message* on his balcony. Chloë complimented his taste – and it went from there. She had a vaguely Italian look with eyes somewhere between green and blue, and long slim legs with dimples beneath each knee that he found inexplicably attractive. He had looked up her bylines in the *South China Post*, and it was clear she'd been a gifted reporter. She was from Salisbury (his neck of the woods) and they shared interests in history, surfing and old school hip-hop. Were it not for the fact that she loved getting wasted, she might have been designed for Jake. Not only that, she *actually liked him*. If Chloë couldn't cure him of heartbreak, nobody could. Jake respected her; he wanted to fall in love with her. He felt if he could achieve this, Jenny would be behind him. He could look upon their love affair with nostalgia instead of tragedy.

Chloë came to sit with him now, producing the *Bangkok Post* and a joint. The lead story was about Ebola – another outbreak was raging in West Africa and Sierra Leone's government couldn't cope. Banditry and rebellion had sprung up in the vacuum, rival warlords turning on each other; Upcountry had become a cyclone of bloodletting and rapine.

Jake didn't read the article, it was all too depressing. But an item on page five caught his eye: the new British Prime Minister Victor Milne had announced the construction of the biggest dockyard in the world on an artificial island in the Thames

Estuary; Milne wanted Britain to dominate global trade once more. Fat chance. That ship has sailed, pal.

When Jake turned the page he gasped. The newspaper rattled in his hands.

"My god," he managed.

The British businessman and historian Michael Beloff has been killed by a bolt of lightning in Jerusalem, his spokesman has announced.

Mr Beloff, who made his fortune in fashion and telecoms before turning his hand to popular history, was struck dead in the garden of his second home by the Wailing Wall yesterday evening, during a grandchild's bar mitzvah. Mr Beloff, whose recent biography of Napoleon was a best-seller ...

Before Chloë could read the story Jake was away and sprinting across the beach.

"What's the matter?" she shouted as he flew across the sand ahead of her. "Why is this important, Jake?"

He was kneeling in their hut when she caught him. The contents of his backpack were strewn across the floor; a yellowing *Telegraph* article was in his hand. Jake's eyes worked across the story like the needle of a seismometer and he sank onto his knuckles.

An important painting of Napoleon has been bought at auction by Michael Beloff, the mobile phone and retail billionaire. The Peace of Amiens, by Antoine Devosge, was painted to commemorate the 1802 treaty signed between Britain and France after an astonishing run of victories made Napoleon the most powerful man in Europe. The peace may not have lasted long, but ..."

The cutting was eighteen months old. The painter had portrayed France as a new Rome; Napoleon assumed the role of Emperor

Augustus. In Napoleon's hand was a scroll, and on that scroll were characters.

Etruscan characters.

Jake was kneading thin air between his thumb and forefinger – as if there was an *ether* to be felt in it. He stared out of their hut, past a gibbous moon hanging low over the sea which winked at him like the eye of a hyena. Past the Milky Way, to outer space.

"They're looking for it again," he said.

Someone was at the door.

"Mister Jake, Mister Jake." It was a teenager who worked at the bar. "Letter for you."

He laughed uneasily. "I don't think so."

"For you, for you." she insisted.

"But nobody knows I'm here. *How the hell can there be a letter for me?*"

3

Evelyn Parr, senior MI6 case officer, stared out over Horse Guards Parade. From this high-up corner of the Foreign Office she could see right into Number 11 Downing Street. Whiteboards were visible on the lower floors, though curtains obscured the view into the Chancellor's flat. Commonwealth flags fluttered along St James's Park and Parr noted the film across the windows that would keep the glass together in a bombing.

"They call this the 'Naughty Room.'" When C smiled it was only the skin moving, not the muscles underneath. "It's where ambassadors from abroad await a ticking off when they've been summoned by the Foreign Secretary."

The chamber had been designed to impose the might of Great Britain on lesser nations, and no expense had been spared on the antique furniture and embossed wallpaper. A captured Enigma machine was a reminder of past glories.

"Like waiting to see the headmaster," said Parr, with a faint smile of her own.

Sir Dennis Amaoko had just been installed as the new Chief of MI6. He was the same age as Parr, although Ghanaian genes and an ascetic lifestyle left him looking half that. C wore a linen suit and brogues from Jermyn Street. There was something python-like about his head: the way it arched down from his collar, the smoothness of the skin. He adjusted his wire-frame spectacles and loosed another skin-deep smile.

"Feeling nervous?" C's accent would have graced the breakfast table at Windsor.

"A bit," Parr admitted. "I've never met a Prime Minister."

"Well, don't be. Everything you did was in the national interest. Victor's a rational man, he'll see that."

There was a cough in the doorway, and there was the Foreign Secretary, Nigel Edmonds. New Foreign Secretary, new C, new Prime Minister. Parr glanced out of the window once more. The changing of the guard.

"Are we ready to go?" said Edmonds.

An order, not a question: the politician didn't like being kept out of the loop like this. The spies were supposed to be *his* foot soldiers, and it peeved him that their secrets were only for the ears of his boss. Perhaps escorting them to Number 10 would claw back some authority. As they left, Parr glanced at the mural in the corridor – *Britannia Pacificatrix*, by Goetze. Britannia stood before a classical colonnade, lording it over supplicating allies. Even when it was painted the image had been wishful thinking, for the sun had already begun to set.

A second mural guarded the door to the Foreign Secretary's room, and when Parr saw it her heart fluttered.

A hooded man, a scroll. The word, *Silence*.

Out on Downing Street she saw tourists peering through the gates, and she let silvery hair fall in front of her face. With her silver trouser suit too she resembled some sort of armour-plated warrior of the service, hardened and implacable. The world's most famous front door opened and amazingly there was the Prime Minister himself, pulling them over the threshold in a flurry of handshakes and how-do-you-dos.

Victor Milne was the consummate post-modern politician, in that amid this age of PR-coached smoothies he was perceived to be *himself*. He made no secret of a privileged upbringing (St Paul's, then Cambridge), indeed he wore it as a badge of honour. Falling in the sea may have done for Kinnock, but Milne's stumble as he took the stage in the final election debate had merely sealed the national affection. Her Majesty's Opposition was in a terrible mess, and Milne had romped home with the biggest majority his party had enjoyed for decades.

"Don't just stand there gawping, come on in," he blustered. "Have a peek around the old bachelor pad."

The Prime Minister led them upstairs, past portraits of Churchill and Lord Palmerston, and into his private quarters.

"All frightfully formal down below," he explained. "Let me tell you, up here's where the real, straining every sinew graft of keeping Great Britain PLC ticking over goes on."

The flat was stark in its modernity, but dirty plates and empty wine bottles jostled for space on the aluminium surfaces. As the Prime Minister rampaged around the open plan kitchen Parr felt a sudden warmth for him. His brown hair was unfashionably cut and despite his diminutive height he had a vague *bigness* without being either fat or muscular. Sloping shoulders contributed to a shambling gait, yet the whole was somehow likeable, and as Milne made tea Parr noted with professional interest how the mysteries of charisma did their work on her. He gestured to a sofa and banged mugs down on the coffee table – he'd forgotten to remove the teabags and there was an oxbow lake of tea in her saucer. The Prime Minister was a Victorianist; she spotted a study of Kipling on his bookshelf. Next to the tome was Baden-Powell's *Scouting for Boys*.

Milne dismissed his Foreign Secretary.

"Right then," he said once the fuming minister had departed. "Who wants to tell me what the Dickens has been going on in my Secret Service?"

The year before the election, MI6 had been gripped by a scandal. Three officers were killed – the first known fatalities on duty in the history of the service – and a fourth had vanished. A computer wizard from the Secret Intelligence Service's listening post GCHQ was about to face trial for breaching the Official Secrets Act over the affair; much to the fury of the *Guardian*, this would be held behind closed doors. Fleet Street had dubbed the crisis 'Indiana Jones-gate', after another newspaper claimed the deaths were related to an archaeological matter. The journalist who had broken the stories had disappeared too – there was initial speculation he'd been killed. But his family weren't making enough of a fuss for that, and neither was the father of the missing spook. So after a while the nationals decided the pair must have simply 'eloped together'. Now Milne was to get his explanation.

C booted up a laptop. "Watch this," he said. "And – brace yourself, Prime Minister."

The footage was black and white; grit and solar flares pebble-dashed the celluloid. They saw a country garden, men wearing Oxford bags. Everything shook as some adjustment was made to the tripod.

"Where are we?" asked Milne.

"Mytchett Place in Surrey," said Parr. "It was an MI6 safe house during the war."

"Are you ready then, old man?" said a voice off-camera. Amusement lingered in the Received Pronunciation accent. "Let's see what you can do."

A figure wandered out in front of the lens, instantly recognisable with his caterpillar eyebrows and thickset skull.

"Rudolf Hess!" exclaimed Milne. "Hitler's number two. That would make this – what, 1941 or something? Just after the peace flight."

C nodded. "Watch this."

Hess began talking not in German but some other tongue, weird beyond comprehension. It veritably bristled with clicks and pops. His eyes rolled upwards in his head; the garden seemed to darken; there was a furious explosion and the picture over-exposed in a flash of white.

"Bloody hell," exclaimed the voice behind the camera. "I say, is everybody all right?"

When the image reformed the camera lay on its side. Blades of grass protruded in front of the lens, fluttering and out of focus. Smoke rose on the far side of the garden. The whites of Hess's eyes were bloody, but his expression was triumphant. A hand came into shot and the film ended.

"That," said Evelyn Parr, "was Hitler's deputy showing our predecessors how to summon a bolt of lightning."

4

"Why the rush?" said Frank Davis.

An MI6 assassin. Six foot three and built like a piece of agricultural machinery, with a spot of white in otherwise steel-grey hair. He seemed to have acquired a limp. Jenny grabbed a stone Buddha from a stall and threw it at him with considerable violence. But Davis ducked the airborne deity and wagged a finger at her.

"You oughtn't to have done that, love," he said. "Bad karma."

The boy caught up with them, no longer so beautiful. His lip was bleeding, one cheek was grazed and he was missing a shoe. He grabbed Jenny by the biceps, but she sank her teeth into his wrist as hard as she could, where sensitive nerves lie near the surface. With a shriek he let go and she kicked him in the groin, pushing him backwards. She ducked underneath Davis's lunge, then she was sprinting again.

A tuk-tuk idled at the far end of Khao San Road and the driver sat up in in his cab. But Jenny was fifty paces away and the boy was in already in pursuit. He nearly had her, she wasn't going to make it.

A tramp was rummaging in cardboard boxes by the side of the street. He leaned in further and casually extended a leg, kicking out at a handcart of deep-fried insects sold to tourists for drunken consumption. This rolled into the path of the boy who collided with it at twenty miles per hour, becoming one with the object: a ball of white and pink that span through space before hitting the ground with a heart-rending crash. An insectoid rain was launched across the pavement, showering two ladyboys who'd been imperiously sauntering down the street. Scorpions entered handbags. Crickets sought cleavages. Their screams were atrocious and they set upon the boy as he lay dazed on the tarmac: pointed toe to the head and stiletto on a flailing hand. Davis batted the first ladyboy in the face with the back of his fist. The second he grabbed by the throat. Thais descended upon the hooligans, engorged with thoughts of retribution. As the fracas became demented Jenny collapsed into the tuk-tuk which lurched away with a clatter of two-stroke engine, front wheel briefly airborne, spiriting the fugitive away into the megalopolis.

5

A feeling of genuine alarm came over Jake as he handled the envelope, like the first shivers that foreshadow tropical illness. And sure enough, it *was* his name: printed on a white label in small capitals.

"Who gave this to you?" he asked.

"Someone leave it by the bar." A massive grin, then the messenger was off.

This was serious. This might mean he had to leave, tonight.

Jake tore open the envelope; four neat white cards slid into his palm, each bearing a quotation. No letter accompanied the cards, no note of the sender, but they had been prepared with obvious care. Jake's mouth was a perfect oval as he studied the first card from every angle.

"I believe in luck. But a wise man neglects nothing which helps his destiny." – Napoleon Bonaparte

He looked at the next.

"Great men seldom fail in perilous enterprises. Is it because they have good luck that they become great? No, being great they have mastered luck." – Napoleon Bonaparte

Both quotes reminded him of something the Roman historian Polybius had written in the second century BC: it was by very accurately assessing their chances that the Romans conceived and carried out their plan to dominate the world. And Jake of all people knew how Rome was able to calculate its odds with such keenness.

The third also bore a quote from Napoleon.

"At Amiens I truly believed the Fates of France, Europe and myself had been fixed." – Napoleon Bonaparte

There was one more card, and Jake swallowed before turning it over.

"I am the instrument of Providence. She will utilise me as long as I achieve her dreams. After that she will shatter me like a glass." – Napoleon Bonaparte

Fate. Destiny. Providence. The belief in it pulsed through the Little Corporal's every word.

6

Parr told the Prime Minister everything. How in 1933, German archaeologists discovered a tomb in northern Italy that held the remains of a prophet of the ancient Etruscans, whose civilisation was the precursor to Rome. How it also contained several scrolls, sealed into jars with beeswax. How these proved to be the *Disciplina Etrusca*, an Etruscan guide to divining the future through the interpretation of bolts of lightning. How Nazi scientists tested the lore and found that it *actually worked*. How this power had helped the Third Reich excel at diplomatic brinksmanship in the 1930s, enabling Hitler to unleash his unstoppable blitzkrieg. *Lightning war.*

Finally Parr described how this had happened before: for it was Etruscan augury that had enabled the cancerous growth of ancient Rome, an expansion that only ceased after the wholesale burning of pagan texts by the Emperor Constantine, who had first made Christianity the Roman state religion. But Constantine had reckoned without the duplicity of Eusebius, a scholar and closet pagan. Eusebius had hidden copies of the *Disciplina* throughout the Old World, leaving clues in his writings to their location. Almost two millennia later Jake Wolsey had followed them.

One might have expected Milne to have laughed Parr from the room. But he was privy to knowledge of how the last case handler had died at the height of the scandal – struck by lightning on the Tower of London. Milne sensed intuitively that what he had just witnessed was *real*, and he understood then the expression that one's skin crawls.

Parr explained that Hess had become disillusioned with Nazi Germany and fled to Britain with the *Disciplina Etrusca*, hiding it in the Tower where he was held prisoner. He had proven to the Secret Service that he could conjure lightning bolts, but without the scroll itself, prophecy was beyond MI6. For seventy years British agents had hunted the *Disciplina* without success. And then this Jake Wolsey had stumbled upon a declassified document citing Churchill's interest in the 'ancient Etruscan matter'. The whole thing had damn near been blown into the open.

It was a few minutes until the politician collected himself. "What's the science behind all this?"

"You might have heard of dark matter?" said Parr.

"Yes. No. Not really. I'm a man of letters."

"Dark matter is what stops the universe collapsing in on itself due to the weight of gravity," she said. "A theoretical concept until recently, when it was proved by a scientist at CERN."

"Now a dead scientist," interjected C.

"What he detected was a universe-wide grid made of tiny filaments of energy. This network acts as a super-fluid, conducting waves faster than speed of light. It developed sentience, functioning as a celestial supercomputer capable of predicting the movement of every atom in existence."

"Developed sentience?" said Milne. "I'm sorry, but how and why would that happen?"

"In our world, things tend towards disorder," said Parr. "For example, if I dropped this mug it would smash into smithereens and tea would go everywhere. Chunks of porcelain and pools of liquid don't leap up and form themselves into a cup of tea. But at the level of the atom and the quark, the reverse is true. Particles tend to *order themselves*. Now, imagine a near-infinity of filaments, arranged on a matrix the size of the universe – with thirteen billion years to develop. This CERN guy reckoned the emergence of sentience – of *consciousness* – was a certainty."

"Foretelling the fates of men was a …" C looked troubled. "A *game* that it played. And this was the prescience Bronze Age Etruscan augurs learned to tap into. It spoke in energy, its own mother element. In bolts of lightning, to be precise."

"Why were Hess's eyes all bloody?" asked Milne. "The man looked absolutely monstrous."

"It seems to be a side-effect of communing with the Network," said C. "The capillaries burst."

Prime Minister Victor Milne sat for a long time, chin on his hand like Rodin's *The Thinker*.

He was remembering the Scottish Referendum.

There had been lightning over Westminster that night too, but curiously not a drop of rain. This country he loved had already thrown away the largest empire the world had ever known; that vote could so easily have shorn it of another third of its size on top. Milne recalled how powerless he'd felt after a shock poll put the nationalists ahead for the first time. Each day as he crossed Westminster Bridge, Big Ben had seemed smaller. Diminished.

Never again.

And on the day of the EU Referendum there was lightning over Parliament again. History was turning. An idea had just occurred to him – he would see how far he could run with it.

"Look at this, Prime Minister," said C.

It was CCTV footage. Jenny crouched beneath the Gherkin, leafing through a scroll; Jake set fire to the manuscript and it was consumed.

"A corner of paper survived," said C.

"Papyrus," interjected Parr.

"We carbon dated it to 800 BC – the same age as the bones in northern Italy."

"So the journalist actually found it," said Milne, and it was possible to observe something beady in his eye, something appraising. "He found a ... an *instruction manual* for predicting the future – and it's lost."

"There is also this."

C passed Milne the *Telegraph*'s story about the *Peace of Amiens*. The politician spotted the Etruscan at once.

"Does this mean *another* copy's out there? And Boney had it? The Little Corporal?" He guffawed, colour returning to his face. "Saucy French rapscallions! Always something up their sleeve."

"We don't know for sure," said C. "The scroll Napoleon's carrying might have been a figment of the painter's imagination."

"It says in the article that the words on the scroll don't correspond to any known Etruscan inscription," said Milne.

"That's true," said Parr. "We've checked."

"Nonetheless ..." Milne leaned inward, the ghost of a smile on his face. "You can't deny Napoleon cut quite a dash in his day." He paused. "Well, come on then, why did you do him in?"

C's face was neutral. "Do who in, Prime Minister?"

"Michael Beloff, the guy who bought the painting. He was a donor of ours, you know. I sat next to him at the Lord Mayor's banquet this year, for Pete's sake."

"That, um, that – ah." C rubbed his nose. "That wasn't us, Prime Minister."

Milne tugged at his hair. "Don't hold out on me, why kill the man?"

"We didn't do it, sir," repeated Parr.

"Then who the hell did kill him?"

"I'm afraid we don't know," said C.

Milne's gaze flitted between the two spooks before settling on Napoleon. "The French? Kept hold of it since Bonaparte's day?"

"They didn't exactly see 1940 coming," said C. "Or the German offensive in 1914. Or Bismarck's invasion come to that. If Napoleon did have a copy, he lost it. He must have – or why invade Russia?"

"Don't march on Moscow, Bernard Montgomery's first rule of war," muttered Milne.

"As far we can ascertain, nobody's had enough of the *Disciplina Etrusca* to master full-on augury since the thirties," said Parr. "And then it was only by pot luck – obtaining a 'master copy', so to speak."

"So who's been chucking lightning bolts at my donor? The Chinese?"

Again Parr saw it: a piercing avarice, shining through that shell of bonhomie. Milne had taken on board knowledge that would shake the world view of most men to its foundations and barely broken stride.

"It's a possibility," she said. "One of their operatives got her hooks into Wolsey a couple of years back. She almost certainly obtained enough text to do … what Hess could do."

"Of course, we can't rule out that the bolt that killed him was sheer coincidence," said C.

"Lightning doesn't strike twice," said Milne, leaping to his feet and pacing the flat. "Tell me about this blasted journalist then. Whatever his name was, Jake-something. What became of him?"

"He's in Thailand," said Parr. "As is our awol spy, for that matter. They think they're in hiding, but we know exactly where they are."

"In any case, I wouldn't worry about Wolsey," said C. "The man's a total shambles. Recovering alcoholic, scatty as hell."

"He does have three qualities that are rather problematic though," said Parr. "Number one, he abides by a very strict code of principles."

"So do we all, I should think," Milne interjected.

"But we are guided solely by the national interest, are we not?" said C. "The greatest good for the British people. This Jake Wolsey is more of a … how shall I put this?"

"A sandal-wearing, limp-wristed pinko?" suggested Milne.

"Your language, not mine – but yes, spot on. Second problem, he's a talented historian. Covered all sorts of historical topics for his newspaper, before he began going down the slippery slope, that is. And third problem. The sandal-wearing, limp-wristed pinko is rather gifted at spotting things other people miss. He found in a matter of weeks what the best and brightest in our organisation had sought for decades without success."

"Why haven't you just bumped them off?" said Milne.

Parr took a sip of tea and winced at the tannin; the teabag floated like a collapsing yacht. "We're attempting a more cerebral approach, sir. Wolsey's going nowhere. The hope is that we might turn his gifts to our advantage."

They discussed the case a while longer, then C asked Parr to leave so he could discuss an unconnected matter.

"Best of British luck to you," said Milne. "Evelyn, isn't it?"

As Parr departed she heard him begin, "Now then, what about all this unpleasantness in Sierra Leone …."

7

The *Peace of Amiens*; the electrocution of Michael Beloff. They had to be linked to the arrival of this sinister little delivery. Jake smoothed the stubble on his cheeks while he took it all in. Could Beloff have dispatched the cards? Is that why he was struck dead? Beloff might have found cuttings of Jake's reportage from two years back, made the connection to that painting of his. Yet Beloff was not an intelligence agency … and if bloody *Beloff* could find him here MI6 would have rubbed him out months ago.

But somebody knew he was there.

It was by very accurately assessing their chances that the Romans conceived and carried out their plan to dominate the world.

Jake searched 'Napoleon and Polybius' on his smartphone and a Google Books entry filled the screen.

Bonaparte eagerly read works of history, particularly Polybius. Fascinated by the ancients, he read every book on Greece and Rome he could find, and became increasingly impressed by the Caesars.

When Jake Googled 'Napoleon and ancient Rome', the search engine was overloaded with hits. With growing consternation he read how after seizing power Napoleon had styled himself 'First Consul', mirroring the consuls who once ruled the Roman Republic. How, like Augustus, he had next proclaimed himself emperor. At his coronation Napoleon had been crowned with a laurel wreath like the Caesars of old, clad in a robe the Tyrian purple of Imperial Rome. Notre Dame was decorated like a Roman temple, and as their standards the soldiers bore bronze eagles, like those that Roman legionaries had once planted around the Mediterranean. Jake pressed his palms into his eyes, hard. Last time he had engaged with this madness he'd nearly been killed. His career was ended, he was a hunted man. He shouldn't be Googling this stuff at all – Jenny would have had a fit. She'd insisted the Etruscan in Napoleon's scroll was coincidence, a classical flourish by an artist with an overactive imagination, perhaps. And yet some macabre fascination drew him back.

A nameless dread was in Jake's stomach as he typed, 'Napoleon and lightning'. His finger hovered over search.

"What is it, Jake?" Chloë peered at the cards.

"Nothing much," he mumbled. "Just a load of random stuff about Napoleon."

"Weird." Her arm trailed around his shoulders like a creeper as she tried to glance at his phone. "Hey! Why won't you let me see? Too busy emailing all your other girlfriends?"

"Don't be silly."

If Jake told her the truth she'd think he was insane. Maybe he was insane.

"Don't look stressed out, man," said Chloë. Have a beer. You're on a tropical beach, Jesus."

"For the millionth time, I don't drink. It doesn't agree with me."

Only when Chloë wandered off did he press search. As page after page of hits filled the screen he felt real fright for the first time: beginning in his gut, rising up the back of his throat.

This was Napoleon after putting the Austrians to the sword in 1800:

We have struck here like lightning. Great events are about to take place.

Next, a line from a French propaganda sheet that is thought to have been authored by Bonaparte himself.

Napoleon flies like lightning and strikes like a thunderbolt.

A third quote hit Jake between the eyes. It was 1814, the war was lost, and Napoleon's regime stared into oblivion. And he had told his marshals:

The sacred fire is extinct.

Yet it was all so circumstantial. And the conclusion that presented itself *couldn't* be true. Because if Napoleon had possessed the mastery of lightning prophecy, why did he lose a battle?

Had *Jenny* sent him this stuff? Was *Jenny* looking for it again? She could hardly post this material on the message board – sending it here would be safer. It had to be her. That meant he was trapped here, waiting for more. Jake held his head in his hands and a few hairs came away in his fingers. He was definitely looking a bit thinner on top.

*

Later that day Jake checked out the *Huffington Post*. At the request of the Sierra Leonean president, Britain was sending in the troops. The United Kingdom would restore order until Ebola was under control; an advance party of Royal Marines was already ashore. The template was Tony Blair's crushing of the West Side Boys in 1997: a humanitarian intervention, in the land of blood diamonds. Union Jacks were being paraded through Freetown by the locals, a red carpet for the former colonial power.

In an indefinable way this story nagged at him too.

8

Eleanor Thompson studied her friend down an expanse of Kensington dinner table. His name was Jacob Serval, and there was something leonine about him. The rugged bearing, the auburn stubble. Serval looked hard and he was harder than he looked: if he was a lion, it was one of the scarred old campaigners of the veldt, battle-worn but dangerous. However his poise – elegant, indolent, one arm draped across the table – more recalled the domestic cat. He looked fantastic in that white shirt, several buttons open to reveal a bronzed chest and a virile explosion of hair. Thompson was a married woman, yet she felt a sordid shiver of lust as she took in a man she could never have. Serval was brooding about K2 again, evidently. Oh, how she wished he'd never set foot on that infernal mountain.

Earlier that evening Serval had been chatting with ease to Fiona, a blonde creature her husband knew from university. Fiona was captivated by him – hair flicks, all the works – and Thompson hoped Serval would reciprocate, might find something worth pursuing in life again. But soon he'd lost interest, staring out of the window while her husband droned on about the London property market. Occasionally Serval would incline his head and smile, as if to say, *fascinating, really, how very interesting*. But Thompson knew he was replaying what happened on that bloody mountain – and how swiftly everything had fallen apart.

Jacob Serval was once the up-and-coming explorer in Britain. Armed with only an iron resolve, he had walked the length of Siberia, departing from the Urals in March and emerging in Kamchatka before winter set in, gaunt and wounded but alive. It was one of the last great feats of exploration. With his dashing looks and aristocratic connections, media interest had come easily. A trek to the source of the Amazon had followed; then two years ago he had tackled K2. With him in the Himalayas was that foolish Australian boy who would be his downfall. The kid had masked altitude sickness during the ascent, desperate to make it to the top. He began dying before Serval's eyes. They were too high, no descent could be fast enough to save him.

So the Australian begged Serval to continue without him, to summit for them both.

Carrying on was meant to be Serval's tribute to his partner, but the papers didn't see it that way. When it emerged he had abandoned a dying man for the summit, Serval went from the dashing young thing of British exploration to a callous careerist. The sponsorship dried up, the expeditions petered out. And now he had that look about him. The look of the *hunted*. The man was barely recognisable.

Only Thompson was wrong – Serval wasn't back on K2 at all. He was thinking about the man whose life he'd ended the previous night.

MI6 had first encountered Serval in a pub near his Kensington bachelor pad a few months after K2, wearing a tatty polo shirt, drinking alone on a weekday afternoon. The meeting was by chance, but at once the recruiting officer knew he was in the presence of an individual who was as hard as steel and could move at any level of British society – both qualities the Secret Intelligence Services had ample use for. He had been trained up in counter-surveillance and the art of violence, then seconded to a team at the forefront of the organisation's realignment under the new government. No longer was MI6 to be concerned solely with gathering information. It was undergoing a swing of the pendulum back towards the role it had during the Second World War: an organisation also charged with engineering *desirable results* by *covert means*.

And so to last night's murder.

For a rabid Anglophobe, the Sierra Leonean foreign minister certainly enjoyed the finer things west London had to offer. A plump but energetic man, Frederick Simpson Turay was in the capital on one of his spending sprees when his file was passed to Serval. The 'bump' Serval crafted went like a dream. One of Turay's vices was a taste for fast cars, and he had hired an Aston Martin DB7 for his stay. So Serval had acquired a 1964 DB5 from the government's car collection: Bond's ride, he noted, relishing the grim little irony. Serval tailgated his target into the carpark of The Dorchester and pulled up next to him, complimenting Turay on his taste in matters automotive. There was a further 'chance encounter' in the hotel bar; they got chatting about cars; Serval bought the politician a drink.

Several single malts later the conversation moved on to high-class prostitutes and the three grams of cocaine Serval had obtained from MI6's 'drugs and thugs' desk. They relocated to Turay's suite to await the appearance of two non-existent hookers. But Turay did not know the cocaine was 99.7% pure. It was soapy and hard to cut, the chandelier light reflected green and violet in its suds as Serval cut up two gargantuan lines. Nor did Turay notice when the Englishman blew *out* through his banknote instead of sniffing *in*, obliterating his own powder.

According to European Union guidance the fatal dose for cocaine is 1.2 grams, although in some individuals death occurs at considerably lower levels. And in the event it wasn't necessary to force him – Turay blew his own head off willingly. He was dead by cardiac arrest within the hour. Serval slipped away; the Met swiftly confirmed they were not looking for anyone else in connection with the death; drug users were warned to be on guard for a very pure batch of cocaine.

This was the reason for Serval's catatonia at the dinner party. There were grounds for the assassination: Turay had been block-ing the British intervention in Sierra Leone. Liquidating him would enable British soldiers and doctors to save many people. But that didn't lessen Serval's desolation that evening. His actions, his hands, his artful plan, had ended another man's life. He had never killed before.

Serval necked half a glass of St Emilion and helped himself to more. He wouldn't find any plonk this decent out in Sierra Leone, that was for sure. For new orders had come through. And he was flying out to Freetown the next morning ...

9

MI6 had messed up. The beautiful boy (his rather splendid name was Alexander Coppock-Davoli) may have joined The Firm after Jenny's departure, but the spymasters had overlooked the fact that his vetting took place while she still worked there. That, and her photographic memory. Two years after passing him in a corridor on the way out of Vauxhall Cross, and she had recognised him instantly.

As per the plan, Jenny left a coded message on the website to warn Jake that MI6 were on to them. Then she planned her route out of Thailand. The aromatherapy practitioner from Leeds had been rumbled, so Jenny considered the remaining two identities in her possession. Jamila Ahmed, a Brummie mother-of-one, was the first. The UK passport Jenny's GCHQ contact had created before his arrest contained a convincing array of stamps from Pakistan and one from Saudi Arabia; he had erased any trace of their creation from MI6's files. Jenny could keep the contact lenses in and fake tan would do the rest. Or there was Frances Dunlop, the flame-haired Scottish lawyer who had plied her trade in Bangkok for two years now, on paper, at least. An easier disguise to pull together in a rush. Jenny assembled her shopping list: smart clothes, proper shoes, glasses, wig. Plus make up – she needed to be paler. And at Bangkok's MBK Centre you can find almost anything.

The key to avoiding man-hunters is random behaviour, so Jenny caught a tuk-tuk towards the mall, got off at a busy inter-section and took a motorbike taxi back the way she had come. She hopped on a second motorbike taxi, hopped off and rode the Skytrain the last two stops.

A European took an interest from the far side of the carriage. Middle-aged, wispy brown hair, pointy nose; rather like a scare-crow. Male attention wasn't unusual for Jenny, but to be on the safe side she extended a foot just before the two sets of sliding doors shut so that hers stayed open, but not his. She nipped off the carriage before he could alight and the train pulled away. (An old trick, but a good one.)

Alec McCabe spoke into his wrist. "She's got off, too fast for me to follow."

"Damn it!" Frank Davis was astride a motorbike half a mile away. "GCHQ, can you assist?"

In Cheltenham three of the UK's top computer geeks monitored CCTV cameras controlled by the Thai police.

"It'll take a moment," said GCHQ. "These systems are just arcane …"

"I'm approaching the station," said Davis. "Where did she head next?"

Back in the West Country the jabbering had risen to a crescendo.

*

Once the biggest mall in Asia, the MBK Centre has since embraced a trajectory of shabby decline. The towering metallic box was fed by walkways down which tourists journeyed towards commercial nirvana. Jenny surfed between them, walking with illogical slowness. If she had a tail, he would be detached from the flow. At an internet café she bought a plane ticket to Israel, then she began perusing clothes stalls. From an upmarket shop she selected two trouser suits, three shirts and a charcoal skirt; at an optician she bought a display pair of horn-rimmed spectacles that lent her a librarian's mien. Finally she headed towards ground level, leaving a trail of radiation with each tread of her left foot; a trail that vibrated invisibly behind her like breadcrumbs threaded through a forest of people.

Six months previously, Coppock-Davoli had let himself into Jenny's apartment and injected a microgram of polonium 210 into the heel of each pair of shoes he could find. This was the radioactive element that killed the Russian dissident Alexander Litvinenko in London, laced in his tea. But polonium produces only alpha particles, and even a sheet of paper placed between isotope and body will prevent harm. That was why Litvinenko's killers had been able to fly all the way from Moscow in close contact with the poison before eliminating him. MI6 could follow her every movement with radiographic scintillators and the rate of decay told them when she had been at a spot with atomic accuracy, just as the Met retraced Litvinenko's last footsteps around London. Davis and Co had been playing Hansel and Gretel all around Bangkok ever since; only by this expedient had a small team kept up with an operative of Jenny's guile. Then Beloff was killed, Coppock-Davoli got spotted and Parr ordered that Jenny's radioactive leash be replaced by something more corporeal.

"Got her," shouted GCHQ. "She went into a shopping centre called Mahboonkrong." There was a murmur in the background. "MBK for short. How fast can you get there?"

"I can see it now," Davis shouted into the blare of horns.

"Me too," panted Alexander Coppock-Davoli. "I'm approaching by foot from the north."

"Good lad," said Davis.

"We can't get eyes inside," GCHQ advised.

"Just tell us if she leaves and we'll do the rest." Davis produced a handheld electronic device; red and yellow bars played across the screen, as if measuring the volume of a piano recital. "She was right here, about twenty minutes ago."

When he dashed past the internet café the coloured lines diminished.

"Hold on, hold it." Davis retraced his steps and ran inside. "She went into this arcade place."

The bars grew frenzied by the eighth computer. A teenager looked up wordlessly from his game.

"Go away," said Davis.

The Thai did not move; Davis grabbed his chair and simply rolled him across the room before tapping at the keyboard.

"I've just emailed you from the computer she was using," he told GCHQ. "Find out what she was up to, eh?"

"I've picked up her trail," Coppock-Davoli interjected. "She was on the ground floor less than a minute ago. Went into a clothes shop. Then she ... wait." A flame of excitement had entered his voice. "She – *she's in the ladies toilets.*"

Davis joined him outside the door. "Ready for this? I'll let you be the one to take her down."

The long handsome face was flushed. "Legend."

A minute passed; no Jenny. Two minutes. Three minutes. Davis checked his GPS and his jaw dropped.

"What is it?" asked Coppock-Davoli.

"These toilets are on an exterior wall."

Davis kicked open the door of the lavatory and stepped inside, ignoring the squeals of outrage. A window was propped open and beyond lay the street. Coppock-Davoli was speechless.

"Now we'll both be in the shit," said Davis.

Half a mile away Jenny placed her purchases in the boot of a taxi with studied nonchalance. She never knew how close she'd been to them – but that was the point of relentless evasive tactics. It was operatives whose standards dropped that got caught, she reflected with a private smile. Those who let their guard down, even for an instant.

The driver closed the boot. "Where you go miss?"

Before Jenny could answer she felt a needle enter her backside and in one swooping lurch her vision melted away like celluloid exposed to flame.

10

Full Moon Party: for two decades now the most savage night of debauchery in Asia. Jake gripped the side of the dragon boat as it closed in on the headland, scudding across the waves. A black bar of land lay ahead, the night above it awash with light and turbulent with the rumble of far-off sound systems. Fatalities were commonplace at Full Moon Party, and Jake hadn't fancied it. But Chloë was quite insistent. They rounded the headland and he saw Haad Rin beach: a mile long, thirty thousand ravers strewn along it already. Hundreds of torches had been lit along the surf and a palisade of orange flickered over the sand.

Like Austerlitz.

Napoleon's most famous victory. On the eve of battle Bonaparte had visited the bivouacs of his ordinary troops. Spontaneously his men had lit torches, illuminating the emperor's path through the encampment. As Jake neared the shore he saw those flames as the Russian czar might have from the opposite hill and the bass rolling off the beach became cannon fire. The booming grew louder as they neared, cannonball and canister shot, bombarding his ears. But it was no longer cannon fire.

It was thunder.

"What do we have to do with Fate? Politics is Fate."
– Napoleon Bonaparte

Three more quotations had arrived that morning. The same embossed card, same expensive-looking typography. On reading the first Jake was consumed by coughing, the taste of bile rancid in his throat. Thoughts of fate never left him as it was: for he already knew there was such a thing as an *actual future* that could be divined via bolts of lightning. And if this was so, how could there be free will? Jake was bound to his rudderless path, as surely as Oedipus must kill his own father. Thinking of it hurt his brain.

Jake tore through the deck like a crack addict at his stash. The next card bore a quotation from Bonaparte's confidant, Joseph Fouché:

"Napoleon believed himself the son of destiny."

And the third was from Pasquier, one of his ministers:

"In 1806, Napoleon reached the peak of his power and glory. But nothing could protect it from dangers brought about by his excessive confidence in his star."

Napoleon's 'star'. Throughout his career, the emperor had constantly referred to it. What form did this star take exactly? What did he mean by this?

Jake felt a cool touch on his arm; Chloë's eyes gleamed orange in the approaching torchlight, like some kind of wildcat. When she kissed him he tasted rum on her mouth, some foul Thai liquor rumoured to contain amphetamines. She'd been pressing the stuff on him all evening.

No thanks.

"You ready for this?" she said.

Jake could make out individual ravers, pagan figures with their body paint and bestial prances along the sand. "Not even in the slightest," he said.

With a soft *thunk* the hull of the boat met sand and Chloë leapt over the side, pulling him after her. Jake glanced at his shins as they crashed through the knee-deep surf.

Ooush.

When he and Jenny first arrived on Koh Phan Ngan a fisherman had taken them to a deserted island a few miles offshore, a glade of palms one metre above sea level at its highest. She had loved him too then, he was certain she did; hand in hand they'd sprinted through the surf, screaming in exuberance. It was without doubt the happiest moment of his life. As he glanced down now, surf erupting up his shins so they resembled Eskimo boots, the memory came to him. Only while that was a thing of beauty, this felt sordid and wrong: like a juju priest's mockery of what had gone before.

Why did he still love Jenny?

She was beautiful, but she didn't know it. She was kind. She had a sense of humour; she was tough and strong and resourceful. And for some reason she had loved him back, just as fiercely. Jake had called her *My One*, as though of the three billion females on the planet, this was the woman fate had intended for him. He had genuinely believed it too, until she left him and belatedly he realised the universe was playing a different game. You don't know what you've got till it's gone: the truest phrase in the English language.

Heartbreak was like a stone he had swallowed, and still the gravity of it reverberated throughout his body with its numbness. This was the opposite of the lightness he'd once felt sprinting through the surf – but now it had been forced down his throat he had no choice but to digest it, though digestion might take years and Jake feared it might yet prove indigestible. The moments when he forgot were like a splash of spring sunshine at the end of bitter winter, only for the memory of it to come gusting in once more. Cold and hard and mean and thin: the bare branches of love's ending.

Chloë was whirling, throwing wild shapes with her body and stamping with bare feet. Every set of male eyes was upon her and she revelled in the attention, her eyes always sliding back to Jake, that wicked smile spreading across her perfect teeth which made him know that later her snakelike legs would writhe around him.

Come on, old man. You haven't got it that bad.

Yet there was something *wrong* when he slept with her. It felt – and Jake was aware this was freaky – as if he was wearing some kind of *mechanical suit* that drove his movements, the touching and the thrusting. Like one of those wheelchairs which stands its user up at the touch of a button. Going through the motions. Yet oddly, his lacklustre performances seemed to drive Chloë to ecstasy.

She kissed him roughly. "Later on, when we get back, things will be absolutely *wild* – I promise you that. Just for tonight, why don't you let go of whatever it is you're always thinking about. You know ... when you're with me, but not quite with me."

Chloë kissed him again, threw herself into the rave, and suddenly Jake understood why she'd packed in her job for this sybaritic existence. Life was for the living. The music took him by the shoulders too and finally he was dancing, letting the rhythm carry him, submitting to the Dionysiac orgy.

While all the strangeness of Jake's inner journey melted away on a tide of music and beats, the woman he still loved was being spirited out of Thailand, and world events were taking shape.

11

Frank Davis systematically led the MI6 psychiatrist through all seventy-one kills he had made as an SAS sniper in Iraq and Afghanistan. He recalled every detail: which part of the anatomy he had shot; how hairy a certain chest was; whether the person stopped moving right away or wriggled about for a bit. When Davis described the very worst things he would sigh and the hoods of his eyelids would flicker up. But his eyebrows barely moved.

"Do any of your killings trouble you?" asked the psychiatrist.

"None." Davis was chewing gum. "No way."

"Did your father ever hit you?"

The assassin's head retracted, but he carried on chewing. "Never. He was a good man."

"Have you ever hesitated before killing someone?"

That threw him. "Once, yeah."

"Tell me about it."

"I was in Basra. This Iraqi fella was crying for his mum and that. Most of them do to be fair, but this guy was 'please-mummying' all over the shop."

"What did you do?"

"I gave him a little bit of time to pull himself together, like."

"And?"

Davis's upper lip rose over his gums, so they momentarily resembled dentures.

"And I shot him in the head."

Victor Milne hit pause, freezing Davis mid-sneer. "I've seen enough," he said. "The man's an absolute psychopath."

The Prime Minister was sitting with Evelyn Parr and C in a secure speech room at Vauxhall Cross, forty feet below the level of the Thames. It was the very chamber where two years previously Parr had first briefed Jenny on the case.

"Frank took out six Chinese secret agents singlehandedly in Ethiopia," said C. "He's the best we've got in the, ahem, 'How To Kill People Department.'"

"We can't replace him," said Parr.

"He's a nasty piece of work," said Milne, waggling Davis's file. "Just imagine this on the front page of tomorrow's *Times*. It's my watch he's offing people on, remember."

"He's a single dad," offered Parr. "Nine-year-old daughter. Apparently he dotes on her – collects her from school every day. All the other mums love him."

Milne massaged his forehead and groaned.

C nodded to the screen. "He goes on to tell our psychiatrist that his life's dream is to have a son. He is human, you know. He just happens to do a very difficult job."

"*Oh-very-well-then.*" Milne's words came in a rush. "Next up?"

"I really must protest about all this," C grumbled. "It's just not the way we do things here. Choice of personnel should be up to us – it's most unusual for a Prime Minister to take such a hands-on approach. As a matter of fact, the last to do so was Blair, in the run up to Iraq."

"And that didn't exactly end well," said Parr.

"To give Tony his dues, he did at least recognise that Britain can't carry on being *supine*," said Milne. "Not if it wants to retain any last vestige of Great Power status. Do you respect my judgement, Dennis?"

There was only one answer C could give. "Of course I do."

"And what's the top priority for our national security – the Islamic State, Putin, or finding this wretched *Disciplina* thingy?"

"The *Disciplina*," said Parr. "Unquestionably."

"Therefore I'd be neglecting my duties if I wasn't across every aspect of the operation. That includes the composition of your team."

C's neck hung with python languor over his collar. *Checkmate.*

"What does this 'Alec McCabe' bring to the party?" asked Milne, opening the next file.

The photograph showed a gaunt man with wispy brown hair and a pointy nose.

"He's our Etruscan expert," said Parr. "He read classics at Oxford – apparently Greek and Latin grammar's a good grounding for the language – and he's got lots of field experience. North Sudan, Georgia, Venezuela."

When Milne saw the photo on the next file he merely said, "Crikey. She's not bad ..."

He moved on to Coppock-Davoli's dossier. "Why take the youngster?"

"He's bright and he's very fit," said Parr. "Plus he's malleable. We don't want another Jenny Frobisher on our hands, do we?"

"Oh good lord no," said Milne.

C produced a laptop. "Talking of which, you wanted to see the CCTV of Frobisher being taken by the Chinese ..."

"Let it roll," said Milne with schoolboy relish.

The images were high resolution. Jenny sashayed towards a taxi with an array of shopping bags; a figure descended on her from behind and she collapsed into his embrace. As the driver pulled away he looked right into the camera.

"Han Chinese, we're ninety-nine percent sure," said C.

"But Bangkok has a ginormous Chinese diaspora," said Milne. "Does it not?"

"GCHQ's been picking up chatter from Beijing too," said Parr. "The termite's nest is stirring, all right."

"Can we see the face of the chap who needles her?"

"This is the only CCTV camera," said Parr. "And his back's to the camera the whole time."

When Milne frowned there was something of the dowager Queen Victoria about him.

"Pull up that footage of Frobisher giving our gang the shake," he said. "You know, before this charming Davis character started duffing up transvestites."

C loaded grainy shots of the Khao San Road.

"Hold it there," said Milne.

At once Coppock-Davoli was caught in full flight, his body a zig-zag that juddered backward and forward between two frames. The insect-seller's handcart was frozen in its emergence and the vagrant's right boot was extended, kicking out at the wagon.

"Let's have a look at that chap," said Milne, jabbing at the tramp with a cone-shaped finger. "Who's he, eh? You tell me that."

C remained very still.

"Go back to the other clip," said Milne.

They were at the shopping centre again; Jenny wilted into her assailant's arms.

"Same bloke?" he demanded.

"Could be," Parr admitted. "Similar shoulders."

Milne went back to Khao San Road, clicking away in frustration. "How does one get a closer look on this infernal contraption?"

Parr zoomed in on the plane of cheekbone discernible through matted dreadlocks.

"I don't think *he's* Chinese," said Milne. "Too dark-skinned. He could be an Arab. Or a black chap, even. I think we're looking at our adversary. How did he know to be there, though? That's the question."

"There's something else," said Parr. "When Frobisher was in the shopping centre she posted something on a car website. Some nonsense about the new Hyundai."

"A message to Wolsey?"

"It has to be."

A thought occurred to the Prime Minister. "Why didn't we lift Beloff before someone zapped him? And his blasted painting, come to think of it?"

"There was no need," said C. "We got a close look at the painting as it went through Heathrow after the auction. We had an academic examine the imagery in microscopic detail. We checked Napoleon's scroll against every other Etruscan inscription in existence in an attempt to identify it. We even X-rayed the canvas to see if anything was hidden under the outer layers of paint. Everything drew a blank."

"Beloff was unaware of his painting's significance at first," said Parr. "He was a Napoleon enthusiast – no interest in the Etruscans whatsoever. But something changed. Overnight he became *fascinated* with them. Googling non-stop, pestering academics, ordering books left, right and centre."

"And a week later he was killed," said C.

"So he found something," said Milne. "He must have. Something in the painting, something we missed. But what?"

"We don't know," said Parr.

"I think you should be out there yourself," said Milne. "To keep an eye on things personally."

"She'll be on a flight to Bangkok this evening," said C.

"Perfect," said Milne. "When it comes to manoeuvring our pawns we ought to take a leaf out of Boney's book, no?"

"You've lost me," said Parr.

"You know – his hat on the field being worth forty thousand

men and all that." A puckish look crept across the Prime
Minister's face. "But what, pray tell, was he keeping under
that hat?"

12

Sitting next to Jacob Serval on the flight to Sierra Leone was a
rotund Englishman in his sixties named Wally. He was ruddy,
bearded and sported a safari suit. He was also extremely drunk
and claimed to be an arms dealer.

Some genius had built the airport on the far side of the estuary from Freetown, and the Foreign Office considered not one
method of crossing to be safe. You could go by aging Soviet
helicopter, but they fell out of the sky. You could go by boat,
but they sank (and there was no coastguard). You could go by
hovercraft, but these burst into flames and then sank. Or – and
this was the most dangerous route of all – you could go by road.
The child in Serval had not died yet: he went by hovercraft.

Freetown by dawn was a scene from some grim fantasy novel.
The mountains loomed from the mist in a world cast a pale grey,
rearing from the Atlantic like a sea monster on its haunches.
And the slums were its scales, a mass of wood and corrugated
iron that teetered over the water on flamingo-leg stilts before
swarming up the mountainside. A helicopter flitted along the
coast with a halo suspended underneath, scanning for minerals
even amid the chaos of a failing state.

Serval was no stranger to Africa, but he could not escape a
feeling of disquiet at being in Sierra Leone now. The previous
civil war had been diabolically nightmarish (the eating of human
hearts; the trailing of intestines across the road) and already
there were reports of the same. Freetown still bore signs of the
last conflict: ruined buildings; a permanent UN court to mete
out punishment for war criminals; a collection of amputees on

their pathetic hand tricycles. Yet for all the ravages of Ebola, it struck him that this was a joyful city. School children in immaculate school uniform and bonnets toddled along; sound systems pounded out dancehall at maximum decibels. A flamboyant police officer with a brilliant smile directed traffic like the conductor of the London Philharmonic. Down Town was laid out in grid formation, but any semblance of order ended there. The streets teemed with illicit money changers and people selling SIM cards. Women with plates of fish or bananas on their heads bustled through the crowds with a roll of the hips. Hand-painted signs were everywhere, ranging from the futile – *No street hawkers, No piss here* – to the inexplicable: *De oldies be de goodies*.

Under a still-wet mural of Victor Milne: *World's Greatest*.

The slot of a red pillar box was choked with weeds, the heavy iron structure too sturdy to be removed. Serval smiled a touch sadly; he nurtured a guilty fondness for memories of Empire. *No shame there*, his father would have boomed.

A further anachronism was the language. Krio was sired by Mende and eighteenth-century English, lending it a quaint and piratical personality. Things didn't happen *often*, but *seldom*; Serval encountered the phrase, 'nefarious acts'. To say good morning one would ask, *How de body?* to which the proper reply is, *De body fine*.

Serval checked into a hotel on the edge of Kroo Town, a fearsome slum running the length of the bay. His hotel used to be a hospital, built by the British, and here again Serval saw traces of the departed power. The cracked toilets were made by Royal Doulton and the iron lift (still functional) was stamped *Made in Birmingham*.

Serval bought a beer and drank it on the roof, staring out over an oily creek that snaked towards the sea. Drank his beer and tried to quell the beating of his heart at what he had to do that evening.

*

Two squaddies guarded the shanty town's perimeter.

"I wouldn't go any further if I were you, mate." A Tyneside accent came through the facemask. "Not pacified yet. And a bit rowdy, like."

"Plus the Ebola," said the second Geordie. "It's in there, all right."

A definite sense of the virus as a *living thing*.

"I can look after myself," said Serval.

The first soldier shrugged. "Suit yourself, mate. But just so as you know, if you get in a ruck we ain't coming in for you."

Serval picked his way along the river bank. The smell was of cheap fuel, effluent and rot. Smoke rose from piles of burning rubbish; pigs snuffled at his feet. Only the rattle of a generator suggested habitation – and the infrequent oil lamps flickering in windows. Further inland the mountains were a patchwork of yellow and black, depending on which neighbourhoods had power that night. A pitch-dark alleyway led into the belly of the slum. Serval switched on his torch and took a few steps in.

Two young men emerged behind him.

They wore vests and baseball caps; muscular arms glinted in the half-light. Serval measured their tread behind him, refusing to increase his pace. When he turned a corner they followed.

Next it was a tooth-whistle. "White man, white man."

Serval turned, appraising the pair who confronted him. One was tall and rangy with crazy teeth, the other short but heavily built, his arms like boa constrictors and carrying a machete. Serval reckoned he could take them, but it might get messy.

"What you problem?" said the short one.

"There's no problem," Serval replied evenly.

"What mek you look foh fight?"

The Englishman felt a certain *exhilaration* spill into his blood. So: this was why some people loved violence the way he loved the wild places.

"I'm not looking for a fight," he said. "I am going for a stroll."

"Him jus' go look round!" the taller man told his friend, as though explaining something to a cretin. He handed Serval the machete. "Here be cutlass."

That's when Serval realised: they didn't want to hurt him. They wanted to help him, they were worried about his welfare. When he thought of that unfamiliar thrill at impending violence he was glad of the night, for his cheeks were burning with shame.

"What are your names?" he asked by way of contrition.

"Me nem Internet," said the shorter one. "Him Action."

Serval went to shake his hand, but he paused.

It's in there, all right.

Internet's head fell. "Body no bad. Me feel well."

For a second time that night Her Majesty's man in Freetown experienced a shadowing of guilt. He gripped Internet's hand and shook it firmly, as Napoleon at Acre had once embraced troops with the plague.

"Na wetin you de do?" said Action.

What do you do?

"Him doctor," said Internet; he still had not released Serval's hand.

"Shut ye mout!" said Action. "Let 'im speak!"

"No, he's right," said Serval. "I am a doctor. Are there sick people here?"

Both men nodded.

"Take me to them."

"For gif me cold beer," said Internet. "You do me, I do you."

"It's a deal."

So they led him to the hut of the dying.

Internet's eyes were wide as he enunciated each horrific syllable: "Ee-bo-*laaa* ..."

Serval donned a plastic suit from his bag, along with mask, gloves and shoe-covers. He used surgical tape to seal the cracks. But their knocks were met by silence. Serval opened the door. It was humid inside. It smelled like bad cheese and the silence oppressed him. At first he thought the room was empty, but there were two shapes lying on foam mattresses, huddled under rags.

"Sir? Madam?"

Nothing.

"Excuse me? Is anybody there?"

The larger shape stirred. Serval lifted the rag and illuminated a face that was terrified and uncomprehending. The woman was very thin, her head shrunken and eyes jaundiced.

Serval lowered the torch. "Sorry to disturb you, Madam."

"Me body." Her voice was hoarse and she swallowed before continuing. "De 'urt."

It hurts.

"I'm a doctor." He raised a syringe.

"Dis merecine?"

Is it medicine?

Serval shook his head. "I need to take some blood, madam."

"You wan' do tes?"

"Yes," he said quietly. "I want to do a test."

Her arm was thin as a snooker cue. Serval slipped the needle into a vein and the syringe filled with blood that glowed obsidian in the darkness. He injected it into a vial and cleaned its exterior with the solution his handler had provided.

There was movement to Serval's left, the lightest of sighs.

"De pikin," the woman whispered.

The child.

Curled up beneath a stained Mickey Mouse blanket was a little girl. Even in sleep her brows were dark and mischievous, and her hair had been plaited into six long thin antennae which sprang up when he lifted the cover. Four years old, he reckoned. Maybe five. She was ridiculously light. (He could have held her in the crook of one arm, run with her. Made her laugh.) The child's head looked obscenely large on such a frame and her skin was mottled with white patches. She was definitely dying. Serval felt a lump in his throat, a prickling in the tip of his nose.

"De pikin," the woman mumbled again.

"I need some blood from her too," he said. "With your permission, of course."

The mother did not protest, but the child stiffened in alarm as the needle glided into her and all six antennae quivered.

Serval stood up to leave.

"What bout de merecine?"

"I don't have any medicine to give you."

"I got pain na me head," she rasped. "Me wetin de pan."

I've got pain in my head. I'm wetting my pants.

"I … I'm sorry."

"De pikin. Which hospital you gon' tek her?"

A fleck of saliva landed on Serval's shin.

"I've got to leave her here, I'm afraid."

The awful implications of this filled the stifling little hut.

"I wish I didn't have to," he added. "I wish that …"

The words trailed away.

The mother whispered, "Me money done-done. I got *notin'*."

"I'll give you money," Serval said softly. "You can have some money."

He passed her a hundred dollar bill. But she barely registered the denomination, slumping into her rags.

"Good luck," he said, absurdly.

Serval ran back to the hotel and showered intensively in a vacant room with the special shampoo his handler had given him. He got out, dried himself and showered again in a second room. He showered a third time in his own bedroom and caught a taxi to Aberdeen district, where the hovercrafts departed. The contact was waiting by the pier, shifting from foot to foot as if the plague rose from the ground, like they believed in the Middle Ages.

"Hope you don't mind if I skip shaking hands, now?" The Welshman laughed nervously, running a hand through long dank hair.

Serval didn't reply. *That little girl. Her flaking skin.*

His colleague took the package with a look turned fearful. "Well, I'll be away then. No sense in staying longer than necessary, is there? I've a flight to Heathrow to catch."

"No, there isn't." The words felt gruff in Serval's throat. "Go on, go."

Only when he was stepping into the shower again did it occur to Serval: British Airways ran the only service to London, and it departed at noon. He smiled for the first time since the descent into Kroo Town. These MI6 types and their secrets!

Later that evening curiosity got the better of Serval, and he looked up the schedules. Only more departure that day: his colleague was flying to Abuja.

Why Nigeria?

Suddenly Serval was tired. Tired of thinking about K2, tired of the look on Frederick Turay's face as he overdosed; tired of all of this. Anyway, his was not to wonder why, his was but to do or die. He was only glad to be helping these people.

13

Here's the funny thing: Jenny awoke from a blissful sleep. No fogginess of mind, no trace of a chemical hangover; she had never felt so rested nor so perfectly alert. If the drug they had selected was the first clue, the cell was the second, a cube of plastic illuminated by a high window. She had been abducted by a team that surpassed professionalism. These guys were absolutists. There was a basin, a lavatory, two wooden chairs that might have been pilfered from a church community centre. Clearly, the shaft of daylight was meant to suggest the possibility of freedom to her unconscious mind. The light was muted through a long thin tunnel, so she couldn't guess the latitude or time of day.

When she sat up there were hairs on her pillow (stress, it had to be). She was wearing a new tracksuit, although her own trainers stood by the bed. There was nothing to do but wait. Whoever came through that door would be a poker player of nuance and sophistication and she wasn't going to surrender an advantage by banging on the door. Jenny stood on her bed and tried to peer through the porthole, but the window was three feet too high. A hatch opened – lunch was a cheese sandwich and an apple. Four hours later the hatch opened again. Another cheese sandwich, another apple.

They kept her like that for two more days.

On the third morning Jenny's body language suggested the first encroachment of despair. Her facial muscles were slack, her legs splayed numbly across the floor. The shaft of light made its third sweep across the wall. That afternoon he came at last, and Jenny was unsurprised to recognise the taxi driver from Bangkok, wearing chinos and a sports jacket with an Ivy League haircut and rimless glasses. A vintage Omega was on his wrist; he resembled a newly-graduated financier.

"Suvarnabhumi Airport, please," she said.

He giggled. "It's a long drive from here. I'm Jamie Fung. Please, let's sit down."

Her interrogator spoke like an International School student, the not-quite American English that rich kids talk from Havana to Hong Kong. If Jenny had to guess at his nationality she'd have said Singaporean. But he could have been from absolutely anywhere. They faced each other on the Church of England seating.

"Who are you, Jamie?"

"Hell, I'll square with you. I'm your opposite number."

"Good for you."

"I'm not going to bother with any fancy 'interrogation technique," he said making quote marks with his fingers, "or any of that crap, because you probably know it all already. I'm just going to sit here and talk with you until you tell me what I want to know. If that takes *years*, that's my loss. But just so you know, that's the score, that's how we'll do it."

Jenny looked away, exposing her neck. As in: *here's my most vulnerable point. I'm not afraid of you.*

"Do you want a coke or something?" said Fung reasonably.

"Listen, buster," she said. "If you're not playing games, don't pretend to be my friend. Spare me the meek and mild act. You're not meek. You're not mild."

Annoyance flared in his pupils. Almost indiscernible, but there. Fung received a text message and she watched him type in the pin number with open scorn.

"I'm going to tell you what we want plainly," said Fung. "The journalist, Jake Wolsey, your old lover. What did he know? MI6, what do they know? Your politicians – what do they know? Tell me all that and we can both go home."

Jenny glanced at his wedding ring. "She'll be waiting a long time."

A wince of frustration at Fung's temple.

They talked for thirteen hours and she told him nothing at all.

*

Jenny was waiting for him at 7 am the next morning: leaning back in her chair, thumbs in her belt hooks and groin thrust forward.

I've got the biggest dick here.

Gladiatorial combat ensued. What really annoyed Fung was the way she stared at the bridge of his nose instead of making eye contact. That, and pointing out each psychological gambit he deployed as he tried it. She was undermining him, whittling him down. The beam of daylight travelled across the wall.

At 2 pm came the first significant engagement. Fung was sitting opposite her with his hands on his knees, like a boy receiving a sermon.

"Why are you using submissive body language?" asked Jenny.

"I am *not!*" Fung roared. "I am *not*, I am *not*, I am *just goddamn not!*"

The rage came from nowhere and Jenny's eyes widened before she collected herself. But Fung had noticed the momentary loss of hauteur, and at 4.17 pm he struck again.

Jenny was studiously ignoring him. Fung poured himself a glass of water, took a sip – and hurled the glass at her. The vessel exploded on the wall behind Jenny's head, showering her with water and shards of glass. She screamed, only gradually reacquiring disdain.

"That was bloody *rude*," she said.

Yet it did not escape Fung's attention that for the next half hour Jenny sat very still, like an animal trying to avoid being seen. Something of the lost child had been brought out by the snap of violence. So he decided to punch her in the face.

He was pacing the room, veering closer with each traverse. Jenny brushed her cheek with the tips of her fingers – a jerky movement – and she shied away from every pass.

When Fung halted a new softness was in his voice. "We won't actually *hurt* you, Jenny. You know that, right?"

"Thank you," she whispered.

Fung punched her in the eye, sending her sprawling off the chair.

"I'm sorry," he said, a lilt in his voice again. "I shouldn't have done that thing, Jenny. That was against the rules."

She was lying face down on the carpet and a tremor went through her. "There are rules?"

"Let me make it up to you," he coaxed her. "Come and sit down. I'll get a hot meal brought up."

"Like hell you will."

"Anything you want, just name it. No conditions. You've had enough cheese sandwiches, right?" His voice was sincere. "Look, I – I won't hit you again. I promise."

"A salad or something," she said grimly. "And a cup of tea."

"It's yours. Just get up off the floor."

Jenny held her palm to her eye and inspected it before slowly standing up.

He charged her.

"No!" she shrieked, dancing back. "Please don't hurt me …"

The interrogator had her up against the wall. Her hands were against his chest, pushing him back. Fung went to head-butt her and she flinched, letting go of his left lapel to shield her cheek.

"*Bitch*!" he shouted again, right in her face.

At this some inner resolve seemed to break and Jenny slid down the wall. Fung towered over her, out of breath, his eyes rolling like those of a strangulated bull.

"Well?" he roared.

"Ok," she managed between sobs. "I'll tell you what you want to know. Just – just give me a moment."

Strange, he reflected, that violence might be enough to break her. When preparing for the duel he hadn't even considered it. He almost felt let down.

She peered at him with a puffy eye; mucus bubbled from one nostril.

"All right," he muttered. "I'm going to fix a salad and a cup of your precious British tea. And when I return you'd better tell me everything. Or we'll *really* get started on you."

He walked out of the room.

Jenny stood up and turned on his mobile phone.

14

Night time on the beach. Jake idly flicked twigs and driftwood onto a campfire as it guttered and collapsed in on itself. He stared out to sea, watching the grey waves crashing in from the gulf and head nodding as he contemplated the Gordian knot of contradictions that was his life.

He didn't want to be here, but there was nowhere to go.

He didn't love his lover, yet he was terrified to leave her.

Plus the woman he *did* love didn't want him any more.

Surely no man in all of history had experienced heartbreak of this magnitude, Jake reflected. Not in the *Iliad* nor the *Epic of Gilgamesh*.

Jake wasn't always this way. He remembered discovering the beach, all those years ago. He'd got lost in the jungle, scooter running out of petrol, the night coming in at tropical speed. He'd needed somewhere to stay, anywhere. That was when he emerged onto this stretch of sand for the first time, drunk on the beauty of the place and cackling with laughter. Jake had been young then, erudite and witty, full of potential.

What happened to that guy?

Finally there was all this Napoleon stuff, and here was the most intractable tangle of all. Three more cards had arrived that morning. March 1809, war against Austria, and Napoleon told his confidant Roederer:

"If it seems I am ready to meet everything, it's because before entering on a challenge I have meditated lengthily, and fore-seen what may happen."

Jake had checked the quote online – once again it was authentic. A shiver of unreality. *Who the hell is sending me this crap?*

He read about the campaign. A month later, when a captured Austrian officer refused to reveal their order of battle, Napoleon had replied: "Don't worry, I know everything anyway."

To the astonishment of the officer he'd gone on to outline the position of every corps in the Austrian army.

The next card bore a quotation from Molé, one of Napoleon's ministers.

"When Napoleon was leading our armies they became irre-sistible, and the generals obeying him all seemed great cap-tains. But when he was absent, those armies found it hard holding their own ..."

The thesis forming in his mind was becoming hard to deny. Finally there was a rumination from Napoleon after final defeat at Waterloo, incarcerated on his island-prison of St Helena in the South Atlantic:

> *"One should never ask more of Fortune than she is able to grant."*

Why was Jake not running? Engaging with this stuff would catapult him once more into the ghastly race between MI6 and the Chinese Secret Service, fix upon him the eye of Fate itself. A capricious entity; when he thought about it a darkness seemed to roll in from the Gulf of Thailand, like a fog. Was he suffering from psychosis? On balance he thought not, though it was certainly a possibility. He briefly considered the insane possibility of having a drink. But that would only further constrict the tangle that enmeshed him. He clenched a fist.

No way.

From nowhere Jake felt a whisper of ambition, of duty, even. The knowledge in his head could prevent terrible crimes, make him the most high profile journalist on the planet. But this was swiftly dampened by a sense of his own inadequacy. If you can't keep a girlfriend, you can't bring down MI6.

"Hello gorgeous." Chloë's eyes danced with some new mischief. "I've got something for you. Come with me."

Her hand ran down his forearm with the touch of lace, tightening around his wrist, and Jake allowed himself to be led down the beach in the twilight. The bar hadn't changed in fifteen years: psychedelic paintings, Bob Marley on the stereo, ultraviolet lights daubing it with a feel of the underworld. Chloë threw herself down on some cushions. Something small and brown was in her fingers.

"Good gracious, you don't give up, do you?" he said. "I don't smoke hashish, never have."

But the knavery in her smile told a different story.

"It's opium, Jake."

Madness, the point of no return. But all of a sudden he felt reckless. What did he have to lose? Fear and temptation enfolded him; when he closed his eyes he heard that deep vibration of the void.

"It'll soothe you," she said gently, as if reading his mind. "It comes from the hill tribes in the north. The high's milder than you might think – it's natural, very organic. It'll bring you some peace."

Or put me out of my misery.

The ultraviolet picked out broken veins on the bridge of Jake's nose, souvenirs of his drinking days. In the purple light the skin resembled the shell of a sea urchin. His shoulders hunched inward as he eyed the drug.

"You're on," he said.

15

Jenny had needed to get close to the inquisitor, that was the key to it. Her only chance was to obtain his phone, get a GPS reading to Jake and pray that he worked out the significance. He was clever, still recklessly in love with her; there was a *chance* he could get her out, however minuscule. Besides, she had nobody else to turn to. But to steal Fung's mobile, she'd needed proximity.

Jenny had assessed Fung as a 'driver': results-driven and competitive, but forceful, a risk taker. To heighten these characteristics she'd simulated an amiable personality type, hidden within a false shell of bravado for him to penetrate. After her goading had provoked a reaction Fung was allowed to unearth the submissive within. Like a hunter taking baby steps towards a watchful prey – seeing if the animal is alert to the meaning of the movements – Jenny gave him the feeling of being in control. When it came to psychology and the power of suggestion, she had once been the most gifted officer at MI6. Fung never stood a chance. He fell for this deception; assumed the role of teacher with child; deduced that information could be elicited by brute aggression. A physical encounter became inevitable. When he had Jenny pinned against she wall, she'd pushed back against his lapels, pressing the phone in his jacket pocket against his body. As he shouted in her face, her forefinger and thumb were extracting it; then it was clamped against his chest only by her palm, so he could still feel it there had he been paying attention. When she removed her hand to shield herself from the head-butt the phone dropped out of Fung's jacket. His sightline was blocked as she turned to protect herself and her left hand caught the phone, which promptly vanished.

Jenny had watched Fung type in his pin number on the first day of the interrogation. Now she keyed it in and the locking screen slid blissfully upward. She was looking at the menu of a BlackBerry with five bars of signal.

When she opened BlackBerry Maps the screen juddered.

There was no GPS signal.

"Don't do this to me."

Jenny restarted the phone. Still no signal.

"Please …" she whispered.

Nothing.

Her captors must have known about MI6's tactic of inserting bugs *inside* their most important targets. A GPS jammer had been installed nearby. Jenny stood rigidly, breathing fast and thinking hard.

The window.

In a single movement she had scrambled onto her bed, stretching to her fullest height to take a photo through the porthole. The image was a smear of light in a sea of dark, like the view from a dislocated telescope. Jenny strained to remain stable, the tendons in her body a single cord. She tried again. A blurred street scene set in outer space. Jenny landed on the floor, uploaded the photograph to the car forum without comment and deleted the image. As Fung walked into the room tears sprang back into her eyes.

Now that the space between them had been broached, getting the phone back into his pocket would be simpler. Jenny could enter his force-field without suspicion. And she was trained in distraction, how to direct the spotlight of someone's attention.

"Your watch," she said.

"What about it?"

"My dad has that exact same one." A convulsion of sobs. "I haven't seen him for two years."

Fung watched – smug, fatuous – as the beaten spook undid the strap, pathetic in her distress. She raised the Omega before her face like a talisman, directing his concentration.

"Daddy," she whispered, collapsing onto his shoulders like a landslide.

Cue hiccups, rasping for breath. Fung pushed her away roughly.

The phone was back in his pocket.

Now it was down to Jake. Whether he still loved her enough to try. Whether he could summon the brilliance that had once outfoxed the entire British Secret Service. Whether he was sober.

16

Chloë produced a length of bamboo with a ceramic-lined hole at one end and plastered a fingernail of opium around the aperture. She held a lighter to it, pulling on the bamboo until the opium bubbled and spat. She exhaled a lungful of smoke, eyelids fluttering, and fell onto her back. A violet cloud dissipated through the eaves of the beach bar as she repeated the preparation.

The smoke tasted sweet, like petals. There was no catch in the back of Jake's throat; he felt a pleasant heaviness in the limbs. From nowhere a measure of contentment materialised.

Chloë loaded up the bamboo, working briskly. "Have another," she said. "In the north the shamans smoke fifty pipes a night. We could go up to five or ten, no worries."

Jake took a second hit, and his neuroses were *pad, pad, padded* down again. As they smoked the high became more cerebral, moving like a beneficent fever from the body into the brain until the night danced with magic. Speaking was an effort, but her voice comforted him.

"Don't stop talking," he said.

"But I can't think of what to say." – Dreamily.

"Read me something," he murmured. "I'd like that."

"You first."

Jake army-crawled to the bookcase, which was a typical back-packer selection: Howard Marks's *Mr Nice*, John Grisham and J.R.R. Tolkien. At random he selected *The Odyssey*.

"Homer? Trippy, baby. Hit me."

He read to her of Calypso the nymph, who enchanted Odysseus with song and sex: detaining him on her island for seven years. Keeping him from his duty and from his wife.

Calypso came to Odysseus sitting upon the shore. He had been weeping. Sweet life was ebbing away in the tears he cried for his lost home. For the nymph had stopped pleasing Odysseus. By night he was forced to sleep with her in the vaulted cave, icy lover. But in daytime he sat on the beach, torturing himself with tears, looking at the sea.

Jake gazed out of the bar, reminded suddenly of himself: thinking about Jenny, as sand slipped through his fingers. Something else was nagging at him, but he couldn't put his finger on it.

"My turn," said Chloë, snatching the volume and letting it fall open.

She recited Odysseus' visit to the island of Circe, a goddess of magic, an enchantress. Jake's grip on that half-formed thought began to loosen before his neurones let go completely, the notion lost to an enfeebled brain.

Circe's house was in a clearing, made of polished stone. Guarding it were wolves and lions Circe had entranced with magical drugs. Circe made a meal of cheese, barley-meal and honey for them. Into it she poured a potion, to make them forget their native land.

It was bothering Jake again, that intuition he could not bring to the forefront of his consciousness. But still Chloë lulled him with her tongue and she loaded up another pipe. His eyes were drawn to her shadow, projected onto the wall behind her, and in the spectral ultraviolet, drugs pulsing through his eyeballs, her tresses dangling, the shadow morphed into *Circe herself*.

At once Jake was alert.

Revelation hit him like water and dazzling ice.

Terror made him cold.

That errant thought had emerged dripping from the fog of his mind, and he examined it and knew it the truth. He had been living in an intelligence trap. And Chloë was an MI6 agent. That explained why such a beauty was interested in him. That explained why she tempted him with booze, tried to wean him onto more powerful substances. He was to be kept here supine, satiated with sex and drugs. His thoughts on Napoleon monitored; lost to his own self more with each passing day. Kept from Jenny, like Odysseus from his Penelope.

Oh Jesus. *Jenny ...*

He hadn't checked the message board for days. Chloë was unaware he had awoken, that he had rediscovered the ability to make *connections*. Just as connections were being made in the air around them. In outer space.

I have to get out of here. This very evening.

Jake lurched to his feet; with panic he realised how high he was.

Chloë stopped reading and put down the book. "You all good, baby?"

"Feeling a bit sick. Need some air. Going for a walk."

Jake knew nothing about this woman – her real name, where she grew up. And they'd *slept together* for crying out loud. So there had been two of them trying to convince him he was making love. She must have loathed it: a sacrifice, for Queen and country. Was MI6 his mysterious correspondent, feeding titbits to his copious intellect to provoke the breakthrough that had eluded them?

Somehow Jake made it onto the beach. The sand was cool on his ankles; the stars were beautiful and beyond counting, each a swivelling diamond set in a blackness somehow potent with menace. And still the opium throbbed through him, heightening in power with each heartbeat. Jake realised he was in a trance. The world was melting ... hard to say if he was asleep or awake ... he was beyond pleasure or fear now, floating down the beach in this chimerical state, through a world that was shimmering.

Trying to remember something.

Perfect silence.

His passport ...

Circe's realm.

17

Jake awoke to sunlight and the sound of waves. He sat up and vomited, retching until his abdomen had turned concave and he was thoroughly emptied out. The beach was unfamiliar – long and windswept, scrubby development strung along it. It looked like the south coast of the island. He had his backpack (good start!), but an unknown towel lay alongside him. He felt the flare of sunburn on his face; he also had no shoes on.

"Hey! Are you ok?" A German tourist, full of motherly concern. "I tried to wake you up, but too much the alcohol last night, I think?"

"Something like that."

"I put this towel on for protecting from the sun, but you are always throwing it away. You just ... take care of yourself. This island is not so safe, you know?"

Jake's memory of events after leaving the bar was like a jigsaw puzzle in the early stages of completion: scattered images on a bed of nothingness. There had been a frustration, something he needed not to forget – something that bled away as he grasped at it.

Passports.

With a rush of terror Jake patted himself down. But there in his pockets were both of his clean passports, procured by Jenny before their flight from London, a bankcard too. He couldn't remember packing them – it might as well have been done by a different person – but years of getting smashed had bequeathed him a highly functional autopilot setting. He had a vague recollection of being on someone's moped. And one image was seared into his mind: crossing Koh Phan Ngan's highest peak, all four corners of the island stretched across the sea like a dark virus, moonlight slick on the water's surface.

Jake hitchhiked into Thong Sala. It was a typical backpacker town: a straggle of bars and beach shops run by weather-beaten ex-pats, Thais in flip-flops zipping about on motorbikes. He found an internet café and logged on to the car forum.

"Oh no." Jake gripped his forehead in his hands. "You idiot, you *idiot.*"

Jenny had posted two messages at the beginning of the week, and he had been so wrapped up in his own thoughts he had not even bothered to check. A surge of anger went through him then – at Chloë, at Beloff, at Antoine Devosge and Napoleon; at himself.

The first message mentioned a Hyundai. *They are on to us.* Then Jake saw the second message, and felt only confusion. The photograph had been taken from an upstairs window. Beyond a security fence topped with razor wire lay an alleyway of yellow stone. The impression was of a medina, somewhere ancient. He and Jenny had codified numerous messages, but she'd never mentioned photographs. He stared at the screen, willing his brain to generate the answer. A funny thing, the mind: command it to produce and the response is sullen. Jake tried to let go, allowing his grey matter to absorb the problem. Disassembling it, examining each component.

The first deduction was that it must mean *something*. Jenny knew the unexpected would freak him out. He smiled – it felt good to be using his head again. What was she telling him?

She was saying …

She was saying *I am here.*

Jake grinned again, had the feeling of progress. The opium hangover retreated another notch. Why was Jenny telling him where she was? Did she miss him?

I've fallen out of love with you, Jake.

Jake felt a whisper of tragedy at the recollection; with an effort he pushed it away. What else could it be? Suddenly his mind became clear.

This is where they are keeping me prisoner.

And therefore:

I need your help.

There was no other answer, and the admixture of anger and fear produced a fresh surge of adrenaline. And he felt another emotion. What was it now, this long-forgotten sensation? It was *hope*. The most important human sentiment, one that trumped loyalty and even love. It was hope that propelled the species out of Africa. It was hope that crossed deserts.

*

The clue was an Orthodox priest, striding along in black robes and a cylindrical hat. A *kalimavkion*, Jake remembered from childhood holidays. What the hell was Jenny doing in Greece? The city was made of yellow stone and graffiti trailed meaninglessly along a near wall; a flying buttress soared over the alleyway at the vanishing point. The middle of a sign on the building opposite protruded over the security fence – it was curved, evidently following the arch of a doorway. Only six letters could be seen above the razor wire: *ian Hos*.

But Googling 'Greece and ian Hos' produced junk. Jake perused images of various Greek cities. Athens looked completely different. Corfu Town bore a resemblance, but wasn't quite right.

It was sunny, no clouds in the sky. Something about the sunshine – the purity? – reminded him of the Middle East.

A sharp inhalation.

That graffiti wasn't some random squiggle. *It was Arabic.*

A translation website offered up a single word in English. Short, offensive and rather like the name of the Danish king Canute. Jake snorted. But still, he was making progress – Jenny *was* somewhere in the Middle East. An impressive bit of intuition, he reckoned. An ancient city in the Middle East where Christians felt safe walking the street. Well, that last bit rounded it down nowadays. Another flash of inspiration: Cairo, the Coptic Quarter! But 'Coptic Cairo and ian Hos' drew another blank in the search engine. He stared at the six letters, willing them to yield. The second word could be 'hostel'. But what about the first? It was a real life crossword. And crosswords were Jake's thing, he could do this!

When he stopped thinking about it the answer came. *Christian Hostel.* But there was no such establishment in Coptic Cairo. And a quick image search showed he was wrong completely – Coptic Cairo was hewn of grey stone, not yellow. Jake stared at the priest, resentful of the nonchalance in his stride.

Where are you?

Come to think of it, there was a Greek Quarter in Istanbul too. But Turkey wasn't an Arabic-speaking country, which made the graffiti out of place. By association, the word 'Armenia' popped into his mind. He searched for images of an Armenian priest.

"Yes!"

Jake's shout alerted a Chinese tourist on the far side of the café. The priest Jenny had photographed wasn't Greek at all – he was Armenian, there was no doubt. But that only deepened the mystery, for they didn't speak Arabic in Armenia either. Where else? In which ancient city could Christians practise freely, where Arabic was spoken with Roman letters on the signs – and an Armenian diaspora in residence too? Jake's chuckle, when it came, was long and dry. Jenny was being held where Christianity began. He was looking at a photograph of Jerusalem.

He stopped laughing.

Mr Beloff was struck dead in the garden of his second home near the Wailing Wall yesterday evening.

Now Jake's searches became more urgent. Google Maps revealed an Armenian Quarter in the Old City; Jake switched to Street View and went exploring. But the alleyway wasn't there. The stone was similar, the architecture, the *feel* of the place. Yet the flying buttress and security fence were nowhere to be seen. Jake slumped onto the desk, staring at the six letters.

Armenian Hostel.

It had to be! With trembling fingers Jake searched for the words, coasting upward on a sense of rising glory. But there was no Armenian Hostel in Jerusalem.

ian Hos.

Three vowels, three consonants, mocking Jake from the screen. What other institution might a priest be leaving? Suddenly – halleluiah, glory be! – the word resolved itself before Jake's eyes.

Hospice.

There was an Armenian Hospice in the Old City.

It stood on the Way of Sorrows, down which Christ bore his cross before the crucifixion. Jake switched to Street View and there it all was. The alleyway with its medieval flagstones, the flying buttress, which he now saw adjoined the Church of the Condemnation. And a fifteen-foot high fence, glinting with razor wire and CCTV cameras. Armed with only a photograph he had pinpointed a single spot on the five hundred million square kilometres of planet earth.

18

"What do you mean, he's disappeared?" Parr had been in Bangkok for an hour and already things were deteriorating.

"He just wandered off last night," said Chloë down the line from Koh Phan Ngan. "I don't know where he is."

Davis stared at the speakerphone. "Hopeless," he mouthed.

Parr had assembled her team in a secure speech room at the modernist British Embassy in Bangkok. Alexander Coppock-Davoli fiddled with his Glastonbury wristband. Alec McCabe – the nascent Etruscanologist – observed the crisis with the detached amusement of a veteran. The Queen Mother looked on in portrait form with a toothy smile, as if she alone knew the answers.

"We nearly had him with the opium," said Chloë. "He was enjoying it for sure. Then he announced he needed some air – and that was the last I saw of him."

"You were out of it too, weren't you, pet?" said Davis.

"That's enough, Frank," said Parr. "Wolsey was hardly going to try the stuff if Chloë didn't, was he?"

"I took my eye off the ball," said Chloë. "I'm sorry."

"What about his trail?" asked Parr.

"He left barefoot."

"Right, so he was out of it, plain and simple," said McCabe. "Gone for a wander somewhere and passed out."

"Maybe he's drowned," said Davis hopefully.

"He took his backpack," said Chloë.

"So he did rumble you," growled Davis. "You must've given the game away while you were out of your tree."

"That's *enough*, Frank," Parr snapped. "Chloë's made a lot of sacrifices on this job. She did well to string him along this long. Wolsey may be a bit shambolic, but as you of all people should know, he's got a good eye. A rather dangerous characteristic, as my predecessor put it."

"He must have worked out about the shoes," muttered McCabe.

"I think he was just wasted, to be honest," said Chloë.

"What's the latest on Frobisher?" asked Parr.

Her trail had led to the airport; but radiation could hardly be tracked through thin air.

"Good news," Coppock-Davoli chipped in. "She uploaded a photograph to that website we're monitoring."

"Photograph of what?"

"A street in Jerusalem," replied Coppock-Davoli. "We worked out where it was taken through the EXIF data stored on the ..."

"I do know how to geo-locate a photo," interrupted Parr.

"No harm in a bit of youthful enthusiasm, eh?" said Davis.

"The question is," mused McCabe, folding one leg over the other, "does Wolsey know how to do it?"

"With Wolsey's level of technical proficiency?" Parr replied. "I doubt it. He could no more extract EXIF data from a photograph than lay a golden egg."

"Could he work it out from the picture, though?"

"Almost impossible, surely?" said Coppock-Davoli.

"I wouldn't put it past him," said Parr. "Not if he's got his thinking cap screwed on again."

"What now?" asked Davis.

"Chloë stays on Koh Phan Ngan to look for Wolsey. He might be lying dead in the jungle for all we know. I'm more concerned about Frobisher – she's considerably more *compos mentis*. So the rest of us are going to Jerusalem to say a rather forthright hello to this mysterious vagrant and his taxi driver chum."

McCabe tapped at his computer. "A Thai Airlines flight to Ben Gurion leaves in two hours."

Parr sighed. "Back the way I came it is then. I do too many air miles ..."

Not far away, a Bangkok Airways flight from the Gulf of Thailand touched down at Suvarnabhumi Airport. A security guard scanned Jake's body – he was relieved and a little surprised the device didn't beep. But an alarming thought occurred to him, and he emptied his backpack onto the floor of a cubicle in the gents to begin a fingertip search. He hovered over a photograph of himself aged nineteen on the back of a pick-up truck in Guatemala. Suntanned, bog brush hair, ridiculously childlike. It was one of a handful he'd snatched from his flat before fleeing the UK. Jake stared deeply into his own eyes: a boy who had no idea what was coming. A boy would meet a girl called Jenny and fall in love with her. A girl who would break his heart.

His father's feet protruded from the pile, but Jake couldn't bring himself to look at the next photograph down. It was two years since he'd seen his parents. He decided to jettison the camera they'd given him for his thirtieth birthday – it would be easy to stow a tracking device inside it. Another minor crumb of sadness sprinkled onto a life turned upside down by the British Secret Service. Finally he examined the backpack.

There was a lump in the material.

Hard yet with a bit of give, like a packet of compacted sand. Jake shook his head in exasperation. Had it always been there? It didn't feel like a bug. But there was nothing else for it: he cut open the material with a pair of nail scissors. A bag of white powder fell into his hands.

Jake's heart was racing.

Heroin, probably, or maybe cocaine. Jake flushed the packet down the toilet and washed his hands. Again he was overcome by MI6's malice – this little insurance policy could have seen him a resident at the Bangkok Hilton for life. Executed, even. And *what* was this fetish for illegal drugs?

A Thai Airways flight to Israel departed in two hours' time. Nice airline. But at short notice it cost a thousand dollars; a Turkish Airlines flight shortly after was half the cost. Jake wrestled with the dilemma. Every hour might be crucial. But his funds were nearly exhausted, and running out of money completely would not improve matters. Besides, he could use the extra time to better become the person in his passport.

It would have been most unfortunate for Jake to have shared a flight with the very people who were hunting him. But his choice to fly Turkish only postponed the inevitable. They were heading to the same place; there would be an encounter. It was written.

19

"You know you're off the beaten track when the women are all wandering around naked," observed Serval.

Captain Andrew Bracknell of the Royal Anglian Regiment glanced at his passenger and smiled. They'd been driving for two hours and it was the first hint of warmth from the gruff intelligence man.

"They certainly do things differently out here," Bracknell admitted. He was young and rosy-cheeked, Afghan Hound thin.

"She's quite fit, though," contributed a private in the back of the Snatch Land Rover.

The subject of discussion was a young woman wearing only a loincloth, squatting by the roadside with a bottle of freshly tapped palm wine. They were lurching down an ochre track through a mess of tousled scrub: palm trees and bush, everything very green, the far-off mountains humps of pistachio against the sky. Huts that had been torched during the current conflict stood alongside burned out buildings of yesteryear, invaded by foliage.

A naked boy burst from the bush and ran alongside. "Ba-boo-nay! Ba-boo-nay!"

Captain Bracknell wound down the window and merrily took up the chant, the squaddies joined in too, and the vehicle rocked on its axles with the cries.

"Ba-boo-nay! Ba-boo-nay!"

The boy looked momentarily perplexed before smiling again. Running and clapping, re-joining the chorus. A snort of laughter erupted from their interpreter's nostrils.

"What is it, Suleiman?" asked Bracknell. "Do share ..."

"Baboonay. Is meaning, 'white man'." The translator surrendered to hysterics.

"So we've all been chanting, 'white man, white man'?" said the other squaddie. "That is brilliant."

"Oh crikey," said Bracknell. "Bit awkward."

Serval looked irritated. "Is this tin can going to keep us in one piece?" He rapped on the door. "Didn't have the best of reputations in Afghanistan."

"Oh, we're safe enough," said Bracknell. "She can take a bit of small arms fire – and they aren't using IEDs yet, thank god."

"Hear, hear," muttered one of the privates darkly.

"Anyway, the militias cleared off from this district last week," said Bracknell. "Only wish I could say the same of where we're headed."

Serval's mind drifted to a shack bar in Freetown last night; the booming laugh of its owner when he'd voiced his destination.

You are going to the south? They will eat you there, man. They will eat you up ...

Serval had been briefed the previous morning. The British Army – supported from the air, battle-hardened after years of war – had smashed the militias with ridiculous ease. The warring sides had dissolved into the bush; Sierra Leone was now a de facto possession of the United Kingdom. But a Liberian warlord was launching cross-border raids into a mining region called Kambui, where the diamonds came from and the coltan that went into people's mobile phones. This had interrupted the flow of minerals; Serval's job was to solve the problem. It must be important, for the call came from C himself.

"Why don't we send the SAS into Liberia?" Serval had asked. "Wipe them all out."

"Liberia's in the US sphere of influence, Sierra Leone's ours," C replied. "We don't want to irritate the Yanks, basically."

Serval laughed. "Sphere of influence? What century is this?"

"It's not a laughing matter, Jacob. We know that we're in Sierra Leone to do good, but a few US senators are getting uppity. 'Neo-colonialism' and all that nonsense."

"That's ridiculous," said Serval. "The locals are over the moon we're here – it's embarrassing, frankly. And neo-colonialism? They can talk ..."

"Well, there it is. The warlord is called Jason Bourne – named himself after some movie character I gather. Rather an unpleasant man. He's currently deep inside Sierra Leone with five hundred drug-addled crazies under his command. They're camped in a wildlife sanctuary called Tiwai Island, on the River Moa. I want you to go and talk to him. It's remote down there – thick jungle, exotic wildlife and what not. I thought the job would be up your street."

"Why don't we just bomb this island sky high?"

"Because another Liberian militia would spring up in the vacuum to carry on the plunder. Sierra Leone needs these resources if it's ever to build itself up again. Bourne's the regional strongman – so let's make him one of ours. Turn him into a bulwark against other war-bands."

"And how exactly am I supposed to do that?"

"Bribery? I don't know, use your brains, that's why we're doing the persuading. Talk to him. Work out what makes him tick. Try and ascertain if he's being encouraged by Washington, for a start. Give him whatever he wants, make whatever assurances he wants. Just get him on side."

"There's another," said one of the privates, hauling Serval back to the present.

An old man squatted in the dust. His cheek had been amputated in the recent past, a mass of volcanic black scab in its place. Serval was surprised to find he had punched the car door, a reflex action.

"And another," said the second squaddie. "Bloody hell, look at that guy."

A man with no hands stood by the track, his wrists swaddled in T-shirts and a chicken nestled in one forearm. As the Land Rover passed he waved a stump in greeting.

"Absolutely appalling," muttered Captain Bracknell. "It doesn't matter how often you see it ..."

As the bush grew denser signs of habitation dwindled. They passed a rusty water tank rising from the foliage like a hot air balloon, a battered WWF sign urging the locals to leave the chimpanzees alone.

They are our friends ...

"What brings a spook to a shithole like this then, mate?" asked one of the squaddies.

"Don't be a silly arse, Daniels," said Bracknell.

Serval made no reply, his soft hair bouncing as the Land Rover picked its way along. He couldn't pinpoint when the landscape changed into proper jungle. But when he wound the window down the rainforest was steaming and screeching with life. This was a place where every species – plant, mammal, reptile or insect – brandished spikes or fangs or deadly venom. Nature at war with itself. The explorer shifted in his seat, keen to get out there. A Chinook flew low overhead; they passed a British Army encampment, the tents a glimpse of order against the chaos of the jungle. Finally they reached the mud hut village where Bracknell had established his field headquarters. A heavy machine gun was emplaced at the far side of the settlement and soldiers played cricket on the red earth, a perversion of an English village scene.

"Welcome to the front line," said Bracknell.

"Where's this island?" said Serval.

"Just over there. You want to take a look now?"

The sky was turning a richer blue.

"I'll have a quick squizz, if it's all the same to you. Before we lose the light."

Bracknell led him through a clearing of waist-level scrub. Bamboo was rampant, each shaft as thick as the arm of a heavyweight boxer. Serval glimpsed water through the shafts, green and steady-flowing.

"We need to be a bit careful now, they're not averse to taking pot shots." Bracknell winked. "Bloody awful aim though."

They stole through the scrub to another machine gun post. Bare-chested squaddies sprawled in a trench, all gleaming muscle and tribal tattoos. A copy of the *Mirror* was handed around and *(What's The Story) Morning Glory?* droned from a stereo. Fifty feet of water separated them from Tiwai Island.

"How big is it?" asked Serval.

"Six clicks long by three wide," Bracknell replied. "It used to be a wildlife reserve before all this kicked off. Chimps and pygmy hippos. Everything eaten now, of course."

They will eat you up.

The trees on the island were fifty feet tall and mushrooming with foliage, like a palisade of molten candles. Palms leaned close enough to the surface of the water to drink from it and a dugout canoe was roped up on the beach. The island was very still.

"Have a closer look if you want," said Bracknell, handing him binoculars. "But, er – only if you've got a strong stomach."

Serval peered through the glasses. What he had taken to be rope was in fact human entrails, draped across the boat. And perched on its bow, eyes swivelled in different directions, was a severed head. It was Wally, whom he had sat next to on the plane from Heathrow.

20

Frank Davis was not predisposed to subtlety, and this was not a
hostage situation – it wouldn't be a disaster if Frobisher ended up
dead. So he had opted to go in hard. He intended to kill every one
of the operatives holding Frobisher captive, and he was looking
forward to this immensely. He sat in a blacked-out Jeep with
Coppock-Davoli and McCabe. They wore masks, UV goggles and
Israeli police uniforms which were bespoke reproductions down
to the bootlaces. Each man carried a silenced MP5 machine pistol.

"The Way of Sorrows," Davis smirked. "Not wrong eh, mates?"

Coppock-Davoli smiled weakly. Sweat had formed beads
around his eye-sockets.

"You nervous, fella?" said Davis.

"Not at all," replied the youngster unconvincingly.

"No need to be. The Chinese are pussies – you could probably
take them singlehandedly."

"We don't actually know it's the Chinese," said McCabe.

"Of course it fucking is."

A black dot skimmed over the street, ducking and weaving
like a dragon fly.

"There she goes," said McCabe.

The drone passed twenty feet above the compound walls before
disappearing from view and attaching itself to the front door of
the safe house itself.

A radio crackled. "The charge is in position," said Parr.

She was on the roof of the Armenian Hospice with a sniper
rifle and a UV scope that could see through the safe house's
reinforced door as if it was glass.

Frank licked his lips. "Now we wait."

"No we don't," said Parr. "Someone's walking towards the
front door. It's a woman. She's fiddling in a handbag. About to
leave the house."

Coppock-Davoli's fingers tightened around his machine pistol. "Relax," Davis soothed him.

Parr's voice had become stiff. "In three, two, one ... get ready, get ready."

At the explosion all three agents were out of the car and sprinting.

*

Damien di Angelo was born into a blue-collar African-American family in the Ellwood district of Baltimore. The gaily-coloured terraces where he grew up could have passed for an Edwardian seaside town, were they not mostly boarded up – his formative years were spent amid the most diabolical crack epidemic in US history. Unusually for the neighbourhood, di Angelo's parents were married. But his mother was an alcoholic and his father suffered from chronic anxiety, while two older brothers resided in Maryland Penitentiary. Two things saved di Angelo from the same. First, he had been born with a very high IQ, and second, he played baseball. The eccentricity of the American education system meant it was the latter that elevated him to the University of Pennsylvania to study law. Displaying a characteristic single-mindedness he prospered, and looked set for a prestigious clerkship in the Supreme Court. But an unexpected veer in direction was in store, for one cold November day he stunned his tutors by announcing he was to join the US Army. And he did it for love.

Di Angelo knew he was gay at thirteen. Like the ancient Greeks, he considered the male torso the ultimate expression of beauty. But in nineties Baltimore that was not a sentiment to be voiced, and he arrived in Pennsylvania having never been kissed. Andy Carlson was the straightest guy in his fraternity: buzz cut, military family, legs like New England oak trees and clean cut as they come. Perhaps that's why a kid from the crack wastelands of Baltimore was drawn to him. Naturally, di

Angelo never expressed his feelings. But they became friends, and when Carlson joined the army and deployed to Iraq, di Angelo followed suit. The need to impress him was imprinted on his psyche.

Then Carlson was hit with a rocket propelled grenade.

He lost a chunk of his torso and was brain damaged by blood loss from a severed femoral artery. When di Angelo visited the family home it was like paying a social call to a tuber. Right then and there he decided to stay in the army. Like Serval summiting K2 for a dying Australian, this was to be his tribute.

Brainpower is valuable in any organisation, but perhaps somewhat rarer in armies than in law firms. It also saves lives; di Angelo rose fast. Soon he was in military intelligence, directing drone strikes in Yemen and Somalia where more than one terrorist had been turned into a 'bugsplat' on his recommendation. The CIA came calling soon after.

This explained how Damien di Angelo came to be in a safe house in Jerusalem with a half-completed Sudoku, thinking about the explosion which turned a love affair with Carlson from fantasy to impossibility.

There was a blast downstairs and the whole building shook.

*

Dr Robin Matthews, the history lecturer from Warwick University, landed in the Holy Land two hours and seven minutes after MI6's team. The documentation Jenny had arranged in London was sound: with his side parting, tweed jacket and elbow patches the toughest immigration officers on earth didn't give Jake a second look.

So: this was Jerusalem. Modern outskirts, brown brick housing developments full of Orthodox Jews in all the clobber, flyovers swooping over every hill, as improbable in their curves as their defiance of gravity. Modern Israel might not be a perfect society, but you certainly can't fault the engineering.

Jerusalem's core was the Old City, wrapped in its shell of Ottoman ramparts. On this small plateau King David was buried and Jesus crucified; Mohammed was raised up to heaven. Jake entered by the Jaffa Gate, past a Mamluk citadel with its crooked minaret. The fort stood on the foundations of Herod's palace, the ancient blocks five times larger than the medieval stones.

Inside the city walls it was calm. The only sign of fault lines were the Israeli Defence Force soldiers, hale twenty-year-olds with shaved heads and perfect teeth. Jake navigated souks manned by shrewd Palestinians, packed with Nigerian pilgrims in multi-coloured robes. He was near her.

There was an explosion two blocks away, too loud for a backfiring car.

Locals deduced terrorism, muscling past in practised silence. At the second explosion their flight became ruthless. The blasts had come from the direction Jake was heading in, and he felt a swooping sensation rise up his windpipe. He broke into a run, against the flow of the crowd.

*

McCabe slapped a charge onto the door in the outer wall, blew that off its hinges too. A nest of video cameras observed the commandos as they darted into the courtyard: guns first, cheeks glued to their weapons, as if the barrels were pulling them on. The safe house was three storeys high and centuries old. The steel door had been propelled into the building, a smoking cave left in its wake. The hit squad fanned across the courtyard, taking position either side of the doorway.

"The woman's lying underneath the door at the end of the corridor," radioed Parr. "She's alive."

Davis raised three fingers.

Two fingers.

One finger.

He and McCabe rotated into the doorway, firing a controlled blast with their machine pistols. The bullets ricocheted off the inch-thick steel, imprinting it with thimbles.

Beneath it Senior Special Agent Wendy Valdez's left shoulder was in tatters.

"I'm hurt bad," she shouted. "I need help here, guys."

Davis paused. "American?"

McCabe nodded grimly. "Sounds like it. Evelyn, do we pull back?"

A hesitation. "Proceed. But for goodness sake, no survivors."

"*Bien sûr, Madame*," said Davis.

He tossed a flash grenade down the corridor, there was a colossal bang and the doorway was illuminated solar white. Davis and McCabe swung in from each side with guns trained and advanced. The door was blackened and bent, wobbling slightly.

"Be careful," shouted Parr. "She's …"

Valdez popped up from beneath the door and got three shots off with a Beretta before Davis blew off the top of her skull with a single bullet that buzzed from the silenced machine pistol like a supersonic bee, opening up a skylight into her brain.

"I'm hit." McCabe's tone was of mild surprise.

"Is it bad?" said Davis.

McCabe touched his shoulder, where blood glistened. "It grazed me."

Jamie Fung emerged from the far end of the corridor and shot McCabe in the stomach. He concertinaed inward, crumpled to the floor and let out a howl of pain. Davis took two paces forward: stepping like a ballerina, shrinking to the left of the corridor. When Fung tried his luck again Davis shot him in the head.

"With me now, Alexander," he said.

Coppock-Davoli stepped into the corridor, mouth gaping at the carnage. McCabe squirmed at his feet, whimpering now and blood foaming between his fingers. A tattered handbag spilled out its contents: phone, molten lipstick, a singed copy of *Eat, Pray, Love*. Blood pooled beneath the warped door; brains were splattered across the far wall. Fung's hand protruded from the end of the corridor, his ring finger twitching.

Cordite hung in the air.

"Evelyn, could you be a sweetheart and us lend a hand?" said Davis mildly.

"I need to cover the exits."

"Evelyn, lend a hand."

Not a question this time – like the captain of an aeroplane, Davis trumped all ranks when it came to matters paramilitary. Forty seconds later she was by his side.

A chunk of skull crunched underfoot.

21

Jenny was attempting to recite every Shakespearean sonnet she'd learned at A Level when the first explosion shook the building, right beneath her. A louder explosion followed at the perimeter wall. Someone was blasting their way in, the wrong way round. This was not how Jake operated. She slapped her palms on the cell door, shook the handle, screamed for them to let her out. The door was opened moments later by a black guy in his thirties, tall and thin with cheekbones like chevrons.

"My colleagues are trying to hold them off," said di Angelo. "We have to go. Right now."

The accent was Eastern Seaboard; so she was with the Americans.

"This is not a goddamn *suggestion*," said di Angelo, levelling a gun at her. "Come with me or we cut our losses."

Jenny could sense his panic. "Okay, you win. Let's go."

As she stepped out of the cell a needle went into her arm and her world became woozy. But it was more of a serum than a knockout blow. She was steered to a spiral staircase, could only comply. They descended, traversed an underground passage, ascended a spiral staircase at the far end and emerged into an antique shop. An American behind the counter was shouting, "Go! Go! Go!"

On the Way of Sorrows the daylight was dazzling.

Jake rounded the corner. There was the hospice, the Church of the Condemnation, the compound with its high walls and razor wire. It was like stepping into the photograph. A rake-thin man walked away at speed, oblivious to Jake's presence. Leaning in to him, obviously drugged, was Jenny. He knew those shoulders like his own reflection. That neck, the fall of her hair.

There are few instances when violence dispensed without warning is the best course of action, but this was one of them. Displayed outside the antique shop was an Ottoman cannon ball, ten kilograms of polished granite. Jake grabbed the missile, caught up with di Angelo and brought it down on his cranium with all his might. Five trickles of blood began at the agent's crown and ran down all sides of his head. He emitted a little moan and sank to the ground.

Jenny had a black eye and her pupils were dilated, but Jake saw a jolt of recognition. She tried to say something, failed.

She tried again: "Jake."

In her good eye a single tear welled, and Jake felt his own vision prickle with salt water too.

"You came," she murmured.

"There was never a doubt, Jenny. Never a doubt."

They were a team again.

A helicopter whizzed overhead as the first wave of soldiers surged into view, the Star of David on their arms.

Jenny was trying to say something else. "Be ... Be ..."

"Be what?" said Jake. "Be careful?"

"Beloff."

22

The door opened enough to reveal a pair of eyes with clods of mascara heavy on the lashes. Black shadows encircled them: the markings of the freshly bereaved. Every journalist knows them.

"Mrs Beloff?"

"Yes? Who are you?"

"I'm so sorry to intrude on you like this. I'm a reporter. I …"

The door clicked shut.

"I thought you were meant to be good at this short of thing?" said Jenny.

She had regained control of her tongue, although the letter S still caused difficulty.

"I'm not really a death knock specialist," he muttered.

"Oh, let me try."

The door opened before Jenny's finger had left the button.

"Leave me alone," said Mrs Beloff. "Or when I return to the UK I'll report you both to Ipso. For intruding on private grief."

The door closed again.

"What now?" said Jenny. "We can't stay here long …"

They were in the Jewish Quarter, a labyrinth of apartment blocks made from a pleasant cream stone, like a particularly well-kept estate back home. This neighbourhood had been destroyed by the Romans, destroyed in the Arab-Israeli War, regenerated each time.

"I'll write her a note," said Jake.

Jenny gave him a blank stare. "Well, that *might* work."

She was making it clear: nothing had changed. Jake sighed. Once the warmth between them was a mighty thing. He jotted down an appeal and posted it through the door, which opened straight away.

"I apologise for my rudeness." The widow's voice was gravelly-Hampstead. "Most journalists are, you'll excuse me, locusts. But come in, Jake Wolsey. You're always welcome in my home."

Ursula Beloff was an expensive-looking woman in her seventies with a pink twinset and a bronze bouffant, like a raddled Jackie Onassis. The house was small, but when Jake entered the sitting room he saw where the money went. The décor was Liberace let loose on Versailles, and that was as nothing compared to the view.

"Wow," said Jenny.

They were looking out over the Wailing Wall, where black-clad figures leaned and bobbed. To their left the Dome of the Rock shone golden in the dying sun; the West Bank Barrier zig-zagged across distant mountains, like the plates along the spine of a stegosaurus. Devosge's *Peace of Amiens* dominated the room and Jake traced the Etruscan characters with his finger.

"A picture's worth a thousand words," he muttered. "Napoleon said that, you know."

Next to it hung a painting of Nelson's *Victory*, pounding a French warship into submission at the Battle of Trafalgar.

The widow went to make tea.

"How did you convince her?" Jenny asked.

"Michael Beloff wrote popular history. And – worse in the eyes of the literati – he was a billionaire businessman. Envy oils the wheels of journalism. He could have been Edward bloody Gibbon and he'd have got a pasting from the broadsheets. But history for the masses is no bad thing, if you ask me. And his last book was a good effort. I gave Beloff his only good review."

"I want to thank you," Mrs Beloff said when she returned. "Not one reporter's asked me about Michael's books, not one. And they were bestsellers! The only interest was from the Foreign Office, if you can believe it."

Jenny met Jake's eye. "Excuse me?"

"That's right, the Foreign Office! A very rude woman. She was meant to help with the formalities, but all she wanted was the notes for Michael's next book. How's that their business? I told her where to go."

"What did she look like, this woman?"

"Oh, my age, slim, silver hair. A real Cruella de Vil."

An uncomfortable silence developed.

"Amazing view you have here," offered Jenny.

"My husband was a very devout man ..." Mrs Beloff's voice wavered. "Until recently. He was happy to pay top dollar to be near Solomon's Temple. What remains of it, at least."

"Until recently?" said Jake.

She sighed. "Off the record?"

"Of course."

"He lost his faith, almost overnight. I ... I don't know why."

Jake met Jenny's eyes again.

"You'll probably think I'm a crazy old bat," Mrs Beloff was saying. "But when your husband turns his back on god like that and then gets struck by lightning" – she looked skyward – "you half wonder ..."

"I don't think you're crazy, Mrs Beloff." Jenny squeezed her hand. "Not at all."

The widow manoeuvred her cup and saucer with a clatter. Her irises were filmy, brown like old stockings.

Suddenly Jake saw how elderly she was.

"I think your husband's next book could have been important," he said.

"You're darn right it could have been important." She clasped three of Jake's fingers in hers. "Michael was the most under-appreciated scholar of our age. But bless you for saying so."

"I want the world to know about it. Would you let *me* see his notes?"

"I'd like that. I ... I trust you, Jake Wolsey." The widow fumbled for a tiny key. "There were documents he was protective of. Things he kept in his safe."

Michael Beloff would have his epitaph.

23

The billionairess had regained her composure by the time she placed a leather box file before him. "It's all yours, darling."

When Jake thought of the madness this Pandora's Box might contain he wanted not to open it.

"It was you who sent me that stuff on the beach," he said to Jenny. "Wasn't it?"

"What stuff?"

"Quotations from Napoleon, all typed up on card. They started arriving two weeks ago. I ..."

His voice died out at the sight of Jenny's face.

"I don't know what you're talking about," she said.

He handed her the bundle and she leafed through the cards with growing consternation.

"Are these quotations genuine?"

"Yes, all of them," he said. "I've checked."

"Jesus god in heaven."

"Then it was MI6," said Jake. "These were meant to rekindle my interest."

Jenny glanced at the side of his head; she looked thoughtful.

"They wanted to use you," she said.

"They planted someone on the beach, you know. Someone who tried to get close to me. I couldn't understand how they did it at first, because I looked up Chloë's bylines in the *South China Post*."

Jenny's eyebrows raised a fraction.

"But after the penny dropped I did some more digging," he went on. "There was a real reporter called Chloë Fleming on that paper a few years ago. She got married, left the profession and took her husband's name. That Chloë Fleming disappeared from the internet. 'My' Chloë stepped into her identity."

"Standard procedure. Once you'd seen her stories you never doubted her, right?"

"Right."

Jake emptied Beloff's folder onto the table. There was an Etruscan alphabet in the pile, a copy of the Brontoscopic Calendar that made a prediction for each day of the year in the event of lightning. He spotted a translation of the Prophecy of Vegoia, an Etruscan prophet who warned of damnation for kings who violate their natural borders.

If anyone extends his own possessions or diminishes those of someone else, for this crime he will be condemned by the gods. The people responsible will be affected by the worst diseases and wounds; they will perish in the heat of the summer; they will be killed off by blight. There will be civil strife. Know that these things happen, when such crimes are committed ...

Jenny drew out several sheets of typed paper tied together with silk ribbon. Beloff had written a timeline of the events he intended to focus on for his publisher, annotated in fountain pen but apparently unsent.

The Battles of Napoleon.
M. N. Beloff.

1796. The campaign against the Austrians in northern Italy was Napoleon's first sole command. An eventual triumph, yes. But was Bonaparte to cast all before him, as in later years? Not a bit of it. The Italian campaign was character-ised by disorganisation and strategic blunders, the young general often saved by sheer luck. Throughout the campaign, Napoleon had to split his force into several groups (clearly he did not know which route the enemy would come from). When one of his commanders marched a division sixty miles in the wrong direction, Bonaparte was forced to call off the siege of Mantua at the cost of two hundred cannon. On another occasion Bonaparte was resting in the town of Lonato with just a thousand men when 3,000 Austrians arrived unexpectedly. He bluffed them into surrendering. But for this ruse, one of the greatest military careers in history could have ended there.

After his first defeat at Bassano, Napoleon conceded: "Maybe my hour has arrived."

And after victory at Arcole, he admitted: "I needed good luck."

"This hardly speaks of a man able to tell the future," said Jenny. Jake nodded seriously and continued reading.

Napoleon's errors were to be expected in an era before satellites, spy planes, the telegraph or the radio. Generals were like blind men – feeling out the terrain with their fingers, fumbling for the enemy. What is remarkable is that for the next fifteen years Napoleon acquired sight.

1798. Like the campaign of two years previously, Napoleon's expedition in Egypt was frequently disastrous. Nelson pulverised his fleet at the Battle of the Nile and the march on the Holy Land was devastated by plague. He tasted defeat again at the siege at Acre. Yet Egypt was a watershed. For subsequently, Napoleon lost no significant engagement until his catastrophic invasion of Russia in 1812. To all intents and purposes, he became invincible.

24

Jake hammered the table with his fist. "So *that's* where he got hold of it. It wasn't only the Rosetta Stone that Napoleon's savants found in Egypt. And it's no wonder Napoleon became an orientalist. They discovered a copy of the *Disciplina Etrusca* too."

"Who were the savants?" asked Jenny.

"The small army of historians and scientists Napoleon bought with him to Egypt."

"But they couldn't have found the *Disciplina*," she said. "The Egyptian campaign was a fiasco – Beloff says so right here. Can't you read?"

Jake felt as if the space between them was a solid. She was miles away from him.

"It would have taken the savants time to translate it, though," he pressed. "Still more to realise the bloody thing worked. And right after the Egypt campaign, Napoleon's run of victories began."

"Correlation is not causation. This isn't evidential Jake, it proves nothing. You're supposed to be a journalist. Could you defend this thesis under cross-examination in the High Court?"

He could not. Outside, a boy was trying to throw a slip of paper into a high-up crack in the Wailing Wall. Prayers are frequently removed from the lower gaps and buried on the Mount of Olives; Jake guessed the youngster's wish was intended to remain in situ.

They carried on reading.

Despite the setbacks in Egypt, Napoleon wrote to his government: "Fortune hasn't abandoned us, not at all – she has served us during this campaign more than ever."

Later he recalled: "In Egypt, I was full of dreams. I saw myself founding a new religion, marching into Asia on an elephant, the new Qur'an in my hand. My time in Egypt was the most beautiful of my life."

An old fear gnawed at Jake. He recalled that during the voyage to Egypt the French fleet had been scattered by weather, passing within twenty miles of Nelson's ships of the line. An encounter would have meant automatic annihilation for the French; by sheer luck Bonaparte slipped past.

It was as if the book wanted to be found.

And there, writ large in Beloff's notes, was further evidence of Napoleon's meteorological good fortune.

By 1799 it was clear the Egyptian campaign was a failure. The Royal Navy had Napoleon blockaded. His capture seemed inevitable. But a north-easterly breeze picked up, the perfect wind to evade Nelson's cruisers. He escaped to Paris, thence to conquer Europe.

Beloff's next focus was Napoleon's second venture into northern Italy, to fight the Austrians once again. It was this campaign that had first marked him out as a Caesar, a Charlemagne.

1800. In conference, Bonaparte asked his private secretary Bourrienne where the key battle of the campaign was going to take place.

"How the devil am I meant to know?" came the reply.

"Here, you fool," said Napoleon, pointing at the River Scrivia on his map.

It was the exact spot where the Battle of Marengo would be fought three months later. The encounter is considered Napoleon's first strategic masterwork.

"We've struck like lightning," Bonaparte told his brother Joseph. "Great events are about to take place."

"It's like Hitler's prophecy before he marched into Austria in 1938," said Jake. "Do you remember it?"

"'I'll appear in Vienna like a spring storm,'" Jenny recited. "'Then you'll see something.'"

Jake was reminded suddenly of Mark Twain's comment. *History doesn't repeat itself, but it does rhyme.*

"We did a great thing by destroying Germany's copy," he said. "We're a good team, you know?"

But Jenny merely pursed her lips, returning to Beloff's timeline, and again Jake was aware of the void between them: to encroach upon this space was to touch the negative ends of two magnets and feel the repulsive force. He leaned on his fists, staring out at the Wailing Wall with all its sadness. The boy's note had dislodged an avalanche of other prayers; he was pawing through the mass of fallen paper, looking for his own.

> *1805. The emperor faced a grand coalition of Britain, Russia and Austria and Great Britain, all bankrolled by English gold. War was coming to central Europe.*
>
> *Napoleon's minister Daru later recalled: "In terse, imperious tones, Napoleon outlined the plan of the campaign up to Vienna. The order of the marches, their durations, the places where columns should converge, surprises, attacks in great force, diverse movements, mistakes by the enemy; everything had been foreseen."*

"Once again, Napoleon knew what was coming," said Jake.

Jenny had turned sallow: that same hue of bad mackerel flesh she had assumed when the veracity of lightning prophecies first hit her two years ago. Then she read of Austerlitz.

> *1805. Napoleon visited the small village of Austerlitz, set amongst rolling hills in what is now the Czech Republic.*
>
> *He told his generals: "Gentlemen, examine this terrain carefully. It will be a battlefield and you will play a part. Study those heights – you will be fighting here in under two months."*
>
> *Battle commenced as prophesied that December.*

On the morning of the battle, Napoleon announced: "Let's finish this war with a thunderclap."

The Bavarian State Archives contain a sketch Napoleon drew before the clash, which illustrates how it proceeded exactly according to his prediction.

He even forecasted the weather.

A low mist hid Napoleon's troops from his enemies at the start of the battle, burned off by the sun at exactly the right moment to reveal the Allies' principal attack. Austerlitz was Napoleon's masterpiece, a synthesis of bluff, movement and coordination. Military historians like to say that no plan survives contact with the enemy. In reality, no enemy could now survive contact with Napoleon's plans.

Jake recalled Full Moon Party beach, that flickering palisade.

"Ok," Jenny murmured. "I admit it, Jake. Napoleon could tell the future. Napoleon had the Book of Thunder too."

Jake's countenance was heavy with the ageless truth. "Michael Beloff realised Napoleon's manoeuvres would have been impossible without modern communications," he said. "Then he became curious about the scroll in his painting and put two and two together."

Jenny looked at him. "You were right all along. I apologise."

Sometimes when you try to connect two negative ends of a magnet, Jake reflected, one spins around. Plus meets minus, opposites attract – and connect. Perhaps Jenny could be turned. He smiled at her shyly, this person both familiar to him and newly strange.

Beneath the Wailing Wall the little boy had found his prayer, and he prepared to throw.

"Napoleon," Jake breathed. "Born to a family of minor landowners in an age before meritocracy – yet he turned himself into the most powerful man on earth. His siblings would include an emperor, three kings, two princesses and a queen. How? The traditional view is he achieved this with genius, ambition and belief – plus that other crucial ingredient. Luck."

"Didn't Napoleon always say he wanted lucky generals?" asked Jenny.

"He certainly did. Only ..." Jake's laugh was empty as he slapped two of the cards on the table.

"I believe in luck. But a wise man neglects nothing which helps his destiny." – Napoleon Bonaparte

"Great men seldom fail in perilous enterprises. Is it because they have good luck that they become great? No, being great they have mastered luck." – Napoleon Bonaparte

"Napoleon did not so much make his own luck as *make luck his own.*"

Jake stared out to the Dome of the Rock, an artery like a rope of steel in his neck.

"I didn't want to do this again," he said at last. "I thought I'd played my part. But sometimes ..."

"Sometimes what?"

He turned to face her. "Sometimes you can't escape your destiny. That I have learned."

"What's your destiny, Jake?"

"Napoleon's ambition cost *three million* lives," he said, gazing at the Wailing Wall where more worshippers gathered. "And his crimes were nothing compared to those of the Third Reich. Corpse upon broken corpse, Bonaparte had a long way to go to catch up with Hitler. Jenny, it's our duty to find out what happened to Napoleon's copy of the *Disciplina Etrusca*. And if it still exists ..."

"I understand." A new fire smouldered in Jenny's eyes. "We must destroy it."

25

A vision had come to Jake: Napoleon Bonaparte, clad in the hooded robe of the Emperor Augustus, the *Pontifex Maximus* of Rome, bridge between earth and the heavens. The hood in which Roman augurs foretold events that were yet to transpire. One hand aloft, consulting the clouds, ready to unleash upon Europe a blitzkrieg of movement and coordination that was not of time. A marvellous, frightening image.

"But we come back to the same old problem," said Jenny. "If Napoleon was a seer, why was he beaten?"

"Let's see what Beloff made of it," said Jake.

The historian's dissection of Bonapartist devilry continued.

1807. At the Battle of Elyau in eastern Prussia, Bonaparte was fought to a standstill by the Czar of Russia. One of the ghastliest engagements in the entire Napoleonic War, it took place amid blizzards so bad that visibility was reduced to ten yards, obliterating the sky from sight. Napoleon abandoned the artful choreography of his previous battles for a crude frontal smash. This ended in a bloody draw, costing him the strategic initiative. The next major battle, Friedland, saw no such climactic difficulties and Napoleon won a brilliant victory over the Czar.

"Bad weather, lightning not visible, no victory," said Jake. "Clear skies – a triumph."

The pages sat heavily on the desk, as if made of iron.

1808. The Peninsular War begins. French armies got bogged down in Spain and Portugal for years, eventually beaten there by the Duke of Wellington. But Napoleon rarely took personal control in Iberia, leaving battlefield command to his generals.

He told his brother Joseph: "This war could be finished in an instant with a clever manoeuvre. But I need to be there for that."

Beloff had underlined the last sentence and added: *keeps it for himself.*

1809. Austria again. At the Battle of Aspern-Essling, Napoleon suffers his first major defeat in a decade. On the day of the battle the fog was so thick that visibility was reduced to the level of Elyau, with identical results.

During this campaign, there were the first signs of ill-health in Napoleon.

Beloff had circled *ill-health* and scrawled: *Vegoia. Borders.*

"But what about the decision to invade Russia?" said Jenny. "Napoleon's greatest mistake – just as it would be Hitler's downfall more than a century later."

"History rhymes," murmured Jake.

"Hess had stolen Hitler's copy of the *Disciplina* and fled to Britain by the German invasion of Russia in 1941," said Jenny. "So he can be excused the blunder. But Napoleon would have had ample opportunity to take the auspices before crossing the border. He must have *known* he would fail."

They consulted Beloff.

1812. As Napoleon crossed the River Niemen and entered Russia his horse shied, throwing him onto the bank.

"It is a bad omen," he said. "A Roman would recoil."

Napoleon was correct in this prediction. The Grande Armée that entered Russia numbered more than 600,000 men – only 27,000 would return. It was perhaps the greatest folly in military history.

Bonaparte's minister Molé later wrote: "Napoleon never discovered where the impossible begins. He only thought about increasing his own glory. Only death could stifle his ambition."

Instructive too are the words of the historian Charles Esdaile on the Napoleonic mind-set: "The emperor could not accept that there were limits, whether military, political, diplomatic or moral to what he could do."

"I understand," said Jake. "I get it. The skies *did* tell Napoleon he would be defeated in Russia. But by that point he was in the grips of such megalomania he decided to go ahead and do it anyway. He could brook no limitations on his power whatsoever – not even from the heavens."

"A self-fulfilling prophecy," said Jenny.

Now they read how Napoleon's foresight had deserted him overnight.

The emperor had predicted Sweden and Turkey would side with him against Russia. On both counts he was wrong: they turned against him. Like Hitler, Napoleon was biting off more than he could chew.

He admitted of the diplomatic coup: "It is very stupid that I did not foresee it."

When the invasion began, the Czar's armies repeatedly dodged French spearheads, escaping encirclement. The Emperor could no longer orchestrate his forces over great distances – and the Russian retreat was a trap he fell head-long into.

Napoleon had never been trapped before.

The Russians finally gave battle at Borodino. That morning, Napoleon declared: "Fortune is a liberal mistress. I have always said this, and now start experiencing it."

He unleashed another unimaginative frontal smash, far from the élan of his earlier triumphs. The resulting charnel house was the bloodiest encounter in the history of warfare until that point and would not be exceeded until the

Marne a century later. The 75,000 dead is equivalent of a full jumbo jet crash-landing into a battlefield five miles square every five minutes for eight hours solid, without a single survivor. Napoleon took the field, but it was a Pyrrhic victory.

The emperor's judgement continued to fail him. He did not foresee the Russians abandoning Moscow and burning it to the ground, depriving his troops of shelter and sustenance. The decision to retreat came too late. And when winter struck, he chose the worst possible route home.

In December 1812, the Czar told a dinner guest: "The spell is broken."

26

"I'm confused," said Jenny. "Imagine you're Napoleon. Out of pride or stroppiness or whatever you've stopped using the *Disciplina*. As a result, you face catastrophe. Wouldn't you admit your mistake and begin using it again right away? Napoleon was a pragmatist, after all. 'A wise man neglects nothing' ..."

"I think that he did," said Jake. "Wellington himself said Napoleon's last campaigns gave him a greater idea of the man's genius than anything that had gone before. But by then it was too late – France was in the position of Nazi Germany in 1945. The emperor was facing a million allied troops with barely 200,000 men. His country was mutinous, broken and bankrupted. There were barely any men left to recruit. He was engulfed."

"You're forgetting something," said Jenny. "Waterloo. The forces in Napoleon's final battle were broadly equal, right? Yet he lost, badly. How come?"

They read of the build-up to Napoleon's final defeat.

1814. After the Allies invaded France, Napoleon surrendered and was banished to the island of Elba. It was a luxurious imprisonment. In return for going quietly, Bonaparte was crowned king of that pleasant Mediterranean island and gifted an annual income of two million Francs from the French state.

But this did not slake his thirst for glory.

1815. Napoleon escaped his gilded cage and landed in France with a few hundred supporters. Soldiers sent to arrest him instead embraced him, with cries of "Vive l'Empereur". Bonaparte was restored to the throne – the Allies had to vanquish him all over again. The so-called 'Hundred Days' was under way. Endgame.

Waterloo was Napoleon's last throw of the dice. Yet when battle was joined in Belgium, the Emperor made some extraordinary mistakes.

1. He did not think the Prussians would reach the battlefield in time. They did.

2. A division that was marching in the opposite direction was not recalled; it would be badly needed.

3. He fought the battle on a wet day, where the soggy ground helped Wellington's defence. The weather was no longer an ally.

4. He delayed his attack until 11 am, hoping the ground would dry out. This gave the Prussians the time they needed to arrive.

5. Napoleon's strategy was another frontal sledgehammer. It was Borodino, not Austerlitz.

At the deciding moment, a suicidally brave cavalry charge led by Napoleon's general Ney captured a walled farmhouse that was the keystone to the battle. Ney begged for reinforcements to take full advantage. Uncharacteristically, Napoleon dithered. By the time he launched his last reserves into the fray, Wellington had plugged the gap. The emperor's last, best chance to win the battle had gone. The Imperial Guard broke for the first time in its history. The tyranny of Napoleon Bonaparte was over.

Napoleon was later to admit he "did not fully understand the battle", blaming it on "extraordinary Fates".
Historians find his decisions on the day incomprehensible.

There ended Beloff's notes.

"At Waterloo Napoleon didn't have the *Disciplina*," said Jake. "He couldn't have. He must have parted with it – at some point between the campaigns of 1814 that wowed the Duke of Wellington and his escape from Elba."

"Maybe he destroyed it?" suggested Jenny. "When he knew he was beaten, when France didn't have enough men to hold back the deluge."

"Or gave it away, even?"

"That doesn't sound much like Napoleon," she said.

Jake stared at Beloff's notes; a peculiar light had come into his eyes.

"When Napoleon was deposed and sent to Elba – he got off pretty lightly, didn't he? This guy was responsible for millions of deaths, yet he's rewarded with a cushy island and an income for life. You didn't see the leading Nazis getting enthroned after the Nuremberg trials. They got hanged, every man-jack of them. Except ..."

"Except Rudolf Hess." That tinge of yellow was in Jenny's cheeks again. "Who was *kept alive*."

"Because he had something to bargain with."

"But if Napoleon haggled his way to Elba with the *Disciplina Etrusca*, who was the recipient?"

"Let's look at this logically," said Jake. "Which country went on to dominate the nineteenth century?"

A silence filled the room, full of foreboding. As one, they turned to the painting of Trafalgar. To the warship in the foreground; to its flag. A flag that once flew over the biggest empire the world has ever seen.

It was the Union Jack.

Part Two

Grandiloquence

(THE PRIME MINISTER)

I have no way of judging the future but by the past.
Edward Gibbon, *The Decline and Fall of the Roman Empire*

27

BEEP. BEEP. BEEP. BEEEEEEP.

PRESENTER 1: *Good morning. This is the Today programme, and these are the headlines from the BBC. Britain will provide the caretaker government of Sierra Leone for the rest of the year, the Prime Minister has announced.*

CLIP (Victor Milne): *"It's just not good enough for us to stomp on the militias and clear off, only for all this mayhem to start again in six months' time. We need to rebuild Sierra Leone's economy so it can provide its own security in the future. The Sierra Leonean president's asked us to stay, the people want us to stay, and we jolly well will stay until the job's done."*

PRES 1: *The Foreign Secretary Nigel Edmonds joins me shortly. I'll be asking him – is it really Britain's place to play the world's policeman? And how does he respond to accusations from some in the Opposition that Britain's embarking on a neo-colonialist adventure?*

PRES 2: *Staying in West Africa, and the first cases of Ebola have been confirmed in Nigeria. The World Health Organisation reports a spate of infections in the north of the country. It comes amid increasing concern about the oil-rich state's ability to fend off the Islamist group Boko Haram. We'll have analysis on whether Africa's biggest economy is becoming the world's biggest failed state.*

PRES 1: *And the US president's vowed to do anything it takes to bring to justice a group of gunmen who shot dead two CIA agents in Jerusalem yesterday afternoon. A third American's been kidnapped – there's speculation Iranian intelligence was behind the assault.*

Victor Milne turned off the radio. "I can't bear to hear Nigel get savaged again."

"Surely the small matter of being on the right side of the argument must help?" said C.

"Not when it's a cretin versus The Rottweiler."

"At least he's not facing that chap." C nodded to Jeremy Paxman's *Empire*, which lay open on the coffee table of the flat above Number 10.

The dissolution of empire was as much a product of what was militarily feasible as its acquisition had been.

"Dear old Paxo," said Milne. "Glad I don't have to lock horns with him any longer."

A clutch of other tomes on Britain's golden age were strewn about the flat and C glanced at the nearest.

By 1909, some 444 million people lived under British rule. The empire included one continent, one sub-continent, 100 peninsulas, 500 promontories, 1,000 lakes, 2,000 rivers and 10,000 islands. Today, that same empire has shrunk to fourteen territories with a combined population not much higher than 200,000.

"A bit of light reading, Prime Minister?"

"Shall we say, research for my next book?"

C peered at another volume.

The post-war Labour Foreign Secretary Herbert Morrison compared independence for African countries to giving a child of ten a latch-key, a bank account and a shotgun.

"How prescient he was," he said.

"Talking of prescience …" began Milne. "The CIA. Your boys didn't exactly see that one coming, eh? An intelligence failure *par excellence*."

"We left no evidence."

"It's blooming obvious we did it! Crikey, a row with the Yanks is all I need."

"Respectfully, they started it," said C. "Besides, Washington won't let it be known we're having a falling out."

"Why on earth not?"

"Because the world and its dog would try to discover what the spat's about. If the Americans *do* know what we're looking for – well, that's the last thing they'd want. Hence Washington briefing against the Iranians, who've got no reputation left to defend."

"I see."

"These tiffs do happen from time to time, Prime Minister. It'll go under the radar, I promise you."

"Apart from all the bodies," snapped Milne. "Not to mention a starring role on Radio 4 this morning. What about our injured man? Mc-something-or-other."

"McCabe. He's going to survive, but the doctors say he'll need a colostomy bag for the rest of his life."

"Poor chap," said Milne. "And Wolsey? Frobisher?"

"We've picked up their trail again. If you want we can snatch them right away."

"No, I don't want."

C frowned. "Why not?"

"Now Wolsey and Frobisher are back together, they'll be trying to find out what happened to Napoleon's *Disciplina Etrusca* – correct?"

C nodded.

"And over the years those lovebirds have proved rather more capable than our own serried ranks of spies and academics when it comes to historical detective work – also correct?"

C's face was grim.

"Then I say, let them get on with it!" said Milne. "If they actually discover anything, we swoop."

"Actually, that's rather a wise plan."

"So do make sure nothing bad happens to them," said Milne. "And let's get to work on this fellow who Wolsey bashed on the head. I want to find out just how well the Americans know their history."

A skin-deep smile. "We have just the man for the job, Prime Minister."

*

Damien di Angelo was tied to a chair at a British military base in Cyprus.

"The worm has turned has it not, fella?" As Davis loomed from the darkness his shoulders were like mountains of shadow, lurching across the wall.

The American jerked against his cords, realised it was futile and relaxed. "Where am I?"

"Where are you?" The fillings in Davis's teeth glinted dully. "You are in a spot of bother, my son."

28

Jake stirred Beloff's notes, wondering what else might be plucked from the devil's cauldron.

Here was a line on Etruscan spirituality:

They believed in mighty spheres of religion, where reason cannot penetrate. The fulfilment and interpretation of omens was devoid of ethical content.

Something else caught his eye:

The fasces, a bundle of sticks symbolic of Roman imperium, is of Etruscan origin. It is the source of our word, 'fascism'.

Then it happened.

Not so much a click or a pop as a *reverse noise* – a vacuum where the sound should have been. Jake was gliding silently through points of light set on a hexagonal grid, marching onwards for eternity.

I'm inside it.

Jake could hear a high-pitched chatter as the singularities communicated with each other and the entire formation trembled as though it had been disturbed, before returning to stillness.

Or it's inside me.

He had no idea how long he had been gliding. It could have been seconds or a month; microns or light years. Maybe he was dead? (Heart attack or stroke.) He heard the beat of the drum, the tramp of jackboots. The blast of the war horn, the rumble of Napoleon's grand battery which was also that of thunder. And behind it all, the hiss and the thrum of creation itself: the background residue of the big bang.

Not a click, not a pop, but a *nothing*.

Suddenly Jake was back, reality rushing in his ears. He was lying on the floor, rigid as a seizure victim and unable to move, eyes wide open as foam gathered in the corners of his mouth.

Jenny was in full panic mode. "Jake? Jake? Speak to me ..."

"It's evil," he managed.

She pressed a glass of water on him and he struggled up. Concern and reserve did battle in her eyes. And there was something else there, something occluded by a cloudiness he could not penetrate. When they were lovers Jake had been in the company of this person constantly; he had understood intuitively her every emotion and desire.

I don't know what's going on inside your head any more.

Some tea had spilled and he watched two droplets become one in a curious blobbing motion, their surface tension now shared. Foretold, as all things were. Now he tore through the pile anew, desperate for a lead, for anything that might suggest how Napoleon disposed of his history of the future or where it came from.

An envelope.

Jake tore it open, withdrew a yellowed letter. It was signed by the father of the greatest Briton.

Randolph Churchill.

The ancient Etruscan matter.

29

Blenheim Palace: December 31, 1883.
My dear Wolff,
   I have had a very curious letter from the Queen.
   Yours ever,
   Randolph S.C.

"Lord Randolph Churchill was a failure as a politician, right?" asked Jenny.

"That's a bit harsh," said Jake. "He was seen as a rising star in the late-Victorian age. A socialite, *bon viveur* and witheringly good speaker – with an impressive moustache to boot. But he was a risk-taker, prone to picking fights he couldn't win. Poor health and reckless decisions ended his career early."

"And who's this Wolff?"

"Sir Henry Drummond Wolff would be my guess," said Jake. "He was another member of Churchill's clique, along with Lord Salisbury and WH Smith – yes, the newsagent. They were the leading Conservatives of the era."

"Beloff must have thought Queen Victoria's 'curious letter' was significant," said Jenny. "Is it in the envelope?"

"No, but there's something else."

He withdrew a folded page, torn from Winston Churchill's biography of his own father.

Perhaps someday it may be possible to publish in complete form the letters which passed between Lord Salisbury and Lord Randolph Churchill during their eventful association. When we consider the profound and secret knowledge of forces at work which both possessed, one cannot imagine any compilation which would more truthfully illuminate the dark and stormy history of those times. All that, however, is a matter for the future.

"Stormy history," whispered Jenny. "A matter for the future."

"If Britain got hold of Napoleon's copy of the *Disciplina Etrusca* at the end of the Napoleonic Wars, did Randolph Churchill learn about it seventy years later? Maybe that was the content of Queen Victoria's 'curious letter' ..."

"The High Court test," Jenny chided him. "You're being grilled by a QC and your job's on the line. Can you defend this theory?"

"Not a chance," Jake admitted. "But imagine for the sake of argument Randolph Churchill *did* know about the Book of Thunder. Instantly half the jigsaw falls into place – because he would have told his son too. And *that's* why Winston Churchill took an interest in 1941, when Rudolf Hess began wittering to MI6 about the ancient Etruscans. *That's* why he gave it the time of day. And it explains something else. Have you ever heard of the famous prediction Winston Churchill made at Harrow when he was seventeen?"

Jenny shook her head.

"Read this," he said, showing her a quotation on his phone that has astonished historians for decades.

I can see vast changes coming over a now peaceful world; great upheavals, terrible struggles; wars such as one cannot imagine; and I tell you London will be in danger – London

*will be attacked and I shall be very prominent in the defence.
I see further ahead than you do. I see into the future. This
country will be subjected to a tremendous invasion, by what
means I do not know, but I tell you I shall be in command
of the defences and I shall save London and England from
disaster. Dreams of the future are blurred but the main
objective is clear. It will fall to me to save the capital and
save the Empire.*

Jake's finger traced an invisible line in the air, meandering
through space: as the *Disciplina Etrusca* had wormed its way
through history, spreading havoc in its wake.

"*That's* why Winnie spent the thirties warning about Hitler
and appeasement," he said. "While the press denounced him as a
warmonger. Because he *knew* what was coming. Churchill, who
stood alone. Cometh the hour, cometh the man."

Jake felt his cheeks bloom with an unexpected glow of pride.
Then he recalled a line from Winston Churchill's Finest Hour
speech and the emotion was replaced with unease.

*But if we fail, then the whole world will sink into the abyss
of a new Dark Age, made more sinister, and perhaps more
protracted, by the lights of perverted science.*

"But this is all speculation," said Jenny. "We've got no evidence
whatsoever that Britain got hold of Napoleon's copy of the
Disciplina. It's just a hunch, based on nothing more than the
fact that we had a good century. And besides, we *know* Britain
doesn't possess it to this day."

Jake wheeled to face her. "How do we know that?"

"Because if Britain's had the Book of Thunder since the fall
of Napoleon, why let two World Wars bankrupt us? How come
we regressed from the global superpower to the sick man of
Europe by the seventies? Why will MI6 stop at nothing to get
it now?"

The stirrings of a blush were discernible on Jake's face.

"The sun set on the British Empire," Jenny pressed. "Britain's place at the top table is based on past glories, not hard power. If Britain did obtain Napoleon's copy of the *Disciplina*, somehow we lost it too, Jake."

"What about Churchill's prediction?"

"It's strange, certainly it's strange. But strange things happen, Jake – coincidences occur. Not everything is meaningful, not everything is foretold."

The blobs of water on the table top had parted again.

"Dreams of the future are *blurred*," read Jake from Winston Churchill's schoolboy prediction. "As in, *not clear*. Not like Napoleon's pinpoint predictions, anyway. So Britain didn't have the *Disciplina* by the Churchills' day – this was more like a ... a long-term forecast, possibly augured before Winston was even born. Randolph Churchill got wind of it though, either from Queen Victoria or in some smoke-filled drawing room. He told the little boy who would one day be Prime Minister, who was destined to save Britain from disaster. The prodigal son."

"All total conjecture, of course," said Jenny.

"It's a lead, though," said Jake. "Trust me, I'm a journalist."

She raised an eyebrow. "No comment on that. Anyway, everything in this file's a bloody lead."

Jake closed the box. "Thank god I wrote a good review of Beloff's book."

"You did it because you're a good man." Jenny accepted his gaze for the first time since the reunion. "A fair man. You refused to follow the pack. You gave Michael Beloff a fair crack of the whip, when everyone else was getting their kicks in."

Her hand flinched on the table and for a joyous heartbeat he thought she was going to place it upon his. She did not.

Jake looked at her hand, so slender, so strong.

Looked at her hand ...

And it came to him.

"Beloff's painting," he said. "We know from the *Telegraph* article that the inscription depicted on Napoleon's scroll is unknown. But what of the *handwriting*?

*

Before they departed, Jake sought Ursula Beloff again. "What was your husband reading in the weeks before his death?"

The widow wrinkled her nose. "I haven't a clue, books were arriving here the whole time. Have a look in his study if it satisfies you."

Jake scrutinised the historian's bookshelves. The recent Etruscan connection was evident: in a library chiefly concerned with the nineteenth century, books on ancient Italy had carved themselves a niche.

And there, slap bang in the middle of Beloff's desk, was a package wrapped in brown string. It was decidedly book-shaped.

"This one arrived two days after Beloff was killed," said Wolsey, studying the postmarks. "Sent from Henry Pordes Books in Charing Cross."

"Knock yourself out," said Mrs Beloff.

Jake tore open the paper to reveal a tome bound in red leather, marbled down the sides.

Napoleon at Fontainebleau and Elba, Being a Journal of Occurrences in 1814-1815 with Notes of Conversations, by Sir Neil Campbell.

"Elba!" Jenny exclaimed. "Napoleon's gilded cage. Where he was held before escaping for his last hurrah and Waterloo."

"Pithy title," said Jake. "This is a first edition, published in 1869. Must be eye-wateringly valuable."

"Michael wouldn't have had it any other way," said Mrs Beloff. "Keep it as a souvenir if you're interested, darling. I ain't gonna read it."

"Sir Neil Campbell was a British colonel," Jake read from inside the cover. "When Napoleon was exiled to Elba after his first abdication – before his escape and restoration to the throne – Campbell was sent to the island to keep an eye on him." He weighed the book in his hands. "This is a first-hand account of Napoleon's imprisonment at exactly the time he disposed of the *Disciplina Etrusca*."

30

Tiwai Island loomed through the mist, a vision of Avalon in the dawn whiteout. Captain Bracknell thought the rebels were more likely to be sober at daybreak, not so erratic. *Less chance of us getting fucked*, as he put it. Serval was glad of the soldier's presence in the dinghy as it buzzed across the waterway, and his eyes narrowed as he scanned for signs of life on the island. A crocodile propelled itself from the bank and arrowed away across the river; Wally's head had disappeared, and Serval imagined the two were not unconnected. The boat sat low in the water, heavy with tins of corned beef and sardines, sacks of sugar and rice. A white flag fluttered at its prow and Suleiman the fixer clucked with anxiety. When they were close enough to see the bloodstains on the canoe, Bracknell cut the engine. The dinghy drifted along the island with the current.

"Flag of truce," shouted Captain Bracknell as reams of trees slid by. "Don't shoot."

The island was still.

"We come in peace," murmured Serval.

A rasping noise above surprised them: a single hornbill, tracing a line through the sky like a Reaper Drone as air vibrated through its wings.

Silence again.

"SBU sir, over there." The translator pointed at movement in the forest.

"SBU?" said Serval.

Bracknell smiled sadly. "Small Boys Unit. Their abbreviation, not ours."

The children emerged silently from the mist, like spirits of the forest arraying themselves along the bank. They were naked or dressed in rags, armed with machetes, Kalashnikovs or bows and arrows. One brandished a golf club. The tallest wore a grimy Real Madrid shirt with Cristiano Ronaldo's name and number on it and a pair of yellow Y-fronts. He said something to a lieutenant and the nine-year-old bent double with a jerk of laughter which evolved into a swaggering dance. Bracknell started the engine and kept it to a low burble, holding the boat stationary.

"Good morning, lads," he shouted.

The resultant dutiful chorus of good mornings could have come from a primary school classroom anywhere in the world.

"I want to talk to Jason Bourne," Bracknell said. "Where's the boss?"

"He sleep pasmak," said Ronaldo, toeing the ground shyly.

"He sleeps late," translated Suleiman.

"It's about time you woke him up then, eh?" shouted Bracknell.

The riverbank blared with hoots and screeches of laughter.

"'im angry, if ahmbohg," the child disclosed, exposing beautiful teeth.

"He gets angry when he's humbugged," said Suleiman.

The child levelled his AK at the boat, wobbling under the weight of it.

"Bang-bang! Bang-bang!"

All three men flinched. More laughter, tiny heads bobbing up and down.

"Come along now." Bracknell raised a bag of sugar to instant silence. "One of you run and fetch Jason Bourne – and I'll give you some of this stuff."

After a huddled conference the smallest child was dispatched, leaping and bouncing away through undergrowth and fallen trees. He returned with three men. One of them was naked, the second had no ears and the third wore a red flat cap, pink sunglasses and a Hawaiian shirt, like a pimp from 1970s Harlem.

"None of these guys are Bourne," Bracknell muttered.

"I know, I've read the file." Serval raised his voice. "I'm coming ashore."

Flat Cap barked something in Mende and the bank bristled with assault rifles. Arrowheads meandered in circles as infant arms strained to keep bowstrings taut.

"I'm coming ashore," Serval repeated calmly. "We're unarmed."

A child lost his grasp on a bowstring and the arrow whistled high into the air at a skewed angle before landing in the river with a plop.

Flat Cap burst into laughter. "You kin kan insai, baboonay."
You can come here, white man.

Bracknell gunned the motor. "You've got some cahoonies, Jacob."

"Not at all."

The dinghy coasted in to land and Serval clambered ashore, offering Flat Cap his hand.

"Jacob. Pleased to meet you. I've brought these gifts, with compliments of the British people."

Flat Cap's eyes went left. "Wetin dis man no ears?"

Serval's hand hung in the air. "Is this a joke? I don't know. Why does he have no ears?"

The naked man giggled. "Jason Bourne dohn eat."
Jason Bourne has eaten them.

"Aw yu lekh am?" Flat Cap asked his comrade.

"How did you like it?" translated Suleiman.

No Ears smiled. His expression was diffident, rather sad.
They will eat you up.

Serval lowered his hand. He was not smiling any more.

"I warn you, you will find me a better friend than an enemy. Fetch Jason Bourne right now."

Flat Cap removed his sunglasses and the men stared into each other's eyes. Serval's face had a fierce intensity and his glare bored into the warrior's skull. The SBU fell silent. Flat Cap swallowed and glanced downward. When he resumed eye contact his smile had become fixed, a little silly.

Serval had not flinched.

Flat Cap nodded toward the jungle. "Kam."

Come ...

"Tell Bourne to come here," ordered Serval.

Flat Cap shook his head.

"He won't come to the water's edge," Bracknell muttered.

The rebel's confidence was returning and he mustered a grin. "Us time you de go?"

"When shall we go?" Suleiman translated smoothly.

"Don't," warned Bracknell. "They'll kill you for sure."

"You return to base," said Serval. "I'm going to make friends with these chaps."

"Jacob, this wasn't part of the plan ..."

"Captain Bracknell. Your orders are to offer me every assistance. I require the services of your very capable translator. That is all. If you don't wish to accompany us, the boat's right there."

Bracknell shook his head and he leaned an elbow on Serval's shoulder. "Oh Jesus. Ooooh Jesus Christ. I should have my head examined."

"Why's that?"

"I'm coming with you, man."

*

The daylight in the jungle was feeble. A few shafts of light sliced through the canopy high above and steam billowed through the trunks. Serval glimpsed the black and white tail of a colobus monkey dangling like a curtain tassel before it darted away. Human excrement glinted in the grass and a naked woman watched them with a dull stare.

"Bush wife," explained Suleiman. He was shaking with fear.

Warriors slumbered on the ground, oblivious to the mosquitoes. Those awake wore New York Raiders caps, basketball shirts and baggy jeans. Their skin was freshly scarified with brown-brown, the potent mixture of gunpowder and cocaine rubbed into sliced bodies. Serval spotted the charred bones of a chimpanzee, scored with knife marks. He was reminded of a line from Kaplan's *The Coming Anarchy.*

A rundown, crowded planet of skinhead Cossack and Juju warriors, influenced by the worst refuse of western pop culture and ancient tribal hatreds will find liberation in violence.

They were led into a clearing. Hammocks were strung from trees; muscles gleamed; ammunition belts were slung over shoulders. Bandanas were worn and joints smouldered between teeth.

"Not small lads, are they?" said Bracknell.

A hush fell over the encampment at Bourne's approach. He was powerful but obese, like a black Pavarotti with his thick beard. He carried a sabre, and the ensemble was piratical in the extreme. He wore the Stars and Stripes as a cape, and on his head was a hot pink rabbit hat, something a twelve-year-old girl would wear. It had long fluffy ears and one glass eye had shattered.

"You must be Mr Bourne," said Serval. "Charmed."

The warlord's smile turned into a sneer, the sneer became into a scowl, then his bloated face was full of violence and he pointed the sabre at Serval.

"*Go insai bak.*"

Yahooing and war cries. Rough hands, grips. Knives and fists. Serval took a blow to the jaw, another to the kidney. He lashed out twice, felt a queer twist of joy as his knuckles connected with a face. (How soft it was! How squishy!) He was jerked off his feet; glimpsed Bracknell on hands and knees, bleeding from the lip. Suleiman stood wonderstruck. They were dragged through the forest at speed, toes brushing the ground, like French aristocrats borne off by the mob. Serval took a meaty blow to the forehead and blacked out completely.

He revived in time to see a bamboo grille in the jungle floor rushing closer. It was opened and headfirst into a latrine he went, crashing into two feet of sewage. Suleiman and Bracknell were flung in after him and the bamboo jaws snapped shut with a rickety crash. This was followed by the tinkle of urine as ten men relieved themselves through the gate. Into Serval's face, his hair.

"I'll kill you!" Serval was white hot and he lunged for the grille so wildly he nearly dislocated a shoulder. "Kill you, kill you, *kill you!*"

Surprise once more, at this thing he'd found in himself. This jet fuel. But the grille was out of reach and the men simply laughed, jiggling the last drops of urine over the prisoners before sauntering away.

The pulse of anger subsided.

"You all right, mate?" Captain Bracknell was wide-eyed.

"Fine." Serval wiped slurry off his cheek with a brawny fore-arm. "Sorry about that."

"Understandable in the circumstances," panted Bracknell through gritted teeth. "We're in a bit of a pickle, but they'll get us out. The British Army's rather good at that sort of thing, actually."

They weren't alone in the pit. A boy of about six shrank against the mud walls, cowering in fright. The wounds where they had whipped him half to death were turning septic. Serval remembered the girl in the slum.

Her flaking skin.

He had absolutely no idea where all this would end.

31

Jerusalem's preeminent forensic handwriting expert resided in Yemin Moche, a neighbourhood of cottages overlooking the walls of the Old City: built as poor houses, now worth millions.

The hillside was presided over, obscurely, by a windmill. Meshi Aberlieb was a Falstaffian figure with a jovial burst of goatee beard who looked like he'd swallowed a barrel. It took the old man three hours to make a leap that had eluded Sotheby's, the *Telegraph*, Michael Beloff and MI6. Aberlieb rose from his study, rolling arthritically back through the little house. He brandished two pieces of paper. The first was a photograph of Beloff's painting, the second was an Etruscan inscription. The words were different. But the script was *exactly the same*.

"Sit, sit," he said.

Aberlieb lowered himself into a rocking chair and smoothed his beard. He sighed contentedly. His eyelids began to droop.

"Mr Aberlieb?" Jenny touched him on the forearm.

Aberlieb awoke with a jerk. "Ah! Yes, yes." He placed half-moon spectacles on the very tip of his nose. "Pardon me, madam. This inscription, this inscription," he raised the two pieces of paper, "I think is by same hand. But this is, ah, not normal case, no. I must make you the warnings."

Jenny nodded, urging him on.

"First warning. You have here *painting* of manuscript, not original. So all depends on painter, yes? If painter is true to life, if has talent. Warning two. In the painting is a small sample, only three sentences. On sample this size, not good evidence in court, no. Judge is laughing at me."

"I see," said Jenny.

"Three. I am expert in Hebrew, Arabic, Roman script. Not this, this Etruscan. This also serious problem, yes? Because I not know which characteristics of the letters belong to the individual, which part of the general style. Is making difficult. No good for court of law. But, ah, you cannot prosecute the dead, yes? Mr Aberlieb have nothing to fear from Napoleon Bonaparte. So I can say, I think I know." He lit a cigar end and puffed away, rocking on his chair. "Mr Aberlieb know."

Jake and Jenny shared a secret smile. They shared a fondness for the human species, in all its wondrous variety.

"So, I find this inscription," said the expert, waving the printout.

Jake was surprised to see strips of linen, adorned with runic letters.

"First of all, I look for signs these two writings are by *different* writers, yes?"

Silence as they awaited the verdict.

"I find nothing, no. Nothing to say is different scribe."

Jake breathed out.

"Second of all, I look for signs that it same person, yes? Here, much to commend the theory. Letter forms are same. Relative height of big and short letters is same. Slope of hand, spacing of letters, also same. Line quality is similar. Motor actions behind the hand movement ..." His head tilted from side to side. "They could be the same man. If painter is good painter."

"How sure are you?" asked Jenny. "Give us a percentage."

"If artist can paint like take photograph, I am eighty to eighty-five per cent sure. Also there is this."

He pointed at a letter in Beloff's painting that resembled a double axe head.

"And also here."

The same symbol on the linen.

"What's the significance?" said Jenny.

"This form of the letter, I cannot find anywhere else, no. Is unique. Maybe it came into use locally for short time before went away. To conclude, Mr Aberlieb think artist was painting this book of linen. One of the missing segments, yes? Because handwriting is same, but words are different."

Something between hope and fear inflated Jake's lungs. "Where's the linen book from?"

"Egypt."

"Egypt," Jake repeated. "Egypt!"

In Egypt I was full of dreams. I saw myself founding a new religion, marching into Asia on an elephant, the new Qur'an in my hand.

"Correlation is not causation, Jake," said Jenny. "But I'll give you this – the correlation here is pretty damn strong …"

Aberlieb handed him the linen book's Wikipedia entry. "I print it for you."

At 1,300 words, the Linen Book of Zagreb is the longest known Etruscan text. The manuscript has been carbon dated to approximately 200 B C, give or take a few decades. Although linen books are thought to have been used widely in the ancient world, it is the only one to survive from antiquity, preserved because it was later used to bandage a mummy in Ptolemaic Egypt. The text is a ritual calendar, an instruction book for religious rites. It formed a part of the Disciplina Etrusca.

Jake blew air into his cheeks before continuing.

The story of its discovery is fascinating. In 1848, a Croatian bureaucrat bought a mummy in Alexandria. When it was unwrapped, an unidentified language was discovered on the linen. Both mummy and bandages were subsequently donated to the Archaeological Museum of Zagreb, where they remain. During the nineteenth century numerous experts examined the linen, including the Victorian explorer Richard Burton, who was interested in the Etruscans. But it was not until 1891 that the writing was proven to be Etruscan. It is not known who wrote the manuscript, nor how it came to be in Egypt. However, there is evidence it originated in northern Italy. The twist of the thread is in a 'Z' direction, typical of that region – whereas Egyptian linen of the period has an 'S' thread. Another curious feature is that the linen was carefully cut into strips with scissors before being wound around the mummy, whereas mummy linen was usually roughly torn.

On palaeographical grounds, academics have speculated that the manuscript was written near Lake Trasimeno in Perugia.

"Why would an Etruscan inscription found by a French general be stashed on an Egyptian mummy?" Jenny pondered.

"A riddle, wrapped in a mystery, inside an enigma," said Jake. "To paraphrase Winston Churchill."

32

Aberlieb had nodded off again, and Jake plucked the smouldering cigar from his fingers before placing it in the ashtray.

"A mummy's the perfect place to hide a fragile document," he said. "The embalming process kept the linen intact for millennia."

"Not that Napoleon got to see it," said Jenny. "The Zagreb inscription was discovered decades after he died."

"But clearly other mummies *were* found by Napoleon's savants – enough to have written the entire *Disciplina* on. The Zagreb mummy was the one that got away."

"It was a stroke of genius to look at the handwriting. So bloody clever, Jake, it's maddening."

"Oh, I don't know about that." He fiddled with his fringe. "Now, what do we know about the mummy itself?"

Jenny buried herself in the article. "Her name was Nesikhonsu. A rich woman with red hair who died aged about forty. A papyrus found with her revealed she was married to a priest of the sun god at the Temple of Karnak in Luxor, some chap called Pakhar-en-Khonsu."

Jake Googled the name. "Pakhar's mummy is in Cairo! At the Museum of Egyptian Antiquities."

"And the bandages?"

"Jenny – it would appear the mummy's never been un-wrapped."

Her face went cold.

"We're at a crossroads, then." Jake kneaded the flesh between his thumb and index finger. "Do we follow Randolph Churchill back to nineteenth-century London, or Pakhar-en-Khonsu all the way to ancient Egypt?"

A glint was in Jenny's eyes. "How's your Arabic?"

Decision made.

"But I don't have any travel documents," she added. "The CIA didn't give me much opportunity to pack. And my clean passport's at the charity I worked for in Bangkok."

"So let's lie low while your old colleagues Fed-Ex it over."

"The CIA and MI6 are both after this thing. They might well have tracked us here. They could look up Mr Aberlieb's web history, work out that Pakhar-en-Khonsu might hold more of the *Disciplina*. We can't risk them getting to Cairo first."

"What do you suggest? They won't let you fly without a passport."

"There are other ways to cross from Israel to Egypt," she said darkly.

When Jake took her meaning his pupils widened with fear and he tugged at his hair.

"Hey!" she caught him by the wrist. "Don't mess it up, you look good with a side parting. It was time you grew out of the whole surfer look, anyway."

A bubble of recklessness rose up. "I thought you said stay focused ..."

Jenny looked away, mouth hardening. She would not meet Jake's eye and rejection glowed on his cheeks.

"Look Jake, I'm grateful that you came for me," she said. "And we need to do this thing together. But for the avoidance of doubt, nothing's changed between us. What I said on the beach still stands."

Memories of that day were stored in the marrow of Jake's bones. Heading for the jungle; turning back to see her standing on their balcony, watching him. A sad wave. Her face white as a china doll.

"You lost your spark, Jake, whiling away the months on that beach. Worrying about that flipping article in the *Telegraph*. I needed more."

You had her, she was yours. And you threw it away.

A crushing sensation in his larynx. There was a danger he might start weeping.

"But I love you, Jenny."

There. Said it.

"And I think I always will," he finished.

"I'm sorry."

An hour after the British couple departed, more visitors knocked on the door of the cottage in Yemin Moshe. Mr Aberlieb sighed and began his journey through the house. But funnily enough, it was another British couple – and if anything, this pair were even more photogenic. The girl had a vaguely Italian look, with mesmerising blue-green eyes. And her partner was an undeniably beautiful boy.

33

Now MI6 was really getting to work. Here was Davis, entering di Angelo's cell. But the CIA man could recognise him only by those looming shoulders, for Davis wore a protective suit, mask and oxygen tank.

"Wakey wakey, sunshine!" Davis's voice sounded as if it had been canned. "Good morning, *guten tag* and *buongiorno!*"

The American lolled on his bed. "Nice clothes, dickhead."

"How was the scran last night, fella?"

"What?"

"The tucker. The nosh. Your fucking supper, matey. How was it?"

"It was ok." Di Angelo explored the stitches in his scalp. "For British food."

"Ouch, that hurt. You couldn't taste the secret ingredient then?"

"What? What are you on about, man?"

"The human plasma in your mashed potato." Davis clapped his hands together. "You've gone and got the Ebola virus, fella."

Di Angelo sat up in bed. "You're shitting me."

"*Contraire, mon frère.* It is you who will be shitting yourself, in the not too distant."

"I don't believe you."

"Believe what you like." Davis grinned happily. "But I can tell you this now. In a few days' time you will most certainly not be – how can I put this? – fit as a fiddle."

"If you're for real you're a fricking psychopath."

Davis chuckled at that. "Let me explain what's going to happen next, chap. Quite soon, your body's going to detect that West African nasty we've put in you. But by then your immune system will have its hands tied behind its back, because the gremlins will have already battered your dendritic cells. Without them, your antibodies won't have the blueprint they need to fight the infection, so the virus will be at it like fluffy bunny rabbits in your bloodstream. At that point your immune system will throw the kitchen sink at it – antibodies, white blood cells, all going bonkers. It's called a cytokine storm – nuclear war in your bloodstream basically. One side-effect is that blood vessels get more permeable. Blood and plasma leak into the surrounding tissue – eyes, nose, ears. Brain. In desperation your body will release nitric oxide to regulate your blood pressure. But that'll make your blood even thinner and cause more damage to your blood vessels. A Catch 22! Your liver will be bang in trouble too, by the way. It'll give up making the proteins blood needs to clot, which means, you've guessed it, yet more bleeding. The long and the short is, you'll be melting from the inside, fella!"

Di Angelo was trying to look unperturbed, but his gaze skittered around the room.

"At some point in all this fun and games, you'll probably start asking me for the doses of ZMapp2 we've got," said Davis. "That's the antidote. It's not a definite cure, but if you get treatment in time you're reasonably likely to survive. Whether you get it will depend on how much you've told me about what you fellas over the pond are up to. The sooner you open your gob, the better your chances. So I would get my skates on if I were you. Sunshine."

And here at the British Embassy in Tel Aviv another interrogation was underway. Mr Aberlieb was tied to a chair in an empty room as Evelyn Parr screamed at him through a two-way mirror. Only the jolly fat man had a stubborn streak and he hadn't caved in, even though he had been kept awake for two days.

And here in provincial Israel were the adorable couple who had tricked their way into his home and drugged him, Alexander Coppock-Davoli and Chloë Smith (née Fleming). Only by dint of Jenny's radioactive left heel were they able to keep up as she and Jake criss-crossed Israel, but the overall direction of travel was clear: south, south, south. Chloë's orders were to protect them from the CIA 'wet boys' that Parr correctly assumed were in Israel. Protect, observe, let them get on with it.

Meanwhile Jacob Serval still languished in his pit, trying to get a smile out of the child as Fleet Street fulminated over the hostage crisis. In Birmingham Alec McCabe was getting used to the gurgling of his colostomy bag, books on Etruscan linguistics spread about the private room at Queen Elizabeth Military Hospital. And at Vauxhall Cross C oversaw all, one eye on West Africa, the other on the Middle East. And *his* boss remained ensconced in Number 10, drinking cup after cup of tea and reading George Orwell.

I did not even know that the British Empire is dying, and still less did I know that it is a great deal better than the younger empires that are going to supplant it.

Reading and thinking and watching his net approval ratings tick higher as Sierra Leone went from basket case to boom-country, as the security situation in Nigeria began to deteriorate.

Only back in Cyprus, there had been a hitch in the Prime Minister's designs. For on the third morning when Davis began taunting di Angelo, he felt suddenly dizzy. His hands went to his mask; he staggered; then he toppled to the floor like a Bamiyan Buddha blown to dust.

The odourless fentanyl derivative had been added to Davis's oxygen tank by two Royal Military Police officers. They had been got to by the CIA, offered $10 million each and a new identity for this single deed. At that moment there was a rocket propelled grenade attack on the base – it would be blamed on the Islamic State – and in the ensuing chaos di Angelo and the traitors simply walked out of the front gate. A UH-60 Black Hawk helicopter, modified to minimise radar noise, picked them up a few miles outside Akrotiri. Thirty minutes later di Angelo was in the medical bay of the USS George HW Bush, lurking in the eastern Mediterranean to facilitate airstrikes on Syria. The rescuers were in the nick of time. For that morning a perplexing ache had rolled over di Angelo's back, and he was getting a sore throat.

In short: it was all kicking off.

34

The renegades in the eye of the storm were drinking coffee at a roadside café near Kiryat Gat, southern Israel. Sir Neil Campbell's memoirs were on the table.

"Read the first two sentences of the book, Jenny."

Having received two wounds, I was prevented from accompanying the Allied Armies on their march to Paris, and did not arrive in the capital until April 9. Even then, I had no knowledge of the arrangements in progress regarding the future destiny of Napoleon.

"Future destiny." Jake nailed his espresso in a single swallow. "Does he mean future destination? Or something else?"

Campbell and Napoleon had met in the French town of Fontainebleau, shortly after the Allies had offered the emperor the crown of Elba and an income for life if he abdicated. Britain alone had objected to the terms. Jenny looked cynical, but she shifted closer to him and together they read Campbell's account of his first encounter with Napoleon Bonaparte.

I saw before me a short, active looking man, who was pacing the length of his apartment, like some wild animal in his cell.

"Almost exactly like ..."

"Rudolf Hess," Jenny interrupted.

After Hitler's deputy had fled to Scotland with Hitler's copy of the *Disciplina* he was assessed by a British psychiatrist. And neither could forget the doctor's first impression.

The face is that of some tormented beast. Bestial, ape or wolf.
Sir Neil's recollections continued.

Napoleon passed high encomiums on Lord Wellington, inquired as to his age, habits etc. When I described his Lordship's great activity, he observed, 'He is a man of energy in war. To carry on war successfully, one must possess the like quality.'

Jake jabbed at the line. "A man of *energy* in war. What energy?"
But Jenny was already leaping down the page.

Napoleon paid many compliments to the British nation for their union and national feelings, in which he considered they excelled from the French.

'Yours is the greatest of nations', he said, 'I esteem it more than any other. I have been your greatest enemy – but I am so no longer. I wished to raise the French nation, but my plans have not succeeded. It is all destiny.'

"Becoming quite the Anglophile," said Jake.

Napoleon constantly expresses the sense he entertains of the superior qualities which the British nation possesses over every other. After continuing in this strain for a long time, Napoleon said France had lost all. He spoke as a spectator, without any present hopes or future interest.

Future interest.

And there was something else: a paragraph that made Jake shiver in the heat of the day.

In remarking on his confidence in his own troops, he referred to me to say candidly if it was not so. 'Tell me Campbell, frankly; is it not true?'

I told him it was; that everyone spoke of 'the Emperor and his guards,' as if there was something in them more than human to be dreaded.

35

The first email had arrived a year back.

From: historystudent@outlook.com
To: KMAACHII@britishmuseum.org

Dear Dr Maachii,
*   I am a private individual who is attempting to become*
fluent in the Etruscan language. I wondered whether you
might provide me with some one-to-one tuition. I happen to
be a public figure however, and I greatly value my privacy.
I therefore require lessons online and anonymously. (I may
also request tuition at antisocial hours.) I realise these are
awkward requirements and you would be remunerated
accordingly. Please let me know if you are interested.
Kind regards,
David

At first Dr Kanisha Maachii penned a refusal, but the enigmatic correspondent begged her to reconsider. That didn't surprise her. Etruscan is an extinct language and only a dozen academics alive are fluent in the tongue; Kanisha supposed her would-be student had been turned down by every Etruscan linguist in the world. She was intrigued though, and David's persistence impressed; still more eye-catching was the sum he suggested. So it was that, half-suspecting a hoax, she agreed.

The alarm went off at 2.45 am, plucking Kanisha from sleep and reintroducing her to a studio flat in Camden Town. She struggled out of bed, turned on her laptop and put the kettle on. Even in her pyjamas Kanisha was striking. Her mother was Scottish, her father an Iranian Zoroastrian who'd fled from the Ayatollah in 1978, and the electric light brought out reds and coppers in the black curls that spilled down her face. Her complexion was somewhere between coffee and rose and her eyes were green. Her nose was unmistakeably of the Achaemenid kings, noble and unrepentant in its dimensions.

The student was waiting on Skype, video function disabled.

"Good morning." The greeting was metallic, warped by voice-disguising software so completely it was rendered sexless. "It's David here."

David Attenborough? David Icke? Kanisha smiled to herself. What a conundrum!

"So, the Mysterious Etruscan," she said. "First up, let's try a little test. I want to see how much you already know. Hold on, I'm sending you an image."

There was a *ping* as the file disappeared into the ether, a fainter one as it landed. It was a picture of a vial inscribed with a dozen jagged letters that looked halfway between Greek and Saxon runes.

"In Etruscan first," she said. "If you please."

After a pause, David read: "*Mlakas se la aska mi eleivana.*"

"Impressive. Translation?"

Three minutes passed before her student replied, "'I am the unguent-bottle of the beautiful Sela.' Ha. Pretty."

Etruscan shares no ancestry with any other known language, but there are grammatical similarities with Latin and Greek: the conjugation of verbs, changing the ends of nouns. And as the lesson progressed Kanisha became certain her pupil was a linguist.

"Can you read me something longer?" said David. "I want to hear it in full flow."

"Sure – I've got a nice grave inscription here."

Her words filled every corner of the room: a peal of sounds that elided wonderfully on the tongue, lapping against each other like waves.

"*Acasce creals trachnalth spureni lucairce ipa ruthcva cathas hermeri slicacheś aprinthvale luthcva cathas pachanac alumnathe hermu melecrapicces puts chim culs leprnal pśl varchti cerine pulalumnath pul hermu huzrnatre pśl ten ci methlunt pul hermu thutuithi mlusna ranvis mlamna mnathuras parnich amci lese hrmier.*"

This was a language of silver thread and war horns and the beaks of dragons, and when Kanisha finished there was silence. She fancied David had closed his eyes.

"Beautiful." A catch in the computerised throat. "It's like Elvish or something."

Kanisha laughed. "Klingon, I've always thought. But I am a Trekkie, I freely confess it. Maybe that's why I'm still single at thirty-three."

"And what does the passage mean?"

"This is the epitaph of Laris Pulenas," Kanisha boomed with mock-gravitas. "Son of Larce, grandson of Larth, grandson of Veltur, great-grandson of Laris Pule, who wrote this book on divination. He held the office of magistrate in this city."

"Divination ..."

Linguistics was forgotten as they discussed Etruscan religion for the first time. David seemed fascinated by this element of the Etruscan world.

36

"Hello, Mo," said Jenny, something like a smile on her face. "Long time no see."

The Palestinian with the trilby and the gold chain turned his collar up. "Is too much you asking me this time, Mrs Jenny."

It was dawn and they were standing by a breezeblock hut outside Sderot, southern Israel. The landscape was flat and surprisingly grassy, dotted with tiny yellow flowers that seemed muted in the half-light. Jake was reminded of Oklahoma.

"The man this side, we bribe him." Mo pulled hard on a cigarette. "The man other side of wall, he is cousin of me. But if Hamas meeting us in tunnel?" He grimaced, drew his thumb across his neck.

"Never mind the histrionics," said Jenny. "Let's just get it over with and we'll leave you in peace."

Mo had been Jenny's first break as a handler: a Hamas fighter she'd recruited for a £45,000 retainer. He was unaware she no longer worked for MI6 – and now Jenny was coming to collect.

"This is a bad life," he lamented.

Mo's eyes were fissures in a desiccated face as he regarded the Israel-Gaza barrier, a fingernail of grey sprouting from the earth. On the eastern horizon a godlier vision arose as red and orange and yellow leached like watercolour paints into a sky still weighted with darkest blue: the rainbow emergence of a new day.

"Come," said Mo. "We go."

A family of six lived in the hut. The mother and father were awake, but their brood filled the single bed with slumber.

"Baksheesh," said the father.

There followed a flow of Arabic too fast for Jenny to follow.

Mo pointed at both of them in turn. "One thousand, one thousand."

"Dollars?" Her eyes were like gunshot. "Mohammed, need I remind you that you're on our payroll?"

"Money is not for me. Is for this man. I say you are good journalists, wanting to help Palestinian people. But still, you have to pay. Not normal, for you use these tunnel. Maybe the Mujahideen killing us if they meeting us. Quickly, quickly."

"One thousand for both of us."

The father acquiesced and dragged the family's brazier to one side – it stood on a paving slab in the cement floor, almost invisible with the ash impacted between the cracks. He eased this out with a poker and hauled it aside.

Rungs disappeared into blackness.

The tunnel had been bored to infiltrate Hamas militants into Israel. It ran for two miles, passing under the barrier to emerge in the Palestinian Territories. Once through, Jake and Jenny had to cross the Gaza Strip, from where a second tunnel entered Egypt. After that, only the jihadi head choppers of Sinai stood between them and Cairo.

Mo went first, descending thirty feet before wriggling into a horizontal shaft. Jake bent double to get in, shoulders scraping both sides of the tunnel. The air tasted noxious with cement and it was pitch black; he felt a flutter of claustrophobia. Yet the workmanship was undeniable. Concrete arches linked overhead like tongue and groove planking, a bespoke fit for this deadly artery. He noted the exquisite smoothness of the concrete. What a thing: to touch the innards of a Hamas attack tunnel.

"One metre digging, is taking one day," Mo enthused. "Construction is taking two years. Cost, two million dollars." His teeth gleamed in the torchlight. "And cement is coming from Israel."

The further they went the hotter it became and Jake strained his ears for Arabic. He couldn't turn around in this space; a backwards evacuation at speed was too nightmarish to contemplate.

Just keep going. Just keep going.

His heartbeat hammered out each step.

They had to be under the Palestinian Territories by now. Would he rather be in the hands of Hamas or MI6? Hard to say. Nobody spoke, each of them wrestling with their own fears. It was silent as a pharaonic burial shaft.

Mo halted. He turned, beaming again. One arm rested on a steel rung. It was a ladder. They were through.

"Is good tunnel, yes?" said Mo.

They emerged into a foxhole. Camouflage netting was slung across it and a mortar was angled towards Israel. Mo lit a cigarette, kissed his cousin on both cheeks and murmured a prayer of thanks.

He turned to Jake and spread his arms. "Welcome to Palestine."

37

Mo's Datsun had the appearance of a car that had been rolled down a hill sideways. The clock had stopped at 365,000 kilometres, the seats were torn to ribbons and the windscreen looked as if it someone had sprayed it with a double-barrelled shotgun. Ahead lay the most disputed strip of land on earth.

The population crush recalled India. People walking five deep on both sides of the road; a preponderance of men; children wearing grubby pyjama bottoms. Tenements teetered on the verge of collapse and steel rods protruded from the breezeblocks like straws from a scarecrow's sleeves. Each storey had to be tenanted before landlords could afford to add a new one, and the effect was of too many shoeboxes piled on top of each other.

Jake engrossed himself in Sir Neil. The book reproduced the soldier's orders from his Foreign Secretary, Lord Castlereagh.

> *You have been selected, on the part of the British Government, to attend the late Chief of the French Government to the island of Elba. You will be accompanied by an Austrian, a Prussian, and a Russian officer of rank; you will conduct yourself with every proper respect to Napoleon, to whose secure asylum in that island it is the wish of his Royal Highness the Prince Regent to afford every protection.*

Sir Neil's memoir continued:

> *Soon afterwards the Allied Commissioners assembled together. It was then that I was first made aware of the exact particulars of the treaty between Napoleon and the Allied Powers.*

"What treaty would that be?" asked Jenny.

"The Treaty of Fontainebleau, in which Napoleon agreed to abdicate in return for the throne of Elba and his family's safety."

Jake read on.

> *The reason of my ignorance appeared to be that the treaty had not as yet been signed by Lord Castlereagh on the part*

of England, on account of certain objections; and I therefore,
as British Commissioner, had received no official intimation
of its existence.

Certain objections.

The exact particulars of the treaty.

Yet even as Jake puzzled this, the words blurred before his eyes. The motion and the heat; the cyclical ticking of the engine; the dawn start. All conspired to sledgehammer him, and his eyelids slid downward irresistibly so that his recollections of the journey were forever woozy. The sun beat through the roof, mingling with the woodiness of Mo's cigarettes and the thickness of his slumber to form dreams of sudden vividness. These were obliterated with each jolt, whereupon he would awake with a gasp at small sounds which were unexpectedly loud. Then Jenny nodded off too and her cheek drifted onto his shoulder.

Jake was instantly awake and he watched Gaza slip over her crown with a gentlemanly crick of the neck.

At noon they reached Rafah, on the Egyptian border. The car stopped in what resembled a haphazard archaeological dig: dozens of quarries set into the earth and shrouded with tarpaulins. These were the smuggling tunnels, built by entrepreneurs to service the needs of the blockaded territories. A steady stream of Arabs emerged bearing suitcases and microwaves.

Mo pointed at Jake and Jenny in turn. "Fifty dollars, fifty dollars."

There was no time to argue – it wasn't unknown for Israeli warplanes to bomb the tunnels, cutting these conveyor belts through the blockade. The entrance was manned by a lad in his twenties called Abdul. Muscular and boyish, a pudding basin haircut; a pleasing gap between his front teeth.

He touched his heart. "*Salaam alaikum.*"

The tunnel was a void in the earth up which a rope jerked as an electric motor rattled and whined. A boy with a sheep arose from the ground like a conjuror's illusion and they replaced him on the platform. When Abdul whistled the machine went into reverse, passing them into the underworld.

"Sometimes, there is power cut!" said Mo cheerily. "And then ..."

"I don't want to know," cut in Jenny.

"Welcome in Lower Gaza," said Abdul when they reached the bottom. "I making this place."

This tunnel was larger and cruder than the last, left to private enterprise rather than the centralised clout of a would-be state. The sides were of rock and earth, the ceiling composed of wooden joists and ill-fitting slabs of cement. These tunnels collapsed frequently, even without the help of Israeli ordnance. Abdul led them past orange lights fed by bird's nests of cables strung along the way. Palestinians passed with a curt nod, laden under foodstuffs and domestic appliances.

Abdul paused and held a hand to his ear. There was noise to Jake's left.

"Drilling!" he said.

Abdul smiled.

"A regular rabbit warren," murmured Jenny.

All the lights went off.

Five seconds passed in which all they could hear was breathing and the clank of far-off drills. The lights came back on with a ping.

"Power cut?" Jake began.

Mo silenced him with a hiss. The lights went off for another five seconds. Then on again. All drilling had ceased. As they were plunged into darkness for the third time the meaning dawned on Jake.

"This is meaning Israeli plane," whispered Abdul. "When lights come on again, we running."

Fear dissolved Jake's stomach and energy squirmed in his calves.

The lights came on.

*

Running for one's life is a surreal experience. The feeling your shins are about to fly off your knees. The detached appreciation that you must continue sprinting at full pelt for an indeterminate time. The thought *this is actually happening*. Jake stumbled on loose rock, ducked beneath a fallen beam, swerved around bundles of clothes and gas cylinders abandoned in the rush. Abdul was in the lead, followed by Jenny; Mo brought up the rear and he hacked and swore. He halted and spat out something black, leaning on the wall.

"Come on mate," Jake panted. "Nearly there."

Jenny and Abdul were diminishing ahead of them.

"Go," Mo wheezed. "I follow."

"I'm not leaving until you do."

The space around them could cease to exist.

"Ok, ok." Respect in Mo's eyes for the first time. "I coming."

Pain lanced through Jake's abdomen as they ran and his stomach quivered with the threat of vomit.

Just keep going. Just keep going.

Nearing them fast: Abdul and Jenny, waiting on another platform and willing them on. Jake's foot hit the metal and it lurched off the ground, swaying and bouncing up the shaft; drawn towards the daylight.

Jake stumbled into an identikit crater. Arabs were strewn across the ground like battle-weary soldiers. Temples were clasped; chests heaved. Cigarettes were lit. An open air market embraced the earthworks. Livestock and sacks of rice, toys and DVDs, soft drinks piled high. Refrigerators wrapped in cellophane formed a wall in the sand. High above them an Israeli fighter plane completed the final swoop of its reconnaissance and banked away north.

Hello, Egypt.

38

There were things in the pit that made Serval shudder. The rings of filth and salt on his skin, sordid and sticky to the touch. The effluent, which rose visibly at the height of the day. The trilobite-like creatures with transparent exoskeletons that wriggled into the mud when he trod on one. Meals consisted of a bucket of fermenting rice with a chunk of fruit bat to be picked over if they were lucky. Hundreds had defecated through the grille.

Serval had befriended the child at last – though he shied away from contact, it was possible to make him laugh. Bracknell was stoic, counting down the days until the SAS swooped; Suleiman awaited events with the unsurpassable patience of the Sierra Leonean people.

On the fourth day the bamboo opened.

"Cam si di." Flat Cap lowered a rope. "A sho yu di chif."

Come here. I will take you to the chief.

Serval took the line and sank his other hand into the side of the pit to claw himself up. The texture was slimy, fine as liver. There were shouts in the jungle – a half-naked woman was being dragged into the foliage by two men. One carried a mop, the other a baseball bat.

"What are they doing with her?" said Serval dangerously.

"Mekin dohn was?" said Flat Cap, his upper lip riding above his teeth in a filthy smile.

"Making her do washing," Suleiman translated.

Serval managed an irritated smile. "I would respectfully ask that you to order your men not to hurt her."

Flat Cap yelled something in Mende and their hoots of laughter echoed about the trees.

*

Jason Bourne squatted on a tatty armchair, a bullfrog on its throne. He still wore the rabbit hat – one ear had wilted – and what light penetrated the canopy pooled on his cheekbones, like moonlight reflected in water. A phalanx of juju warriors was arrayed around him, the wonky court of this despotic jungle fiefdom.

"Aw it di kaka yonder?" the warlord enquired politely.

The courtiers stifled giggles.

"How is it eating shit over there?" translated Suleiman.

Serval did not smile. "That child is going to die soon."

Bourne nodded. "Smohl smohl."

Little by little.

The explorer drew a single tapering breath. "Hell's teeth, man, he's a *little boy*. Keep us prisoner if you must. But set the child free."

The warlord's voice was scornful. "Una de tohk tumas."

The man with no ears tittered nervously.

"You talk too much," said Suleiman.

"First time I've heard that one," said Serval. "What is it that you *want*, Mr Bourne? What's your cause? Are you fighting for socialism? Your religion?"

"Noto buk wo dis." A dismissive tone.

Not a book war, this.

"Do a deal with me," said Serval. "Whatever the Americans are giving you, we'll double it. All we ask is that you go back to Liberia. And stop other war-bands from coming into our country."

Our country?

"Du yaa no wes me tehm," said Bourne.

"Please don't waste my time," Suleiman translated.

"We'll supply you with weapons too," said Serval. "Your SBUs are armed with bows and arrows. Hardly befitting, is it? For a man of your reputation."

Bourne's lower lip glistened.

"We'll train your men too," Serval added. "You'll be the most powerful boss-man in Liberia."

Bourne looked thoughtful as he whispered into the non-ear of his underling.

"Supplies by air every month," Serval pressed. "Ammunition and food. Coca Cola, American cigarettes. And as a show of good faith, two hundred thousand dollars. It's on the other side of the river in new hundred dollar bills."

"Yu sabi tokh to pohsin," Bourne admitted.

"You know how to talk to a person," said Suleiman.

"But yu go gi me bunya."

But you must give me extra.

"An go an kam, an go an kam."

You help me and I'll help you.

Serval's mind whizzed. "Good whisky from Scotland. Suits from London for yourself and your lieutenants."

"Yu go ebul bruk mi klos?"

There was another stirring of laughter.

Will you also be able to launder my clothes?

Now Serval did smile. They were getting on, this was actually working.

"Oo, oo," chuckled Bourne. "Bad no de."

"Ok, ok. Not bad."

"Only know this." Serval's back was very straight. "If you double-cross us, we'll bomb you off the face of the earth."

The warlord laughed again, a booming resonance taken up by his entourage.

"An go an kam," he said.

You help me, I'll help you.

"I do have a final condition," said Serval.

Everything went quiet.

"The boy. Let him go."

The response was startling. Bourne's face changed from levity to dark and deadly anger and he ejected a stream of guttural Mende. The clearing echoed with the *snicket* of Kalashnikovs being released from safety mode and a hubbub spread out through the camp like ripples in a pond.

"They say the boy is a witch," whispered Suleiman.

"Seht yu moth!" Spittle on Bourne's chin. "Lehf mi."

Shut your mouth, leave me.

Serval's audience was terminated and he was dragged off through the forest. He was half way back to the latrine when he saw the woman.

Her head had been bashed in.

It happened again: a visible pulse of anger, exploding in his vision like a solar bomb. And the next thing he was fighting. An elbow to No Ears' jaw with a *crack* that felled him at once. Fingers into someone's eyeballs, raking down, provoking a scream that filled Serval with the lust for more. A fist into a temple, a knee to the groin. Suddenly his hand was around Flat Cap's neck, and he thrilled to the feel of it as he squeezed, constricting the vertebrae: he felt the grain of the bones as they ground in his grip. Kicks and punches assailed Serval, but the rage was in him and he wouldn't release that soft throat, only crushing and compressing until he heard a satisfying *click* ...

The fury subsided.

He had gone over the edge, like a man pushed beyond endurance by sexual pleasure. Resignation flooded through him and he let go of No Ears, sinking into oblivion as the Kalashnikov butts came cascading down.

When Serval awoke he was back in the latrine. Bracknell wound strips of shirt around his temple; Suleiman's face was a series of marshmallows, puffy and engorged. The child looked on uncomprehendingly.

"They say ..." Bracknell peered into Serval's eyes, as if trying to spy the homunculus within.

"They say what, damn it?"

"They say that you killed a man."

Jacob Serval digested this information. And he felt – nothing.

39

Tellingly, nobody would rent them a car to cross Sinai, so they were forced to buy one. It wasn't long before Jenny spied a 2004 Mercedes C-Class – and after colourful negotiations the trader agreed to sell it for $3,000.

Jake glanced at a more elderly specimen. "But we could get a car for half that ..."

"And do you want to break down halfway across? Look, if you're worried about the money, don't be. There are always ways."

He caught her eye but not her meaning. Mo refused to accompany them; Jake had the sense of standing on the last toehold of safety before swimming a gulf of sharks. He started towards the driver's door.

"What do you think you're doing?" said Jenny. "I drive."

He summoned jauntiness and strolled to the other side.

It was the *indifference* in her voice that hurt him, the presumption he would obey – as though he were a teenage cash-handler at a toll booth. He couldn't work out if it was hauteur by design, or worse: how she considered him now. They eased out of the terminus, through a roadblock manned by soldiers left slack-jawed at the sight of westerners entering Islamist territory. A tarmac road arrowed through a desert of kopjes that boiled with stone. Jake was reminded of Ethiopia, their drive through bandit territory two years back. This was infinitely more dangerous.

He mustered a grin. "Once more unto the breach."

"We'll be fine."

She stamped on the accelerator and they roared into the jaws of the Islamist death cult.

*

No wisp of green, no glint of water. The desert was torn through by hernias of jagged red rock; it had a destructed, devastated beauty. The only signs of life were the Bedouin tents, but even these had an abandoned air, doors flapping listlessly in the desert shimmer. Jenny kept up a constant hundred miles per hour, the car bounding and skipping on its tyres; Jake let his eyes relax until the mountains became a single smudge of speed. He had the vision of a spectral army with Napoleon at its head, marching in the other direction to defeat in the Levant, as yet without mastery of the Book of Thunder.

Sir Neil's diaries jiggled on his lap. Bonaparte was at Fontainebleau, saying his last goodbyes before the journey to the Mediterranean.

Napoleon was in the habit of receiving regularly The Moniteur *and hearing everything that went on at Paris; he felt bitterly the sarcasms that appeared in the newspapers about himself. He gave away manuscripts etc. to different officers, and directed others to be transmitted to favourites.*

"Wait a minute …" said Jake. "It says he ordered for 'manuscripts' to be transmitted to favourites."

Jenny's gaze darted from road to page and the car oscillated on its course. "What does it say next?"

In contrast with the treatment he had received from the Provisional Government of France, Napoleon spoke in grateful terms of the liberal disposition evinced towards him by the Ministers of HRH the Prince Regent, although he has always been the avowed enemy of the British nation.

"It almost reminds me of Hitler," said Jake. "You know, that weird respect he had for the English throughout the war."

And here was another parallel between the great monsters of the nineteenth and twentieth centuries.

> *Napoleon has frequently spoken to me of the invasion of England, and stated that he never intended to make the attempt without a superiority of fleet to protect the flotilla.*

It presaged exactly Hitler's stillborn invasion of Britain, foiled by the Hurricanes and Spitfires of the RAF. Jake stared from the window as the lifelessness flew by.

"History doesn't repeat itself, but it does rhyme," he muttered.

They passed a few burned-out cars. Then it was a crucifixion, the victim reduced to no more than blackened fibres by the sun, stretched out across the frame.

"This is a horrible place," said Jenny.

Jake retreated to the diaries.

Of Napoleon's conveyance to Elba on a Royal Navy ship-of-the-line, Sir Neil had written:

> *The Russian and Prussian Commissioners accompanied the rest of the party on board the HMS Undaunted, but they quitted the ship before she weighed anchor, as their instructions did not allow of their proceeding further.*

"So the only Allied commissioner who accompanied Napoleon to Elba was a Brit," said Jake.

Two vehicles appeared in their rear-view mirror.

"Who are they?" said Jenny. "Can you get a proper look?"

One Toyota pickup truck, one BMW saloon, the black flag of ISIS fluttering madly from a passenger window. Through the pall of dust Jake glimpsed masked men.

"Oh Jesus, they're jihadis. Holy crap, Jenny."

She inched the speed higher and the truck fell back, but the BMW responded with a jerk of pace – then began drawing sickeningly closer. An assault rifle was dangled from the passenger window.

Crack-crack-crack-crack-crack!

Bullet holes danced across the windscreen and they ducked to avoid the fusillade. Jenny was steering blind and the car shimmied on its tyres. When she peered over the bonnet it was to see a burned-out oil tanker scissoring across the road, galloping to meet them. She pulled hard left. Jake was slammed against the door, head snapped to one side by the G-force. The Mercedes lurched off the road, and for five petrifying seconds it was on two wheels, flirting with letting go and launching itself into a roll.

They were on a knife-edge of gravity.

With a *crunch* the car was back on four wheels. The windscreen shattered, the cockpit became a gale; wind and sand and bits of stone whizzed into hair and eyes, and Jake gritted his teeth as shards of windscreen sliced his ear, his gums, an eyelid. The Mercedes still flung itself across the desert, redoubtable, noble as a chariot. But chunks of rock rent its underside in a cacophony of bangs and their speed fell away. The impact was audible above it all. Too late had the dust clouds thrown up behind them parted before the BMW. The oil tanker approached with vindictive speed and the driver hit the barrier at 120 miles per hour, compacting the saloon into a block of tangled metal. A cascade of steam and dust was launched into the air; the pickup rounded the barrier and set off across the desert, better suited to rough ground than the saloon.

Crack-crack-crack-crack-crack!

Wing mirror taken off, dashboard smashed to pieces, headrest pulped in a blizzard of foam. There was a terrifying *bang*, right under Jake's feet. The back left wheel became an oblong and they began wobbling along at high speed.

"Blown tyre," shouted Jenny.

Now sixty miles per hour, now fifty, now forty. Before them lay only desert – the nearest mountains were five miles distant. Still the car lost speed. Even if they made it to the ridge and lost the gunmen in the ravines the heat was a death sentence of its own. Now thirty miles per hour. Twenty-five.

"We're goners," said Jake. "We've had it for sure."

"Be calm," said Jenny. "Whatever happens next, we're more likely to live if we keep our heads."

As the stricken vehicle coasted to stationary, Jake turned to look at their would-be executioners. So he was looking right into the driver's eyes when, apropos of nothing, the pickup exploded into a ball of billowing orange flame.

40

"Gosh, that was a bit exhilarating." Victor Milne was on the edge of his seat and gripping the armrests. "Let's watch it again."

Once more the GCHQ operations room admired the crazed curve of the Mercedes as it hurtled across the desert; the impact of the BMW; the debris as it was catapulted over the tanker like spray on a harbour wall. The technician cut from the satellite feed to the Reaper drone's camera. It was black and white footage, barren topography slipping silently beneath as the murderous device overhauled the two vehicles with ease. A corkscrew of smoke was visible as the Hellfire missile descended and the screen whited out.

As Jake and Jenny had begun their traverse of Islamic State territory, Milne was addressing the floor at Honda's factory in Swindon.

"This country was once the factory of the world," he cried. "And with the whopping new docks we're making in the Thames? Having thrown off the shackles of the EU? With a workforce as brilliant as you lot? There's no blooming reason on earth it shouldn't be so again."

There was a murmur as Milne punched the air. He was the first politician since Thatcher to truly connect with blue-collar aspiration, with Essex Man. There was something of Disraeli in the one nation politics he espoused; in his opportunism too. Although unlike the Victorian statesman, *ideology* could be glimpsed behind the pragmatism. Then C's message arrived and with masterful discretion his spinners wrapped up the visit.

The nearest place to monitor the action was GCHQ, and Milne was driven at high speed to that giant aluminium snail, curled up on the edge of the leafy Gloucestershire countryside with its antennae twitching. Now he watched rapt as two figures emerged from the Mercedes. (There was a crater where the pickup had been.) Jake lay on the ground, the heaving of his lungs visible from space.

"Do you know *why* I decided to get into politics?" asked Milne as Jenny removed the spare wheel from the boot.

"Go on," said C.

"To prevent things getting broken."

The spymaster prepared for a monologue.

"I'll never forget something my uncle told me," Milne began. "As he was carving the lamb, he said this. It's just not good enough to turn out and vote every five years and spend the rest of the time twiddling your thumbs, while wretched bloody do-gooders set about wrecking the joint. You have to actually get out there and stop it happening."

"And if the wheel's already come off?"

Jenny's repair was complete.

"Well, you put it back on again."

Food arrived from Pizza Express, and Milne and C sat like old pals before the cup final as the Mercedes crossed the Suez Canal. The car stopped at a roadblock; policemen inspected the bullet holes; cash changed hands and they continued.

"Corruption," said C. "Originally meaning, 'rotten'. Such a good word for it, I've always thought."

"Nations have their illnesses, as people do," said Milne.

"A Napoleonic quotation, if I'm not much mistaken?"

That earned the politician's most indulgent smile.

"And is Britain sickening in your opinion?" asked C.

"Oh, for more than two *saecula*, now."

The spymaster frowned. "*Saecula*?"

"Sorry, classical education getting the better of me. It's an Etruscan word. Two lifetimes."

"Talking of sick nations, this Sierra Leone situation needs a decision." C used his glasses as a conductor's baton, emphasising each syllable. "Our man's health will be failing. We really ought to get him out."

"Not yet. The coltan raids have abated – this frightful Jason Bourne chap must be at least considering his proposal. Get him on side and we've sewn up half the country. Don't let the clamour in the press bother you – the *Telegraph* just wants an excuse to knock up one of those fun hostage rescue graphics. You know, the ones with all the arrows and explosions and little cartoon helicopters."

"Respectfully, Prime Minister, you're not the one in a malarial latrine."

Milne snorted. "Now, what's the security situation in northern Nigeria?"

"Business as usual. Barbarians on the rampage, girls unable to go to school, beheadings all over the shop."

"Can the Nigerian Army regain control?"

"Not with Ebola to contend with too," said the spymaster.

"Great Britain has a responsibility in that part of the world," sighed Milne. "It's part of the Commonwealth, after all. I wonder, Dennis, I wonder."

"What do you wonder, Prime Minister?"

A martial gleam had come into his eyes. "I wonder whether we shouldn't have another little war of our own ..."

41

Everything in Cairo acquired a golden aspect in the sunlight: monuments, streets, buildings, faces. It reminded Damien di Angelo of looking through yellow sunglasses, and only when the CIA man rose above the sprawl did the effect diminish. From the spire of a Downtown minaret, gold faded into the steel grey of a hundred thousand clapped-out Fiats. Di Angelo could discern the Pyramids of Giza through the haze – where Napoleon fought a battle, where he did not, in fact, shoot off the sphinx's nose. The streets below him were a multitudinous drone of horns, arguing and mingling with each other; the city smelled musty, like an old cupboard in the summer.

Di Angelo was no longer infectious. He wore robes and a headscarf around his face and a latex callus mimicked the 'prayer bump' acquired by the devout through friction between forehead and prayer mat. Once again his disguise had been too good for Frobisher – and Wolsey was only interested in whatever the heck book he was reading.

That morning Frobisher had collected a package from some dive hotel on the Midan Talaat Harb. The receptionist had revealed the stamps were from Thailand: new documentation, di Angelo surmised. Frobisher confirmed this by purchasing a hijab and emerging, newly olive-skinned, from the Marriott Cairo.

Maryland's decision came through in late afternoon as the targets were ambling about outside the Egyptian Museum.

Di Angelo had inveigled himself into a gaggle of old-timers playing draughts. Behind him the traffic ground around Tahrir Square, a few protesters straggled about. The museum itself was pink and foursquare, embellished with columns, and pharaohs and lions dotted the courtyard, like the concourse of a junkshop. Egypt had more of this stuff than it knew what to do with. Di Angelo watched children playing with foam pellet guns, dodging the rockets as they came arcing by.

A newspaper story came back to him.

EDGEWORTH – The family of a US soldier left brain damaged after he was hit by a rocket-propelled grenade in Iraq harbor fears his fate was completely avoidable.

Second Lieutenant Andy Carlson was injured four years ago in the Sadr City neighborhood of Baghdad. But his father's now revealed they were only ambushed after corrupt local police forewarned the insurgents ...

Di Angelo realised he had closed his eyes. When he looked up Wolsey and Frobisher were still studying the upper floors, and the journalist pointed at an open window. Hell, if he didn't know better he'd say they were *casing the joint.* Di Angelo stayed in position as the pair entered. Six CIA agents followed them into the building. At 7 pm Frobisher re-emerged, blending so perfectly with the sea of demure Egyptian women spilling from the museum that he nearly missed her.

Wolsey didn't come out.

Di Angelo watched as the last museum-goers got evicted. The sun fell swiftly; the doors were locked; the windows of the museum were filled with darkness, segueing from orange into black. He smiled: it promised to be an interesting evening. The journalist was still inside.

*

After the theft of a £30m van Gogh from Cairo in 2010, it was decided that Egyptian museums should adopt new security protocols. One of these was the immediate reporting of alarms directly to the police chief of Cairo. And Babnouda Fanous was in for a very bad night's sleep.

When he was awoken for the first time, Fanous did not hesitate. He was a Coptic Christian, which meant the blood of the pharaohs flowed through his veins – how he reviled those philistines who'd looted the Egyptian Museum after Mubarak's downfall. But when he arrived, a dozen police cars already there, it was to learn of a false alarm. A laser had been tripped in the east wing, CCTV footage had been consulted (all the cameras were functional these days) and nobody could be seen. Everyone went home.

An hour later the alarm went off again; the dozen police cars and Babnouda Fanous returned. The same laser had been tripped, but the CCTV showed no intruder on the ground floor. One wag suggested it was Tutankhamun himself. Fanous guffawed, pointed out that King Tut was on the first floor, and they all went home again.

Fanous's humour deserted him the third time it happened and he arrived at 4.30 am in a towering rage, dressed no longer in his police uniform, but tracksuit bottoms and an old shirt. The laser tripwire was misfiring *again*. That gallery contained nothing too valuable – a stone sarcophagus only a forklift truck could remove and some pre-dynastic pottery – so Fanous ordered its alarm to be disabled. His son graduated from medical school the next morning and he didn't want to look like crap in the photos.

As Fanous placed his head on the pillow for the third time, an unpleasant thought occurred to him. Wasn't there access to the storerooms from that gallery? The police chief considered the dilemma. There was nothing priceless in the basement either. And besides, even if an intruder *did* get down there, hundreds of laser tripwires formed an invisible thicket between the basement and the nearest exit from the museum. Fanous fell asleep thinking how he would tell his friends that his eldest son was now a doctor. Perhaps he might become a surgeon one day. Or even move to Europe?

42

As Jake felt the form of a reed in the darkness he sensed the fall of a hammer onto a chisel more than two millennia ago. The angle of inflection, the ring of bronze on stone; the scent of dust and sweat on an artisan's hand. A kinetic instant, frozen in granite, the author forgotten. A duckling, a vulture, a finger, a hand holding a stick and a seated man. This was hieroglyphic braille, though Jake could not know he was touching a word as old as civilisation.

Itja.

Thief.

Jake lit up his phone and the interior of the sarcophagus was illuminated pale blue, the hieroglyphs cast into dramatic relief. It was 5.30 am. Time to try again. On hands and knees he heaved the lid ajar, an Atlas beneath clouds of stone. But this time when he threw a paper ball from the coffin, he was greeted only by the rattle of paper onto marble. No longer was the museum transformed into noise and light.

He emerged into the gallery.

Cabinets of black and red pots lined the room and funerary urns were dotted about, each big enough to accommodate an adult male, leering faces contoured into the clay. As Jake padded through the room the exhilaration of the cat burglar was in him, a child's thrill at treading in a forbidden place. A doorway led down to the cellars, wherein dwelt the mummy of Pakhar-en-Khonsu. The door was locked. The gargoyle on the nearest urn gurned at Jake through the gloom, urging him on. He took two steps backward and kicked the door in. A splintering noise, the shriek of old metal, the scent of brittle varnish flaking away. No alarm sounded, and he descended.

Moments later the lid of the nearest urn was lifted aloft and a figure unfolded itself from the vessel to prowl invisibly through the gallery. Special Agent Bradley Günther listened at the doorway and half-nodded in approval, like a gourmand sampling a rare and expensive dish. There was something of the razorblade to his face; those angled cheekbones. A garrotte dropped into his hand as he followed Jake into the vault.

*

The storerooms resembled an auctioneer's warehouse, arte-
facts stacked high and without theme. Discoveries that shake
Egyptology were made down there regularly, and Jake's spirits
sank as he explored forgotten vaults of untold wares. He crept
through a chamber of statuary, the antiquities shrouded beneath
sheets as if awaiting removal. The next corridor was lined with
wooden drawers – Jake opened one to reveal shards of pottery,
each marked with a scrawl of ink. Papyrus was pricey in the
ancient world, so notes, bills and rude cartoons of one's boss were
executed on potsherds instead. Jake appreciated once more the
swoop of an ancient hand, had the feeling of touching history.
Behind him he heard a noise and he shrank behind the shelves,
mopped up by the shadows. But no cry of challenge followed,
no swinging light of a janitor's torch. The corridor was dark
and still, like an oil painting that has aged badly and regressed
into murk. He swallowed, heard a click inside his skull. Thrill
had turned to fear now: he wanted to get this done. In the next
vault the mummies were stacked on shelves, a library of them
sleeping away the afterlife like sailors in bunkbeds. Caskets
lined the walls too, staring drunkenly at the ceiling. His phone
illuminated painted eyes and patterned breasts, each as fabulous
and intricate as a bird of paradise.

This place is crazy ...

Günther watched as Jake hunted through the collection. It was
decidedly *not* in the Brit's interest to find something. If he did,
the American would obtain it by murder. The garrotte hung
limply, an inverted ankh in the assassin's hand.

Jake had found something.

A Ptolemaic casket with hair of cobalt blue. He checked the
serial number and swallowed. He was staring at the celestial
vessel of Pakhar-en-Khonsu. The mummy was wishbone-light
as Jake laid it on the floor, all moisture purged long ago from
both wood and corpse. But the casket was sealed with beeswax;
he needed a tool. Back he went, heading for the corridor of the

many shelves. The about-turn took Günther by surprise – he had no time to retreat, so instead he simply faced the wall. Jake walked right past.

As Jake entered the corridor he thought he saw a light extinguished at the far end. The adrenaline was immediate, blaring in his veins, but the harder he listened the more the soundlessness confused his ears. Where that flash had been was only darkness, and Jake wondered if he had seen it at all.

The cord dangled in Günther's fist.

Jake select a pointed sherd before returning to the High Priest and using it to scrape the beeswax from the join in the casket. He clawed his fingers into the crack and heaved. The ancient wood parted with a *croak* and the top half clattered onto the floor, echoing through the basement. The tomb robber froze. But there were no footsteps, no rushing torchlight, and he let his eyes be pulled downward. Linen stretched over a gasping face; Jake had the impression of a ghoul, surfacing for air.

"Hello friend," he whispered.

No writing upon the bandages. But what about on the *inside*?

There was nothing else for it, so Jake began tearing at the bandages. A surreal moment, this act of desecration, this violation of every code by which he'd lived. The destruction of something ancient was as anathema to him as punching an elderly relative in the face at Sunday lunch. As Jake unrolled the bandages like twine from a spool the priest rotated in his casket. A spindly forearm revealed itself before snapping into dust, sheared bone protruding. Next the priest's face became visible, puckered and grey, the one-toothed mouth a maw of bewilderment. A fossilised chest came into view: skinny, pathetic beyond description. The linen spilling onto the floor was unmarked. But something wasn't right. Jake tugged at the linen, admiring its fineness and its strength. He'd handled ancient fabric at university and it crumbled at the touch.

These bandages have been replaced.

A new sickness overcame Jake then, a darker torpor. A sense he was being laughed at, played for a fool by predecessors who thought many moves ahead. Jake pocketed a strip of linen and photographed the casket – the priest was no more than a pile of filth amid bundles of lacerated swaddling. He swept the bandages back into their case and fiddled the halves back together; he needed to return to his hiding place before the museum awoke.

Special Agent Günther prepared to strangle him.

*

Günther heard each of Jake's footsteps as though it was the crash of cymbals, his consciousness vivid in a way most men never know: the heightened wakefulness of a killer of men.

A blade was drawn across his throat.

He sighed and knew at once that he was a dead man. The slice was so surgical it had caused a mere lancing of pain, though Günther felt clearly the warm slick of blood flooding across his breast. The sensation was almost pleasant. He had only seconds to appreciate this, only seconds to think of his wife Alice who was undergoing fertility treatment in Tennessee, before the blade of the stiletto was thrust into his earhole up to the hilt. Günther quivered on the end of the dagger, skewered through the brain and dead as Pakhar-en-Khonsu himself.

The beautiful boy's first murder had gone as Davis had predicted. Training and instinct had taken over; a nasty moment followed by the satisfaction of a job well done. His mentor would be proud. Alexander Coppock-Davoli hauled the corpse from sight moments before Jake passed by, the burglar unaware this evil had transpired at all. Jake returned to the gallery and clambered into his sarcophagus. Coppock-Davoli followed at a safe distance: the boy who had lost his innocence.

43

On the seventh day, they came for Serval again. Both Suleiman and Captain Bracknell were wild with fever and dehydration; helicopters passed, but rescue attempt came there none. That morning Bracknell had actually used the phrase, 'We're gonna die here, man.'

Serval remained unaffected. The explorer's constitution was every bit as unbreakable as his will, and though he would have appreciated a shower he felt he could take another fortnight. Not so the child. Serval reckoned that without medical attention he had days to live. Then one stifling afternoon, the bamboo cage was thrown open.

It was No Ears. "Kohmoht, wit-man."

"Come out, white man," Suleiman translated.

"I know, I got that," said Serval.

He hauled himself up.

"An de bohboh," said No Ears.

"And the small boy."

The interpreter handed the infant up to Serval, who plucked him out by the wrists. Suleiman clambered up too and they left Bracknell lying comatose in the pit. Serval rested his hand on the child's head as they walked, a skullcap on the tiny cranium. It was the first time the boy had not shied away from contact and they might have been father and son on a day-trip were it not for the guns, the air of menace, the stoned meander of the boy's footsteps. They stopped beneath an African Greenheart tree, fifty metres tall, and No Ears said something in Mende.

"He says this tree, the bark is a magic bark," said Suleiman. "They using it to make tea. In the tea, they are placing the ..."

His words petered out.

"Placing what?" said Serval.

No Ears's grin was brilliant, the whites of his eyes fully encircling the pupils.

"Placing the skin of child," muttered Suleiman. "This tea, if you drinking, is making you popular. Is making you, like ..." he sought the word.

"Charismatic?" suggested Serval.

"Yes, charismatic. At election time in our country, no parents are letting the children onto the street. Because the Honourables, they are wanting to make this tea."

This detail had the ring of truth to it.

No Ears giggled and said something with the air of a punchline.

"But of course, I am not a member of this secret society," translated Suleiman.

Holy Mary mother of Christ, Serval thought. Travel in sub-Saharan Africa is ... well, it's definitely not like being in Thailand. *They will eat you up.*

He was led to an abandoned research station. Spent shotgun cartridges were everywhere and a satellite dish lay on the ground: it was a scene from a zombie movie. Jason Bourne squatted in the doorway of the nearest hut, bush wives perched on each side of him. His distended stomach protruded grotesquely from his vest.

"Mr Bourne," said Serval grimly. "And how are we today?"

The warlord patted his stomach. "Rohtin behleh."

"Rotting belly," said Suleiman. "It is meaning, 'glutton.'"

"Not at all," said Serval. "You look in fine condition."

The toad king's eyes glittered as he calculated the sincerity of the remark. "Butu."

Suleiman and the boy threw themselves to ground; Serval remained erect.

"Bow down," whispered the translator.

"Butu," the warlord repeated more dangerously, a gravelled hiss from the back of his throat.

"Bow down," pleaded Suleiman, who was grasping the dirt. "Please bow down."

But Serval did not move and Bourne physically bristled at the challenge. A new wildness was in Bourne's eyes; the juju warriors shifted on their feet. The bush wives looked between the males in patent terror.

One finger at a time, the warlord clenched his fist. "*Butu!*"

With the sigh of an adult wearying of childish games, Serval bowed his head. All around the compound tension went out of shoulders and necks, a single breath released.

Bourne cleared his throat. "Dis wok ya, a go ebul am."

"This work," said Suleiman. "I am able to do it."

"Good. That's excellent news."

"A noh lehk dat wan de." Bourne pointed at the boy.

"But I don't like that one there."

"He's my friend." Serval put an arm around the youngster but the boy, sensing danger, pulled away.

"Yu de gi ram to me," Bourne smirked.

"You will give him to me," said Suleiman.

"Fo de *it*."

"*For the eating.*"

"Tell me, Suleiman," Serval muttered sideways. "What's Mende for the phrase, 'Not on your nelly'?"

The translator shook his head rapidly.

"Di pikin, ram dai," said Bourne reasonably.

"The child, he will die anyway."

"Yu de kohstamohnt," he went on. "Me di makit uman."

"You are the customer, I am the market man."

"A want see di *wit-man* mek di sara."

"I want to see the *white man* make the sacrifice ..."

Slowly the price of cooperation dawned on Serval. On top of the money and arms and the fine clothes from London, he himself had to kill the boy. A test, a challenge, a symbol of devotion. The throb of anger that went through him was so powerful this time that his knees trembled, and for a few moments he saw nothing at all.

The research station reformed itself and a giddy sickness was in him as he realised what he was about to do.

*

The boy would die anyway, nothing could stop that. By this single action – this *mercy* – he could end the barbarism in western Sierra Leone. The ends justify the means: did this not underpin every civilisation from Rome to the British Empire? He would put down the boy, as gently as he could. He would release him from all this. And one day he would kill Jason Bourne too. Serval swore this to himself with silent vehemence.

"De bohboh," the warload coaxed him. "De bohboh, de bohboh, de bohboh ..."

Serval kneeled down and opened his arms. The boy was trusting now, as if sensing deliverance; willingly he entered the explorer's embrace. Serval enfolded the diminutive frame in his limbs. He wrapped one hand around the child's jaw, the other around his left shoulder. He leaned into the child's ear and whispered that he was sorry. Then he jerked his arms counter-clockwise, so the bohboh's neck went *click* and he fell asleep.

When Serval stood his cheeks were wet with tears.

"Ohlman de pan in you wa-ala," Jason Bourne was telling one of his bush wives matter-of-factly.

Every man has his troubles.

Serval was free to go.

He staggered through the jungle to fetch Captain Bracknell, struck dumb at what he had done. He focussed on his shoes, trying not to think of the face of his father. Then a funny thing happened. He thought of the ground beneath his feet, the wealth it contained. What could be done with it, the transformative power of civilisation at the barrel of a gun. His paces became surer. And this fury he had discovered in himself was back: no longer in peaks and troughs but in the background, ticking through him at a residual level, like pneumatic fluid powering his cyborg stride. Another image came to Serval: that red pillar box in Freetown, slot choked with weeds. The weeds would be removed soon, and the people better for it. For the ends do justify the means. Rome wasn't built in a day; you can't make an omelette without breaking eggs.

White man's burden, he thought.

He would do what needed to be done.

Bracknell had revived by the time the explorer returned.

"We're free to go," said Serval.

The captain brightened. "Thank god for that. What happened?"

"Nothing important. Now get out of that stinking bloody pit, will you?"

They will eat you up.

In Tel Aviv, Mr Aberlieb had started to talk.

44

Dr Marie-Elise Babineaux placed the scrap of linen into a quartz tube with some copper oxide and silver wire. She attached a vacuum line to expel the air and used a blowtorch to seal it, placing the tube in an industrial furnace. This resembled a domestic appliance from a space station, crudely joined in the manner of specialist devices. The laboratory was elegant with long windows through which the Cairo sunlight spilled, reminding Jake of physics classes at school in Bath.

L'Institut Français d'Archéologie Orientale was the only place in Egypt to offer radiocarbon dating. It inhabited a handsome nineteenth-century mansion south of Tahrir Square, in one of Cairo's most fashionable districts. Jake and Jenny had stepped with trepidation through the parqueted entrance hall, passing Egyptian mummies in display cases and a library full of French archaeologists. They made it to the laboratory unchallenged, where Jake introduced himself as Dr Robin Matthews of Warwick University.

Dr Babineaux was a tiny Frenchwoman in her fifties with chic silver hair and darting eyes, like a rather pretty sparrow. *Oui*, for €330 the tests were possible but approval from the Egyptian Supreme Council of Antiquities was required. Oh, and there was a two-week waiting list. Jenny offered a €5,000 donation that would fund a PhD student for months; paperwork was no longer required.

"But how can we afford it?" Jake murmured.

"I told you, there are ways and means to get money," she replied cryptically.

At 900 degrees centigrade the copper oxide caused the textile to combust. The tube now contained carbon dioxide and a little water, which Dr Babineaux mixed with hydrogen and iron powder inside a graphite reaction vessel. This was a tube of burnished aluminium: another spaceship part.

As the mixture was heated Jake continued through Sir Neil's memoirs; folded page corners and scuffmarks denoted his progress through the book. The commissioner had recounted a meeting with Wellington.

Enlarging upon the influence Napoleon possessed over the minds of French soldiers in the field, Wellington said that under him they performed what no other chief could obtain from them ...

A French trill interrupted his reading. "Aha! The next stage is complete."

The carbon absorbed from the atmosphere by a flax plant long ago was now deposited on the iron powder as graphite. From there the equipment got even more space age. Dr Babineaux placed the graphite into a tiny aluminium bullet and inserted it into a metal disc rather like the cylinder of a revolver. This was placed into the accelerator, a tangle of aluminium tubes and drums. The carbon was blasted with a caesium beam into the Mass Spectrometry Accelerator where magnets separated the isotopes into C12, C13 and C14. Only the last was allowed through into the final snarl of metal tubing.

As the C14 was analysed Jake returned to the diaries.

"Wait a minute," he said. "Listen to this ..."

It was another missive from the British Foreign Secretary, Lord Castlereagh:

> *You have already been informed of the Act of Abdication passed by Bonaparte, and of the assurance given him of a pecuniary provision of six millions, with safe asylum in the island of Elba. The Act in question was to be given up on the due execution of engagements, with respect to the proposed arrangement.*

"What *proposed arrangement*?" said Jake.

"Who knows?" said Jenny. "The treaty must have run to pages and pages."

Dr Babineaux frowned as she studied the data spilling down her screen. "You said this is from a Ptolemaic mummy, Dr Matthews?"

"That's right."

She shook her head. "That is archeologically unacceptable. This textile is not antique."

A tightening in Jake's throat.

"I calculate this sample to be from the early modern era."

"How precise can you be?" asked Jenny.

Dr Babineaux studied her graph. "With a margin of ten years error either side, I calculate that this linen dates from the year 1797."

The year before Napoleon set sail for Egypt. Jake wanted to awake from something real, like a man told his wife has died in a car accident. Jenny shot him a look full of hunted understanding. This mummy *had* been discovered by Bonaparte's savants. Unwrapped, the inscription on its bandages added to the growing corpus of the *Disciplina Etrusca* that Napoleon was assembling from dozens of mummies, each embalmed with the Book of Thunder as their amulet.

But why was it done?

"Do not be too surprised," said Dr Babineaux, detecting despondency. "After all, you must know how vibrant was the market for forgeries, even in the eighteenth century. Very many were fabricated for the European collector. After two centuries the patina they have acquired can convince even the experts."

"It's not a forgery," Jake uttered.

"Please, Dr Matthews."

But Jake only stared at the screen with its array of graphs and figures; data that told him a different story. Of a discovery; a deception; of the coordination of the *Grande Armée* over vast distances, the forging of an empire.

"You have a photograph of the mummy, perhaps?" asked the Frenchwoman. "Maybe I can give a second opinion?"

One thing Jake had learned as a journalist was this: always take an expert opinion when it's offered.

"My, my, my ..." said Dr Babineaux as she studied the photographs. "What a mess. Grave-robbers, a terrible breed they are. But this *is* a real mummy! I know this casket, it's in the Egyptian Museum, here in Cairo. And my colleagues did *this*? Dr Matthews, I am truly appalled."

Jake looked at his fingernails.

"The sample must have been contaminated," Dr Babineaux was saying. "Though how material from that era got onto the linen I cannot imagine. I cleaned it most thoroughly under the microscope. Are you also studying the Viennese mummy?"

Silence in the room.

"Viennese mummy?" repeated Jenny.

"You did not know about this? But it is a very famous mummy indeed." Suspicion in those sparrow eyes now. "I do not understand how you cannot know about this."

"He's the expert," Jenny blustered.

"Well?" Dr Babineaux said to Jake.

"I, er – I don't know either."

The archaeologist looked dismayed at the state of Anglo-Saxon higher education.

"There are *three* mummies that Egyptologists have found a connection between," she said. "Pakhar-en-Khonsu, whose remains have been violated so unacceptably. His wife, now in Croatia, and even you must have heard of her."

"The Zagreb Linen," said Jake.

Dr Babineaux looked relieved. "That is correct. And the third mummy is on display at the Kunsthistorisches Museum in Vienna."

The disclosure reverberated through them like the news of a coming apocalypse.

She pointed to the hieroglyphs on the casket with a varnished fingernail. "You can see him mentioned here – a little boy." A motherly look came over Dr Babineaux as she contemplated an ancient family's tragedy. "He was their son."

"We have to go there," said Jenny.

This museum-breaking lark was fast becoming a spate.

45

For once Kanisha Maachii's mysterious protégé had called in the daytime, and the linguist was ensconced in the confusing spiral of outbuildings that surround the British Museum. A facsimile of the Zagreb Linen was laid out before her – David's suggestion.

"*Zichri lu*," her student began, and although she had spent a decade studying Etruscan it sent a shiver through her to hear it pronounced so beautifully.

"Meaning?"

"Let it be written," her pupil said with relish.

Reading right to left and with mutual passion, they translated the material. Etruscan is so obscure – and the sources so limited – that the meaning of many phrases in the linen book remains disputed. But it was like discussing the topic with a world expert, and again she sensed David's formidable intelligence.

"*Aiser-sic-seuc.*"

Gods of light and darkness.

"*Farthan.*"

Genius, as in of the dark gods.

"*Zathrumiś flerchva Nethunsl śucri therezi-c.*"

Kanisha found she was nodding along with the cadence, lips slightly parted. "Very nice. And your translation?"

"In the month of Cel, offerings to Nethuns must be made and immolated."

"Perfect," she admitted. "Absolutely perfect. Where Cel is equivalent to our month of September, and Nethuns equated to Neptune."

"I thought the Etruscans didn't believe in the Roman pantheon?" said David. "Etruscan gods were invisible and omnipresent – like an ether, almost."

Ether: from the Latin *aether*, meaning upper air. And so like *aiser*, the Etruscan word for god.

"That was the case at the beginning of Etruscan civilisation," said Kanisha. "But by the time the Zagreb Linen was made in the second century B C, the Etruscan lands had been absorbed into Rome. It was standard practice that when Rome engulfed a new culture, their priests equated each of their gods with a Roman equivalent."

"What sort of offerings would have been made?"

"Oh, the usual stuff. Pigs and goats, a bit of barley meal perhaps. Or a nice amphora of ..."

"*Vinum!*" David interrupted, the exclamation startling through the voice-disguising software. "Wine. I see it written here. Why's that word been underlined?"

"Remember, this book was originally intended for chanting," she said. "Phrases needing emphasis were marked up, to aid the *fulguriator.*"

"Good to know," David muttered.

"Time for a test," she said. "According to the linen, what are the 'sacred priesthood of the citadel and the community' instructed to do?"

There was a humming as David skimmed the ancient document. "Bow to the temples of the people, to the cities and districts and hearths."

Wow. He's a faster reader than I am.

"That line," said David. "It seems familiar."

"As well it might," she said. "It's thought to refer to the Prophecy of Vegoia."

"Vegoia," David repeated.

"The prophet who warned of damnation for –"

"For kings who violate borders," David interrupted.

"I should have known you'd be clued up on Vegoia," Kanisha chuckled. "If only the Romans were too, maybe they'd still be with us."

Silence down the line.

Let it be written …

46

The history lecturer from Warwick and the Yorkshire-bred Pakistani were doing a spot of sightseeing in the cultural capital of Europe.

Neither Jake nor Jenny had set foot in the continent for two years. It was May, still nippy at Vienna's altitude, and he found the forgotten sensation of coldness pleasant. The streets looked ludicrously clean, although the first person Jake saw out of the train station was squatting on the pavement with a sign saying, *Ich hab Hunger.*

Vienna had survived World War Two relatively unblemished and lavish nineteenth-century apartment blocks unfurled themselves for street after street, sausage stands on every corner. What else struck Jake about Vienna? There was the smoking, for a start. The Egyptians liked a fag, but there it was a male-only pursuit. In Vienna *everybody* was at it, indoors too, and cafés that had not missed a day's trade in a century were fumigation chambers. Cobbles, trams, statues everywhere: Brahms; Adam Smith; Christopher Columbus; Goethe. Plus coiffured battalions of immaculate old ladies in pearls and full make-up. It is said Vienna has a moth problem caused by the sheer weight of fur coats.

Jake's confidence was coming back. At a shop a cashier had asked him in English if he'd like a bag.

"No thanks." Then just for the heck of it, "Would *you* like a bag?"

Bemusement, hilarity. It felt good to be spontaneous and daft again, to find people responded. He had charm, damn it!

Beer.

Unexpectedly Jake felt the old urge. He could ditch Jenny and sneak off, have *just one beer*. It was sold on every street, supped outside cafés by those who would never suffer this imbroglio of temptations and doubts. But he would not allow himself to slither back down to weeks at a time in the drunk-hungover cycle.

*

The Kunsthistorisches Museum was a magnificent example of Baroque architecture. Children blew bubbles and men sold candy floss; pony traps clattered along, piloted by drivers in Lovat tweed greatcoats and bowler hats.

"Do you think we're being tailed?" asked Jake.

"Do you know, I think we've shaken them," Jenny replied.

"But we won't let our guard down, right?" said Jake.

"Of course not."

A hair detached itself from her scalp to drift away on the breeze.

There was an hour-long queue for the museum and Jake opened Sir Neil's diaries as they waited.

"This is it!" he exclaimed.

An Asian couple glanced around, but Jake didn't notice them. A new darkness was under his eyes and his cheeks seemed more sunken than before.

My remaining with Napoleon after the departure of the other Commissioners was in obedience to Lord Castlereagh's instructions; there was another article of the treaty not fulfilled. It was not till this very day that Lord Castlereagh gave a qualified accession to certain portions of the Treaty of Fontainebleau. His Royal Highness the Prince Regent, having knowledge of the contents of the said treaty, accedes to the same in the name of His Majesty, as respects the stipulations relative to the possession in sovereignty of the island of Elba.

"It's all here." Jake's fingers were very white as they clasped the tome. "After Napoleon was defeated in 1814, he negotiated a sweet deal with Russia and Austria – the crown of Elba and a lifelong income. The only sticking point was the Brits, Napoleon's most implacable enemy. They wanted to send him to St Helena, at the ends of the earth and somewhere he could never return from – which is where he eventually ended up after Waterloo. So Napoleon bargained for Elba with the only thing he had left. Handing over the *Disciplina Etrusca* was the 'stipulation' for possessing Elba. That was the other 'article of the treaty not fulfilled.'"

Before Jenny could answer Jake was racing back through the book again.

"It says it here in black and white," he exclaimed. "This is the moment."

He gave away manuscripts etc. to different officers present at Fontainebleau, and directed others to be transmitted to various favourites.

"Napoleon cut the deal at Fontainebleau, before he headed south to the Mediterranean. Within a couple of months, Castlereagh had satisfied himself the thing worked, so the Prince Regent assented to the treaty."

"Maybe ..."

"Not maybe," shouted Jake. "Definitely! Look here."

There were backward glances from another Chinese couple as he scrabbled through the work.

"On the way to Elba, Napoleon gets worried he'll be attacked by North African pirates. But Lord Castlereagh *knew* it wouldn't happen."

Another letter from the Foreign Secretary:

I cannot foresee that any enemy can molest the French corvette, on board of which it is proposed that Napoleon should proceed to his destination.

"After that assurance, Bonaparte knows he has nothing to fear," said Jake.

Napoleon next adverted to the threats of the Algerians, but cursorily, and did not seem apprehensive; he said that if it was intended to adhere to the treaty entered into at Fontainebleau, he would not be molested by them.

"And finally this," said Jake.

England, Napoleon said, did now as she pleased; the other Powers were nothing in comparison. 'No Power can make war against England and she will do as she likes.'

It was the birth of British hegemony.

"Napoleon did hand over the *Disciplina*," she said. "He felt betrayed by France. He'd grown to respect his old enemy. So he played kingmaker in the game of nations."

"Only he grew to regret the decision," said Jake. "He got bored on Elba, set sail for France and retook the throne. But when the 'Hundred Days' culminated in Waterloo ..."

"Napoleon got trounced by the Duke of Wellington," Jenny finished. "He fought the worst battle of his life, strewn with all those errors that baffled Michael Beloff. Defeated once and for all, it was off to St Helena where he sickened and died."

"But if Britain had the Book of Thunder," said Jake, "how do you explain the slide to war in 1914? Why didn't Chamberlain confront Hitler early in the 1930s? What about the calamity of Suez, the invasion of the Falklands, the Iraq War? Recent history hardly speaks of a Britain able to tell the future."

"I should have thought that's perfectly obvious," said Jenny. "Because somehow, we lost it too."

47

It was one of the most beautiful galleries in Europe. The murals were inspired by pharaonic tombs: lines of two-dimensional figures inching along the walls, tastefully done. Two columns from an Egyptian palace supported the ceiling, encoded in hieroglyphs like magical palm trees. There were sarcophagi with sides that were a foot of solid granite; steles were arrayed about, grave-markers of the far-off dead. A slab of temple wall bisected the room, embroidered with stars that twinkled in the stone as they must have done on a night long ago in the Middle Kingdom. And the centre of the room: the child.

He lay horizontally in a display case, peering up through the glass like a premature baby in an incubator. The face of the casket had been smashed in long ago, this instant of violence frozen in splintered wood. A golden mask remained beatific within the jagged frame. Ancient grave robbers were the purported culprits, and the label explained that this mask had replaced a missing original in the nineteenth century. An outer layer of linen enclosed the bandages, embellished with ancient spells.

Another unwrapping job.

A little door was set into the base of the cabinet – the compartment beneath the display shelf could be used for storage. Suddenly it occurred to Jake. If he was able to wriggle through the door, he'd be lying *directly underneath the mummy.*

"I need tools," he said.

At a hardware shop off the Ringstrasse he acquired chisel, torch, Stanley knife and hacksaw. Jenny selected a sledgehammer.

"What's that for?" asked Jake.

"We're running out of money, remember?"

"You're going to get money ... with *that*?"

Numerous possibilities presented themselves, none of them good. But Jenny merely arched an eyebrow and would not be drawn on the topic any further. She sawed off the handle, left with the only sledgehammer's head. As they departed the strap of her handbag was cutting into her shoulder.

*

Amid the gothic and the baroque, the art nouveau and the renaissance, the building Jenny led him to was a cube of featureless cement. It was 100 feet wide at the base and 150 feet high; circular turrets protruded over each corner, like Mickey Mouse ears eavesdropping on the rooftops.

It's a *flakturm*," explained Jenny. "A flak tower – built with slave labour by the Nazis to shoot down Lancaster bombers. During air raids forty thousand civilians could fit inside."

"It's hideous," said Jake.

"Yup. But the amount of explosives it would take to blow it up would flatten every other building in sight. Like it or not, they're stuck with it."

"Like a reminder of their crimes."

During the fifties the tower had been converted to an aquarium. Several school trips were booked in and the next available tickets were for two hours hence. To kill time they visited the Belvedere, a Habsburg palace and one of the finest art galleries in the world. And as they took in Monet and Schiele, Gauguin and Munch, it felt increasingly like a date.

Be funny. Be funny.

They were admiring Gustav Klimt's unfinished painting of Adam and Eve.

"There are two types of people in the world," said Jake. "Those who need closure."

Five seconds passed before the penny dropped and Jenny laughed out loud.

"You're a funny man, Jake."

"Oh, I don't know about that," he said, rubbing his fringe.

"And also brave. There, I've said it."

"Now you really are pulling my leg."

"You are," she insisted. "What you did in Jerusalem was brave. What you did in Cairo was brave too. And I know courage – please don't take this the wrong way – courage doesn't come naturally to you. Which makes it all the braver, if that makes any sense at all."

She had Jake's complete attention.

"You're a good man," she went on, regretful now. "And I … sometimes I think I've been so stupid."

Where had this all come from? Jake felt a tightening in his chest, his life swirling about him. The majesty of Klimt, the gallery with its handsome ceilings, the view over palace gardens; all had faded into a different dimension.

"I'm telling you this because I really need you to know …"

"Know what?"

"It's not you, it's me."

Jake felt a horrid prickling high up on his cheeks, had the sensation of his guts slithering out through the soles of his feet.

Beer.

"Horrific cliché, but true," she said with a smile, as though he should be delighted by all this. "You're a special person, Jake. You'll make someone very happy one day."

"Thanks," he managed. "But I'm really not that special, am I? Or you wouldn't be pushing me away like this."

He saw something move behind her face, some thought he could not access.

"You don't understand," she said. "I've just got something else going on."

"Some*one* else?" It came out hotter than he intended.

"No! I'm just not in the right place. Plus you're too bloody good for me. You're like a, I don't know, a ray of decency, Jake, you really are. An occasionally hopeless ray, but a decent one nonetheless."

She was trying to tell him something, but he couldn't work out what.

"Let's get out of here," he said. "I'm not in the mood for art any more."

She looked downwards, biting her lip. "I'm sorry if I've upset you Jake, that wasn't my intention."

Jake was already pounding away through the gallery.

He stopped dead.

Bonaparte confronted him.

48

Napoleon Crossing the Alps, by Jacques-Louis David: the most famous of all depictions of the emperor. The image caught Jake by the throat, and thoughts of Jenny left him. They stood to admire this astonishing man who once bestrode the world, who created the modern French state, its laws and institutions; whose puzzles they were yet unpicking. The canvas illustrated one of Napoleon's greatest triumphs. In 1800, on the way to

Marengo, his army had crossed the Saint-Bernard Pass – a remarkable accomplishment. Napoleon sat astride a rearing white charger before a sky that churned with the violence of an incoming storm. He pointed towards the heavens – in gratitude? – and the artist had added the name Hannibal, carved into a rock in the left of the painting. It was an explicit association between Napoleon and the great Carthaginian general who had led his elephants that same way millennia before to make war on Rome.

History rhymes.

Jake grabbed Jenny's arm.

"Ow!" she said. "What is it?"

"I understand now. It all makes sense."

"Understand what?"

"Why the *Disciplina* was hidden in Egypt in the first place. Napoleon knew too, he's acknowledging it in this painting."

"So tell me."

"When Hannibal crossed the Alps in the third century BC, he took the Romans totally by surprise," said Jake. "They must have ignored the warnings of their augurs, thinking such a feat was impossible. Hannibal rampaged up and down the Italian peninsula for fifteen years, besieging cities, looting homes, annihilating the Roman army at Cannae in northern Italy. Only after slaves were sacrificed for the first time in centuries was the Network appeased. Hannibal met his Waterloo."

"I know, I remember all this from last time. Your point is?"

"Do you remember how old the Zagreb Linen was?"

Jenny recalled the Wikipedia article.

The manuscript has been dated to approximately 200 BC, give or take a few decades.

"It was made at the same time as Hannibal's invasion," she said.

Jake smiled grimly. "And where?"

There is evidence it originated in northern Italy. The twist of the thread is in a 'Z' direction, typical of that region – whereas Egyptian linen of the period has an 'S' thread. On palaeographical grounds, academics have speculated that the manuscript was written in the region of Lake Trasimeno in Perugia.

"Perugia," said Jenny dully, seeing it all. "Northern Italy. Where the Battle of Cannae took place."

"The Romans thought they were going to lose the war," said Jake. "It looked like the end of the Republic. So they copied the entire *Disciplina* onto linen, cutting it neatly into strips. They sent it far away for safekeeping. To Egypt – where it could be retrieved once Hannibal had gone."

During his last hunt for the Book of Thunder, Jake had relied upon the analytical capabilities of the human brain, equal to any ancient witchery. But he had also learned to let his instinct guide him: the whisperings of the Network to which he'd become slightly attuned. And in his gut, he knew.

This is what had happened.

*

Hammerheads darted, giant grouper lurked and a moray eel in leopard print shimmered past like a hologram. A reef shark lying on the floor of the tank glanced at Jake with dog-like eyes.

"Look, why are we here?" he said. "It's clearly not to look at the fish."

Jenny didn't reply – instead she led him to the roof of the Nazi fortress. They stepped out onto the turrets, high above Vienna. The *clink-clink-clink* of traffic lights about to change drifted up from the streets, oddly foreign sounding, and rising from the rooftops a mile away was the *flakturm*'s control tower, like a UFO on a stalk with its beard of modern aerials and satellite dishes. To the south-east, there were mountains. Over there Napoleon had lost one of his only battles, on a day when the fog obscured the sky. Fitting, that they should solve half of the Napoleon Complex in this city, a place so integral to the Bonaparte story. Over those mountains Romans had once tramped too, heading to annihilate the tribes of central Europe. Different emperor;

same pagan science. Just as both empires had been to Egypt, powerful waves breaking upon the same beaches.

Smash!

The sound of metal on concrete swept Jake from his abstraction. Jenny was taking a hammer to the side of the tower.

Smash!

A hole had been opened in the fabric of the *flakturm*. A cavity lay within.

Tinkle!

Jenny tidied up the lip of the hollow with swift, efficient movements. She reached inside and withdrew a hessian sack that clunked dully in her grasp; her wrists trembled under the load.

"X marks the spot," she said.

"What is it?" said Jake.

"Our war chest. Come on, let's get out of here. I'll tell you later."

It was gold bullion.

During the Cold War, MI6 stashed arms and gold throughout central Europe for the resistance cells that would kick into life if the Soviets overran the continent. Jenny knew the location of several of these caches. Back at the hotel, Jake turned the tiny ingots over in his hands. Together they amounted to the deposit on a two-bedroom London flat.

And something else of significance was to happen on that strangest of days. Jenny announced she was going for a stroll, an odd fancy when the streets held danger. But Jake's offer to accompany her was declined.

He would not normally have followed her – stalking wasn't his style. But her behaviour had not been right all day. Something was going on. He *had* to find out what.

Jake tailed her for two blocks, aware that it was madness, that she was trained to spot this kind of thing. But before she did, she went into a shop – and emerged carrying something that shocked him.

A bottle of red wine. And Jenny was a teetotaller.

I've just got something else going on, Jake.

An old flame, right here in Vienna – she had a rendezvous with him that very night. Now all the oddness of Jenny's behaviour was explained in ghastly technicolour. That was why she'd been compelled to make that strange little speech at the Belvedere. It also explained the notion that a ten out of ten girl could ever have been his. For she never had been, not entirely – evidently a part of her mind had been here in Vienna all that time. *That* was why she'd left him. The jealousy was a physical thing: it rattled in Jake's windpipe, weakened his ankles. He went and got hideously drunk.

Jake was observed on this binge by MI6, by the CIA, and also by the Chinese Secret Service.

All three agencies were about to spectacularly collide.

49

Jake was reacquainted with reality by a knocking at his door. It took him a few seconds to remember where he was, but then it came to him.

Oh god. I got wasted last night.

The base of his skull was agony: it felt as if a piece of shrapnel was lodged in there, the pain pulsing from it in waves. The room was still spinning and he felt dirty.

"Jake? Are you in there?"

He could remember the beginning of the bar crawl. Speed-drinking pints; chasing them with scotch whiskies; changing location after each few drinks so the bar staff wouldn't know he was getting drunk alone. Memories became fragmentary before diminishing into nothingness, save for the obscure recollection of propping up the bar in some dive at 3 am and discussing the vicissitudes of women with a pony-tailed Hungarian. Jake sat up in bed. He was still wearing all his clothes (they reeked of fags) and his stomach felt as if it contained toxic waste. With a lurch he thought he was going to be sick.

Another knock.

"I'll be out in a minute ..." he managed.

Jake retreated under the cover in the foetal position, a teenager again. He didn't want to venture into a world full of danger, full of pain. He only wanted to stay in this place of warmth and of safety. He closed his eyes and before he knew it he was slipping back into dreams.

"Jake! It's half past ten."

Wide awake again, Jake had a craving to be at his old flat in Battersea. Impossible! The door handle turned and to his horror he realised he hadn't locked it. Before he could leap out of bed, Jenny confronted him. She appraised his crazed hair, the ruddy eyes.

"You got battered last night," she said slowly. "Didn't you?"

"Jenny, I ..."

"There's no point denying it – I can see it in your face. It's in your posture, I can hear it in your *voice*."

"You can talk."

But the comeback was as meaningless as it was petulant. He must have consumed five times more than her – and at least she had the dignity of company.

"What the hell do you mean by that?" she snapped.

"Oh ... never mind." He slumped back into bed.

Jenny sighed and shook her head. "God, it's so bloody *sad*, Jake. Right. I'm going to the museum to do what needs to be done. With or without you."

The door slammed.

He didn't *have* to do this.

He could sleep for a few hours, go to an art gallery and then have lunch somewhere nice, a bottle of wine to wash it down. Forget all about the Etruscans, leave Jenny to her destiny.

Destiny.

Now: if he chose that path, was it always predetermined?

Self-evidently yes. Because how else could it be foretold? That was another factor in favour of a lubricated lunch – it would not actually be *his* choice to get back on the booze, in a sense. But that would be a self-fulfilling prophecy. Jake wrestled with the dilemma, thoughts tumbling over themselves in his head.

I was born with special gifts. I see things other people miss.

Jake's hands went to his cranium, which thumped with pain in time with his heartbeat. But there was an apologia to his touch now.

Only I can do this.

He looked at the wretched pile of coins and crumpled bank-notes cast across the table. Pisshead's pockets, they called it at university. Any idiot can spend a lifetime getting smashed.

"Don't go without me!" he shouted. "I'm coming with you."

Jake got out of bed and flattened his hair under the tap in the bathroom sink. As he changed his shirt he noticed his torso in the mirror, just beginning its first slide into middle age. That said, he was in fairly good shape. Recoverable.

Jesus!!!

That moment when you lose concentration on a dual car-riageway and drift two feet into the opposite lane. And a car is coming, and you jerk out of its path in the nick of time. And as the Doppler effect of the other vehicle fades away and your car regains its smooth line of travel, you think what you might have lost: all those decades of accumulated memories in your brain, joys and sadness, wisdom and laughter. A working body. A future. This was such a moment.

He had pulled back from it.

50

Snatched from life too young, the child awaited them. Jake peered at the golden mask, envisaging the fragile head contained within.

He kneeled to adjust a shoelace. "Coast clear?"

A middle-aged Chinese fellow with little round spectacles ambled from the room. They were completely alone.

"Coast's clear," said Jenny.

He opened his backpack, which was full of house bricks. "Behold, the feline grace of an international museum robber."

With a *smunch* the door of the display case was bashed open.

"Careful," hissed Jenny.

A couple in their twenties had wandered in, Chinese again. The girl had improbably thin legs; her companion looked rather geeky and shepherded her out with the bewildered protectiveness of a man who can't quite believe he has a girlfriend.

"Ok, get in there," hissed Jenny.

After a flurry of wriggles Jake was lying inside the cabinet with his chin in the dust, assailed by the smell of the musty and the forgotten. Jenny slammed the door shut and he was in darkness. The mummy lay on a panel two inches above his head.

"Well done," came her muffled voice. "That was quite impressive."

"Years of training, my dear."

Jake switched on his torch and positioned the chisel against the side of the panel. He readied a brick.

"Coast clear?" he said.

"Coast clear. But if I tap, stop work right away."

"Got it."

Bash.

The chisel splintered up through the panel and a chink of daylight shone into the cavity, catching on motes in the air.

Bash.

More light, more sawdust.

Tap.

A swish of footsteps approached. Definitely female. And they sounded – Jake didn't know why – as if the feet were turned outwards. A security guard? The metronome veered away through the gallery in an arbitrary curve before vanishing. He fed the hacksaw through the gap and began to cut, sawdust cascading over his face. Soon he had sawed down the length of one side.

Tap.

Spanish voices, female, teenage. Jake heard laughter and the corralling of feet, a sudden silence, a release into chatter. Photographs being taken. When the voices had dissipated he continued; the incision worked its way around all four sides of the panel and Jake propped up each corner with a brick turned on its end. After twenty minutes he had cut the wood free: it had become a table top balanced on teetering bricks.

"Coast clear?" he said.

"Coast clear."

Jake knocked two bricks over, one side of the panel dropped like a trapdoor and the mummy rolled into the compartment with a clunk. He fiddled the panel up and wedged it back in place. The mask peered at him through its ruff of splintered wood. There was something beseeching in its gaze, like a child witnessing his father behaving badly. Jake prised open the casket and the panel was briefly lifted off its bricks. He removed the facemask and sliced away the outer linen sheet.

The bandages were unmarked.

Not this again …

Jake severed a bandage at the neck and began to unwind. The boy weighed no more than a few bags of sugar and when he lifted him there was a dry snap. One shoulder now pointed backwards at a bad angle.

"I'm sorry," he whispered.

He carried on unwrapping.

Tap.

"Hi guys." It was Jenny talking. "Can I help you?"

Jake held his breath, the child frozen in his embrace – like it was under his spell.

"Oh, we're just taking in the show, honey." A Mid-West accent. "It's just a whole lotta dead people, right?"

"And where are you from, darling?"

The second voice was a New Yorker. Possibly gay, Jake reckoned, though his gaydar was far from infallible. As Jenny made small talk he unwound the child's bandages with the delicacy of a man removing a core from a nuclear reactor. The head emerged, tiny and shrunken.

A third set of footsteps approached.

Jenny at her most ballsy: "You again? Look, will you kindly bugger off?"

"Hey Jenny. How y'all doing, guys? Charles, Steve?"

Jake had the sudden understanding that it was the man from Jerusalem. He hadn't the foggiest clue what to do next.

*

In the next room Frank Davis patted the back of Coppock-Davoli's head. "You ready, fella?"

The boy's cheeks were flushed. "Yah, let's do this."

"Atta boy. Ladies?"

Heckler and Koch pistols emerged from handbags.

"Let's get cracking then, eh?" From his backpack Davis produced a Desert Eagle .357 pistol, practically a foot long. "Cheers, all."

Coppock-Davoli snapped the safety catch on his Beretta and all four of them simply walked into the gallery.

51

Vauxhall Cross was very still from outside – like a modernist folly, not a real fortress of espionage where real spies did real business. But the corridors within pulsed with energy, and nowhere was that truer than in the incident room where Victor Milne and his acolytes awaited developments. Only Milne himself seemed at ease, and he sat with leg over knee skim-reading the

Times. The leader column noted that banditry in Sierra Leone had been virtually eliminated, but it ended on a note of caution.

> *Tony Blair's adventure in the country was a triumph too, but sadly only whetted his zeal for meddling in the affairs of other countries – with calamitous consequences. The Prime Minister rides as high in the opinion polls as his predecessor did in 1999. Let us hope he learns from Mr Blair's hubris ...*

When the Prime Minister turned the page C flinched: Milne was caricatured as Queen Victoria, trying to apportion West Africa with a carving knife as the president of Nigeria fended him off. The previous evening Nigeria had refused the offer of British military assistance in tackling Boko Haram. With Ebola seemingly back under control, President Adeyemi thought he could defeat the northern insurrection alone. The cartoon was captioned, *Empire Mark Three?*

But Milne merely chortled. "Ha! The cartoonist really caught me, eh Dennis? Quite the compliment actually, being likened to dear old Queen Vic. I'll get that one framed for the lavatory."

"*Are* you trying to rebuild the British Empire, Prime Minister?" asked C.

"Don't be so silly." Two seconds' silence. "Even though it was undoubtedly a force for good."

"What do you mean?"

"Consider this. In 1955, British GDP per capita was eight times that of Zambia. Now it's twenty-eight times more. Let's be clear, whatever Africa's troubles in the last seventy years, they can't be laid at our doorstep."

C said nothing.

"Look at India, man," Milne enthused. "We bestowed railways, courts, democracy and a civil service upon that rabble. We multiplied the amount of irrigated land by eight times, increased Indian life expectancy by eleven years and ran a bureaucracy with barely a trace of corruption. Now regard the political quagmire in

Bangladesh or Pakistan. Or in east London for that matter. Even the damned Taj Mahal was falling down until a Brit stumped up for the repairs."

The spymaster polished his glasses and leaned his head to one side, evaluating the Prime Minister.

"In the late Victorian Age," Milne continued, "– and things were already on the slide then, by the way – there was this idea floating about that if Britain wanted to maintain her pre-eminence, she had to stop thinking of herself as a European country. Great Britain must no longer be a collection of islands in the North Sea. She must consider herself a *worldwide state* – or she would be overtaken. A mind-bending idea really, isn't it? That Britain could be not a European country at all. That it might transcend its own continent."

He stopped talking as one of C's subordinates drew near.

"Anything from Vienna?" asked C.

"Not yet."

"The greatest wickedness the politically correct ever wrought," mused Milne once the minion had departed, "and by god there have been a few, was convincing us that the Empire was a Bad Thing. It wasn't. And the world is poorer for it. So are the British people – lowered and traduced, shorn of dignity and self-respect." He snorted. "If only you could *see* the dregs I have to shake hands with in our high streets and town centres. What happened to us!? A Victorian would be appalled. To conclude, the Empire was a Good Thing. Now, *hypothetically speaking* of course, might I enjoy your support in bringing it back?"

"You don't have to tell me about the benefits of Empire," C said at last. "My grandfather ran a palm oil export company in Ghana. At independence we were Britain's model colony, the richest country in West Africa. By the time his business was seized Ghana was in penury. We'd suffered half-a-dozen coups and the corruption was as bad as anywhere on earth. Next I consider the education my father and I received from Britain. Great Britain. I'll do what I can, Prime Minister. MI6 is at your disposal. Moreover …" C breathed in, and a brief callousness flickered in his pupils. "Well, it's exciting, isn't it, Prime Minister? Your hypothetical project, that is. The ambition of it."

"If Wolsey finds what we're looking for, by golly we will *change history*," exclaimed Milne. "You and I, Dennis."

As the two men composed themselves the junior spy returned, brandishing a piece of paper.

"From Vienna, sir."

C read the dispatch with increasing concern.

52

The sight that confronted the MI6 team as they entered the gallery was this: Jenny, her hands spread on the glass of an empty display case. The first American, twenty stone in weight and rosy-cheeked, his white-blond hair whisked into a Mr Whippy peak. An East Village style hipster with a pencil moustache, denim jacket rolled up at the sleeves to reveal tattooed forearms, and a haircut involving various fins and shaved bits. Damien di Angelo, with his hands in his pockets. And finally Jake, shame-facedly extricating himself from the cabinet.

Parr closed in on the big guy, Chloë went for the hipster, Davis took di Angelo.

Before any of them could react all three had a pistol barrel pressed into the back of their skulls. Five pairs of hands raised above shoulder height; Coppock-Davoli took a few steps back, pistol tracking back and forth. A *fait accompli*.

"Hello, mate," Davis said to di Angelo, twisting the barrel into the American's skin where the neck met the skull. "You feeling a bit perkier?"

A security guard wandered in and stood with mouth gaping, looking dumbly from protagonist to protagonist.

"Oh, what do *you* want?" said Davis.

Gunfire erupted from three sides of the room and the air was full of blood of the freshly-slain.

*

In the initial maelstrom nobody knew what was happening or who was firing at them. The hipster took a bullet to the cheek, head jerked back, gore splattered across the cabinet. His colleague was hit twice in the gut and once in the chest. The machine pistols were silenced, and their rounds emitted a futuristic *pweut-pweut-pweut* sound, like faeries of death, flitting about the room. There was the crack of bullets into granite, the splinter of wood and shatter of glass.

A single round shattered Parr's left elbow and her forearm dangled. Jenny threw herself to the floor; di Angelo dived into a granite sarcophagus, a bullet skimming the heel off one shoe. Chloë flung herself behind the slab of temple wall as a scattering of bullet holes peppered the ancient stars, and the rest of the MI6 team made it behind the two columns, cowering into twin triangles of cover. Jake and Jenny were close enough to touch noses, and for an instant they looked right into each other's eyes.

Blam-blam-blam-blam-blam. Blam-blam-blam-blam.

A new firearm speaking, the machinegun fire briefly curtailed. Jake switched his phone to camera and used it as a periscope to peep over the cabinet. Davis was leaning against the column, loading a magazine into a cartoonishly huge handgun. Parr grimaced as Coppock-Davoli wound a strip of his shirt around her elbow. And by god, if it wasn't *Chloë*. She squatted with her back against the slab of granite, a pistol clasped in both hands, eyes screwed shut as she summoned up courage to return fire. In all three doorways Jake glimpsed Chinese agents, the little black holes of their silencers flickering wickedly with white light. The air shimmered with disturbance.

Blam-blam-blam-blam-blam.

A scream in the far corner of the gallery; a drop in the volume of Chinese fire. Now Davis would whittle them down. Jake had seen this done before.

"This is our chance," Jenny shouted through the cacophony. "While they're fighting each other ..."

An explosion rocked the centre of the gallery, horrendously loud. The whole gallery shook and a cascade of plaster bled from the ceiling. Jake chanced his camera again. The Chinese agents had fired a grenade round at the column which was blackened now, a crack running down it. Coppock-Davoli's face was contorted in noiseless terror and his eyes blinked very fast. He had lost two fingers.

Blam-blam-blam-blam-blam-blam-blam-blam-blam.

A female shriek this time.

"How the hell are we meant to get out?" shouted Jake.

"Like this."

Jenny grabbed the bundle of linen; Jake couldn't help but noticed it was unmarked. And these were modern textiles. Early modern, to be precise. A plummeting sensation, even amid the heat of battle.

Napoleon got there first.

Jenny wound the bandages around one of the bricks and sparked a cigarette lighter. "When I throw this thing, we sprint for the nearest door," she said. "Got it?"

Jake nodded wordlessly. There was a fifty-fifty chance he was about to be killed. The textiles flared up immediately and Jenny tossed the burning bundle high across the gallery. For the duration of its flight all gunfire ceased; it was briefly possible to hear alarms. They made a dash for it. The ensuing moments went very slowly.

In Jake's peripheral vision, an impression of Chloë, darting for the flaming bundle. Her colleagues providing covering fire now, giving it everything. Blood all over the walls. Bodies everywhere. Chloë grabbed the burning linen and dived into the protection of the sarcophagus. Immediately Davis and

Coppock-Davoli stopped firing and in a spasm of clarity Jake realised the Chinese gunmen were no longer pinned down. He and Jenny were metres from the door, marooned in space. The reaction that saved them was sheer instinct. Jake wrenched a granite stele off the wall – the grave marker was the size of a small door, and it landed upright with a thud. Adrenaline gave him the strength to pivot it like a shield and bullets smashed into the stone, nearly knocking him off his feet. Jenny rushed to help support the weight and they dragged it closer to the exit. The skinny-legged Chinese woman lay in the doorway, boss-eyed, a bullet hole in her forehead. Then several things happened in quick succession that changed the battle completely.

On his own initiative – impetuous, keen to impress – Coppock-Davoli dashed after Jake and Jenny. He was instantly picked up off the floor by a hail of gunfire and cast the length of the gallery, landing with a half-yelled *glerk*. A look of tragedy came into Davis's eyes, followed by a fervour that made his pupils flash with violence and his face turn puce with rage. Suddenly a shotgun was in his hand and he strode from cover like a man of iron, too engorged with thoughts of vengeance to care whether he lived or died. The shotgun snapped and blasted and the Chinese agents disintegrated into red as explosive shells tore grapefruit-sized craters out of them. The Chinese team broke before the onslaught, fleeing deeper into the museum. The battle proceeded into the Greek and Roman galleries, but the rules and objectives had changed. Now it was Davis versus the People's Republic of China, Davis bent on the destruction of every Chinese agent he could find, and none could stand before him. He pursued them through a gallery of red-figure vases – this was the *really* posh stuff. Shattering of pottery, snapping of bone, smattering of wine-dark blood into a double-handled drinking cup, where it submerged a painting of the bloodlust of Achilles after the death of Patroclus.

Achilles leaped like a god bent on atrocious deeds, destroying right and left.

Sad groans arose, and the crystal tide grew red with blood.

The hurricane continued into the next gallery. A bearded Cypriot warrior with an archaic smile and beard of ringlets was blown clean in half by Davis's shotgun. Behind it hid the agent with the tiny round glasses. He was blown in half too. Red slugs were splattered across a statuette of Asclepius the healer. A bust of Aristotle observed the carnage mildly; the philosopher's pupil, Alexander the Great, would have been in awe. In the next gallery the Chinese attempted to make a stand. Sub-machinegun fire tore through three glass cabinets and six panes of glass. Oil lamps, votive figures, leering heads – all were catapulted around the room in a blizzard of terracotta. With three stamps of his shotgun Davis quieted the dissent once more.

Who art thou, daring thus to oppose me?

Unhappy men are they who encounter me in a fight.

Jake and Jenny were forgotten. They ran down a fire escape and dived into the first vehicle they could, which was a pony and trap. The wheels span into a blur and they were away. Behind them the museum was a box of booms and explosions, rooms illuminated momentarily, smoke pouring from windows. Scores of people streamed from the building. Not one of them was Chinese.

"Napoleon found all the inscriptions," said Jenny as they clattered through the neoclassical Heldenplatz Gate. "Everything except the Zagreb Linen."

"We took the wrong path," said Jake.

Jenny leaned towards the driver. "Can you drop us at a train station for the airport?"

"Where are we going?" asked Jake.

They were passing the balcony where Hitler announced the *Anschluss* between Germany and Austria.

"We're going to the UK," said Jenny. "We're going to learn all we can about Randolph Churchill and his 'curious letter' from

Queen Victoria. We're going to discover why the sun set on the British Empire. We're going to find out what became of Britain's *Disciplina Etrusca* after the map was painted red, and then we'll burn it to ashes so this can never happen again. We're going back, Jake. We're going home."

Part Three

The Augur

(?)

The weary titan staggers under the too vast orb of its fate. We have borne the burden for many years ... it is time our children should assist us to support it!
                                    Joseph Chamberlain, Edwardian politician

53

Serval. Back in London, drinking alone in the afternoon at the Windsor Castle in Kensington, where they first recruited him. Only it wasn't beer at his elbow now, it was an expensive single malt. The tatty polo shirt had gone too, replaced with a tailored number from Huntsman of Savile Row, from where the first crate had just been dispatched to the steaming rainforests of Sierra Leone. A change in the way Serval appraised people too, as they bustled about the pub. A new *pitilessness*. The previous night he had chatted up an acquaintance, slept with her and then told her he loved her just for the hell of it. He had felt her wilt in his arms; he wasn't returning her calls.

His encrypted mobile rang and he put down the *Financial Times*.

"Jacob. It's C. How are you? Recuperating well?"

"Not too bad, sir," said Serval.

He looked the picture of health.

"Would you come to see me right away? We have need of your famous powers of persuasion."

Serval left the dram unfinished and caught a black cab to Vauxhall Cross. Thirty minutes later he was sitting in a Secure Speech Room with C and a woman he'd never seen before. She was silver-haired and impassive; her left arm was in a sling. C didn't introduce her and Serval didn't ask.

"First things first," said C. "The situation in Sierra Leone's improved *dramatically*. You've saved a lot of lives and heartache. Well done."

Serval made no comment.

"Now I've got another task for you. More of the same, I'm afraid."

"Ebola and African wars. That my beat then?"

A skin deep smile. "You're aware this drug ZMapp which was so effective a couple of years ago has had little effect on the outbreaks in Nigeria and Sierra Leone?"

"Yup."

"Well, its descendant, ZMapp2, has been much more efficacious." C wound a signet ring around his little finger. "But there's not much ZMapp2 about, and it's time-consuming to manufacture – only a couple of pharm companies make it right now. It goes without saying that one of those is in London, and they've just agreed a big sale to the Nigerian government. I want you to persuade them to think again."

"Respectfully, sir, why would we want to do that? Aren't things grim enough in Nigeria right now?"

"I want it to go to Sierra Leone instead. It's like fighting fires – you put out one before tackling the next."

"I've seen what this virus does to people," said Serval.

That little girl; her flaking skin.

"I hope you're not questioning our judgement?" C had turned severe. "You've seen the Prime Minister's ethical foreign policy yourself. Munificent to a fault, especially when it comes to the Commonwealth. This is for the best."

Serval shrugged. "You got it."

"The owner's a man called Abdul Khan," said C, tossing a folder onto the table. "You might have heard of him?"

Serval opened the file. "*Sunday Times Rich List* ... worth £500 million ... and he lives in – Walthamstow, east London? That doesn't seem like a natural fit."

"He's a devout Muslim, Labour councillor, pillar of the local Pakistani population. Wants to be seen to be staying in 'the community'. He also likes getting pissed. If that helps."

"It helps."

The silver-haired woman had said nothing, only studied him.

*

And so to east London. It was strange going on the Tube again, and everything he saw on the other side he did not like. Row after row of godawful chicken shops, all crammed with customers. Firms of solicitors specialising in immigration and criminal law; a grimy cash and carry furniture shop, now defunct. Groups of Bulgarians drinking super-strength lager; men with beards spilling out of a mosque in a converted shop, their burka-clad wives watching from a distance. It felt more foreign than Freetown, a place he'd be ashamed to tell his father he had bought a flat in.

Serval was aware he was thinking *differently* now, that he was what some might call a xenophobe. Well, who cares? He knew such thoughts were out of step with the times, but let them come, he no longer cared. The savagery he'd witnessed had *shown him* something: about the value of Anglo-Saxon civilisation, as opposed to that of other peoples. That Britain had built a country people wanted to live in was no longer a mark of success, but of failure. The country was an importer, not exporter, of human stock. Invaded, not invaders. Serval realised he was going to enjoy this job, blackmailing this hypocrite. He agreed wholeheartedly with the Prime Minister's goal, so far as he understood it: the rebuilding of British global prestige by interventions abroad.

Harold Macmillan came to mind.

This is the choice – the slide into a shoddy and slushy socialism, or the march to the third British Empire?

Britain had chosen hip replacements over Harrier Jump Jets, and the result was its own diminishment. Plus the descent of lesser nations like Sierra Leone into the chaos he had witnessed and made right.

As Serval neared Walthamstow Village the houses got grander and better tended. He even saw the odd English person – yummy mummies with prams and dungarees. But Khan's mansion was the biggest of all: a sprawling hotchpotch of columns and pediments. Bit otiose, his father would have said. A bloody great

Bentley was parked up outside and some idiot had pebble-dashed the house in decades past. The other side of the street was a shabby row of post-war two-up two-downs, mostly converted into flats. Two were for sale, both top floor. Helpful. Serval peered at the upper windows, evaluating the potential crow's nests.

The door of the first flat was opened by a tired-looking woman in her forties with a fag in her mouth.

She did something to her hair. "Oh, hello! Can I help you?"

"Good afternoon. Are you Annabel?"

"Sorry, I think you've got the wrong house."

Serval apologised with courtly manners and tried the second flat. Nobody answered. It was still light, so he went to the pub. A couple of respectable families were having a natter on the benches outside St Mary's Church; opposite stood a newly restored fifteenth-century house, the timber frame visible. This is it, thought Serval, not quite engulfed yet. The England I am fighting for.

He returned after nightfall. A cat fled before the heavy fall of his feet as he marched up the garden path. Still nobody answered at the flat, and no lights were on either. He was over the fence in a single bound, climbed a drainpipe at the back and smashed the window of the upstairs bathroom. Inside it was just as he'd hoped: the flat was bare of furniture or possessions. Serval trotted to the bedroom at the front of the property. From there he could see into all sixteen windows of Khan's mansion, and just as he'd suspected it was rammed full of grannies and cousins and little children. His father would have disapproved of the interior decoration – huge mirrors, modern rugs, all frightfully showy. Like a Premiership footballer's gaff.

Serval produced a Nikon D5100 SLR camera with a 30-300mm lens worth £34,000. He opened the window and scanned the house, lurking back so he was invisible from outside. A little skip of the heart as he saw Khan himself, dressed in flowing gown and slippers. Serval tracked him through the house, then lost him.

It was a while until he saw the target again, padding along the landing. He re-emerged in the dining room for supper and Serval felt his pulse quicken. But bottles of Fanta were being set on the table; kids were everywhere. He realised he was in for a wait.

Only he was wrong.

For after supper Khan retired to his study, exactly opposite Serval's vantage point. And to Serval's exquisite joy, he produced a bottle of twelve-year-old Caol Ila single malt. Nice drop, that. The lens was so powerful he could read the tasting notes. *Oily and tarry.* Serval took a dozen shots as the businessman leaned back in his chair, savouring the dram. He noted with disapproval that Khan took ice. Just when he thought the images could not possibly be stronger, into the study walked a woman wearing a full burka. Serval snapped her standing by Khan with his glass in hand, the whisky bottle in the foreground. Ouch. Khan gave the woman some £20 notes – her pocket money? – and she departed. Moments later the front door opened and she left in the company of a male, trailing off down the road behind him. Typical socialist, thought Serval as he stared at the drinker in his study. Do as I say, not as I do.

54

After the places they had been, it felt faintly ludicrous being back in England. Churchill College lay in the Cambridge suburbs, and each detail was as strange as it was familiar. The tidiness of the streets, the mundanity of the double yellow lines; dog-walkers and pigeons and estate agents' boards, caravans parked in driveways.

They had changed identity again. Jake had cropped his hair and wore a rocker's denim jacket; Jenny had acquired leather jacket, heavy-rimmed glasses and a nose ring. He'd been too bruised to bring up her Vienna rendezvous, but the sight of hale young chaps in rugger shirts with ravishing girlfriends did his raging sense of inadequacy no favours.

Churchill College was like an architect's sketch from the 1950s, tessellated, boxy and very pristine. The library and archive was a minimalist fender of cement set amid manicured lawns. Jake glanced at its motto.

Connecting the past, present and future.

"Rather apt, eh?" he said.

Jenny smiled, and some of the tension between them dissipated.

Books on Churchills from the un-extraordinary to the illustrious lined the walls. A bust of Winston himself dominated the room, and a slightly famous TV historian busied himself with some documents. The archivist, a mousy thing with an endearing smile, did not know of the 'most curious letter'. But she retrieved the rolls of microfilm on which most of Lord Randolph's surviving correspondence was stored and led them to a side-room. The microfilm viewer was huge and clunky, humming like some piece of Soviet industrial equipment. Jake fiddled the first microfilm onto a spindle and a letter from 10 Downing Street filled the screen, the address in a gothic font, the message handwritten. At the touch of a button it zoomed off to the left to be replaced by another missive. They spooled to the month of Wolff's letter.

"There!" said Jenny.

Lord Randolph's handwriting was beyond the pale and it took them several minutes to decipher.

Blenheim Palace: January 2, 1884.
My dear Wolff,
    You are not slow to take a hint, therefore your failure to understand my letter is, I think, a pretence. When I receive 'very curious letters from political personages' I have hitherto sent them to you without delay. Your cautious behaviour seemed to call for similar caution on my part. I therefore

wrote to you that I had received a very curious letter from the Queen, which I should not show you when we met, and I shall not.

Yours ever,
RANDOLPH S. C.

"Getting there," said Jenny.

She wrested the buttons from Jake and continued back through the archive. But Queen Victoria's letter was absent.

"It's been removed," said Jake.

*

They worked through the thousands of letters this most raffish of lords had rattled off in his lifetime. Most bore the address of some Kensington club or other. But just as the eyes of crocodiles in the reeds are revealed by torchlight, they began to see things: half-insinuations, little clues.

Politics is not a science of the past; politics is a science of the future.

Jake and Jenny glanced up, each ensuring that the other had understood the import of the line. They read on.

In 1886, Lord Randolph had told a correspondent: *I feel much in the dark as to the future.*

And the British Army's defeat by Afghan tribesmen at the Battle of Maiwand was *mainly attributable to want of foresight.*

Then they read a speech Lord Randolph had delivered to the House of Commons.

6th August 1886.
The most unpardonable crime is not to look ahead and make provision for the future. The Government of England cannot from its very nature look far ahead; it is always a policy of hand to mouth. The sky overhead, to the careless observer, seemed very blue. Yet there was much which ought to have

warned and to have roused. All this time the cloud grew
bigger, the darkness nearer and blacker; yet counsellors slum-
bered and slept, taking no thought for the morrow, ignorant
of the future which was shaping itself.

"Blimey," said Jake. "The government *cannot by its nature* look
ahead. It was *ignorant* of the future. And look at all the references
to storms and clouds. Those in the know would have realised
exactly what he was referring to. Britain was no longer able to
foretell the future."

"So by 1886, Britain *had* lost the *Disciplina*," said Jenny. "But
how? What became of it?"

He had no answer.

Here were Lord Randolph's musings on the Foreign Secretary
of the day, Sir Stafford Northcote.

Northcote's character was estimable, his talents were distin-
guished; but heedless of the warnings of Nature, he struggled
gallantly forward until he died in harness beneath burdens
he was utterly unable to sustain.

"The warnings of nature are bolts of lightning," said Jake. "They
must be. But the Foreign Secretary was unable to read them.
By Lord Randolph's time, augury was a science that Britain
had *lost*."

"He uses the same turn of phrase in this letter," said Jenny.
"The warnings of nature unheeded once more."

Mr Gladstone has reserved a conspiracy against the honour
of Britain more nefarious than any of those other designs
and plots which, during the last quarter of a century, have
occupied his imagination. Let a credulous electorate give him
a majority, and this Minister will complacently retire to that
repose for which he tells us 'nature cries aloud'. Nature, to
whose cries he has turned a stone-deaf ear.

"William Ewart Gladstone was arguably the greatest Victorian politician," said Jake. "He was a Liberal, highly principled, already a legend by the time Randolph Churchill erupted onto the scene. He dominated British politics for decades and served four times as Prime Minister."

Gladstone's *Encyclopaedia Britannica* entry showed an austere face: snow-white sideburns, furious brow. This was not a man to be trifled with. For leisure he used to cut down trees; Queen Victoria had detested him, claiming he addressed her like a public meeting.

"Gladstone was nicknamed the Grand Old Man," Jenny read. "G.O.M. for short. And he was a ..."

Her words petered out.

"A devout Christian," Jake finished. "Of course! He used to wander the streets by night, lecturing prostitutes on the error of their ways."

"So hardly one to engage with a pagan science. Could *that* be why he turned a 'stone-deaf ear' to the cries of Nature?"

"But the High Court test," said Jenny. "It doesn't pass."

"Gladstone's QC would take me to the cleaners," Jake admitted.

There the archive ended.

A man ducked into the room, glanced at them and walked out again. Jenny glared at the vacated doorway.

"What is it?" asked Jake.

"On the sky train in Bangkok a guy took an interest in me. MI6 was my guess."

"And?"

She jutted her chin in the direction of the departed man. "I only saw the back of his head – but it was the same hair. Sort of ... wispy."

"How can you be so sure?"

"Because I've got –"

"Oh yeah. A photographic memory."

"Time to go," she said.

"Did you find what you're looking for?" the archivist asked as they left.

Jake shook his head.

"Well – the originals are stored at the Cambridge University Library. They've got some letters that we haven't."

He turned to Jenny. Long moments passed.

"Come on," she said. "Let's get this done."

55

They meandered through the Backs, those so unexpected pastures strung along the River Cam. Cows grazed among ornate lampposts and iron gates enclosed the cloisters of the most ancient colleges; the greens were carved up by gurgling streams, bejewelled with glades of forget-me-nots and tangled grass. But Jenny was alive only to the picnicking students, the cars that passed, a council worker emptying bins, subjecting each of them to her scrutiny. And Jake was lost in his own thoughts: the sense that, after so many false leads, they had clicked into the groove at last. This was the loose end that would unravel the mystery; as he paced across the common he had the sense his own footsteps were getting ahead of him, whirring away into the future and beyond his control. Was the success of this endeavour not preordained anyway? Jake looked at a fingernail of moon, suspended high up in the blue sky like an eyelash.

Maybe I should sacrifice to it?

He shivered at what he had just contemplated. Become a *fulguriator*? Loathsome.

If Hitler invaded hell, I would at least make a favourable reference to the devil in the House of Commons.

Dear Churchill. Jake pushed quotation away, immersing himself in the present.

*

Cambridge University Library was somewhere between a US penitentiary and an oversized crematorium, a Gargantua of brick with a single gigantic chimney looming over it. Two girls gossiped on the steps, both gorgeous: one Mediterranean, the other with chestnut hair and very fair skin. Their smiles pained Jake, their glossy hair was not of this earth. Both were absorbed in the riotousness of being young and desired.

"He said [inaudible]," gushed one of them.

"He said *what*!?"

"He did!"

"No way!" Hand to clavicle.

Girls like this were meant for someone else, not for him, and their being his was as fantastical as rock stardom. It was a glum reader who registered at reception. If Jake couldn't make Jenny rediscover what they had possessed together, he would never find happiness. He was sure this was his fate.

Chinese students in Cambridge hoodies clogged the corridors, but the only reader in the manuscripts room was a bloke with baggy jeans and greasy hair poring over a medieval codex that looked as if it had been found under a hedge. Randolph Churchill's correspondence arrived – the originals, bound in volumes of blue leather the size of a paving slab. Jake turned the pages, and there were the titans of the Victorian age. Gladstone and W.H. Smith, Lord Rosebery and Joseph Chamberlain. Disraeli too, his signature a curlicued 'D' – flamboyant as the man himself. Their very pens had touched these pieces of paper. As fast as Jake dared, he manipulated the folios.

No curious letter from Queen Victoria.

His heart was heavy all of a sudden. If these statesmen were referring to a shared secret knowledge, surely *nothing* would be spelled out? Anything revealing would be a state secret, classified beyond even cabinet level. Together he and Jenny worked though the volumes, seeking out mention of Gladstone.

> *There was no master mind pervading and controlling every branch of the Administration. Organisation went to the dogs. A stupefying degree of over-confidence, a fatally erroneous estimate of Mr. Gladstone — these causes, all of them preventable, slowly but surely worked the ruin.*

"No master mind," said Jake, "pervading and controlling."

A sudden iciness, leaching off the page.

"What's Randolph talking about, 'worked the ruin'?" she said. "I thought Britain was at the height of its power in the 1880s."

"Don't you believe it," he replied. "The Victorian boom came to an abrupt end in 1870, to be replaced with a decade-long depression. There were signs that Britain was slowing down compared to Germany and the States, even then."

Jenny turned the page to find another assassination of Gladstone by Lord Randolph, this time addressing electors in 1885:

> *Irish troubles, Colonial losses, Indian dangers, costly wars, fruitless sacrifice of many heroes. Mr Gladstone's Government was the author of these disasters. The policy of the Tory Party is to evolve such forces as may enable the mother country to rear that Imperial federation of the subjects of the Queen which many wise and far-seeing minds regard as essential to the perpetuation of our power.*

"Randolph wants Britain to once more gain the *forces* that can allow British imperium to flourish again," he said. "Which *far-seeing minds* know will guarantee British hegemony."

Seeing into the room: Alex McCabe, he of the pointy nose and wispy hair, taking high resolution photographs of their reading material from an upper window as his colostomy gurgled and rumbled.

56

Abdul Khan switched the radio on as he eased the Bentley out of the drive. Talk Sport, as ever – he was a huge Liverpool fan.

Weather now – and Britain's battening down the hatches, with a big storm system coming in off the Atlantic later this afternoon ...

The sky over Walthamstow wasn't menacing though, and Khan hoped he might get his afternoon game of tennis in yet. The company didn't take much running these days – that explained why he was off to the office at a leisurely 10 am. He would do two hours' light work and go to his tennis club before the storm broke; after that he had a date with his eldest daughter Fadwa on New Bond Street. Handbag shopping. He slowed at the end of his street, looked right, looked left. Respectability demanded the girls cover up, of course. But that didn't mean they couldn't have nice things –

The passenger door opened.

Khan turned, hot with anger. "What the hell are you doing?" he shouted.

But the man simply got in and closed the door. Serval. Blackmailer, killer of a child; peace dove of Sierra Leone; empire builder. Taking in the musculature and expensive tailoring Khan felt fury slide into terror, and a single horrifying word came to mind.

Kidnap.

"Drive the car," said Serval.

Khan cleared his throat, gave a useless half-nod and nosed the Bentley out of his street, past St Mary's Church and the Tudor House.

"Pull in here," suggested Serval. "I want to show you something." Khan acquiesced.

A brown envelope was in his fingers and Khan felt a surge of relief – it would be a business offer, something dodgy. A trademark infringement, or a bribe. But photographs spilled from the emissary's envelope. Of him.

"Doesn't look great, does it?" said Serval. "I daresay in the wrong hands these images would prove a little – *fissile*."

That was it? A tawdry attempt to wring a bit of money from him? Khan had expected more from a – well, not a gentleman, but someone of breeding. *There's blood there*, his Lord on the Board would have said. Khan felt his courage return and he sat up in the driver's seat. He was a fine-looking man with a beard of silken white and a long, noble face whose hollow cheeks recalled the roots of an oak tree.

"Let me tell you something," he said with growing bellicosity. "Nobody, *nobody* blackmails Abdul Khan. Do I make myself clear, you scumbag, you piece of trash?"

Serval gazed into Khan's soul. "I do," he said.

There was something Teutonic in that stare: the robotic, strictly-business appraisal of the concentration camp guard, not an ounce of humanity. What childhood could have produced such a man? Khan almost felt sorry for him.

"Copies go to every mosque in east London unless you do as I say," Serval continued. "And to the local rag. And the *Daily Mail*, who I gather you had a bit of a contretemps with a couple of years ago. We'll see how that goes down with the *community*."

A twist to the word 'community', as though it tasted unpleasant in his mouth. Khan knew then he was dealing with a racist, somebody who hated Muslims.

"So tell me," he said.

"ZMapp2."

Khan frowned. "What about it?"

"The shipment to Abuja on Friday. It doesn't go."

A gap appeared between Khan's lips. "Who are you?"

Serval adjusted his position so that his jacket fell open, and on seeing the black metal holstered inside Khan's pupils flared. Surrender washed through him, every bit as ineluctable as flooding upon the fields of his childhood in Pakistan. He slipped the envelope into the glove box.

"Ok. I don't mind who you are. I really don't want to know at all, in fact."

"Sell it to Sierra Leone instead."

"But they need it more in Nigeria. People are dying."

"I really don't give a damn."

"We've signed a contract," Khan said pathetically.

"I daresay you'll find some way to wriggle out of it."

An extremist, devoid of pity or scruples; this man will stop at nothing. Khan's hands fell to his knees with a slap. He was reasonably fit, but his thighs looked thin and wizened in their Paul Smith cladding. He suddenly realised he was becoming elderly.

"Ok then," he sighed.

"Glad we're in agreement." Serval extended a hand. "Pleasure doing business."

Khan's palms remained planted on his legs. His head tilted back and a little anger returned to his eyes, some nobility to those mahogany features.

"I'll do what you want," he said. "But I prefer not to shake your hand."

A dusting of respect in Serval's gaze for the first time. "Suit yourself."

Khan glanced at the glove box. "Can I keep those?"

A snort of amusement this time. "If it makes you feel better, old fruit." Serval opened the door. "One more thing. You know what'll happen if you make a fuss, don't you?"

Khan glanced at Serval's jacket and nodded.

"Tell me."

The businessman tried to speak, but the sides of his throat had stuck together.

"Tell me," Serval growled again.

"You'll kill me," whispered Khan.

Serval got out of the car, closed the door and walked briskly away.

Khan recomposed himself. His breath was coming in gasps and there were sweat patches under the armpits of his silk shirt. The radio refilled the enclosed space; he realised it had been burbling away the whole time. He dabbed at his forehead with a turquoise handkerchief and started the car. As he drove towards his office in Pimlico that morning, he was no longer thinking about tennis or Anfield or shopping trips on New Bond Street. A single dilemma churned through his mind.

What the hell will I tell the Nigerians?

57

Lord Randolph's speech grew explicit.

Gladstone is like Macbeth before the murder of Duncan; he plunges the knife into the heart of the British Empire as a thief in the night.

"A thief in the night." Jake rubbed his eyes and blinked. "So, we think from Sir Neil Campbell's diaries that Napoleon gave the *Disciplina* to the British Foreign Office, in return for the throne of Elba and the safety of his family. Almost overnight, Britain becomes the world's superpower. For most of the century it dominates world trade and industry, imposes a *Pax Britannica* – a 'British peace' – across the globe. Unrivalled since the *Pax Romana* of old." Jake laughed suddenly and rolled his eyes. "A peculiarly British use of a dire power, isn't it?"

"What do you mean?"

"We didn't use the Book of Thunder to conquer the world, like Hitler or Napoleon. Actually, Britain added very little to its empire between 1815 and 1870. Only the odd strategic trading base – Singapore, Hong Kong, Aden, Lagos. It was in the 1880s that the final Scramble for Africa happened, Randolph

Churchill's day. And we think the *Disciplina* was lost to them by then."

A thought was niggling at him, something about borders, but it was embryonic and he could not grasp it.

"Instead of conquest, the Brits used the *Disciplina* to keep the other Great Powers in check through diplomacy," he said. "Maintaining the balance of power, using the peace to amass great wealth through trade and industrial might. In those days, a level playing field was all Britain needed to assure commercial primacy. Then Gladstone enters Number 10, a Christian who would have no truck with a pagan text. At once Britain's economic fortunes changed. It lost that geopolitical nous that had held the other great powers in perfect balance for sixty years. On the contrary, Gladstone's foreign policy was a disaster. In the Transvaal, the British Army was humiliated by Boer farmers. He was outwitted during the Great Game in Afghanistan by Russia – the Pandjeh Incident. He allowed General Gordon to be destroyed by fanatical tribesmen at Khartoum in the Sudan, it was a major scandal at the time."

A quietness came into Jenny's voice as she read the end of the speech. "But Randolph thought it might be found again."

The time may be at hand when the path of honour and safety is illuminated by the light of other days. It may be that this dark cloud will pass away without breaking.

The light of other days; this dark cloud. Jenny mouthed the words.

If it does, I believe you and your descendants will be safe for a long time to come. I believe this storm will blow over. And if it should be within the design of Providence, I do not hesitate to tell you that there will not be wanting those of position and influence in England who would be willing to share your fortunes and your fate.

Storms. Providence. Fortune. Fate. It was like a pronouncement of Napoleon Bonaparte. On the next page, oddly, was a letter to Lord Randolph from …

"Richard Burton!" exclaimed Jenny.

During the nineteenth century, numerous experts examined the Zagreb Linen – including the Victorian explorer Richard Burton …

"Burton was one of the nutters who nearly died hunting for the source of the Nile," said Jake. "Well, this has got to be worth a read."

October 15th, 1886
My Lord,
  Since the £300 a year to which I think I am entitled is hardly equivalent of years of hard work in anything but wholesome climates, I beg you to favour me by placing my name on the civil list for a pension of £300 a year. There are precedents for such a privilege, but I would not quote names unless called upon. I have had several kind letters, expressing their conviction of the reasonable nature of my request; the general idea being mine is an exceptional case.
  I am your most obedient humble servant,
  Richard Burton.

"A begging letter from the second most famous British explorer of the Victorian age to the father of Winston Churchill," said Jake. "Men who *both* have an Etruscan connection. Coincidence?"

"We just don't know."

Jenny continued through the papers. She paused at a speech Lord Randolph had made to electors in Paddington.

Since 1868, have you enjoyed domestic security or foreign credit? Lawlessness and disorder have been supreme. The blame must be borne by the man who is Minister now. Under the baneful insecurity which is inseparably connected with his name, your trade has gone from bad to worse, your

Parliament has become demoralised, your foreign credit shaken, your colonies alienated, your Indian Empire imperilled. What frightful and irreparable Imperial catastrophe is necessary to tear the British people from the influence of this idol, which has brought upon them unnumbered woes? The hero of the Transvaal surrender, the betrayer of Khartoum, the person guilty of the death of Gordon, the patentee of the Panjdeh shame. Known to the country under various aliases – 'The People's William,' 'the Grand Old Man.'

"Here it is," said Jenny. "He spells it out for us – 1868. The year Gladstone destroyed the *Disciplina*."

"The year he first became Prime Minister," said Jake. "And almost right away the Great Victorian Boom is over, the rot sets in."

"So Lord Randolph *did* know about it. *That* was the content of Queen Victoria's 'curious letter'?"

"Do you know what?" Jake smiled warily. "I think I could defend this argument."

58

"Where are Gladstone's papers kept?" Jenny asked.

Jake studied his phone. "North Wales. At Gladstone's Library in Flintshire – he established it himself."

Her brain whirred, analysing practicality and risk.

"Not worth it," she said at last. "But we are in a library. It probably has books …"

"Oh yeah," said Jake. "Eight *million* of them."

Political history was on the fourth floor. Light flooded through big arched windows and library noises eddied about: a flapping like wings, the lowest baritone of murmur. They selected two dozen volumes on Gladstone and set to work.

"Look at this letter," Jake said. "It's 1862, and Gladstone's Chancellor of the Exchequer – the coming man in British politics."

I see the elements of future power and good; I also see the elements of danger and mischief. The forces brought into unrestrained play are by far too gigantic to be controlled.

"This is interesting," said Jenny, who was studying another volume. "Another note from Gladstone. He was staying in Scotland at the time."

I am come in from a nineteen mile walk to the Lake of Lochnagar, fresh as a lark! The Queen sent me a message not to go up Lochnagar if there was mist; and mist there was, with rain to boot. You forgot to tell me for what pious object you picked Lord P's pocket.

"Picked his pocket for a *pious object*," said Jake.

"Like a 'thief in the night,'" said Jenny. "But who's 'Lord P'?"

"Ah. That would be Lord Palmerston, another of the century's great Prime Ministers. He was in office for decades. Palmerston was a Liberal, like Gladstone. But there the similarities end. They absolutely hated each other. Palmerston was swashbuckling, full of bluster – and solely concerned with advancing British interests, ethical foreign policy be damned. The Opium War was Palmerston's doing, China forced to accommodate British drug dealers at the barrel of a gun. 'Gunboat diplomacy' was the approach. Sail the fleet to the country you're having a row with, blockade its ports – and if your demands aren't met, then flatten their cities. It was very effective."

"He sounds like a charmer."

"To be fair, he was a doughty opponent of the slave trade. And wildly popular too. His finest hour was the ..."

Jake's words seized in his throat.

"The what?"

"The *Civis Romanus sum* speech."

"I am a Roman citizen," Jenny translated.

She looked up the passage in Hansard.

The Roman in days of old held himself free from indignity. He could say Civis Romanus sum; *so also a British subject, in whatever land he may be, shall feel confident the watchful eye and strong arm of England will protect him against injustice and wrong.*

The watchful eye. Again Jake felt a chilliness bleed out of the ink.

"So, that's Palmerston," he said. "A rogue by modern standards, but a veritable institution in Victorian times. And a good candidate for a custodian of the *Disciplina* I'd say, given his foreign policy. Queen Victoria loved him."

Jenny studied a photograph of Palmerston in his dotage. He had sideburns of wiry white, hooded eyelids and a stern little mouth that betrayed an inkling of humour.

"What became of him?" asked Jenny.

"He died of old age in 1865 while still in Number 10, knowing for certain Gladstone would replace him."

"This is intriguing," said Jenny. "More entries from Gladstone's diary."

October 21st, 1864. A letter from Lord Palmerston holds out a dark prospect.

October 22nd – Wrote my reply to Lord Palmerston in a rather decisive tone, for I feel conscious of right and of necessity.

"Read this one too," said Jake. "It's a letter to Gladstone from Richard Cobden, the great Liberal thinker. He was writing just before Palmerston's death."

Unconsciously, you have administered to the support of a system which has no better foundation than a gigantic delusion.

"And Gladstone's reply?"

You say unconsciously. I am afraid that in one respect this is too favourable a description. I suppose the duty of choosing the lesser evil binds me; the difficulty is to determine what the lesser evil is.

"Here we have it." Jenny closed the book, held it to her chest. "The very moment Gladstone is contemplating doing something drastic."

"Destroying the *Disciplina Etrusca* ..."

"Though it would be to Britain's great cost."

"Because it was the right thing to do," Jake finished. "He was one of us, Jenny."

Then Jenny discovered the pamphlet. A blood vessel on the knuckle of her thumb was beating in time with her heart.

"What is it?" said Jake.

A mirthless smile. "If there was even a scintilla of doubt that Gladstone turned his back on the *Disciplina,* it just rode right out of town."

The pamphlet was the sort of thing once sold to the masses for a few coins: the political Twitter campaign of its day. Low-grade paper, blotchy printing. It had been published in 1886 by Edward Stanford of Charing Cross.

Our Premier: Lord Palmerston's Forecast Verified.

Many years before Mr Gladstone had achieved world-wide reputation, Lord Palmerston was reported to have thus spoken: "That man will live to be Prime Minister, but if he does, he will ruin the country."

*That Mr Gladstone was considered a reckless and danger-
ous politician is beyond doubt. Mr Laing, MP for the Wick
Boroughs, says he was "engaged in writing the first chapter
in the Decline and Fall of the British Empire."*

*Those who believe in a Providence ordering the destiny
of nations must believe in the means, that is to say, in the
men providentially used for the purpose. We may reasonably
infer that if England, after a career of unequalled prosperity
and glory, be destined to succumb, to be dismembered and
dishonoured,*

> When that dread day come as it must,
> And Britain's power lies prostrate in the dust

*She will find a statesman to play the part. Those who hold
with Lord Palmerston that Mr Gladstone is destined to
ruin England can now refer to the past as some index to the
future. History tells us of a "William the Silent" who saved
his country. Future history will tell us of a "William the
Eloquent", who did the reverse. Such a man may be wholly
wanting in the political foresight without which all statecraft
is work in the dark.*

"Political *foresight*," Jake muttered. "And without it? Leading a
country is like wandering through history with your eyes shut.
Like Napoleon trying to coordinate his armies without the Book
of Thunder."

*Tis, of course, no surprise to those who always believed Lord
Palmerston's prediction. What is our course, if we would
contend against the evil destiny of which Mr Gladstone is
the blind instrument? Get rid of the physician.*

*The political epitaph of the Premier will doubtless be
laudatory. Yet Truth will add – BUT HE RUINED THE
EMPIRE.*

There was movement on the other side of the bookcase. A man, walking away from them, glimpsed in the gaps between the volumes. Now: what was it about that figure – dark-skinned, robes and skullcap – that reminded Jake of di Angelo? Was it the build? The potency of his movements?

Jenny followed his gaze.

"Oh hell," she said.

*

Out of the library. Through the Backs once more, a cow shying away from the sprinting figures. Past the Mathematical Bridge, so rickety for a structure designed by Newton. Along the riverside, where punt owners hauled plastic sheets over their vessels, for the sky had turned sullen and the first pinpricks of moisture were dotting Jake's face. Over the river, approaching a T-junction, the limestone finery of Corpus Christi College to their left. A silver Ford Focus glided into their path. Four men in the car, staring *right at him*.

The car was hit side on by a white Ford Transit.

Sprinting again. Blindly, desperately, deeper into the maze of colleges and courtyards as the rain hammered down, cold searing Jake's cheeks.

"Again they find us!" Jenny shouted. And more wildly, into the downpour, baring her teeth: "*How*?"

Above them came the first suggestion of thunder. The rumblings of a daemon whose puzzle was being unpicked.

We are not amused.

The denseness of the cloud was like a tumour, a vortex of black. Another rumble above, another sweep of rain across the cobbled street. Jake didn't want the thunder to break. Oh, more than anything he'd ever wished for he didn't want the thunder to break. But still he ran towards it.

59

David began the lesson by apologising for the time.

"Not a prob," said Kanisha, glancing at the art deco cocktail cabinet she had just bought at a ruinously expensive antique shop in Primrose Hill.

"I was hoping you could help me identify a couple of Etruscan letters," David said.

"Sure," she said. "They're probably in a local dialect – or character forms that fell out of use. Ping them over."

David sent her a hand-drawn image.

"Well, the first one's *almost* a late Etruscan Z," she said after a moment. "It looks like two stick men, one of them sitting down. But it's not quite right. I'd need to see the full sentence for context."

The resulting silence was somehow deliberative, then the inscription landed.

"Where did you get this, David?"

A pause. "Why?"

"I don't recognise the inscription, that's all. I thought I'd seen everything that's been discovered. And new finds get reported in the journals."

"It's from a hand mirror I stumbled across at the National Archaeological Museum, in Umbria."

"Tin did not make the world, he is a young god," she read softly. "He commands the sacred thunder."

Kanisha's translation was answered immediately by a flicker of light to the north-west, as though the night sky was responding to her. She counted to three before the thunder was audible – somewhere over Willesden, perhaps.

"That was freaky," she said.

"What was freaky?" said David.

"Oh, there's a big storm here. The timing of the last thunderbolt was – dramatic, to say the least. You sketched this inscription yourself?"

"Yep."

"That would be why the letters have little errors in them, it's no wonder you're having problems."

"I see."

"Why didn't you take a photograph?"

"My phone ran out of battery," said David.

"Are there any more sentences?"

Another calculation. "Yes. Actually, I could do with some help on those too."

David sent her the passage, and as the storm roiled unabated they translated the handbook of an Etruscan soothsayer.

> *Know that these things must be done to divine the will of the gods:*
>
> > *The fulguriator commences lustratio, great sacrifice of appeasement.*
> > *The boar-piglet is offered, to cleanse and purge.*
> > *The priest sacrifices to Tages, mysterious being, half-boy, half-sage, who sprang from the earth.*
> > *He sacrifices also to Vegoia, who taught us how to interpret lightning.*

"Lightning!" exclaimed Kanisha, touching the last word on the screen. "*Trutnvt* …"

"*Trutnvt*," David repeated, a cold fondness in his pronunciation of the word.

Kanisha skimmed through the inscription. The term was all over it.

> *On his head, the fulguriator places the sacred hood, square and fringed.*
> > *With his staff, he demarks the visible heavens into sixteen parts, one for each of the dark gods.*

Nine gods are they who through the sacred lightning.
Tin, lord of them all, throws three of bolts of lightning.
The benign lightning shall serve as a warning.
The lightning that does both good and harm, and this needs
the approval of Dii Consentes, the pitiless ones.
Finally, the lightning of destruction.

Kanisha's skin had turned porcelain – it made her hair seem darker, her citrine pupils more colourless. She translated the final sentence carefully.

"Bring forth lightning," she whispered. "Bright, shining, free from alloy."

She was answered by a detonation right overhead.

*

When the lesson was over Kanisha made a cup of tea. She took a sip, then upon reflection tossed it down the sink. Instead she poured a hefty Jameson's, peering at herself in the mirror. In the flickering light her image was phantasmal.

"What the *hell*?" she whispered.

It wasn't the lightning that had shaken her. It was the inscription.

Trutnvt.

Kanisha sipped her whiskey and laughed. Ah, the touching naivety of the amateur archaeologist! For the Etruscan word *trutnvt* is only known to modernity from the epitaph of a single Etruscan, who lived at a town called Pesaro on the Adriatic. Apart from that – and by sheer bad luck – not one example of the word for lightning has been discovered by archaeologists. David's passage ought to be the most famous in the field, an equal of the Zagreb Linen. This was the most explicit description of Etruscan lightning ritual she had read. So David was lying. Either her pupil had fabricated it, or it hadn't come from the National Archaeological Museum of Umbria, but somewhere else entirely.

And this was undoubtedly a passage from the *Disciplina Etrusca*. Not the first book, which dealt with the examination of livers. Nor the second, concerning the founding of cities. It was from the third, the *Libri Fulgurales*. Book of Thunder.

A final explosion rattled her window panes.

60

"I don't know why things changed," Jenny murmured.

Jake glanced up from his espresso, the morning clatter of the Imperial War Museum café retreating.

"But I'll try to do things differently. I'll try to bring back the – the old me."

This can't be happening. Can it?

"Jenny, I –"

"I've been such an idiot," she continued unrelentingly.

"But you haven't," he gushed, leaning forward and gripping the table. "It's only natural. We've been through some terrible experiences ..."

"You're joking!" she interrupted. "They almost caught us in Cambridge. They nearly got us in Vienna too. They actually did get me in Bangkok. None of this would have happened before. But they seem to know where we are, whatever I try."

Oh. I'm the idiot.

Jake necked his espresso, taking grim satisfaction from the bitter kick in the throat that made his head want to click sideways.

Their first fifteen hours in London had been spent on the move, meandering through the West End as Jenny planned her pounce on their destination: eyeing up the prize as a cat might a morsel within swiping distance of the cook. They'd had three hours sleep – first Jake, in a corridor at St Thomas's Hospital, then Jenny at an all-night café in Soho. It was odd being back in London, Jake's home for ten years, and he noted how mental habits of old reasserted themselves. Foremost among these was the masochistic appraisal of happy couples (with concomitant feelings of despair). The boyfriend on the Tube, kneading a lock of his girlfriend's hair and gazing at the back of her skull while she looked away, bored, her profile Grecian and imperious. And at Tottenham Court Road Station a Jamaican girl with rich skin tones and long slender legs, chic leather jacket, russet Afro haircut. Jake hadn't needed to see her face to know she was smoking hot, but as they overtook he cast a sly glance at her bloke. Pot-belly, skin-tight white polo neck, head like a meatball.

Why not me?

And all the time he heard Jenny's footsteps beside him, each click reminding him of what had been.

When Jake looked up from his empty espresso cup Jenny had tears in her eyes. He was astonished. He had only seen her cry twice – on the death of her mother and during her rescue in Jerusalem, when her mind was addled with drugs.

"What is it?" he said.

"My hair." A few strands of sunlight were in Jenny's fingers. "It's falling out. Must be the stress. It's not that I'm vain, you know that, right? But Jake – I'm not sure how much longer I can carry on like this. I'm just not."

"It happened to me too," he said. "In Thailand."

"It *what*?"

"My hair started falling out, whole clumps of it. I guess it was stress too. And – well, losing you, frankly."

"But it's not falling out any more?"

Jake's hand went to his skull. "Erm – no. Not now you mention it."

Her eyes whizzed across his frame. "Do you still have the clothes you had in Thailand?"

"All of them. Why?"

Jenny's hands ran down her own body, fingers quivering, as if something about it disgusted her.

"Did you leave anything behind?"

He frowned, remembering that dreamlike escape: waking on the far side of the island, sunburn on his face. "Shoes," he said. "I left without any shoes on."

Jenny tore off her trainers, inspecting the soles like a jeweller with a loupe. There was a pinprick on the heel. She begged a knife from the kitchen and gouged at it. A grain of something rolled onto the table top. Something metallic, with an oily, multi-coloured sheen. She reared from the table as though it was a hissing scorpion.

"Oh my god," she said. "I feel sick."

"What is it?"

"How could they be so wicked?" she whispered. "So callous ..."

"What is that thing?"

"It's how they've been keeping track of us – and slowly poisoning us too."

"I don't understand."

"It's polonium 210, Jake. I'm radioactive."

61

Di Angelo admitted defeat at Tavistock Square in Bloomsbury. Only one of his team could still walk – it had proved impossible to tail Frobisher in a city of alleyways and multitudes, of snickets and sliding doors. He sat on a bench and called Virginia, asking to be patched through to the director of the CIA. The hold music was the *New World Symphony*. A Georgian terrace hemmed in one side of the gardens, now a hall of residence; the students ambling out looked no more than children. The daylight was pallid, yet the tulips hummed with colour, yellows and purples and reds. Brits did gardening well, he had to admit it. A cross-legged statue of Gandhi levitated above the blooms, daffodils laid in his arms. The road on the far side looked familiar from somewhere; suddenly it came to him. This was where the bus had exploded on 7/7, he remembered it from the news. Interesting juxtaposition – the Great Soul and the slaughter of office workers. That said, Gandhi was no stranger to terrorism.

"Sir? The director notes the urgency of your call and asks you to phone back in twenty minutes."

"Huh?"

"I'm sorry, sir. The Vice President's with us today and there's a presentation going on. Have a good day, sir."

Di Angelo dialled a number he knew by heart.

"This is the Carlson residence." The voice was courteous, weary yet unbowed. Prematurely old.

"It's Damien, sir."

"Damien. Good to hear from you, son."

Di Angelo could picture Andy Carlson Senior's big round belly clothed in the habitual short-sleeved check shirt: proper granddaddy material. Wire-frame aviators like his own, but from the first time around. He heard the creak of a chair, an exhalation of breath pushed out by the diaphragm.

"How's Andy, sir?" said di Angelo.

"Oh, same as ever, no better, no worse. Sleeping a lot." His voice trailed away. "Mandy's gotten him a trendy new haircut. Her friend's daughter did it as a favour. Guess he looks real cool. Not that Andy cared about that kind of thing."

They talked about bedsores; discussed the progress of neurology; assured each other he might yet recover. Di Angelo promised he would visit New England next time he was in the States; the older man said he knew he would and gamely tried to find out where di Angelo was deployed, vivacity in his voice for the first time.

Di Angelo glanced at his wristwatch. "Sir – it's been good talking to you. But I've another call to make."

"You're a good man, Damien. None of his other friends come around any more, you know that?"

"I'm sorry to hear that. Andy deserves better."

"Not even his old girlfriend. She's got herself a new man, not that I hold that against her."

"I'm sorry."

"Damien ..." a reluctance entered Carlson's voice. "I want to ask you something, son."

Sudden intensity.

"Did you ever feel anything for my boy that went *beyond* friendship?"

Di Angelo froze on the bench.

"It's the twenty-first century and all. Gays even allowed in the army now."

He heard the old man sigh, pictured the mottled shaving rash on his throat.

"Oh, I know Andy wasn't that way inclined," Carlson continued. "A new girl on his arm every week, that was my boy. But son – I just want to know." He swallowed. This was difficult for him to say. "Son, if that's how you felt, if that's how you feel – well, Mandy and I don't mind."

Di Angelo breathed out. "Thank you, sir."

"Andy would be proud of what you're doing, if he could still think. Fighting for freedom. I never got the opportunity, me. Too young for Vietnam, too old for I-raq. All those years under the flag, and I never got the chance to do my bit for America."

Another sigh; di Angelo sensed the old man's ribcage heaving up and down. Deep in the house he heard the chime of a clock, the one in their hallway.

Carlson was meandering on. "Oh, I know people ain't too sweet on the I-raq war nowadays. But I still like to think ..."

"Yes, sir?"

"I like to think my boy died – because he may as well have died that day, it's sure as heck no life he's got now – well, I like to think that he died doing his duty."

A heavy silence. The old man swallowed again. This was as close as he could come to tears.

"I think so too, sir," said di Angelo.

"Son?"

"Yes, sir?" A catch in di Angelo's throat he was unused to.

"You can keep on visiting us, son. Me and Mandy would like that."

"Thank you, sir."

Suddenly there were tears in his eyes, and the colours of the daffodils were diffracted into a thousand shards, as if he were peering through a kaleidoscope.

"Sir?" he managed.

"Yes, Damien?"

"It means a lot to me. You saying those things."

"You just carry on doing your bit for freedom and goodness, son. That's all we ask."

∗

Di Angelo phoned Virginia again and this time he got patched through right away.

"Damien." Robert Ardrey's voice sounded polished somehow, like aluminium. "Progress?"

"I've lost them again," he said. "It's goddamn hard with only two of us. Do you have any updates for me?"

"Someone'll be in touch when we get something. I hear the weather over there's taken a turn for the worse?"

"Storms yesterday. More predicted for this afternoon. When am I getting my reinforcements?"

"He'll be at your disposal shortly."

"Robert –"

"*Sir*." A slice to this interjection.

"Sir. Respectfully, sir, I hope it's the right kind of operative."

"Explain yourself."

"You keep giving me clever people. I don't need clever people. I'm a clever person. I need *deadly* people. No more thinkers. Your thinkers have been getting their ass whooped, it's embarrassing. We're *America* for Chrissakes."

Robert Ardrey considered this.

62

Like a shark swishing closer as it calculates when to bite, Jenny had been circling an institution that makes the Great Library of Alexandria look like a council book van. A place holding 150 million titles, four hundred miles of shelves – and the papers of a statesman who in the Victorian age was as much of an institution as Queen Victoria herself. Confident in her spy-craft once more, at last Jenny felt they could approach this monument to erudition.

With its modern red brickwork and sloping roofs, the British Library reminded Jake of an overgrown Scandinavian leisure centre. Clouds still stretched from each of London's tangled horizons, the stratus rumpled into banks like hard wet sand on a beach. The only two people in the manuscripts room were old men; neither glanced at them. Within half an hour the first portfolio was brought up. For once, handwriting in a period before the typewriter was not their enemy – Palmerston's script was considered an exemplar of taste and cultivation.

1861. to the President of the Board of Trade.
My Dear Milner Gibson,
   It is wise when the weather is fine to put one's house in watertight condition against the time when foul weather may come on. The reports from our manufacturing districts are at present good; the mills are working, and the people are in full employment. But we must expect a change towards the end of next autumn, and during the winter and spring of next year. This year's crop must be less plentiful than that of last year.
   Yours sincerely,
   Palmerston.

"The weather references are pretty pointed," said Jenny.

"Do you know what I think we've got here?" said Jake.

"Go on."

"A day to day *example* of the auguries being consulted."

"Remarkable document."

They surfed through the life and times of Britain's most buccaneering Prime Minister.

"Here's another augury," said Jake. "At a – er – rather higher level."

It was a letter from Palmerston to Queen Victoria.

New Year's Day 1861.
This autumn and winter have been productive of events which future years are not likely to repeat. The capture of Peking by British troops; the union of Italy; and the approaching dissolution in America of the great northern Confederation by secession of the southern States. These are events full of importance for the future. Speaking confidentially to your Majesty with regard to the future, Lord Palmerston would think himself doing better service by recommending the House of Lords for Mr Gladstone ...

"A summary of the year's events and a flavour of things to come," said Jenny. "All of the predictions accurate, of course."

"And there's that man again," said Jake. "Gladstone. And with *regard to the future*, Palmerston wants him put out to pasture in the House of Lords. Where he can't do too much damage."

"What was the Queen's reply?"

He pointed out a sentence with a white-gloved hand.

There is nothing but clouds and causes of deep anxiety.

Here was a Palmerstonian prophecy for his Foreign Secretary, Lord John Russell.

September 13, 1865
My Dear Russell,
    Russia will, in due time, become a power almost as great as
the old Roman Empire. She can become mistress of all Asia,
except British India, whenever she chooses to take it; and
when railways shall have abridged distances, her command
of men will become enormous, her pecuniary means gigantic,
and power of transporting armies over great distances most
formidable.

"Deadly accurate once again," said Jenny.

"Because he *knew* what would come to pass," said Jake. "But
to hoi polloi? Palmerston must have smacked of genius. Like
Hitler in the thirties. Check this out – it's a speech the local MP
for Northamptonshire gave at a banquet where Lady Palmerston
cut the first sod for a new railway."

The noble lord seems to be always engaged in the game of
chuck-farthing, and it is invariably 'Heads I win, tails you
lose.' Whenever it comes up 'head', the noble lord very prop-
erly has all the credit. I do not mean to say that he is guilty
of unfair play, but the people, it is evident, are determined
to give him all the halfpence.

"So those outside the cabinet had no idea," said Jenny.

"No. They could only marvel at the rise and rise of British
power."

"Here's another," said Jenny.

It was a letter from Palmerston, expressing concern about
French naval investment.

My Dear Russell,
    It would be unwise for any English Government to shut its
eyes to these symptoms, and not to make all due preparations
for the gale which the political barometer thus indicates.

'Barometer' – an instrument for measuring atmospheric pressure, used in forecasting the weather.

"What you're holding is nothing less than the day-to-day dissemination of thunder prophecy throughout the machinery of the state," said Jake. "Bloody hell, just look at the language he uses. If Palmerston got any more explicit he'd be shouting out incantations to Tages himself."

"Jake – he did get more explicit."

In her hand was a letter Palmerston wrote to the British Ambassador at Paris, analysing a pronouncement by the French foreign minister, Thouvenel.

We must not take the language of Thouvenel as ordinances from the Book of Fate.

"He mentioned it," said Jake. "Palmerston actually mentioned it."

63

They found three more letters. Documents that left as much unsaid as said, by authors who knew well the secrets of the Cabinet and the British Empire.

The first was from Prince Albert to Lord Palmerston.

June 1860.
The Queen has received Lord Palmerston's letter giving an account of the Cabinet. She is very sorry to hear Mr Gladstone cannot raise himself to a statesmanlike view, but relieved Lord Palmerston is determined to place the safety of the country above all other considerations. The Queen feels sure we must take steps.
Prince Albert.

Jake frowned. "What steps?"

The second letter was from Palmerston to Sir George Lewis, a member of his Cabinet.

November 1860
My Dear Lewis,
*   You broached yesterday what seems political heresy. You said you dissented from the maxim that prevention is better than cure, and that, instead of trying to prevent an evil, we ought to wait till it had happened, and then apply the remedy. I beg to submit that the prevention of evil is the proper function of statesmen. There are endless instances of conflicts which might have been prevented by timely vigour.*
*   Yours sincerely,*
*   Palmerston.*

It recalled something Gladstone had written.

I suppose the duty of choosing the lesser evil binds me; the difficulty is to determine what the lesser evil is.

The third letter was Sir George's response.

My Dear Palmerston,
*   If the evil is certain, a wise statesman will, if he can, prevent it. If the evil is proximate and can be averted, undoubtedly prevention is better than cure. The cure may be simple and inexpensive. If we do not insure systematically, we do nothing.*
*   Believe me,*
*   Yours very sincerely,*
*   G.C. Lewis.*

Jake had put his finger on the gossamer thread: the silvery trace of the Book of Thunder's passage through the nineteenth century.

"Do you realise what this is?" There was an intensity in his eyes. "Do you understand what they're saying to each other?"

"I think so ..."

"First Prince Albert warns Palmerston about Gladstone's plans. He reminds Palmerston that the Queen thought they needed to take steps. So Palmerston discussed what to do with Lewis – making clear how Britain had used the Book of Thunder to uphold the *Pax Britannica*. Britain wasn't involved in a major war from the fall of Napoleon until World War One. Instead it made dozens of 'timely' interventions. Like – like our meddling in Sierra Leone right now."

"And in the third letter, Lewis concedes the point," said Jenny. "He admits that they must 'insure systematically'."

"Insure against the Bible-basher Gladstone. Victoria *knew* he would destroy the pagan texts, and to hell with the consequences. Just like the Roman Christians, burning Etruscan manuscripts in the fourth century A D."

"But this wasn't something Victoria could countenance," said Jenny.

"Nope – Queen Vic wasn't above a bit of realpolitik. She liked being top dog."

"So what insurance was put in place?"

"I don't know," Jake admitted. "But Randolph Churchill did. In the 1880s he intimated the *Disciplina* could be found again. Don't you remember?"

The time may be at hand when the path of honour and safety is illuminated by the light of other days. It may be that this dark cloud will pass away without breaking. I believe this storm will blow over.

Instinctively they glanced at the skylights. Rivulets of water coursed down the panes – the glass itself seemed to be flowing. The sky above was blackened and angry, like a bruise. Jake had the premonition of something fomenting up there, some outburst due to break.

Jenny touched the folio. "If there's an answer to be found, it's here."

As they neared the date of Palmerston's death, Jake sensed in the lord's words his vitality and mental powers weakening; he had the eerie feeling that he too was a fortune teller, knowing the year Palmerston would expire and the events that would succeed him. But the only document that gave them pause was a speech he had given to rural voters at Tiverton.

> *The old Romans had a fable about a great wrestler, who when thrown upon the ground, mother earth gave additional vigour and he got up stronger. I hope mother earth will send me back stronger than when I came here.*

"The Roman reference could be an allusion," Jake admitted. "And the theme. This idea of losing a power, only for it to come back stronger. But more than that? It tells us nothing."

And there Palmerston's life and correspondence came to an end.

64

It was dusk when they emerged from Westminster Underground under a sky troubled enough to have been brewed up by Turner. Jenny's aunt had a pied-à-terre nearby in Waterloo, but spent most of her time rusticating in Provence. If her lights were off they would break in – Jenny thought another night in hospital corridors might exhaust them to the point of making mistakes. The plan was to head west, circling through the maze of terraced streets tucked behind Millbank before grabbing a black cab over Lambeth Bridge the rest of the way.

Only they didn't get that far.

Jake saw it in Parliament Square: a statue of George Canning, the Prime Minister in the 1820s. He was wearing a toga and holding a scroll.

But it's so blatant.

Next to him it was Lord Derby, another Victorian Prime Minister. He also clasped a scroll and wore a mantle on his back, fringed like the hoods of Etruscan augurs. The thunder that had been building all day welled up afresh over the north-west horizon, like timpani presaging the charge in Holst's evocation of Mars. Disraeli held a scroll as well, and he too wore a hood – like the one found in Napoleon's baggage train at Waterloo. A scroll was in the hand of Robert Peel, founder of the modern Conservative Party and the Metropolitan Police, and with growing disquiet Jake saw how his fingers gestured towards a hooded cloak rumpled upon a Roman column.

"Do you see it, Jenny? Every one of them ..."

She nodded, whispering to herself, her cheeks very white against the gloom. Wind whipped against Jake's face, and the spire of Big Ben was a witch's hat over a cyclopean eye.

"All of them knew!" Jake's shout was unhinged. "It's so obvious!"

Still the thunder grew, and Big Ben tolled through the gathering tempest. The world's most famous clock, the world's most famous chimes, a stone's throw from the world's most famous front door, with the most famous woman alive living down the road. How was such pre-eminence achieved by an unprepossessing island in the North Sea?

Jake knew.

As the thunder swelled overhead he looked between the long-dead statesmen. No Gladstone here, but Winston Churchill took pride of place, leaning on his cane and scowling at the Houses of Parliament. Next to him stood Palmerston. He held no scroll, wore no hooded garment; but one hand was stretched out in supplication like the Emperor Augustus himself. And as Jake watched, the lightning struck at last.

A cataclysm of sound.

A dagger of white, horrendously close.

The lightning struck a spot somewhere behind the Treasury. Parliament Square was illuminated and the bronze eyeballs of the statesmen glared at Jake with pupils of purple flame. From Jake and Jenny's vantage point beneath Palmerston's plinth, the bolt passed right behind the statue's outstretched hand, so that it looked briefly as if the lord was *wielding* it, a javelin of energy connecting the heavens to whatever Whitehall building the lightning had struck.

The thunder died away; the storm had made its point. The ring of statues that had seemed so alive, so knowing, were metal again. Shouts of wonderment were offered up by the tourists; the humdrum of buses and black taxis resumed. Big Ben stopped tolling.

There were more film crews than usual on College Green.

65

Extracts from Hansard:

House of Commons
Thursday 12th May
The House met at half-past Two o'clock
PRAYERS
[Mr Speaker in the Chair]
Business of the House

Ordered,
    That the Speaker shall put the Questions necessary to dispose the Motion in the name of the Prime Minister relating to military intervention in Nigeria.

Mr Speaker: *To move the Motion, I call the Prime Minister.*

2.36pm

The Prime Minister (Mr Victor Milne): *My right honourable friends, there is no disease on earth more abhorrent than Ebola – except, perhaps, that of militant Islamic extremism. Yet as I speak to you today, swathes of West Africa face both of these scourges simultaneously.*

The deeds of the Islamists are well-known. Kidnapping young girls. The butchery of entire villages, for the crime of holding to their Christian beliefs. The slaying of all those who won't sign up to this perversion of Islam, which is a religion of peace. And in Nigeria, this has been combined with the most virulent strain of Ebola yet seen. Only this morning, the World Health Organisation confirmed new cases in Kuno, Gombe and Kaduna. There are 25,000 infections in northern Nigeria and half will end in death. This is the backdrop to which the Nigerian president has finally requested military and humanitarian assistance. Nigeria is a friend, an ally and a member of the Commonwealth. Ties of history and language bind us. When the Nigerian people request our help, we are compelled to agree. I urge you to support this motion.

3.14pm

The Leader of the Opposition (Ms Alison Tovey): *I start by joining the Prime Minister in condemnation of the barbarity perpetrated by Boko Haram in Nigeria. I'd like to add my admiration for our valiant doctors and nurses already working there with various charities, risking their lives to halt Ebola's spread.*

Mr Speaker, surely none of us here doubt the Prime Minister's good intentions. And this house has a noble tradition of putting unity ahead of party politics in matters of foreign policy. But the question facing us is whether a second military action in Africa within the space of eighteen months is wise; whether it adheres to the letter and spirit of international law; and whether we aren't better advised, given recent history, to seek a full UN mandate.

So we must be clear-eyed about the bitter cost this road map to war will bring to bear on the exceptional men and women of our armed forces. And we must consider how going it alone will be seen by the international community. The Attorney General's advice is that it must be clear there is no alternative to unilateral use of force. That is a demanding condition. I remain unconvinced it has been met.

3.16pm

The Prime Minister: *I respect, of course, my Right Honourable friend's concerns. But I simply point out to her that while the UN haggles over a resolution, people are dying. So let's be clear, if her party votes against this resolution, each day's delay is blood on her hands.*

[Interruption]

6.58pm

Mr Elwin Knight (SNP) (Airdrie & Shotts): *The Prime Minister no doubt much enjoys playing the global statesman, not to mention the recent boost in his poll ratings. But by rushing to yet another war, and at a time when Britain has set out no timetable for relinquishing government in Sierra Leone, I put this to him. Rather than a humanitarian intervention, are we not witnessing nothing less than the birth of a new British Empire?*

[Interruption]

Mr Elwin Knight: *I will not give way. I put it to the Prime Minister that his politics belong in the nineteenth century, not the twenty-first, and that modern Britons will be rightly ashamed of his actions.*

[Interruption]

Mr Speaker: *Order.*

· The Prime Minister: *Mr Speaker, I find it somewhat rich to be lectured on Britishness by a man whose party's sole aim is to destroy our United Kingdom.*

[Interruption]

9.20pm

Mr Alex Holmes (North Wiltshire): *I do not question the Prime Minister's casus belli. It is a brave and honourable thing he proposes. I also credit the Prime Minister with his commitment to spending four per cent of GDP on defence, twice the level of our Nato allies. However my constituents, many of whom are servicemen and women, harbour grave concerns about the cost in blood which must be borne by our Armed Forces. Nigeria's a dozen times the size of Sierra Leone. And we're asking our brave fighting men and women to tackle a full-scale Islamic insurgency, sponsored, no doubt, by oil money from the Gulf. That means roadside bombs, suicide attacks and all the rest. How can the Prime Minister assure the house that we won't find ourselves bogged down for a decade or more? How many troops will he commit, and above all, what is the exit strategy?*

The Prime Minister: *I'm sure my friend wouldn't expect me to discuss operational details. But I do acknowledge that the shadow of Iraq and Afghanistan looms large over these proceedings. So let's be clear – those wars were protracted, costly, and in the case of Iraq should never have happened. But does this mean Britain ought to forever abrogate its duties and responsibilities to the world? I put it to the house that Posterity would judge us most unkindly, were we to take such a course. As the Queen's first minister, I feel keenly the weight of history on my shoulders. And I believe it's fair to say this country's contribution to the happiness of this world over the centuries is rivalled by none. Yes, governments of the past have made mistakes. But we must learn from those mistakes, and I hope we can call on a greater wisdom to ensure our future actions are the correct ones.*

10.37pm *[Noise of thunder clearly audible in the Chamber]*

Dr Rupert Paige (Lib Dem) (Ceredigion): *Am I alone in feeling a sense of unreality in these proceedings?*

11.15pm The Leader of the Opposition: *What concerns me most is that the Prime Minister still refuses to be drawn on whether a caretaker government arrangement might be countenanced in Nigeria. Therefore let me put it to him directly. For the record, Prime Minister – do you rule out a takeover in Nigeria too? Because given our colonial past, such a course would make people all around the world very uncomfortable indeed.*
   [Interruption]
   Mr Speaker: *Order, order. The house will come to order.*
   The Prime Minister: *Mr Speaker, we live in unpredictable times. I'm sure that, on reflection, my right honourable friend will see why it would be foolhardy in the extreme for me to rule out any course of action, disagreeable or not. After all, it's not as if any of us can see the future …*

11.30pm

The House divided.

11.57pm

Mr Speaker: *Order, order. The house will come to order. Mr Dennison, calm yourself please. The ayes to the right, 357. The noes to the left, 221. So the ayes have it, the ayes have it.*
   [Interruption]
   The Prime Minister: *Thank you Mr Speaker. Mr Speaker, I passionately believe in the wisdom of this house. So I am not surprised that members agree with the overwhelming case for military action. As one of my predecessors once said, in ancient times a Roman citizen could proclaim, 'Civis Romanus sum' and know*

they were protected from barbarity, where so ever they may reside.
I believe that a citizen of the Commonwealth should be able to
say the same, safe in the knowledge that the strong arm and the
long reach of Great Britain ...

66

Sir Mark Hellier KBE, Permanent Undersecretary at the Foreign
Office, closed in on Walkers of Whitehall. One of three Foreign
Office pubs, it had once been a bank, and the frontage with its
many windows always struck Sir Mark as rather too grand for the
alleyway it was tucked down. Sir Mark was flame-haired, his face
intelligent but weak-chinned; a decent man, he was at Walkers
to meet a mandarin from the Department for International
Development. It had been decided that the vast and controversial
sums Britain gave Nigeria in aid must be used more coercively.
Getting the blighters to do what we tell them, his minister had put
it. DFID was bound to kick back against that, hence this early
parlay with his opposite number over a lubricating gin and tonic.

Walkers had a patina of boozy comfort. There were mirrors
along one wall, a good selection of whiskies and a passable mural
of the Palace of Westminster. The clientele was mostly civil servants and political apparatchiks with their peculiarly baby-faced
look, although a few tourists had wandered in. A husband and
wife from Leicestershire or somewhere, both dripping in gold.
Probably ran a chain of pound shops. Three Chinese guys in
brightly coloured cagoules. And ...

No.

Surely not.

Jennifer Frobisher.

That March, Sir Mark had been drawn into a power struggle
between the Foreign Office and Number 10. The row began after
the chief of MI6 had gone over the Foreign Secretary's head and

straight to the Prime Minister with a briefing on the spy scandal
that was headline news under the last government. Not knowing
what his espiocracy were up to drove the minister quite mad.
Chagrined, desperate to reclaim territory, the Foreign Secretary
had ordered Sir Mark to learn all he could about the case. But
there was a ring of steel around the files, sterile corridors in all
directions. And now the awol spook had simply sauntered into
a pub on Whitehall.

As Sir Mark stood dumbfounded, a man with a shaved head
and ripped T-shirt joined her. His face looked oddly familiar.
Coyly, innocently, like a man glancing at text messages full
of sweet nothings from his wife, the diplomat sought images
on his mobile. And good heavens, it *was* him: Jake Wolsey,
the very reporter who'd eloped with Frobisher. A sensational
development, a matter of national security, no less. He needed
to inform MI6. But not before attempting a little espionage of
his own.

The mandarin sauntered to the bar. He ordered a single gin
and tonic with one cube of ice. He sipped it within earshot of
the pair, *The Times* tucked under one arm, like a pastiche of
an eavesdropper. Wolsey was doing the talking, and Sir Mark
began to hear words.

"... get hold of restricted documents?"

In the mirror behind the bar, he lip-read Frobisher's reply:
Yes, then *what documents?* – a circle with a glimpse of tongue
for the 'ocu', flash of teeth at the end. The treachery was plain
as a memorandum in his minister's red box.

Wolsey leaned in closer, and Sir Mark heard the following,
baffling sentence: "Anything concerning Lord Palmerston that's
classified top secret."

Palmerston? *Palmerston*?

Yet Frobisher did not guffaw. Instead she said something
he couldn't hear, offered a prim handshake and they departed.

Sir Mark had to move fast. He would tell MI6 everything,
of course. But not before he had requested these documents,

if such things existed. As the Foreign Secretary was technically C's boss, there was no breach of protocol here – Sir Mark was merely doing his duty, expediting the speedy delivery of relevant files to those who might need them. But this course of action had the distinct bonus that the department might inveigle itself once more into a most intriguing case.

He had fallen into Jenny's trap.

*

If the evil is certain, a wise statesman will, if he can, prevent it. The cure may be simple and inexpensive.

Whatever cure against Gladstone's machinations Palmerston had cooked up to 'insure systematically', it wasn't to be found at the British Library. Anything that went beyond obscure allusion would still be classified top secret, held close by the Foreign Office or MI6. What, then, should be the tweezer to extract classified documents from the fortified morass of the British state archives? Step forward Sir Mark Hellier KBE, well-intentioned but territorial, altogether unsuited to the vicissitudes of spy-craft. And with her insider knowledge of the Foreign Office and a contact there from her MI6 days to obtain both the minister's engagements plus those of his top civil servant, Jenny had formulated her plan. When they left Walkers of Whitehall, it was in search of a beautician. She needed to become Jamila Ahmed once again.

67

Armed only with outrageous bluff, they were about to enter the second-most secure ministry, stroll through concentric rings of security and penetrate its very heart. An eye of the needle within the eye of the needle. Only then might they discover if

Sir Mark had taken their bait; if their fishing expedition had been successful at all.

King Charles Street was quiet at 7 pm. A few tourists clustered beneath the bombastic figure of Clive of India: a bounder by modern standards, but few had done more for the Empire. Scaffolding masked part of the Foreign Office, a van parked nearby.

Bonsers, est 1963. Experienced in historic roofing and joinery repairs.

A pleasant security guard manned reception.

"Dr Robin Matthews from Warwick University," said Jake. "I've got an appointment with the press office."

He had telephoned requesting to inspect the famous Goetze murals adorning the interior of the ministry for a forthcoming book. The press officer, a failed journalist turned lazy, told him to "pop the request in an email" so he could forward the request with a click and forget about it rather than bother taking notes. But that put them in a quandary – an email from a personal account would look suspicious. In the end Jenny set up an account with the address 'robin.matthews@warwick.acc.uk'. The extra 'c' was the giveaway, but naturally the highly-paid press officer hadn't noticed. They hoped.

Julian Waverly was a slapdash figure with curly hair, two-day stubble and a worn woolly jumper. He was starting a night shift in the press office, hence the lack of suit. Jake considered the dullness of gaze, the indolent handshake. If this guy was leading them into captivity, he was doing it well. They passed through an X-Ray machine and Waverley ushered them across a courtyard into the main building. This had serious grandeur: antique furniture and chandeliers, lavish ceilings and portraits of forgotten imperialists. Through one door Jake glimpsed life-sized paintings of Wellington and Lord Nelson, the old rivals glaring at each other across a room, Foreign Office humour. But the straitened public sector was visible too, in the acrylic carpets, the temporary doors made of plywood, panes of security glass with crosshatched wire inside, a trace of the NHS amongst walnut and gilt.

"I'd show you the Locarno Rooms," Waverley said. "A few decent paintings in there. But there's a function on tonight."

"Oh?" said Jenny, though she already knew.

"A retirement do for the ambassador to Argentina. Not the easiest posting," he added with a weak smile.

They were led to the innermost sanctum of the Foreign Office, the holy of holies. A staircase swept up towards a blue dome sheathed in signs of the zodiac and symbols of British imperium. It led to a long gallery in reds and purples, off which was arrayed the private secretary's office, the special advisers' office and finally the Foreign Secretary's room. Goetze's murals pronounced the might of a Great Power; to Jake's right was the painting Parr had stood before on the day she was summoned to Number 10.

Beneath Britannia, a scroll proclaimed:

Mistress of the seas
She sends her sons into distant lands

But Jake wasn't looking at it.

He was looking at the mural above the Foreign Secretary's door.

A more sinister apparition, this; redolent of secrecy and enigma. The male figure was clad in a hooded robe of blue, like Augustus once wore, like that found in the baggage train of Napoleon after Waterloo. He held a scroll, which unfurled down the wall. But the scroll was blank and he held a finger to his lips. Above his head, a second scroll bore a single word.

Silence.

Jake was transfixed. The reds and maroons had taken on the aspect of gore; he had the sensation of being a tiny blood cell within some oversized heart, an organ that constricted around him and crushed him with wealth that seemed suddenly grotesque. Obtained by trickery, by force and black magic. For this was the heart of a body with brains and arms – and fists. The

British State, once at the centre of a spider's web whose strands stretched from the orient to wildest Africa. As neurones in the brain connect; as the invisible fronds of the Network commune across the vastness of space.

*

"Is the Foreign Secretary in there?" asked Jenny.

"Oh, probably," Waverley waved a hand, affecting indifference at proximity to power. "Most evenings he spends a couple of hours working through the red boxes before he goes home. Have you seen enough of the murals?"

Jake laughed. "Gosh, no. I need at least a few hours. My thesis is on the symbolism of ..."

"A few *hours*?" Waverley interjected. "Sorry, no – I'm a busy man. And I can't just leave you here by yourself."

"Excuse me," said Jenny, "but your wages are paid with *our* taxes. We *own* these paintings."

Waverley stared at the uppity Brummie in her ludicrous sunglasses.

"Oh all right," he sighed, looking at his watch. "It's coming up to half seven. I'll give you two hours, then you really will have to go."

As Jake and Jenny went through the motions of inspecting the artwork the press officer fiddled with his mobile, releasing the occasional harrumph. Half an hour went by. Then it was an hour. Jake glanced at the Foreign Secretary's door. Not a sound had come from within. They had sixty minutes left to get inside.

"Is this the ambassador's waiting room?" asked Jenny, nodding at the next door along.

"Yup," said Waverley. "I call it the naughty room."

"Can I look inside?"

Another sigh – it was as if all the disappointments in the press officer's life had to be periodically vented through his mouth. "Come on, then."

He stepped inside. Jenny followed and closed the door, leaving Jake in the corridor.

"Hey," snapped Waverley. "I told you, I can't just leave him there. It's a high security building, you're my responsibility."

Together they inspected the Enigma machine, cooed at the view across towards the Admiralty, peered out onto Downing Street. It was 8.40 pm when they returned to the murals; fifty minutes left. Ten more minutes slipped by. Abruptly the Foreign Secretary's door opened and out stumbled the minister. Nigel Edmonds had spent the day being harangued by Berlin, Paris, Washington and Beijing, and he didn't even glance at Waverley, who'd snapped to attention. He pattered off in the direction of the Locarno Rooms, clearing his throat and adjusting a tie. They had one leaving speech's length to get inside his office.

"I need to pray," said Jenny.

Waverley was fiddling with his phone again. "What?"

"I need to pray," she repeated. "Where's your prayer room?"

"I'm not sure we've got one."

"You're joking. This is a public building. You've got to have a prayer room."

Waverley looked flustered. "I ... I really don't think we do, madam."

"Anywhere will do, then. Any room facing east."

The press officer's head flapped uselessly from left to right.

"East is that way," Jenny snapped, pointing down the corridor.

"Errr," said Waverly. "Errr ..."

"Otherwise I'll miss *adhan*. Call to prayer," she added, as if addressing a dunce.

The man looked petrified. "Ok, let's go. I'll find you an empty office."

They began walking, but after a few paces Waverley halted. "You have to come too, mate," he told Jake. "How many times do I have to tell you?"

"Are you crazy?" Jenny snapped. "He's male. That would be *haram*. Are you even *aware* of diversity?"

It was more than the civil servant's job was worth to have that sort of complaint made. Guilty or not, these things stuck. He raised his hands in surrender.

"Don't go anywhere," he shouted like a drowning man as Jenny frogmarched him down the corridor.

Jake knocked on the Foreign Secretary's door. Nobody answered and he stepped inside.

As Jenny knew, the door to the Minister of State's room is habitually left unlocked, with no additional security measures. The only Foreign Secretaries in recent times to use a computer were David Miliband and Philip Hammond (Beckett, Straw and Hague refused to touch one) and no files are stored there; it is essentially a glorified meeting room, somewhere the minister can work without distractions. The only confidential documents ever present are those in the ...

Red boxes.

Three of them awaited him on the Foreign Secretary's desk, charmingly scuffed and bashed. The middle one was open and papers had been extracted. Jake strode across the room, dizzy with unreality. This was madder than anything he had attempted in his journalistic career by some distance. He photographed the pile and began working through it. The dispatches were from all over the world, each with a handwritten précis from the private secretary. A memo on escalating gang violence in El Salvador. Something about a missing backpacker in Nepal. Jake finished the pile and returned it to its original state, using the photograph as a guide. There were more double takes as he worked through the second box. A CIA man in Washington with a British grandfather had a gambling problem. The President of Venezuela, publicly recalcitrant, was making confidential overtures to Britain. This was interesting stuff, and Jake was hit by another head-rush at the enormity of the act.

I am rifling through the papers of a serving Foreign Secretary.

But everything had been written that day, and he felt a sickly desperation as he opened the third box.

On the top of the pile was a very old document.

A pale blue stamp described the contents as *most secret*.

It was a receipt, dated 1865 and detailing £10,000 for the Royal Geographical Society so it might pursue 'agreed additional activities' while searching for the source of the Nile. And it was authorised by Palmerston.

Jake replaced the memo, closed the box and walked out of the room. His eyes were drawn to Britannia.

She sends her sons into distant lands.

68

Damien di Angelo was gazing towards the City of London from Waterloo Bridge when he became aware of a presence beside him.

"I'm looking for my daughter." A Louisiana drawl. "She has a shaved head. Have you seen her?"

"There was a woman here by that description about twenty minutes ago. But she went away."

"You must be Damien. I'm Arnold Deissler."

Di Angelo turned to face him. About fifty, tall but stooped, even more skeletal than he. Yet Deissler's forearms were a tangle of veins, crevices dividing up the extensor muscles: they were the limbs of a man who did a hundred press ups each morning. He wore black loafers with two tassels on each which di Angelo found rather vulgar.

Deissler stared past St Paul's. "One, two, three …" his counting diminished to a whisper "… fifteen, sixteen, seventeen …" Deissler's eyes were like almonds, set at a slight angle on his seed-shaped face. "… twenty-five, twenty-six, twenty-seven cranes," he finished. "This city's going up. Must be doing something right here, Brexit or no Brexit."

"Where are Wolsey and Frobisher?" asked di Angelo.

"I'll know soon."

A mud-lark ambled out onto the spit of sand beneath the South Bank and both men turned, leaning on the railings to face Westminster.

"The mother of Parliaments," said Deissler. "And yet for the international clout it has nowadays, we might as well be looking at the Forum of ancient Rome."

"Or those guys." Di Angelo nodded at Cleopatra's Needle and Deissler laughed dryly.

"It was taken to Alexandria by Augustus, and the Brits got hold of it during the Napoleonic Wars." The teeth in Deissler's lower jaw were pointed, like those of a guppy. "These darn civilisations have been toppling each other for as long as history."

"So let's make sure *that* domino doesn't get back up again," said di Angelo, staring at the Palace of Westminster.

Deissler chuckled. "I just wouldn't have believed it. We've got Putin in Russia. We've got Iran still building a bomb, no matter what anyone says. And which country makes a bid for global domination? The damn Brits. I mean come on, you're kidding me, right!?"

The bark of a motorbike carried across the water.

"Someone's having fun," said di Angelo.

Deissler's head cocked to one side. "Just so you know, it's been decided we've got nothing more to gain by following Wolsey."

"If you say so."

"You ok with that?"

"'Course I'm ok with it, man."

A gay couple walked past, one black, the other South Asian. They weren't touching, but there was that *closeness* between them, the one-inch gap that said so much.

"What does freedom mean to you, Damien?"

"It means the world to me," said di Angelo, surprised at the vehemence in his own voice.

You just carry on doing your bit for freedom and goodness, son. That's all we ask.

The couple's hands had found each other. In New York nobody would have batted an eyelid, but di Angelo would not have recommended it in the projects of Baltimore.

"I know what you're thinking," said Deissler.

Either he was observant or it was in di Angelo's file. Or probably both.

"But the British gave up defending the torch of freedom a long time ago," he continued. "And there's nobody else who can be trusted with it but us."

Di Angelo nodded slowly.

"Waterloo," said Deissler, gripping the railings with both hands. "A bridge named after a battle. Kinda ironic, don't you think?"

"True-say. But the coalition which defeated Napoleon that day gave Europe a century of peace."

"That's it, man!" His eyes twinkled. "You got it. Now, I do believe their Chinatown's not too far that way. Let's go get something to eat."

69

"How did you know it would be there?" said Jake.

Jenny studied the workmen on King Charles Street, civil servants smoking outside the Treasury. "Call it a hunch."

Armed police loitered too, and Jake felt a fresh kick of adrenaline. Then again, there were always armed police in Whitehall.

"Richard Burton," he said as they marched towards Big Ben. "The explorer. It has to be him."

But Jenny had eyes only for the ragged band of protesters at Parliament Square, Stop the War banners denouncing the last night's Nigeria vote. Tourists posed beneath Churchill, flashing victory signs; nobody bothered with Palmerston.

A helicopter hung overhead, as if suspended in fluid. Then again, there were always helicopters over SW1.

"If Burton *was* tied up with the Book of Thunder, it explains two great unanswered questions of Victorian exploration," said Jake as they crossed Westminster Bridge.

A white Ford Transit van lumbered past, holding Jenny's attention. She scrutinised a phalanx of Italian tourists, bristling with selfie sticks like hoplite warriors. A Chinese couple in wedding gear posed for a photographer.

Then again, there were always Chinese couples posing in wedding gear on Westminster Bridge.

"Things that have puzzled every historian of the source of the Nile explorers," he said.

A man in kilt and sporran stood sentinel beneath Big Ben with his bagpipes. Listening to those entangled notes, Jake felt a spasm of pride for all Union had achieved: in commerce and invention, in democracy. In exploration.

The helicopter was over College Green now, boss-eyed in the air as it angled towards them.

"Let's get out of here," said Jenny.

They caught a black cab, ditched it; caught another, abandoned that too; sprinted around the block and clambered into her aunt's flat through the kitchen window.

"Now then," said Jenny. "You were saying something about Richard Burton?"

*

"Richard Burton, Nile explorer, lived 1821 to 1890. In a century of great British eccentrics, he was up there with the best." Jake grinned. "Actually, that's underplaying it. The man was a total wrong 'un."

Jenny couldn't help but smile.

Jake sought his Wikipedia page. "Striking chap, no?"

The face was *fierce* – dark hair, drooping moustache, eyes of ice

that smouldered in his skull. There was something exotic about
him, something of the Romany gypsy perhaps. An expression
of scarcely-concealed menace was completed by scars on both
cheeks.

"He was speared by a Somali tribesman," said Jake. "And still
made it back to his boat, the haft protruding from both sides of
his face."

"Tell me more."

"Where to even start? Burton's entire life was a whirlwind
of salty behaviour. At fifteen he was busted for writing steamy
letters to prostitutes. At nineteen he was smoking opium. On
his first day at Oxford, he challenged a man to a duel. Next
he became a spy in Pakistan, and there *nothing* was off limits.
Bonking local girls, smoking bhang, diving into the homosexual
brothels of Karachi ... he even filed reports to his superiors
on the relative merits and demerits of young boys versus
eunuchs."

"Good lord," Jenny exclaimed.

"He said there was more to grab hold of with the former."

"*Good lord!*"

"Next it was off to the Middle East to penetrate the innermost
shrine of Mecca disguised as an Afghan Sufi, freshly circum-
cised, his skin stained with walnut juice. If he'd got caught,
he was a dead man. He spoke twenty languages and wrote
a translation of the Kama Sutra that was ... *provocative*, by
Victorian standards. I suppose he'd get called a troll today – but
he was rakish and daring with it. 'Ruffian Dick', he was known
as. He scandalised Victorian society to the point of combus-
tion and did not give one single crap. Actually, he revelled
in it. This was sex, drugs and exploration. Frankly, I almost
admire the man."

"He definitely sounds a bit rum," she laughed. "But what's
Burton got to do with the *Disciplina*?"

Jake looked excitable. "What do you know about the hunt for
the Nile's source?"

"Only that Stanley found Livingstone, for some reason. And said, 'Dr Livingstone I presume?' Plus it was a Victorian obsession."

"The quest for the source of the White Nile goes back to ancient times," said Jake. "When Alexander the Great met sooth-sayers at Karnak Temple in Luxor he asked what causes the Nile to rise. The ancient Greek geographer Ptolemy wrote of twin sources near the 'Mountains of the Moon.'"

A world map was on the kitchen wall and he traced the Nile south through Egypt to Sudan, where the mighty river split. The Blue Nile rises in Ethiopia, but the river's more venerable source traces its heritage further, to Africa's very core. A violent wilderness when Burton visited, from which civilisation had flowed.

"The Romans tried to reach the source and failed," Jake continued. "The mind-boggling fact is that in the Victorian age, a time of steamships and railways and the telegraph, we knew less about central Africa than the surface of Mars. Everyone who tried to penetrate it died of fever or was killed by wild animals or hacked to pieces by warring tribes. And yet, out of that unknown flowed the longest river on earth to arrive fully formed in Egypt, the very fulcrum of the British Empire. It's like us not knowing where the M1 comes from."

"Wow," Jenny admitted.

"This is where the White Nile begins." Jake pointed at the central African watershed. "The Great Lakes region. Although to call them lakes is pushing it. They're really inland seas, albeit fresh water. Victorian explorers had heard of them from Arab slaving parties – the debate over which one fed the Nile was fierce. But to visit them meant years in the wild, laid up for months at a time with malaria or detained at the pleasure of a local king. Each lake had to be circumnavigated to see if a river flowed from it and followed until it indisputably became the Nile. David Livingstone reckoned it began at Lake Bangweulu, now in Zambia. Burton favoured Lake Tanganyika, the long thin one separating Tanzania and the Congo. But they were both wrong." Jake indicated a tiny triangular country. "The true source is Burundi, flowing north into Lake Victoria. That lake feeds the Nile. And the discoverer of Lake Victoria was a bloke called John Hanning Speke – Burton's assistant."

"What's the relevance of this receipt?"

"You're Lord Palmerston. Ask yourself, where would you hide a text that's so remote not even a Prime Minister could lay his hands on it? Somewhere *beyond* the ends of the earth. And a destination with a ready-made cover story to boot."

The old Romans had a fable about a great wrestler, who when thrown upon the ground, mother earth gave additional vigour and he got up stronger.

"He had it buried there," said Jake. "That's where it was supposed to remain until Gladstone died, and a less pious Prime Minister took power. No doubt talk of it was handed down by word of mouth, in smoky Victorian drawing rooms. That's how they 'insured systematically'. That's what Lord Randolph alluded to. Those were the 'agreed additional activities.'"

The time may be at hand when the path of honour and safety is illuminated by the light of other days.

"And those were the rumours Winston Churchill remembered," said Jenny. "When MI6 contacted him in 1941 about Hess and the 'ancient Etruscan matter.'"

70

"But how do we know Burton's our man?" said Jenny. "Many a Brit was hunting for the source of the Nile, right?"

"Indeed. But the evidence that Burton was Palmerston's agent is insurmountable. Firstly, he was interested in the Etruscans. He actually *inspected* the Zagreb Linen, it's documented fact. Secondly, there's that begging letter from Burton we found in Randolph Churchill's papers."

*Since the £300 a year to which I think I am entitled is hardly
equivalent of years of hard work in anything but wholesome
climates, I beg you to favour me by placing my name on the
civil list for a pension of £300.*

"Climates don't get much more unwholesome than central
Africa," said Jake. "The man deserved a Rolex, a sailing boat
and a gold-plated pension, I'd say. But finally, at a stroke all the
mysteries of Burton's African expedition are explained."

"What mysteries?"

"Burton had publicly argued – incorrectly, as it happens – that
the Nile's true source was Lake Tanganyika. It took him and
Speke months of horrific cross-country travel to get there and
try to prove it. Burton nearly died from malaria, Speke almost
lost his sight and went permanently deaf in one ear after a beetle
crawled into it."

"Right ..."

"But they made it to Lake Tanganyika nonetheless, the first
Europeans to set eyes on it. Then a local tribesman told them
something sensational. At the north end of the lake was a major
river. If this river flowed *outwards*, it looked a bloody good bet
for the Nile. So off they went by canoe, nineteen days of solid
paddling. But according to Burton's account, just six hours
from the river, a chieftain told them the river flowed *into* Lake
Tanganyika, not out of it. Ergo it couldn't be the Nile. Now, what
would you do in that position?"

"I'd continue on and check for myself," said Jenny.

"Exactly. But they *turned back*. One of the great mysteries of
exploration has been why Burton's resolution wavered at this
crucial moment, so close to his goal. Why not carry on for six
more hours to see it with his own eyes? After all, the account of a
savage was hardly going to be enough for the Royal Geographical
Society."

"Because that wasn't really his goal," whispered Jenny. "He
was there to bury the *Disciplina*."

Jake jabbed at Lake Tanganyika. "And *that's* where we'll find it."

"But what was Burton's excuse? Supposedly he was there to find the source. How did he explain the decision to go back home?"

"He claimed they were running short of 'African money' – the cloth and beads that expeditions used to pay their way with local tribes. That response has never stood up to scrutiny, as an Arab slaver they'd encountered had already proposed to supply them with more cloth and beads. For lack of any better explanation, historians have surmised that he simply wimped out. Which given Burton's previous form seems somewhat unlikely. And another mystery is explained. The two explorers then heard about a huge uncharted lake to the north. But Burton, a lifelong glory hunter, *didn't bother* to go and visit it. He let Speke go there alone. So it was Speke, not Burton, who discovered the *true* source of the Nile, which he named Lake Victoria."

"I understand," said Jenny. "Burton's job was done, but he could have died at any moment. He needed to preserve himself – once Gladstone was gone, he might have to go back there and get it. Hunting for the Nile would have been reckless sightseeing by comparison."

"And one final enigma is laid to rest," said Jake. "After their journey, Burton and Speke fell out spectacularly. The bone of contention was 'whose' lake was the source of the Nile. Was it Lake Tanganyika, claimed by Burton as the leader of the expedition there? Or Lake Victoria, which Speke discovered alone? Nobody could say conclusively, because neither lake had been circumnavigated. So a showdown was arranged – the Great Nile Debate. Speke and Burton would slug it out with their theories in a public hall. It caused a sensation, even the great Livingstone attended for good measure. Only it never happened."

"Why not?"

"Because the morning of the debate, Speke was killed."

*

"Killed?" Jenny exclaimed. "How?"

"In what we hacks like to call 'mysterious circumstances'. Speke was a passionate hunter, and the morning of the debate he was on a grouse shoot. Allegedly he dropped his shotgun while clambering over a drystone wall, and blasted himself in the chest. He died within the hour. This guy had shot game in deepest Africa, manhandled firearms through the most evil swamps and jungles on the planet without mishap. And he shoots himself dead climbing over a wall in a country estate? Somehow, I don't think so."

Jenny took this in.

"The argument's raged for a century," said Jake. "Was it an accident? Or was Speke so worried about the debate that he committed suicide? But now we know. It was *Burton* who killed him. Or more likely, some agent of the Foreign Office acting on his behalf. Because Speke was about to spill the beans on Burton's *real* reason for being in Africa."

Jake thought of the mural over the Foreign Secretary's door. The hood of a seer, an empty scroll.

Silence.

She sends her sons into distant lands.

"What if Burton had died in Africa?" said Jenny. "The *Disciplina* would have been lost forever."

"But therein was the genius," said Jake. "All the Nile explorers wrote a stream of journals and letters that were sent back to Zanzibar via Arab slaving parties and on to London. The idea was that any geographical discoveries would be recorded in the event that they did die. If Burton had snuffed it, his diaries would have got to the Royal Geographical Society sooner or later, with its close links to the Foreign Office."

Jenny's little finger was tapping on the kitchen table and her collar bones heaved up and down with agitation. He had always considered her stronger than him, but something in the quickness of her breath – this *compulsion* to find it – spoke of weakness.

"And do you know what else?" said Jake. "Nobody's ever seen Burton's original journals from that expedition. Because his widow *destroyed them after he died.*"

"But how do we know Lord Randolph didn't follow through with the plan?" said Jenny. "How do we know Burton didn't exhume the *Disciplina* in the 1880s?"

"History's your answer there. The Foreign Office used to run the world – it hardly has much swagger nowadays, does it? Despite the best efforts of the Prime Minister. If Burton had dug up the *Disciplina* as per the plan, Britain would still rule the waves."

"Strange," Jenny mused, "that the book should end up in Africa again. The Romans had already hidden that very same copy in Egypt, when Hannibal was on the march. Three centuries later, Eusebius would send another to Ethiopia for safe-keeping."

"It's almost as though it was *drawn* there." Jake stared at the map. "Where man first began."

For the first time, he saw how the continent resembled a human skull in profile. The bulge of West Africa was the occipital bone, the twin protrusions of the Mozambique coast were the nose and mouth and the bight of Tanzania was the eye socket. Lake Victoria was the eye itself.

"We have to go there," muttered Jenny.

71

"Will there be anything else, gentlemen?" asked the chairman of the Joint Intelligence Committee.

C answered with a curt half-shake of his head and the chiefs of MI5 and GCHQ followed suite.

"In that case, let's get to it. Good luck, everybody."

There was a rustling of papers and the committee shuffled from the egg-shaped room deep within the Cabinet Office. The

Wednesday afternoon meeting was always a serious affair, but today something else could be detected amongst the all-male group of spies, military advisers and civil servants. *Excitement*. They were embarking upon a war.

C remained seated, and as Sir Mark Hellier manoeuvred past he raised a finger. The spymaster waited until they were alone, whereupon the Prime Minister walked in with Evelyn Parr.

"This is one of my top people," said C. "She's been through your statement. She's going to tell you something."

"I want my minister to be here," Sir Mark began, but Milne thumped the table and all the glassware rattled.

"Just *listen to her*, will you?" he shouted.

Spilt water spread across the mahogany, like an expanding empire.

"Yes, Prime Minister," said Sir Mark.

"You fell into an intelligence trap," said Parr coldly. "You were *meant* to overhear Frobisher. And while you and the minister were at that dratted drinks reception, Wolsey got into his office. He gained access to his red boxes."

Sir Mark's face had turned redder with each word.

"I tender my resignation," he said.

"Oh do can it, you twit," said Milne.

"They saw that file you requested," said Parr. "And got away."

Water was dripping onto Sir Mark's knees.

"This is the worst security breach since the Cambridge spy ring," observed C mildly.

The diplomat was rigid in his chair, water spreading up his thigh. "What now?"

"Now nothing," said Milne. "We've had quite enough scandals in the Secret Intelligence Service for one decade. Don't resign, whatever you do. Stay put for eighteen months, and if we get away with it we'll fob you off with early retirement."

"But if this does get out, god help you," muttered C. "You'll be thrown you to the wolves."

"A prosecution and the loss of your knighthood, at the very least," said Milne. "Now get out."

Sir Mark departed unsteadily, handing himself from chair to chair.

"That should shut him up," said C.

Milne was already roaming around the room, touching the walls, peering into a pot plant in search of bugs. Like many Prime Ministers, contact with the Secret Services brought out the schoolboy in him.

"So, the famous Jic." He pronounced it as a single word, as is intelligence custom. "Nice to glimpse the reality behind the mystique. Why were they interested in Palmerston?"

"We don't know," said C.

"What are these 'agreed additional activities'?"

"We don't know that either."

A buzz at the door. "Call for Evelyn Parr ..."

Parr left the room to take it – the walls were made of lead and five feet thick.

She returned seconds later. "Our friends Jamila Ahmed and Dr Robin Matthews have just booked flights to Tanzania."

Milne sat heavily, ransacking his hair with both hands. "Please can somebody explain to me why this ruddy duo are constantly two steps ahead of us?"

"It's Wolsey," said C. "He's good. And she's good at keeping him alive."

"Then you'd better get out there and give her some help. Until we've worked out what their hunch is, anyway. And take – oh, what's his name? That Sierra Leone chappie who's doing such good work. The explorer man."

"You can go now, Evelyn," said C.

She departed.

"You mean Serval," said C. "I was about to send him back to Sierra Leone, actually. For the – the next stage."

"But it's the *same project*. Don't you realise that, Dennis? Obtaining the *Disciplina*, our West African imbroglio. It's the same damned thing." Milne was smiling again. "I think I've done pretty respectably so far in that part of the world actually, considering my successes have come from nothing but opportunism and *muddling through*, in the grand British tradition. With a dash of ruthlessness on the side. A bit like how the original empire was built." He smiled sadly. "When India became independent, the empire lost four-fifths of its citizens at a stroke of a pen. Nowadays she's a country of a billion."

C said nothing.

"The jewel in the crown," Milne continued. "But to get her back, hypothetically speaking of course, my brinkmanship would have to exceed anything done by a statesman since – well, the thirties, I suppose. So we stake everything on Wolsey. On Africa and the *Disciplina Etrusca*. You must have someone else with a silver tongue who can go back to Freetown for us and finish the job?"

"Actually, yes," C began.

But Milne's mind was already running onto the next thing. "You'd better take me through what was discussed at today's committee," he said.

C detailed targets suggested for the first round of air strikes in Nigeria; the plight of fifteen British oil workers being held by the Islamists; intercepts of communications between worried Eurozone heads of state. Their allies, nominally.

"Ah, Europe," said Milne. "What a shower. Thank the lord for the innate good sense of the British electorate. Do you know, ours was the first form of world government since the Roman Empire that actually *worked*. And incidentally, the denarius was Europe's last effective single currency."

C wondered for the first time whether the Prime Minister was clinically insane. But there was no turning back now – his best chance of avoiding The Hague was to see the damned thing through.

He decided on levity. "Well, let's hope for a global *coup d'état*. With you playing the part of Queen Victoria perhaps, Prime Minister?"

"I did *not* usurp the crown." Milne had executed another frightening change of mood; he was paraphrasing Napoleon and C knew what was coming. "I found it in the *gutter*. I picked it up with my sword. But it was the people of the Commonwealth who placed it on my head ..."

72

Reach out and take it!

Stealth tactics, distraction, feints and intimidation; nothing was off-limits in this campaign of aggravated burglary. The monkey had been prowling around Jake's tent in ever-decreasing circles as it plotted food raids. Now it stole along a branch to where a pomegranate quivered on a length of vine, where Jake had hung it to test the creature's intelligence. The monkey yanked the creeper and judged it at the limit of its bodyweight. It sat on the branch, scheming away.

Go on!

Greed got the better of caution as the monkey reached for the creeper again. Suddenly a second monkey appeared from stage left, barrelling across the ground and leaping into the air to snatch the pomegranate like a slam dunking basketball player.

Jake heard Jenny turn a page in her tent.

He sighed, left his own tent and padded down a lightly wooded slope. Two zebra rested their necks against each other in an apparent act of love and their foal picked its way through the tree trunks with ballerina grace. He'd always assumed zebra were essentially horses with stripes, but up close he saw how unearthly their markings were, the untameable look in their eyes. These were beasts. How wonderful to be back in Africa. At the bottom of the slope Lake Tanganyika stretched before him: an inland sea of calmest pewter surrounded by hills that hummed with emerald. Wavelets lapped a spit of orange sand;

it was a paradise, and he felt a stab of sympathy for John Speke, half-blinded when he reached this spot.

After landing in Dar-es-Salaam they had caught an internal flight to western Tanzania, completing in two short hours a journey that took Burton and Speke eight months of suffering. In Burton's day, Kigoma was an Arab slaving settlement – now it was a town of single-story buildings scattered over steep hills. This was the wild west of Tanzania, where the only white faces were aid workers and two miles into the bush you could find mud huts and cottage gardens, families living much as they would have done in Burton's day. Jake hired the most powerful motorbike he could find, an old 300cc KTM off roader, and they rode out to the forested campsite with its permanent tents. Here they would encounter few locals (and be invisible from space).

Across the water Jake could see the mountains of eastern Congo, black bastions whose severity was somehow suggestive of the land they guarded. He turned north, towards Burundi – there was fresh unrest in that ever-troubled state too.

"I know where it is!" Jenny's voice carried through the trees.

She was sitting up in her tent, her eyes shining. Since arriving they had been scouring Burton's published journals for a literary X marks the spot.

It's a puzzle. And the words are the clues.

"I know where it is," she repeated.

Burton had recorded his walk inland from the coast with a 'compass traverse', a linear diagram giving a description of the topography at mile intervals and a compass reading whenever obstacles forced a change in bearing. At his most northerly point on Lake Tanganyika there were coordinates and a symbol resembling an eye.

"The point where he turned back," said Jenny. "And look at his journal entry for that day."

Burton's handwriting was minuscule, individual letters little more than a bump.

A gale appeared to be brewing in the north here – the place of storms. We landed at a steep ghaut, where the crews swarmed up a ladder of rock. It was one of those portentous evenings of the tropics, a calm before the tempest, unnaturally quiet. The sky was dull and gloomy, glimmerings of lurid lightning cut by light masses of mist.

"The place of storms," Jake reflected. "Portentous indeed."

"What's a 'ghaut'?"

"Like the Indian 'ghat' – a river used for bathing. So we're looking for a small river with a bathing spot on the shores of Lake Tanganyika with a natural set of rock steps."

"And we have the coordinates – let's hope Burton's measurements were accurate."

"He was in the army," said Jake. "Map-making was taught to all officers."

"Should be simple, then …"

Six hundred miles away, Parr and Davis boarded a flight to Kigoma; Serval was on a British Airways flight over the Red Sea. Jenny was correct that MI6 had not found them, but the Americans were in the country too. And they had more precise intelligence.

73

Trutnvt.

Such a brutish word, to describe the divine – it was like something a troll would be called. Now it obsessed Kanisha. She thought about *trutnvt* on the Northern Line; she thought about *trutnvt* as she lectured; it came to her in her dreams.

First, the benign lighting, and this shall serve as a warning.

David had not invented the passage. The form and metre were beyond reproach, the archaism too authentic. And the ritual corresponded with all known sources for the period. Most importantly, her intuition told her the passage was authentic – and as any Bonham's expert will tell you, whether it *feels* right is the litmus test. Only a dozen scholars alive could have attempted such a forgery; it would have been easier to fake the Hitler Diaries. Which meant David had acquired the most dynamite Etruscan passage that had yet come to light.

Who was he?

Not from an established institution, that was for sure. There would be no need for the cloak-and-dagger stuff; a museum or university would be singing it from the rooftops. More likely David was a private collector. Or an amateur archaeologist who had uncovered something extraordinary but wanted to hold on to it.

Was there more?

This was the pertinent question. And she couldn't let David's find be lost to the study of serious archaeologists. This was her shot at greatness. A direct approach would scare him into breaking contact; whatever he'd found would be lost to archaeology. So she prepared a trap.

A midday lesson for once: Kanisha was at a café on Great Russell Street. David read Etruscan perfectly now – but goodness, how he fretted about pronunciation. Although nobody knows for certain how it sounded, Kanisha had been sharing the best guesses thrown up over generations of research.

David studied a perfume bottle. "'Mi suntheruza spurias mlakas'. I am the little container of Spuria the beautiful."

"Good. But we don't think they pronounced 'th' like we do. It's a solid 't', and the 'h' is a bit windy. 'Sun-*tuu*-eruza'. Think of the Cockney in *My Fair Lady*, pronouncing the 'h' on words where it's supposed to be silent. Like honourable."

"Thanks, Kanisha, that's bloody useful."

Bloody. So David was a Brit. Or antipodean, come to think of it. And *useful* – odd choice of word in the circumstances.

"By the way, there's a webpage you might be interested in," she said. "It's got some interesting stuff on Vegoia."

"Oh *really*?"

The Prophecies of Vegoia held a fascination for David – all that talk of natural borders.

"It's on the King's College London website," she said. "One of their lecturers was Vegoia mad. He died a couple of years back, sadly, but his research is still online. I'll send you a link ..."

Skype is so secure that even Foreign Office staff use it. But perhaps David could be induced to visit an external website. A tracking device could be added to this page: a few lines of code that would record a visitor's IP address, their unique location on the internet. Kanisha didn't know a thing about computers, but her brother Bastavary worked in IT and agreed to help.

A new website would be suspicious, so Bastavary launched a 'brute force attack' against King's College London's server, spamming its server with millions of numbers and letters until it found the administrator's password. After a few hours, they were in. They created a new page about Vegoia with a bit of metadata attached instructing it not to be indexed on any search engine. That meant nobody could find it without being sent the link directly – whoever clicked on that page was their man. It only remained to see whether David would bite.

74

The dinghy bounced and skipped across the water, its outboard motor a high-pitched buzz in the hot still air. Jake was at the tiller – boats were his dad's thing so he knew how to handle one – and Jenny studied the map on her phone as they closed in on Burton's coordinates. Equatorial sun seared through a thin wash of cloud, turning the day into a haze so that the waves glinted a milky yellow. They hugged the Tanzanian side of the lake, a tangle of fishing villages strung along ruddy bays, the occasional cargo ship rusting on the sands. Naked children played in the water and fishermen punted dugout canoes.

"Another mile if Burton's coordinates are accurate," said Jenny.

"They will be."

Jake let the sun warm his face. He had the sudden conviction they *would* find the Book of Thunder here. They would burn it, that very day. They would celebrate; Jenny would come back to him.

"Look there!"

Jake followed her finger to where a stream issued into the lake, like a ribbon of brass in the sunlight threaded down the hills. When he saw the rocks half way down he felt as if his heart had been clenched in a fist. It was exactly as Burton described. Jenny had caught the sun, but there was a blush of triumph on her face too.

"I couldn't have done it without you," she said. "Absolute first rate investigative journalism."

Now Jake's own face turned red. He landed the boat, immediately spotted by three children who sprinted toward the foreigners. But the parabola of the two older boys' run converged and they hurtled into each other, heads colliding with an audible crack. One burst into tears, the other started laughing, and the tiny one charged straight through the middle before leaping into the air and wrapping his limbs around Jake with a delighted shriek.

*

A fishing village was strung along the river. One hut was an old cargo container with windows cut into it; another was made from oil barrels cut into strips and hammered straight, their circular tops lining the gunnels like the shields of a Viking ship.

"Such resourcefulness," said Jake.

"We explore?" Jake ventured to an old man who was repairing fishing nets.

"Hakuna matata," he replied.

As they walked away Jake grinned. "They actually say that here? Excellent."

They were singing as they walked to the river. *It means no worries, for the rest of your days …*

Nobody was swimming and soon Jake saw why. Two eyes protruded from the water, like black marbles shrink-wrapped in greyish skin.

"Up periscope," said Jenny with a faint smile.

The eyes retracted and the whole lake swelled as the hippo moved off.

"Subtle," said Jake.

"A master of subterfuge."

Villagers gathered as they examined the outcrop. One of the children held a corner of Jake's shirt proprietorially, tears drying on his cheeks. There were natural handholds and grooves in the rock, leading down to the river.

"We landed at a steep ghaut," intoned Jenny, projecting like a poet. "Where the crews swarmed up a ladder of rock."

"We're standing at the exact spot where Burton turned back," said Jake. "The furthest any European had penetrated into Africa at that time."

"Place of storms," said Jenny reverentially.

They had expected to find Burton's initials, or that eye symbol from his notepad. But the rock was devoid of markings.

"What if it's beneath?" said Jake. "We'll need dynamite."

"Don't be an idiot. How could Burton and Speke have shifted a rock this big?"

"I'll tell you what I'd have done," said Jake. "I'd have buried the *Disciplina* and planted a tree. Something with longevity."

"Look around you."

The riverbank was overgrown with bamboo and the occasional acacia, but nothing close to a century old.

"Anyway, what do you think would happen to a big tree here?"

Two fishermen sitting on a dugout canoe smiled and waved. Jake willed his brain to action, looking from notebook to the landscape and back to the notebook. Nothing. He opened a biography of Burton, looking up the infamous decision to turn back.

He paused.

His chin fell to his chest.

He sat down heavily on the riverbank, feet crashing into the water.

"Idiots." Jake laughed, long and hard and bitter. "We're total idiots."

"What do you mean?"

"It can't have been Burton. He's nothing to do with Palmerston's 'additional activities.'"

"But he has to be!" Something akin to anger in her voice. "All the Etruscan connections, the letter to Randolph Churchill."

"Coincidence." Jake's laugh had turned blasé, like someone told a daft joke. "All coincidence, my dear."

"But how do you know?"

Jake turned to face her. "Because Burton came here in 1858. And the invoice for travel expenses we found in the Foreign Office was dated 1865. The dates don't match up."

She sat down beside him. "We are idiots."

The littlest child blew a raspberry at them.

75

Freedom. Democracy.

Chloë stared at the words daubed on the hull of a fisherman's boat. But the paint was peeling and the jagged outline of a British warship lurked offshore.

"Are you ready, dear?" Dame Dot Whalley was the new governor of Sierra Leone. "Now might be a good moment for introductions."

Any sense of tranquillity vanished and the hubbub of the reception was in Chloë's ears again. The Queen's Birthday Party: a red-letter day in the Foreign Office calendar. An annual bash is thrown at every embassy to strengthen bilateral relations between the UK and its guest country – though in this case of course, those distinctions were blurred. Whalley had chosen a showy beachfront restaurant outside Freetown for this year's celebration, where the breeze made the climate manageable for men wearing suits. The Sierra Leonean elite mingled with British businessmen who had done well from the new order. The chief executive of British Petroleum was there – it was drilling offshore – as was the boss of British American Tobacco. Waiters bore canapés (lobster or rare beef on miniature Yorkshire puddings) and Pimm's was served; the tinkling of a grand piano weaved through the bodies. British soldiers kept the beggars and amputees at a respectable distance.

Chloë glimpsed the president's son talking to a Royal Marines major, evidently bored.

"There he is," said Whalley. "Into battle, dear."

The governor was statuesque, feet planted wide apart, sky blue blazer with portcullis pin signifying her time as an MP. With her pleated skirt and impressive bosom she had the air of a headmistress.

The last two days had been a whirlwind of forms to be filled in, medical and dental checks, political briefings. Chloë was glad to be off the Etruscan case. She'd hoped for something a bit less ... nasty. Then with sinking heart she'd been told to get close to the president's son.

Is that all I'm good for?

The job had come from C himself though. It had to be important.

Whalley touched the target on the elbow. "Alex? This is Chloë Aspinal, my new second secretary."

Alex Conteh beamed. "It is my pleasure! Please, welcome to Sweet Salone, Chloë."

He was short with a very round head, rumples of skin piled up on the cranium.

Chloë allowed her hand to be cupped with both of his. "A pleasure to meet you too, your excellency."

West African 'Big Men' expect the obsequies laid on thick.

"Chloë's here to look after our mining concessions," said Whalley, following the script. "I thought you might be a good person for her to know."

"But of course!" cried Conteh. "This is my little concern too. My father's mining company, I have run it for him for five years now."

"And I think I'm right in saying that you both studied English at Oxford," said Whalley.

Conteh's eyebrows shot up and he emitted a high-pitched "*Ee*" – the characteristic West African exclamation from Banjul to Brazzaville.

But before Chloë could reply they heard the roar of powerful engines and a frisson of excitement went through the crowd. The chairman of Jaguar had arrived in a 1950s XK120 Roadster, four brand new F Types in his convoy. The new roads made sports cars a viable proposition in the capital at least, and Conteh scampered away to have a look.

"I tried," sighed Whalley.

Chloë had to let *him* do the pursuing. She worked the room, keeping the princeling on her radar; ignoring him completely. A bottle-blonde Sierra Leonean woman had Conteh in her embrace now, all billowing dress and nail extensions. Chloë had that sweaty, sickly feeling of a career opportunity slipping away. Only once did Conteh look in her direction; he appeared to have a limited attention span.

It was dark when Chloë tried again. The bolder partygoers were waltzing. She stood close enough that he noticed her and stared out to sea, the breeze stirring her long silk dress to reveal a few inches of calf. The *Freedom* canoe had disappeared.

Conteh was beside her.

"So tell me, Chloë, which college did you study at? I am a proud Balliol man."

She deployed her most dazzling smile: the one that had almost entangled Jake. But before she could reply she was interrupted by the bash of a gong. The piano fell silent and a hundred heads turned. It was the 600th anniversary of Shakespeare's death, and some inspired soul had arranged for a scene from *The Tempest* to be performed. The cast were from the local International School: half British, half rich Sierra Leonean. The perfect showcasing of this special new relationship. Tables were cleared and the crowd gathered around.

When she recognised the scene, Chloë saw her chance.

> *Some sports are painful.*
> *Some kinds of baseness, Are nobly undergone.*

For this to work, she had to be directly opposite Conteh. She manoeuvred around the circle, lifting elbows and stepping over feet.

> *This my mean task,*
> *Would be as heavy to me as odious.*

Ferdinand's famous line was imminent. It had to be natural when she entered Conteh's line of sight, feel like his lead.

> *Poor worm, thou art infected!*
> *This visitation shows it.*

She was in position. She composed herself, letting a lock of lustrous chestnut brown hair fall across her chest. Far more ravishing than mortal man deserves.

The very instant that I saw you, did
My heart fly to your service.

At that exact moment Conteh's eyes were pulled to hers, by
that inexplicable force-field of attraction. Chloë held his gaze,
looked away – and blanked him for the rest of the evening. But
the damage was done, and sure enough three days later the
invitation came. The pretext was some new diamond contract
he wanted to discuss.

To make me slave to it.

76

"It's up there," said Jenny. "Watching us."
  "Or He."
  "Or She."
  Night had fallen on that side of Africa, and they were looking
at the stars from the hill above their campsite. Jake set much store
by Jenny's sixth sense, honed on scores of MI6 operations, and
when she had suggested removing to the upper slopes there was
no argument. Two shooting stars crossed the lake, then a third,
like a child catching up with its parents. The celestial voyagers
were mimicked by a manmade traveller as a satellite trundled
across the heavens.
  They were lying on soft grass, a gap between their bodies.
Close but not too close; and in that space Jake detected the conflict within her. He recalled her tears in Jerusalem – it was one of
the most powerful moments of his life. He had been convinced
they would be one again. And she'd voiced such respect for him
in Vienna, only to pull back. Had she taken him up here merely
as a precaution? Or did part of her *want* them to be alone in
such a setting? Then there was that other thing, that reluctance

he could sense but not explain. It was almost as though she felt *she* was not worthy of *him*, ludicrous though that might seem.

The man in Vienna? Something she had done?

He would forgive her almost anything.

Jake lay back on the grass and stared at the constellations. Taurus, Orion's Belt, Cancer. The stars burned through the black velvet of the heavens as if they were pinpricks, revealing a higher power behind.

"How strange it is," Jenny muttered.

"What's strange?"

"That even now, some people believe that the arrangement of balls of flaming gas configures your destiny."

Jake remembered Pasquier.

There was nothing to shield Napoleon from dangers brought on by his excessive confidence in his star.

"Strange?" he said. "No stranger than our fates being foretold by thunder."

What he did not say: the same fate that pushes us together, although you try to leave me. Like two positive magnets forced to touch. And sometimes when you do this, one turns. Plus meets minus, and connects. Fate had forced them to do this thing. What was the end design?

Another shooting star hurried after its family and he saw Jenny following it by the movement of her chin.

"What does your future hold, Jake?"

"I honestly dread to imagine."

"If someone could tell you – would you want to know?"

"No."

He closed his eyes, thinking not of his future but his past: the wild and elemental journey he had been on. National newspaper reporter; drunk; hunted man; bearer of a knowledge shared by a dozen people alive.

"*Jake ...*" she hissed.

He sat bolt upright. But no Chinese agents were ghosting through the undergrowth: he was looking at a caracal, pointed ears trembling with surprise at human presence on the hilltop. The cat darted off into the bush.

"Amazing place," said Jake.

Jenny drew her knees to her chest and stared towards the Congo. In the moonlight she had something of the Navaho Indian about her – a watchfulness, that nobility. He turned to the constellations again, thinking of all the explorers who had crisscrossed this land with those stars as their compass. There was the Southern Cross, four points of light forming the crucifix of Jesus. Which led to thoughts of …

"Oh my god," he said.

"Another caracal?"

"No. No! David Livingstone."

"Livingstone? What about him?"

"Additional agreed activities. Maybe Livingstone was Palmerston's man."

"But he *can't* have been," said Jenny. "Wasn't he a Christian missionary? Hardly a candidate for tramping around Africa to bury pagan texts."

"You wouldn't have thought Eusebius the sort either," said Jake. "A Christian scholar – and he kept the *Disciplina* from Emperor Constantine's bonfires."

Jenny checked her phone. "No signal. It's just coming up to 10 pm – if we go into town now we might be in time."

"For what?"

"To get online. I think we need to do some reading."

77

Kigoma's internet café was a breezeblock hovel with a cheery painting of a computer outside. It boasted two infirm Amstrads with yellowed housing, the letters long ago rubbed from the keyboards. A fan stirred the air and mosquitoes gambolled around a naked lightbulb. It took an age to warm up the machines and the internet connection was lamentable. But at once things began to leap out at them.

"Livingstone set off on his hunt for the source of the Nile in January 1866," read Jake. "That was three months after the death of Palmerston."

"The dates line up perfectly."

"And Jenny …"

It was a line by the historian Tim Jeal.

Stanley wrote that he sensed 'something seer-like' in Livingstone.

"You'd better tell me about Stanley and Livingstone's meeting," said Jenny. "What was it all about?"

"Dr Livingstone was hands down the greatest explorer of the age," said Jake. "A living legend. But during his final expedition he disappeared off the face of the earth. The smart money had it that he'd perished – and a brash young American called Henry Stanley was sent by the *New York Herald* to find him. Stanley knew nothing about African exploration, but he did have resources – and true grit."

"And Stanley actually found him."

"Astonishingly, yes. He tracked Livingstone down at a slaving settlement called Ujiji, very close to here. Livingstone was destitute, his stash of beads and copper having been stolen. That's when Stanley came out with the most famous line in the history of exploration."

"Dr Livingstone, I presume?"

Jake nodded. "Although many suspect he never actually spoke the words, because the pages in his diary describing their first encounter were ripped out. Cynics think he dreamt up some memorable first words long after the event. After travelling together for a while, Stanley went back to civilisation to file his story – but Livingstone kept on going. He finally died a couple of years later."

A power cut interrupted him. Two seconds later the lightbulb came on; it took thirty minutes to get the computers going again.

"Hello ..." muttered Jenny, staring at another article. "It says here that when they parted, the doctor instructed Stanley to take his diaries back to London for authentication. Not by the Royal Geographical Society. By the *Foreign Office*."

"Authentication," Jake repeated dubiously.

"Are those diaries published?"

"Of course – thank god for the nineteenth-century mania for diary writing."

"And Google Books," she said.

"If it ever loads ..."

The lightbulb went *plink*, the machines groaned and everything turned off again.

"Oh, Africa," said Jake to the darkness.

*

When the power came back they explored the doctor's journals.

"Livingstone said quite explicitly that finding the source is not actually important," said Jenny.

> *The Nile sources are valuable only as a means of enabling me to open my mouth with power among men. It is this power which I hope to apply to remedy an enormous evil.*

"We can take a guess at the power he's referring to," said Jenny. "But what's this enormous evil he's on about?"

"The slave trade," said Jake. "It all falls into place."

"How come?"

"Christianity wasn't the only thing that drove Livingstone," said Jake. "His life's work was to fight the Arab slave trade, which still flourished in Africa. He hoped that charting the African interior would open it up to ethical commerce and prosperity might follow, replacing the slave trade. To his mind, if the African people could be 'civilised', they might be strong enough to repel Arab slavers. Livingstone's goal was, in his own words, to *bring the light* to the African continent."

The only sound was the clatter of the fan and the rasping of insects outside.

"I think you might be right." Jenny's voice was tight. "Livingstone named the source of a river he discovered out here after Palmerston. Check out his reason."

I honoured the name of the good Lord Palmerston, in remembrance of his unwearied labour for the abolition of the Slave Trade. It pleases me, here in the wilds, to place my little garland of love on his tomb.

I have shed light of another kind, and am fain to believe I have performed a small part in the grand revolution which our Maker has been for ages carrying on.

"When Livingstone was brought into the Foreign Office's secret, he knew it had to be kept safe from Gladstone," said Jake. "Gladstone was emphatically *not* an imperialist. But ever since he was a young man, Livingstone had believed colonies were the best way to spread Christianity and trade in Africa. Like Palmerston, like Queen Victoria herself, Livingstone was a believer in *Empire*."

78

And suddenly Jake saw it very clearly. Rome; Napoleonic France; Victorian Britain; Nazi Germany. All had possessed the Book of Thunder at some point, but they had something else in common too. They were imperial powers. The Network and the actions of its devotees *tended towards empire*. That reminded Jake of something a quantum physicist had told him – the man who had first detected the consciousness's presence.

It is true that at our level – the level of planets, snooker balls, people – objects tend towards disorder. If you knock a plate off a table it shatters to thousands of pieces. You don't see shards of china leaping off the floor and reforming themselves. But at the level of the quark and the electron the opposite is true. Particles tend to order themselves ...

This was a game it played, and Jake renewed his vow to destroy the *Disciplina*. For freedom – and also for humanity. Because after imperium comes collapse, as night follows day, the whole ghastly cycle laced with death and anguish. Jake considered everything happening in the world at that moment. He hadn't been able to follow politics much recently, but he'd seen enough to know the Prime Minister had quite the Napoleon Complex. The *Disciplina* in the hands of Victor Milne? Jake shuddered to think of it.

A Third World War.

"Read this." Jenny interrupted his thoughts. "Another snippet from Livingstone's journal. He's haemorrhaging from cholera and on the brink of death."

An artery gives off a copious stream and takes away my strength; nothing earthly will make me give up my work in despair. Oh! How I long to be permitted by the Over Power to finish my work.

"The 'Over Power'. Doesn't that sound like a description of ..." Her eyes went up.

Jake heard the thrum of the Network within his skull.

"It does," he managed.

She looked at him curiously. Outside they could hear the distant rumble of thunder – but storms were a daily occurrence in central Africa. Jake tried to ignore it.

Jenny was staring at the screen.

"So it was Livingstone," she said.

25th October, 1870. In this journey I have endeavoured to follow with unswerving fidelity the line of duty, though my route has been torturous. Mine has been a calm, hopeful endeavour to do the work that has been given me to do. I had a strong presentiment through the first three years that I should never live through the enterprise. And an eager desire spellbound me. For if I could confirm the Sacred Oracles, I should not grudge one whit all the labour expended.

"Livingstone meant to do good," said Jake. "But the Over Power played him for a fool, had him do its bidding. All the time Livingstone was trekking through Africa he was, I don't know … *laying its eggs*. So it could spawn again, in our world. Today."

Jenny scratched her forearms. "Ugh. What a horrible analogy."

"Then let's firebomb the nest."

She nodded slowly. Her eyes were like the surface of Lake Tanganyika when the morning sunlight hit it, turning water into jade.

"We'll succeed where Burton failed," he said.

"How do you mean?"

"Lord Randolph must have sent Burton to collect it after Gladstone died – who better than a grizzled explorer who'd already been to the Great Lakes region? Remember Burton's letter to Lord Randolph?"

I beg you to favour me by placing my name on the civil list for a pension of £300. There are precedents for such a privilege, but I would not quote names unless called upon.

"The 'precedent for the privilege' must be Livingstone. And he's threatening to reveal the real reason for the return expedition if Churchill doesn't give him a pension of his own."

"But if Burton didn't find it, how are we supposed to?"

"Burton was tramping on foot through a malarial warzone infested by cannibalistic tribes."

"We're being hunted too, Jake."

"Touché."

"Anyway, let's get looking." Jenny returned to Livingstone's journal. "Because there must be *something* here. Some clue as to where he buried it."

At 3 am there was another power cut. They stood in the doorway to watch an inky mass of cloud over the lake, from which concentric rings of lighter-coloured nebula emanated like a magical void, or the flesh of some preternatural jellyfish. Without warning there was a crack of thunder like the splitting of rock, right overhead. Lightning raced from the north-west – tongue of dragon, flicking out across the water. It tore the heavens in two and a curtain of rain fell straight through the gap; the surface of Lake Tanganyika became murky and disturbed, the Congo beyond the water swallowed up by grey.

"The Over Power," whispered Jenny.

"It's angry."

*

It was 4 am when Jake spotted something else in Livingstone's diary.

The heathen philosophers were content with mere guesses at the future. The elder prophets were content with the Divine support in life and death.

The later prophets advance further: "Awake and sing, ye that dwell in the dust. The earth shall cast out her dead."

This seems a forecast of the future.

An ambassador at Istanbul was shown a hornbill spoon, and asked if it were really the bill of the Phoenix.

"God is great," said the Turk. "This is the phoenix of which we have heard so often."

"Prophets, forecasts of the future, the earth shall cast out her dead," said Jake. "You can't get much more of a signpost than that."

The good news was that Dr Livingstone had provided directions and coordinates. The bad news was that they were in Burundi. Which according to the BBC website was on the verge of civil war.

"I really didn't want to go there," said Jake.

79

"I'm Jacob. How do you do?"

"All right, fella? I'm Frank. Sit yourself down."

Their handshake was like the grinding of tectonic plates, and Parr smiled as the alpha males got acquainted. The friendly psychopath and the one-time explorer, projecting all the old school English reserve of Speke himself. It would be an interesting relationship. They sat under a tattered tarpaulin at Kigoma's central roundabout, half a mile from the internet café. An elderly Muslim gent boiled up coffee over charcoal in battered kettles, swatting flies from his face with a loop of horsehair.

"What do you make of it all, Jacob?" said Parr.

"The country?"

"The case."

Serval turned away, so she could see only his jawline and crow's feet. He was not smiling.

"Bloody screwy business," he said.

"You're telling me, son," said Davis, grinning widely.

"Mind you, it's as nothing compared to ..."

A little boy wearing a pirated Chelsea strip bounced past with an exaggerated stride, and Serval's voice trailed away.

"Nothing compared to *what* exactly?" Parr asked.

"Oh, never mind. Coffee!"

The old man blinked and shuffled off.

"Please," added Serval, remembering his upbringing. "Uncle. Salaam alaikum."

"Alaikum salaam." The elder's smile returned as he busied himself with pots.

"If I didn't know better I'd think I was off my rocker," said Davis.

"It's true, though," said Parr. "Every word."

Serval watched the little boy disappear over the hill.

"Took me a bit of getting used to, matey," Davis continued. "I don't mind saying …"

He was interrupted by roars and shrieks and the beeping of horns. A wedding party had crested the hill on a cavalcade of motorbikes and began circling the roundabout. The bride rode side-saddle, dress trailing by the back wheel.

"They just don't give a fuck," Davis laughed. "Evelyn was saying you're an old hand here in Bongo Bongo Land – so we'll be in safe hands if we have to go marching into the jungle, eh?"

Another forgotten something stirred in the explorer. "I'm an Amazonist actually. But the same principles apply. I walked across Siberia once as well."

Davis looked impressed. "I was in the army. SAS. Iraq and Afghan. Tora Bora in 2001 and siege of Saddam's palace."

Serval yawned. "Have we tracked this journalist and his girlie down yet? The ones we're playing phantom bodyguard to."

"Not yet," said Parr. "No one could get to Dar-es-Salaam airport in time for an interception, and it took a few more hours to work out they got an internal flight."

"We've got satellites crossing every hour," said Davis. "I'd say give it …"

Parr's phone rang and she stood up, passed a hand through silvery hair. "Thanks. Right. Yes of course, right away."

"Got 'em?" said Davis.

"They're an hour north – on motorbike. We need to get going."

Nobody moved.

"That's *now*, guys."

Davis leapt to his feet. "What's happening?"

"They're being chased."

80

The onrush of air battered Jake's head like the fists of a boxer. There had been no time to grab a helmet and a 100 mile per hour gale was in his ears; bugs became hailstones on his bare hands, skinning the knuckles. The casing of the engine was furnace hot – it seared his legs – and the tarmac was a blur that snaked and whistled beneath him. Jenny had her sunglasses on, but still she sheltered behind his bulk.

Up into the highlands they flew, bearing ever northwards: to Burundi. The mountains were triangles of green, sails of cloud streaming from their peaks as if they were on fire, Lake Tanganyika a plane of beaten silver visible through gaps in the range. In his wing mirror Jake saw the CIA agents on their BMW GS1200: the daddy of off-road bikes. Their pot shots were futile at a mile's distance – Jake had to maintain the gap. The Americans had the faster bike, he and Jenny weighed less; that left the BMW a slight speed advantage. But if there was one thing on god's earth Jake knew he was good at, it was riding a motorbike. When he approached a left bend he pushed the handlebars slightly to the *right*, leaning left to follow the curve – a technique known as counter-steering. This added traction, allowing him to corner at ferocious speed. What scared Jake more than gunfire was their lack of protective clothing. A tumble now would turn the road into a gigantic belt sander. Skin and flesh would be shorn from their bodies, their bones smashed as if by sledge hammers.

The distance between the two machines was unchanging.

Jenny had seemed distracted during the last hour at the internet café. She stood by the door, as if sensing what was on the other side, and she said four little words that electrified him.

"Out the back. Now."

As they ran through the stock room the front door was kicked open. They hurdled the owner, dozing on his veranda; hurtled through a vegetable garden, scrambled over a wall. Back into the street, where their scrambler was parked. Dawn had broken and the chase was on.

*

"They knew we were there!" Jenny shouted above the wind. "They always know …"

Women bearing bundles of firewood on their heads zipped past, then a crocodile of schoolgirls in hijabs.

"But you anticipated it," shouted Jake. "You're amazing."

She clung to his waist more tightly. "You're driving really well, Jake."

The words were torn from her mouth by the gale and deposited a hundred metres behind them. They overtook a motorbike with an oil barrel tethered on the back.

"What happens when we run out of petrol?" shouted Jake.

"I'm hoping we get to the border first."

"What happens at the border?"

She didn't answer. Jake had shooting pains in his forearms from the vibrations; at least it was a good road, compliments of the European Union. He considered what was coming. Burundi: fifth poorest nation on earth.

Suddenly they were at the border. Soldiers with Kalashnikovs manned a barrier, flagging them down. The Tanzanian flag fluttered above a low whitewashed building. The BMW was closing fast and he looked at Jenny for guidance.

"We've got to stop," she said. "They can't do anything with all these soldiers around."

Into passport control. The official took their documents, yawned and placed them on the desk. He scratched his nose.

"Actually, we are in a bit of a rush," said Jake. "If you don't mind."

The guard's nostrils flared. "There is not a rush here, sir."

"Of course not, no. Silly of me to ask."

"Never a rush."

"Sorry."

He shrugged and stamped both passports.

In the doorway Jake brushed shoulders with di Angelo. They did not make eye contact. The barrier was lifted, the tarmac ended. The buffer zone was eucalyptus forest, planted as a cash crop, and the motorbike bounced across muddy ground. Children peeped from the trees, grubbier than the Tanzanian youngsters, wearing torn floral dresses or rags. Soldiers were strewn about the Burundian border post in plastic chairs, in various states of repose. Their flag might have been dreamt up by Evelyn Waugh, and a police officer sweltered in a battered kiosk checking passports.

There was a queue.

The Americans joined them. Awkward silence.

"Nice ride, chaps?" asked Jake.

Di Angelo shook his head slowly.

"Blew away the cobwebs, I trust?"

He could detect Jenny's amusement.

Deissler smiled. "Pleasant enough."

Jake studied the insect head, those pointy teeth. His pupils were inscrutable behind sunglasses, but he had the air of someone who acknowledged how frightful he looked and worked with it. Revelled in it, even.

This man has been sent here with the express purpose of killing me.

"We'll see y'all in Burundi," said di Angelo.

"Oh, and do ride safe, boys," Deissler added.

The officer stamped their passports, but when Jake started for his bike he was called back.

"*Vérifier*," said the guard.

"*Vérifier?*" Jake repeated.

The guard pointed at a lean-to with a green cross sign. "Check."

A civilian sat at a table – to Jake's horror he saw a box of plastic gloves. The Burundian pointed a strange plastic gun right at Jake's face.

"*Œil*," he said.

"It means 'eye'," Jenny offered. "Lean in towards him."

Jake complied and the man zapped him in the pupil before inspecting a panel on the gun.

"*C'est bien*," he said pleasantly.

The process was repeated on Jenny, who murmured something in French and slipped him a $100 note.

What the hell is going on?

Up went the second set of barriers and they accelerated away, past a rusted sign that dangled by one corner.

Welcome to Burundi.

Bienvenue en Burundi.

Behind them the CIA team had got into difficulties.

"Would you like to tell me what all that was about?" Jake shouted as the scrambler lurched from bump to rut.

"He was checking your temperature," said Jenny. "Because of the Ebola outbreak, I guess. If you'd had a temperature they'd have done more tests."

"And the money?"

"Ah." She stifled laughter.

"What did you do?"

"I chucked him a little bribe."

Jake sensed devilment. "Go on."

She mimed the donning of a plastic glove. "Let's just say that right now our CIA friends are being subjected to some additional checks all of their own. Quite invasive ones, actually …"

81

Huw Edwards wore all the gravitas that had made him the BBC's go-to anchor for state occasions. And this was a state occasion of the oldest sort.

"We'll go now to our correspondent who's close to the front line," he told the viewers of the Six O'Clock News. "So Ben, what can you tell us?"

The cameras cut to a dusk scene in Nigeria. A pall of smoke hung over a landscape the colour of lion's flanks; the steady clatter of heavy machine guns was punctuated by the occasional explosion.

"Well, Huw, it certainly seems the waiting is over." The reporter looked unfeasibly dashing in body armour and helmet. "Because after a week of punishing airstrikes, earlier we saw the Challenger 2 tanks of the Household Cavalry simply *pouring* over the front line and into the bush, where I understand battle was met and is ongoing about two miles behind where I'm standing now. All day long we've seen footage of explosions in the stronghold of Kano – this is shock and awe, mark two. But it's worth just pausing for a moment to reflect how these scenes will be playing in households of families all around the Islamic world tonight. Because by my reckoning this is the eighth Muslim country since 9/11 we've seen some sort of British military action in. Let's count them. Afghanistan, Iraq of course, Yemen, Syria, Libya, Pakistan ..."

Three Eurofighter Typhoons streaked overhead, so low the sound was like a detonation and the reporter was sent staggering backwards.

"Oh *wow*," he exclaimed, knowing instantly this was a clip destined to be used in BBC News montages for decades. "And there you have it, Huw, a visceral demonstration of British military power. And *that's* why the Prime Minister is so confident that this war can be won in a matter of weeks ..."

He was interrupted as the director cut back to New Broadcasting House.

Huw Edwards was looking sombre. "And we're interrupting Ben there to bring you some very sad news, namely that of the first death of a British serviceman in this conflict. The Ministry of Defence has just told us a soldier serving with the 4th Battalion The Rifles was killed in an explosion earlier today. His family have been informed."

Kanisha switched off the television. She couldn't bear it. She was no lover of fanatical Islam – her father had suffered enough at the hands of the mullahs – but this felt *bad*, like Milne's own Iraq. He'd probably avoid a Chilcot Inquiry though; Milne had the Midas touch when it came to foreign policy. The international community had harrumphed about Operation Hausa Freedom, but basically decided to do nothing. That morning she'd read in the *Spectator* that the French were contemplating further involvement in Mali, their "Gallic dignity piqued" by the energies of these Anglo-Saxon rivals in West Africa.

Her brother rang.

"You watching the news?" she said.

"I know, madness. Listen up – you're gonna love me. You are going to *luuurve* me. Remember that little trap we set?"

Politics was forgotten. "Tell me!"

"Somebody clicked on our page yesterday."

"Where are they?"

"That's the weird bit – Tanzania. The IP address was an internet café in a little town called Kigoma. Middle of nowhere sort of place."

"How very strange."

The plot thickens.

Kanisha emailed her boss with a request for emergency leave.

82

Say hello to the Hutus.

They were mostly shorter and more powerful than Tanzanians, many with heavy cheekbones and beetling brows that lent a severity to faces already marked by hard-living. Expressions were stony, as if to say: what are *you* doing here? But men and women alike tended to have long, elegant eyelashes, and when Jake waved their faces were transformed into smiles.

The things they passed amply demonstrated the gulf between a poor country and one reduced to complete and utter beggary. A long-abandoned refugee camp; a faded banner that read *Pour réunification d'enlevées*. Like all Belgian colonies, this one had been left in a cataclysmic state: divide and rule had bequeathed decades of internecine warfare between Hutus and Tutsis. What hope had they? Jake sped through a border town with a scent of Mad Max in the wind and wound down mountains fringed with fir at the peaks, before evolving into a piebald tousle of red and green. The haphazard demarcations of subsistence farming were everywhere, a mud hut standing sentinel over each patch. They descended onto a plain of palm trees that stretched to Lake Tanganyika before heading north on the single arterial highway. The population was dense, crushed between water and mountain. The hoe was the implement of choice here; women balanced them on their heads as they walked, a synergy of posture and poise. Soldiers languished at hundred metre intervals. The strip of flat land grew narrower still, cramming ever more people into diminishing space. Bicycles were used for freight, piled high with bananas and wheels nearly buckling as the hauliers pushed them along. Jake saw one with ten foam mattresses on it, a gust of wind away from taking off. Another was overloaded with sacks and had capsized onto its back end, the front wheel spinning uselessly in the air. Battalions of schoolchildren hoed the land;

few of them wore uniform. As darkness fell the crowds melted away, leaving only soldiers. A convoy passed in the other direction – evidently a politician, for the blacked out Land Cruiser was followed by pickup trucks full of soldiers, each sporting a heavy machine gun.

"Big Man politics," suggested Jake. "They have to project power."

"On the contrary, a very sensible protection against a *coup d'état*," Jenny replied. "Now, turn off here."

He veered down a dusty track past bush and shacks. At once the motorbike was engulfed by children, running alongside and jumping for glee. They chanted a single word, over and over again.

"*Livingstone, Livingstone, Livingstone.*"

"Where is Livingstone?" said Jenny. "*Où est* Livingstone?"

But the children only jumped and scampered. "*Livingstone, Livingstone, Livingstone.*"

"What a guy," said Jake. "Dead for a century and a half, still a legend."

They were led down a path engorged with vegetation. The bush rasped with insects and the undergrowth rustled as indeterminate fauna scrambled for safety. Livingstone's coordinates took the pair through a forest of baobab and acacia, scattered with chunks of white crystal that threatened to sprain ankles.

"Jake …" Jenny gripped his biceps. "Livingstone's diary."

West through open forest; very undulating, the path full of angular fragments of quartz. We see mountains in the distance. A broad range of light grey granite; there are deep dells on the top filled with gigantic trees. Some trees appear with enormous roots, buttresses in fact. On the left a valley filled with primeval forests, into which elephants when wounded escape completely.

And there behind them was the mountain range. Kapok trees still stood at the peak, their sail-like roots silhouetted against a starry sky. Right on cue a valley opened up to their left, though the elephants were long departed.

"We are walking in the footsteps of Livingstone himself," said Jake.

An ambassador at Istanbul was shown a hornbill spoon, and asked if it were really the bill of the Phoenix.

"God is great," said the Turk. "This is the phoenix of which we have heard so often."

Did the phoenix not refer to the Book of Thunder, a firebird 'dwelling in the dust' to be cyclically reborn? Just as the Book of Thunder had regenerated throughout history. And Etruscan lore had an association with Istanbul: it was there that two years previously Jake found a passage of the *Disciplina* in the city's Roman underbelly. But what of the hornbill spoon? In Livingstone's day, local tribes used that bird's beak as a utensil. But he couldn't understand …

"The hornbill!" shouted Jenny. "There it is."

They had emerged into a clearing. In it stood a single rock, like a monolith of Stonehenge, its bulbous sides recalling unequivocally the hornbill's beak. Children led them by the hand, like a young couple submitting to the altar of pagan sacrifice. Words were carved into the granite.

LIVINGSTONE
STANLEY
25-XI-1871

"So they came here together," said Jake.
"But that makes no sense …"

*

"Would Livingstone have let Stanley in on his secret?" asked Jenny.

"I doubt it. But Livingstone could have waited until he was alone to bury the *Disciplina*. Stanley would disappear for days at a time hunting big game."

"*If* anything's buried here," said Jenny.

"Hmmm." Jake glanced at the eldest child, a beautiful girl of ten with a shaved head. She clutched the broken tip of a machete. "*Aidez-moi, s'il vous plaît?*"

The girl nodded and blinked. "*Oui. Pour-quoi?*"

He turned to Jenny. "What's the French for shovel?"

83

Chloë counted the playboy's breaths slowing down by the second hand of his carriage clock. Only six inhalations per minute now, softer each time. This was how a child slept: zephyrs of tranquillity escaping him as he entered catatonia. When Chloë was certain he was under, she slipped out of bed and padded across the room. She located her skirt (he had *ripped* it down, *thrown* it across the room) and from the waistband she extracted a tiny USB drive. She turned on his laptop and opened the password reset wizard. In went the USB drive, which tried ten million combinations per minute. His desktop was a shot of an infinity pool on the French Riviera; five clicks later she had copied the entire contents of his computer and the USB stick went back into her skirt. Conteh had a spaced-out smile on his face as she slid into bed next to him, his eyelids fractionally parted, hand on groin.

The laptop was thought to contain evidence of Conteh's lurid financial interests. But it wasn't connected to the internet, physical space being the best protection against hacking. Only one member of his staff was allowed into his room, and she was deemed unreliable. That was why Chloë had become the new second secretary at the British Embassy. The government wanted some hold on Conteh and his father, though why she knew not.

Now she had the data.

Chloë should have been exhilarated; this was proper, old school espionage. Instead she felt dirty, like a prostitute. She *was* a prostitute. A sexual weapon of Great Britain, wielded to expedite outcomes she wasn't privy to, taking it on blind faith that they were Worth It. It hadn't been so bad with Jake. He was palpably decent, nice enough looking. And what they were after had the power to change the world. But Conteh was *horrid* – an arrogant lover, violent in his thrusting and tearing. He had licked her cheek. She looked at him now, dissecting each detail of the scrunched up face before her. White lines of spittle had formed in each corner of his mouth.

C had assured her the gamma-hydroxybutyrate would knock him out before he was able to perform. MI6 knew his bodyweight and calculated the dosage; she slipped the powder into his cognac exactly as directed. But Conteh was so randy he'd barely noticed it, the primordial desire to mate trumping even chemistry. If she snubbed him she might not get another invite. So she had made a split-second decision: Chloë Aspinal (née Smith, née Fleming) lay back and thought of England.

Only there was a snag. For when Conteh awoke he had an announcement to make, and with rising distress Chloë watched him sink onto one knee.

"I want to marry you." He giggled wildly, threw himself on the bed. "Miss Chloë, I love you very much indeed. I have never, ever met a lady like you."

Silken boxer shorts swelled by the second; a dozen sloppy kisses assailed her and she shuddered involuntarily.

Conteh pulled back, as if stung. "What's the matter? Don't you love me any more, Miss Chloë? Last night you were *hot* for me I think, yes?"

Opiate bliss slid across his face at the recollection. It was her duty to lead him on, to see whether further advantage could be eked from this situation.

After he'd had his way with her again, Conteh became expansive. He talked of their future, made grand plans. Chloë had seen this look dozens of times before: he had fallen head over heels in love.

"First I must tell my fiancée. Oh golly golly, that will cause a stink."

The woman at the reception with the bottle blonde hair. Another innocent about to receive a broken heart with compliments of Vauxhall Cross.

Conteh was prattling on. "She is from an important family here. But never mind, eh? A worm, I am infected. This my mean task is heavy and odious."

"Don't do it."

"Why?" A flicker of anger. "Don't you love me too, Chloë?"

"I … yes, yes I suppose I do."

"Let me tell you about the life we can have together, you and I." His voice had become throaty. "Your family – they are rich?"

"They're comfortably enough off."

"And me. Do you think I am a rich man?"

She looked at the expanses of gold leaf, the fish tank, the gigantic plasma screen.

"Oh, you're a very rich man," she said, channelling dreaminess.

"It is not so. I can tell you truthfully, I have maybe ten million dollars. But soon, I will be a very rich man. I will be like Mr Abramovich, and have a yacht and a football club. Would you like to be the wife of a billionaire, Chloë? Is that what you have always dreamed of?"

"Yes," she said.

No, she thought. I'd like a nice-looking guy who's a solicitor or an architect. Someone from the Home Counties perhaps, a rugby player type who wants children and dogs.

"In one year's time, we can both be billionaires," he whispered.

"How?"

A crafty look was his eyes. "This Ebola that has killed so many. Did you think it was a *natural* thing?"

She frowned. "Of course it was natural."

A high-pitched chuckle. "Oh, but there was nothing natural about this outbreak."

"What the hell do you mean?"

It came out sharper than she'd intended, but Conteh was at sea on dreams of wealth and of her.

"Your British Secret Service planted it here, Chloë."

*

She burst out laughing.

"Oh, you are all the same, you British, you white people," Conteh spat. "Did you not think that we Sierra Leoneans could have a secret service too? Did you think we black people are too stupid?"

"I don't think you're stupid," she said. "I think you're wonderful." That placated him.

"So." He took her hand. "Let me tell you. We followed a Welshman. He was pretending to be a doctor. We watched him with his needles, his vaccines, here in Freetown, Upcountry. But everyone he treated – they fell sick, Chloë."

"I don't believe you. It's the most ludicrous story I've ever heard."

"But I have the proof." Conteh's eyes went to his laptop. "Photographs. And, how do you say it in English? Intercepts and suchlike."

"But why on earth would we do that?" she persisted. "We were the ones out here helping the sick."

"Because *you people* want to take over here again," he hissed. "This was always the plan. And the disease has helped you do so – has it not?"

She couldn't deny it.

"If you have evidence," she began, "… why keep it quiet?"

Something approaching shame in Conteh's face then, but his chest swelled with fresh reserves of bombast.

"How much do you want to be a billionaire, Chloë?"

She smiled bravely. "Lots and lots."

"Me too. Lots and lots and lots. It's not such a fun life here, being the big fish in a small pond. So my father and I, we had a plan. Not so stupid after all. That's why we decided. We will *let them* take over. We will gather our evidence. And the British Secret Service will have no choice. Ten billion of your taxpayers' pounds will be the down-payment for our silence, and it will only be the start. That is *our money*, Chloë! Our money, you and I!"

She smiled sadly. Oh, but you are mistaken, Alex Conteh. If what you say is true, you and your scheming father won't see a penny. They'll assassinate you both for sure.

On the other side of the room: the laptop, violated, just as she had been. Chloë's gaze returned to the hem of her skirt.

84

"The World Health Organisation is able to declare the end of an Ebola outbreak after forty-two days with no new cases," said the director-general with the chic haircut and the extravagant Swiss-French accent. "This represents twice the maximum incubation period for Ebola. I can confirm ..." and here Natalie Le Clerc paused, revelling in the moment, "that today Sierra Leone reached the forty-two day mark. And it is therefore an *Ebola free country*."

She slapped her hands on the lectern and the press conference erupted into cheers.

"The World Health Organisation commends the British government," she continued. "Without its strong leadership and the exemplary engagement with traditional leaders, I would not be in a position to make this declaration. However many deaths may have occurred, I do not doubt that without British help it could have been so much worse. That's why it gives me great pleasure to introduce a very special man, who landed in Geneva only one hour ago to share with us this special moment. Ladies and gentlemen, I give you – the Prime Minister of Great Britain."

Victor Milne hurried onto the stage, grinning like a Cub Scout in receipt of a nationwide trophy. He pecked the Swiss on both cheeks and gave her a third on the smacker for good measure, then swung to face the blaze of flashes, little pewter eyes scanning for journalists of note.

"Thank you for those kind words, Madame Le Clerc," said Milne. "You do me too much honour."

Abruptly the smile fell from his face and in that instant, reared up before the World Health Organisation logo – a world map, serpent coiled around it – he resembled some diabolical mega-villain in his lair.

The room fell quiet.

"This is a big moment for Sierra Leone," he said. "But it's also a time for reflection on the enormous sacrifice made by the many British doctors and nurses who laid down their lives to get us to this point. And of course, on the heroism of Britain's Armed Forces that made this selfless work possible. Because without stability, there can be no medical response. Without peace, no advancement. Without security, no eradication of this ghastly, frightful, murderous disease."

Le Clerc was nodding in agreement.

"But this is no time for complacency," Milne continued. "Because we've got another fight on our hands, a bigger fight. For I say to the Nigerian people, *we will not rest until your country is Ebola free too.*"

The director began clapping.

"And wherever Ebola may blight in the future, whatever corner of the world that may be in, I make the same free and frank offer of British help in those lands. In times gone past, Europeans looked at the world and asked what it might do for them. In this brighter age, we must ask the world what we can do for its people."

Furious scribbling in notepads.

"But I did not come here today merely to talk about Ebola. I also came to address the people of Sierra Leone directly. Because

Ebola is not the only pestilence stalking that beautiful country. Malaria kills twice as many people each year, as do typhoid and cholera. In our short time in Sierra Leone, we've seen great strides in sanitation and health education. But the work's only half done. I want to see a Sierra Leone where every town has its own hospital, every village a doctor, every bed a mosquito net. My dear people of Sierra Leone, you are our brothers and our sisters. That's why I make this further offer. Give our doctors the honour of continued residence in your mountains and forests, and we the British people *will not rest* until the life expectancy in Sierra Leone is equal to any state in Western Europe. That is our pledge."

Another round of applause filled the room. The director-general was wreathed in smiles, giddy at the unexpected commitment. Even Milne was flushed.

"Thank you, thank you," he said. "Let me finish by paraphrasing another great Prime Minister ..." At once Milne realised the gaffe – *another* – and he hesitated, calculating the damage. They would hang that one around his neck. But the crowd was in a frenzy and he bulldozed on. "Where there is discord, may we bring harmony. Where there is despair ..."

*

Milne was led from the building on a wave of triumph.

"Is this to be your legacy, Prime Minister?"

"What do you make of all this talk of a Nobel Peace Prize, Prime Minister?"

"Where's the money for this going to come from, Prime Minister?"

The money? Why, *from Sierra Leone herself* of course. From the coltan and the oil rigs, from the diamond mines and rubber plantations. From the vast maws they would tear in virgin rainforest for copper and gold, from the newly-cleared plains where cows would graze and coffee would thrive. And all of it run by a nationalised capitalism, taking as its model the China of the last decade, faltering though that country's economy finally was. Because when the Book of Fate was his, Britain would *do it better*. That would pay for a few poxy mosquito nets, with billions to spare. And thence to Nigeria, already tumbling into his grasp. And thence to India, which he couldn't snaffle unaided – but if he knew in advance what ruses would succeed? He'd be unstoppable. And thence – who knows? No country on earth could not be Britain's again, could not be his. But he brooked no more questions, he stopped for no man, surging through the throng of reporters like a galleon in full sail.

Only when he reached his car did the jubilation wither. It was replaced by *hunger*. His spymaster was in the back; and Milne had bigger fish to fry.

"So tell me," he said as the BMW slalomed through the streets at high speed, the police driver piloting it with the pomp of a gold medal winning skier.

"We're going to the British Consulate General," said C. "Things are moving in Burundi."

85

"I know what you're thinking," said Jenny.

Jake was panting and he stood with his hands on his waist, like a footballer calculating an eighty-ninth minute free kick.

"What am I thinking?"

"That we are perpetrating an act of archaeological vandalism."

An hour's labour had produced a three-foot pit under the stone; one decent push and it would topple. A dozen children looked on in wonderment.

"You know me too well."

They heaved, and it fell in slow motion – before crashing into the dirt with a *whump* that engulfed them in dust. The night was full of screeches of disbelief from the Burundian contingent. A bowl of compacted earth was revealed, undisturbed for a century.

Jake began digging once more.

"What is that thing?" Milne studied their progress via geostationary satellite.

"A monument," said C. "Engraved by Stanley and Livingstone when they camped there."

"Stanley and Livingstone? Why them?"

C was a study in ignorance. "I'm sure we'll have some theories soon. But more pressingly ..."

He selected another feed. A motorbike, two riders, speeding along the lake.

"The CIA," he said.

"How far away?"

"Twenty miles. So give it fifteen minutes, at these speeds."

"Do they know Wolsey's location?"

"Most probably," said C.

"Where's our side?"

"They crossed into Burundi an hour ago. It'll be another hour before they arrive. Executive decision time."

The screen cut to a map of eastern Africa; a green dot moved steadily west at Mach Two, closing on Burundi.

"I scrambled a Eurofighter from HMS Queen Elizabeth," said C. "She's lying off the coast of Tanzania."

"So you've unilaterally invaded the airspace of a sovereign nation," muttered Milne.

"You were giving a speech."

"Not to worry, you did the right thing. How long before it can intercept the Yanks?"

"We should reach the location with two minutes to spare. Then it's a Brimstone missile, if you see fit. That makes it thirteen ..." he checked his watch. "No, twelve minutes to make the call."

"Saints preserve us." Milne stood up and stuffed both hands in his pockets. "I didn't get into politics to kill Americans, you know."

"Hold on, wait ..." C had returned to the first satellite. "Something's happening, sir."

"Jake. Look behind you."

He continued pumping the spade into the ground, earth cascading over one shoulder.

"Jake," she hissed again.

Crunch.

Metal hit metal, just below the surface. When Jake turned his smile fell away like a stage curtain. Ten men stood there, armed with Kalashnikovs, Belgian FN FAL rifles, old revolvers and just for good measure one pitchfork.

He dropped the spade.

"Rebels," said C. "Or a pro-government militia. In practical terms it doesn't really matter which."

"What's their prognosis?" said Milne.

"It's an African civil war – so total lottery. Killed, arrested or kidnapped. Unless Frobisher can talk her way out of it."

"You are *spies*." The commander's face was a web of scar from some ancient immolation. One ear had been burned away completely, the other melted down until only a spire remained: like the ear of a goblin.

He enunciated with a slow hatred. "Spies, sent here to help the usurper."

"We're not spies," said Jenny calmly. "We're archaeologists."

"Archaeologists?" His head flinched to one side like a cockatoo. "What meaning you, archaeologists?"

"Historians," said Jake. "From a university in England. Here to study this monument."

He reached for his wallet, but the movement startled them and every barrel pointed at his head.

"Please leave this to me," said Jenny.

"This is *war*," shouted the commander. "What history guy is coming to a war? No. You are foreign maggots, here to meddle in our affairs. Are you not?"

"Sir," began Jenny. "I can assure you that ..."

But the commander's attention was no longer with her. His gaze had fallen to the hole; to the spot where the moonlight played on an alien surface beneath the topsoil.

Something metallic.

86

"What about dropping a Brimstone on them?" asked the Prime Minister.

C sized up the distance between the soldiers and their captives. He had overseen the Kill List and vaporised enough British passport holders of dubious loyalty to have a good working knowledge of air-to-surface missiles. Their accuracy, the dispersal of the explosion, shrapnel spread.

"Heads we take out the militia, tails we kill everybody there," he said. "Not *such* a disastrous result, perhaps?"

Milne looked contemplative. "Unless they've actually discovered something. We don't want that getting fragged too, do we?"

"Good point, as ever." C picked up his phone. "Sir Alan?"

With a pop they were through to the RAF Deputy Commander of Operations. "Dennis."

"Does your plane have machine guns?" asked C.

"Damned silly question, Dennis. Single Mauser cannon on board. Will serve up mincemeat at the touch of a button."

C ignored the impertinence. "Disregard the motorbike for now, we've got some human targets for you. Ten men, stationary, on the shore of the lake."

They heard a puff of air on the receiver, like a mechanic peering into a troublesome engine.

"Rather difficult, I'm afraid. The plane's just cleared a big range – he needs to lose a lot of height. He'd have to turn two sides of a triangle and flatten out over Lake Tanganyika to get a clear run, with a pretty hair-raising ascent to avoid the mountains on the way back. He'd also pop up on the radar of about four more countries. Why not just blow them up?"

"They're standing two metres away from a man and a woman we'd rather leave unharmed. Can you take out one group but not the other?"

"You're talking about a supersonic jet, not an attack helicopter," he scoffed. "That cannon spits out 1,700 rounds a minute. And we'll be shooting at speeds of, ooh I don't know, 800 miles an hour on the final approach."

"Can it be done?"

"We can try – but I certainly couldn't *guarantee* we won't hit them." Milne gave C the thumbs up.

"I'm sending you the coordinates now," said C.

"How soon is this meant to happen?"

"As soon as bloody possible!"

"We'll need three minutes to line up the shot."

"The motorbike's three minutes and twenty seconds away," C told Milne.

Diamonds of perspiration had formed on Milne's brow. "Why must these things always have to be so effing tight?"

The commander's eyes had become round as bowls. "What are you digging there?"

"I told you," said Jenny patiently. "We're archaeologists."

"*Vous et vous*," he snapped at two of his men. "*Déterrez!*"

One used the spade, the other the pitchfork, and within a minute a rectangle of metal had been uncovered in the soil.

"Pick it!" the commander urged, frantic now. "Pick it out of the ground!"

But the men were unable to get any purchase and their fingernails slid uselessly on the metal.

"*C'est trop lourd*," one of them gasped.

Four more militiamen joined in the struggle and inch by ungainly inch the object was exhumed.

It was a chest.

A claw of steel was in Jake's abdomen, clamping and constricting.

The old Romans had a fable ...

"*C'est très très lourd*," panted a fighter.

Behind the commander's big glinting eyes an awakening was taking place. He stared from Jake to Jenny and back to the chest.

"Treasure! You are treasure hunters!"

Jenny shook her head, but the captain was having none of it.

"That is why you came here at time of war. It is *British gold*, from the olden times!"

He seized the spade and began clanging at the padlock.

"The chest's made of lead," Jenny observed. "That's why it was so heavy."

Another tightening of the screw.

They heard a jet plane passing low over the lake, away to the north. It was obliterated by a gunshot as the commander blasted the padlock, and the chest was prised open with a screech of long unmolested hinges. Jake peered over the bobbing heads.

It was empty.

"Empty!" The captain's eyes goggled with fury.

Unexpectedly a change came over him. His mouth erupted into a face-splitting grin revealing the gap between his front two teeth, fleetingly adorable, and he roared with laughter.

"Empty! You risk everything to come here – for nothing!"

In Geneva the Prime Minister's sweat was flowing freely.

The motorbike was a mile away. Over the lake, the sound of jet engines pushed to their limits. Up in space, one of the most sophisticated lenses ever made swivelled and contracted as it fought for a view into the chest.

RAF Command pushed Milne for a decision.

"Leave here," said the militiaman. "Once you have paid your, ahem, 'fine.'"

A Eurofighter Typhoon took shape in the gloom before rushing towards them with dizzying speed. The group had begun to disperse and at the last possible moment Milne called off the strike. The plane jerked abruptly higher, passing two hundred feet overhead with a supersonic crack and a roar of powerful engines. Unnoticed in the pandemonium: a motorbike, two miles inland and making for the capital. The red of its taillights zigged and zagged like a firefly, growing fainter before disappearing completely.

Jake studied the diamond wing-shape as it gained altitude before passing over the mountains, becoming lost amongst cloud.

"That was a Eurofighter," he said. "I didn't think they had those out here."

"Neither did I," said Jenny shrewdly. "Neither did I."

87

"I'm looking for a man."

Instantly Kanisha knew she'd made a mistake – two days in Africa and she'd had a dozen proposals. The café owner's eyebrows ricocheted up his forehead and he opened his mouth.

"His name's David," she cut in. "He was online here on Monday. But you seem nice too."

Eric Bafadhili was a corpulent man wearing a jazzy shirt. He doubled with laughter and high fived her. "No problem, madam. Your David, he is surely a lucky man. He was here? In this shop?"

"In this shop."

Kanisha liked Kigoma. It ran at a balmy and languorous pace, the inhabitants drifting up and down the sloped streets as if by process of convection. In the tattered market the hunks of beef had an attendant beard of flies, shimmering and oily, and women in brightly-coloured robes squatted in the dust with the day's catch, cackling to each other. A policeman strolled around the corner and in a flash the women were gone, spoiled fish and rolling vegetables in their wake.

"What can he do?" Bafadhili's face was a picture of resignation. "They are not permitted to sell here, and yet they come. So, your David. What does he look like?"

"I – er, I don't know."

"You *don't know*? What is this?"

"He's a colleague." She surprised herself with the fluency of her lying. "But I've never met him. He's gone missing. I need to track him down."

"He is British too?"

Another twitch of embarrassment. "I ... I think so."

"Eeesh, you crazy, lady! Let me see ..." He counted back the days on his fingers. "Monday. Yes, I had several white men on Monday."

"Several." *Great.* "What did they look like?"

"First man is easy to describe. He is very tall and strong. Grey hair, but with a white spot, here." Bafadhili touched his temple. "Always saying, *hello mate, hello mate,* like this."

Kanisha giggled.

"He was with another man. Orange hair, but not orange-orange. Brown also. Like ..."

"Auburn?"

"Yes, auburn. He has small beard, not shaving for one week only. He is also very strong. But not a friendly man. A bit ... tired. In his eyes, you know? I think he had a sick soul. Englishmen, both of them. I think maybe policemen. Or soldiers."

Not academics, anyway.

"Later it was two Americans. One of them is old and thin, like a man who has not eaten for a *whole week*." The businessman's voice turned shrill at the thought of it. "His friend was a black man, like me. Very tall, and his face is like this."

As Bafadhili sucked his cheeks in Kanisha stifled another laugh.

"Man number five," the café owner continued. "A very polite man, very friendly man. Also English – a *gentleman*, as you might say. Has brown hair, cut like so-so."

He did a commendable impression of a pair of clippers.

"Right," said Kanisha, thinking this was her man. "How old?"

"Maybe 35? But dressing like the respectable type. I say he is college professor or some-such."

Definitely her man.

"Did you get a name for this guy?"

The shopkeeper was downcast. "Oh. No. But I know where he went ..."

"Wow! How do you know that?"

"This nice man, he asked me directions to Burundi. I tell him not to go, it is very dangerous. Not safe like here in Tanzania. But that is where he was going with his girlfriend and he would not listen."

"Damn. That's problematic."

"And the American men ..." Something in his manner alerted Kanisha to an incoming revelation. "They were following him. So also to Burundi, I think."

She frowned. *What the flip was going on here?*

"Do you know where in Burundi?"

"I'm afraid that I do not. But please, madam. What is this all about?"

She smiled. "Dude – it's complicated."

So, Burundi. That was that: she could no more go there than rock up in northern Nigeria and say hello.

88

Together Jake and Jenny admired the anarchy of a truly benighted developing world capital. Rugged mountains surrounded Bujumbura, pooling the heat and the moisture, and the rains had churned the unpaved streets into an urban Glastonbury. Untold multitudes squelched through the mud. The shops were low and gaudily painted – he saw a *Magasin la Chance*, an *Optique la Merveille* – and the roof of the central market had caved in long ago as a result not of shelling, but poor construction and design. Pickups were parked in every available space, so the *Centre Ville* resembled a gigantic car park. Through this obstacle course milled the population, doing their best to replicate normality as all hell broke loose outside city limits. Presiding over the scene was what remained of the army, a rag-tag collection of teenagers with heavy weapons.

"If we ever get married ..." said Jake.

Jenny looked up sharply.

He grinned. "This is where I'm coming for the stag do."

Jenny reckoned Bujumbura was safer than the countryside, where anything could happen. But the habitually gung-ho *Lonely Planet* did not make good reading.

The capital isn't exactly the safest city in the region, so keep your wits about you. It is imperative to use a taxi or private vehicle once the sun goes down.

By night it was a scary place, devoid of any street lighting whatsoever: trips and falls were as much of a hazard as the muggers. Their hotel was both grotty and ruinously expensive, prices skewed by UN staff, though all had departed. Now they sat with a morning coffee, marvelling at Bujumbura's take on rush hour.

"Mill hour," said Jake. "If you will. Not much rushing. Plenty of milling about."

"How could the chest be empty?" Jenny lamented for the fifteenth time. "It makes no sense ..."

"Because it was a decoy?"

She considered this. "Why would Livingstone plant a decoy?"

"His journals were being ferried back to Whitehall by many hands – through Zanzibar and Aden on the way. Those places were hardly short of rogues and chancers in Livingstone's day. They might be seen by anyone."

"So what?"

"So he needed to be sure nobody could follow his clues without full state support. Only the largesse of a nation would be enough to finance and execute an expedition to several locations somewhere like this."

Jenny sighed. "Which means we're light years from finding it."

"But we're getting *closer*." Jake grabbed her hand and held it, and she did not pull away. "Think how far we've traced it. From Italy in the time of Hannibal. To Egypt, where it lay undisturbed until Napoleon's expedition. From Paris to Westminster, as recorded by Sir Neil Campbell – and right on through the imperial age in all its grandeur. And not to Burton, but Livingstone. That chest is the *proof* we were correct. It's an amazing bit of detective work we've done, Jenny, and we've done it with the intelligence services of three countries out to get us."

He could have sworn her lower lip wobbled. "*We* didn't do it. You did it."

"I couldn't have done it without you."

She lifted his fingers from her hand one by one and withdrew it. "If the monument *was* a decoy – let's read."

They dived back into Livingstone's field journals.

"What about this?" suggested Jenny. "It's describing his stay in Zanzibar, before he ventured into the mainland."

The explorer had reproduced a letter to the Sultan from the Governor of Bombay, Sir Henry Bartle Frere.

Your Highness is already aware of the benevolent objects of Dr
Livingstone's life and labours, and I feel assured your Highness
will direct every aid to be given which may further the designs
to which he has devoted himself, and which are viewed with
the warmest interest by Her Majesty's Government.

"What do you think?" said Jenny. "The 'benevolent objects' could
be the annals of the *Disciplina Etrusca*. Could he have hidden it
at his house in Zanzibar? An elaborate double bluff?"

Jake studied the page for a long time.

"No, I don't think so," he said at last. "First, I doubt the
Governor of India would have been privy to a secret this explosive – let alone an Arab Sultan. Second, it would defeat the
entire object of hiding it somewhere fantastically remote. A
future owner carries out renovations and bingo, a roadmap of
the future is in his hands."

They continued through the pages. Encounters with wild
animals; depictions of tribal culture; moments of real beauty. At
one of his lowest malarial ebbs, the doctor had written:

As I sat in the rain a little tree-frog half an inch long leaped
onto a grassy leaf, and began a tune as loud as that of many
birds, and very sweet; it was surprising to hear so much music
out of so small a musician.

"So small a musician," Jake murmured. "That's lovely."

Damn it, he really liked the man! Perhaps he felt an affinity
with him – a fellow traveller, bound to his mission in the belief
he was doing good.

"What about this?" said Jenny, indicating another entry.

Jake thumped the table. "That's it. It's there. That's where he
buried it."

The land of Kanagumbé is a loop formed by the river, and is
large. The chief is believed to possess great power of divination,

even of killing unfaithful women. We passed near the rounded masses Ngozo and Mekanga. They are over 2,000 feet above the plain and nearly bare. The striae seem as if the rock had been partially molten: at times the strike is north and south, at others east and west. It is as if the striae had been stirred with a rod. The tattoo of the tribe resembles the drawings of the old Egyptians; wavy lines, such as the ancients made.

The *strike*. And in Jake's mind those lines of the old Egyptians were not wavy, but jagged. Bolts of lightning, such as the ancients made.

It was time for the daily storm.

89

"Well how are we meant to get across that, then?" said Davis.

Serval's pupils contracted as he measured the breadth of the swamp. "I don't know. I'm not altogether sure that we can." And *sotto voce*: "It's not meant to bloody well be here."

He silently cursed the vagaries of African cartography. The wide flat river they'd just crossed was marked, sweeping through the landscape in a stately curve; also delineated were the headlands up ahead, 2,000 feet of bare pink rock protruding from the bush. Evelyn Parr was up on those heights with a CheyTac Intervention sniper rifle on the lookout for Americans or Chinese. The intermediate ground was described as light forest – instead they faced a morass of black water, walls of undergrowth erupting from the quagmire. The treeline indicated where decent ground began, half a mile yonder. It might as well have been an infinity away.

Serval radioed Parr. "We've got a problem."

"I know, I can see. You're going to have to cross."

"Evelyn, do you have any idea ..."

"I've seen the Americans," she interrupted. "They're about a mile behind Wolsey and closing."

Jake and Jenny had spent the morning sheltering from the thunderstorms in Bujumbura. After lunch they departed, driving for three hours to the edge of the habitable plain separating Lake Tanganyika and the highlands. Now they were skirting the pink cliffs. Davis and Serval had kept to the low ground, so they could get close if Wolsey found anything. And now this. Serval shook his head slowly as he contemplated the undertaking.

"I thought you were a bleeding explorer," said Davis. "Surely you can get across these things?"

"Normally I go around them."

The band of swamp stretched out of sight in both directions.

"I am ordering you to cross," snapped Parr.

"So be it," said Serval. "If England's becoming so cowardly that travel shall cease in dangerous countries because some fall victim to it, then it's time to roll up the English flag and admit the decline of the English spirit."

"What's that?" said Davis.

"Just something an explorer said in the nineteenth century." Serval cut himself a stick and handed him another. "I'll lead. Step *exactly* where I step. If you can tread on reeds or vegetation, do so. We're going to be knee deep in this stuff, so the key is to start lifting one leg while the other is sinking in – like you're *gliding* across. It's all in the technique. Never ever put all of your weight on one foot."

"Understood, fella."

"And if you go into quicksand, for god's sake don't thrash about. Keep calm and drop onto your hands and knees. Better messy than de…" Serval hesitated. "Than in quicksand. Try to float and make your surface area as big as possible."

"Will there be wild animals in there?"

"We're in Africa. Of course there'll be bloody wild animals."

Davis wore a gaping smile; the bugger was actually enjoying this.

"But this undergrowth looks a bit thick for hippos," said Serval. "We can count that as a blessing."

"We don't have all day," chimed in Parr.

"Do you want us to make it across or not?" shouted Serval. "Believe me, it's better we have this conversation now, rather than out there in ten minutes time when things are going wrong." He turned to Davis. "Look Frank, this is going to be hard work. The suction's a killer. It'll be like gravity times ten – three hundred yards an hour will be good going. Are you ready for this?"

"As I'll ever be, sunshine!" He slapped his hands together and rubbed them. "But before we crack on, be straight with me. How risky is this?"

"We'll be absolutely fine."

Serval's face was pale as he plotted a route through.

90

One hour into the swamp. The sky had turned cloudless; the sun beat their faces remorselessly; each step was a battle of wills with the mire, which sought to draw them into the wetlands and hold them there. Both men were sweating and covered in glutinous black mud. When they paused for breath the swamp was very silent. Steam rose; it smelled of rot. Serval was glad they'd chosen Kalashnikovs – the Viet Cong used to submerge these guns in swamps for months before rinsing them off and doing battle. The British SA80 would have been as much use as a broomstick by now.

The reeds were getting thicker, and Serval advanced with his back to the wall of vegetation. This provided protection from the leaves – they were sharp as a kitchen knife – and the trampled causeway helped them maintain a straight bearing, for god forbid that they should lose orientation. Neither man spoke for a long time, each of them engaged with his own thoughts, his

own deals with the almighty. Without warning the wall of vegetation gave way and Serval pitched backwards into a clearing
of stagnant water. At once he was on his front, spreading out all
four limbs – but the ground held.

Davis was in stitches. "You were shitting yourself, mate."

He urinated into the swamp in great curving arcs, the noise of
urine hitting the water obscenely loudly in the still of the swamp.

"You finished?" said Serval.

Sploosh.

Without warning Serval dived at Davis's feet, grabbing something that was slimy and sinuous and rough. A juvenile crocodile
was in his hands and he had it by the tail.

"Holy *shit*!" screamed Davis. "Shit, shit, *shit!*"

Serval clung to the thrashing reptile and swung it like a baseball bat, its cranium smacking into a tree trunk with a *thwack*,
once, twice, three times. He lobbed the lifeless creature away.

"Now who's shitting himself?" he said.

Davis was shaken, and as they inched forward he began talking
about his daughter. It was the first hint of emotion Serval had
seen in the man.

The explorer endured it for ten minutes, then he snarled,
"Look, will you please *shut up* about your daughter, all right?
I *don't care*. I just want to concentrate and get us through this
swamp in one bloody piece. Is that too much to ask?"

Davis was taken aback. "All right fella, keep your knickers
on …"

It was an hour before they neared terra firma – a hillock of
grass, a single mud hut perched upon it like a pimple. Beyond
lay a rice paddy.

"We've only gone and made it," grinned Frank.

"Don't count your chickens before they're on dry land."

Thirty metres of swamp separated them from the grass,
worryingly free of vegetation. Little streamlets cut their way
through the mud.

"We've got to be more careful now than ever," said Serval. "Avoid the mudflats – flowing water is safer. Step in the middle of the streams, not the sides. And remember, *glide.*"

He checked the consistency with his stick, took a deep breath and stepped into the still black waters. At once he was in it up to the waist. He collapsed forward onto his chest and hauled his legs out with an audible slurp.

"I'm ok," he gasped. "We're going to have to slither for the last stretch though."

Davis panted with anticipation.

Ten minutes later they were across. They sat on the grass, staring at the terrain they had navigated, chests heaving and teeth very white against their muddy cheeks. Perspiration cut channels down their faces.

Davis offered the explorer his hand. "You played a blinder there, fella."

A rare smile. "Frank, I don't mind telling you – that was the most dangerous thing I've attempted in my entire life."

"You cheeky bugger! I thought you said it wasn't risky ..."

A ragged figure rose up behind Serval and before he could react a machete came scything into his back. They heard the shear of metal into bone, the hiss of a collapsing lung. Davis shot their attacker between the eyes and he keeled over backwards, body twitching on the ground.

"Oh hell." Bright blood escaped from Serval's mouth. "Rebel?"

"A fucking farmer for fuck's sake," said Davis. "Maybe he thought *we* were the rebels."

"I'm dead." Serval coughed and another glut of blood erupted down his chin. "Had it for sure."

"Let's have a little look-see," said Davis.

The machete had opened up a foot-long gash, slicing through four of Serval's ribs and sailing on into his torso. His lung had been reduced to a tattered bag in a heap at the bottom of his chest cavity, like a popped balloon. Red bubbles foamed from the wound as swamp water seeped in.

"You're gonna be right as rain." Davis tore his shirt into strips and bound up the injury. "Heart's on the other side, remember?"

Davis's breath smelt milky, almost pleasant.

Serval blacked out.

"Wakey, wakey, sunshine." Davis slapped him around the face. "Wake up! Don't go to sleep!"

Serval's eyelids flickered open. "Lung gone," he managed. "Collapsed for sure."

"You only need one, mate. In Afghanistan I saw a guy walk a whole morning with a punctured lung. Besides, we've got work to do. You can hardly stay here, can you? Can you get up? Come on, that's it. Brave soldier." He hauled the explorer to his feet. "Take a few steps."

The world was spinning, but Serval did as he was told.

"See?"

"You're right. I think I can make it."

"You are one double hard bastard, fella," said Davis approvingly.

As the pair staggered towards the cliffs Serval spat bloodily on the farmer's corpse.

It was all a far cry from climbing mountains.

91

Jake walked through a forest of tall slender trees, ancient without malice. The canopy was sparse and the ground was covered in springy grass, lime green in the generous sunlight. Butterflies danced through the glade, chased by bejewelled birds. There was an air of *secrecy* about the place, hemmed in by the cliffs, a feeling of the sacred, and he lagged behind Jenny, admiring the shafts of yellow light that dappled fallen branches, scenting the aromas of baking timber and blossom. Idly he imagined picnicking there, with an old fashioned hamper. They would dine on cantaloupe melon and serrano ham and share a bottle of prosecco, if he could still drink. After that they would make love, here in this Eden. But each new layer of his imaginings was another step into fantasy: none of these things could be. Only the woodland was there for him to appreciate on the way to somewhere else. The difference between dreams and reality.

"Hurry up," said Jenny.

They skirted the cliff-face, closing on Dr Livingstone's coordinates. Jake glimpsed the grassy summits of Ngozo and Mekanga through the canopy. The cliffs below were scored by sediments of purples and reds and indigos, shot through with streaks of volcanic pink in a geological firework display. Jenny wore her Jackie O sunglasses, their departure lounge glamour out of place in this bucolic setting. The trees thinned out until they were crossing grassland.

Jake halted. "Oh god."

"What is it?"

"Look at the cliff."

Some grand tectonic movement in eons past had yanked the lines of strata from horizontal to near upright.

The striae seem as if the rock had been partially molten: at times the strike is north and south, at others east and west.

"Do you see what I see?" Jake's voice was reverential as he indicated a line of sediment that slashed vertically down the cliff. A violent series of upheavals had smashed the strata into a concertina of red and pink zigzags.

"A bolt of lightning," said Jenny.

The tattoo of the tribe resembles the drawings of the old Egyptians; wavy lines, such as the ancients made.

They followed the strike as it lanced down the rock-face to earth itself at the base. And there, nearly obscured by bushes, was a cave. Lightning, pointing the way.

"It's perfect," she whispered.

*

Parr was ensconced in long grass at the summit of the cliff as they entered; a conference with Vauxhall Cross was in progress.

"Where are the Americans?" said C.

"I lost sight of them. I'm afraid I don't know where they are."

"Frank and Jacob?"

"Not far away. Jacob's been injured by a farmer, quite badly."

There was a murmur in the background – the Prime Minister, she supposed.

"Well, we've got no choice," said C. "We can't rule out their finding something. And we mustn't let our rivals get it if they do. It's time to reveal our hand."

"Send the guys in?"

"As soon as they arrive. If Wolsey and Frobisher have struck lucky they'll know what to do. And if there's nothing to be found, have Frank extract everything they know. All interrogative techniques are on the table."

"Understood."

"Wolsey might even join us – stranger things have happened at sea. You stay in position and cover the approaches. Could the CIA sneak past?"

"I'm looking at fifty metres of open grassland with barely a rock to hide behind. It's a killing ground, sir."

"Which means we've got all the time in the world." Another background murmur. "If the Yanks emerge, shoot them down. That's straight from the PM."

Parr took her cheek from the rifle butt, blinked and resumed position, peering through the trunks with the telescopic sight. She had never *personally* killed anyone before, but she knew that she could. Foliage swayed and Parr jerked the rifle left. But it was Serval and Davis, mud already drying into flakes on their clothes. The explorer was pale and he favoured his right side, but his mouth was a grim little line of determination as they followed Jake and Jenny into the cavern.

92

In the clapped-out bar of a Freetown hotel, Chloë turned on a laptop she'd purchased from a junkshop. It whined and grumbled as Windows 2003 loaded; the only other noise was the refrigerator, which rattled away as if furious about something. A sign over the bar read *Optimistic Elite Social Klub* and the barman – elderly, impeccably dressed in green waistcoat and pinstripe trousers – snoozed on his stool. She was his only customer.

Once the computer had roused itself Chloë inserted the pen drive. She dared not examine Conteh's files in her room at the British High Commission, which was surely monitored. The juicy files were protected, but the folders all had the same password as his laptop, *ferrari_1*. It wasn't long before she discovered his books – more money was flowing through his bank accounts than the average Sierra Leonean earned in a hundred lifetimes. Chloë was not a forensic accountant, but if these dollars were clean then she was Esther Rantzen. Yet evidence of a far ranker crime was not to be found. She felt lighter with each folder examined and found innocent, ashamed for doubting the service: the guilty rush of love of a wife whose investigations prove her husband faithful.

Porn.

Surprise, surprise, Conteh had a folder of the stuff. This would be worth a look. On the off chance it was something especially foul it might be another tool for MI6 to blackmail him with; she had no doubt now he was a venal ruler, best cast down.

"Let's see what you're into," she whispered.

But *ferrari_1* did not work.

Chloë ordered another beer as the software toiled. It took five minutes – a serious password, this one. Finally an old fashioned *beep* told her the skeleton key had done its work. Thirty random letters and digits, several of them capitalised. Now the file had her undivided attention.

She was in.

There were image files.

But this was not pornography. The first was a grainy image of a man walking away from the camera as he entered Kroo Town slum. It had been shot at night and was two months old. The next image showed the same man, back still to the camera, discussing something with two Sierra Leoneans; one carried a machete. But the third photograph revealed him. A handsome face. Mid-to-late thirties. Hair brown or auburn, though it was hard to be certain in the light. An athletic build; five-day stubble. She didn't recognise him. The fourth shot showed the same man donning plastic suit and gloves and there followed a photograph apparently taken inside, a mother and daughter, huddled in their rags. Chloë didn't need a medical degree to see that they were dying. Her heart beat faster, hormones of fear and unease spiking in her bloodstream.

The next set of photos began in similar vein: somebody's back, though this man was slighter with long lank hair. The second photograph was sneaked through a window as he injected a brawny Sierra Leonean in the forearm. And the third image was a full frontal shot as he left the building.

She recognised him.

His name was Dai Elliot. He was MI6, a Welshman. They had trained together at Gosport. In the next photograph that same Sierra Leonean was no longer brawny; indeed he was barely recognisable. As Chloë read the deceased's account – how a British doctor had administered a polio vaccination, and immediately he'd contracted Ebola – she felt sick.

On through the dossier Chloë went. Here was the first guy again, meeting Dai at the hovercraft port in Aberdeen, handing him something. Then it was a photograph of the Welshman later that evening in Lungi International, boarding a flight to Abuja. A copy of his boarding pass, though he had been travelling as a Mr Andrew Edwards. Press cuttings pertaining to the Ebola breakout in northern Nigeria, which began three days later.

This was sick, a crime against humanity.

Chloë Rachael Smith closed the laptop. She closed her eyes. She sat very still in the Optimistic Elite Social Klub as her beer got warm and flat; sat there with her head in her hands thinking about what she stood for and the kind of person she wanted to be.

93

The cleft in the rock was just high enough to crawl through. Jake braced himself for the reek of urine, anticipated empty beer cans or needles. But the cave was virgin pure: like something created on the Third Day. The floor was sandy beneath his fingers and the rock was smooth, the temperature of his own skin. He was reminded of the Hamas attack tunnel, only here he felt again that strange sensation of peace. Had Livingstone crawled this way, generations before him? Were his loyal African guides behind him to the last, bemoaning the Scot's eccentricities as they shoved and dragged a leaden chest down the passageway?

Lead. If the last chest was only a decoy, why was it made of lead?

Jake heard a tapering breath escape Jenny's lips; he was reminded of someone bracing themselves to jump from the highest board. The passage had broadened out now – Jake could no longer touch rock overhead. When he switched his phone to torch he saw they were in a cavern, sixty feet to the far end and twenty feet high. Stalactites hung from the ceiling and organ pipes rose, the lurid shapes somewhere between a boneyard and an alien garden. Several passageways led off from the main hall, and in the darkness he heard a *drip-drip-drip*.

"Wow," said Jenny, stepping into the cavern. "It's like a cathedral."

"My thoughts exactly." Jake's words bounced off the walls, becoming lost in resonance. "What do you think we're looking for?"

"An inscription, I guess."

The walls were a mesh of intertwined mineral deposits and Jake touched a flowstone of stalactite cords, matted together like a druid's beard. The first branch of the cave system was a spider's leg which tapered into nothingness. No trace of the doctor's hand could be found.

"Jake …"

"What is it?"

"Just – be ready, ok?"

"Be ready? For what?"

"This is an enclosed space," she said. "We're vulnerable here."

Jake felt the first prickle of alarm. He tried to cling to the beauty of the place, to absorb its calmness. They ventured the second passage, and with the redness of the stone he felt like Jonah, venturing down the throat of the whale.

"If they did catch us here …" she muttered.

"Yes?"

"If we did have to fight – just leave it to me. You hide."

He laughed. "Jenny, you know me better than that."

"*Please.*"

"No." Firmly, an end to the matter.

Something had changed in the cave, some subtle shift in atmosphere. It retained a beauty, but a deadly one, that of an iceberg. They had reached the end of the second corridor and a spider the size of Jake's hand scuttled away into the darkness.

Livingstone …

Jake let the name course through his body.

Were you here?

He felt a little tug inside him as they returned to the central chamber, and as they entered the third branch the sensation became stronger. He let it draw him on. Livingstone *had* walked this way, with his battered blue cap and weary tread.

Something foreign emerged from the gloom, some form that did not belong in this subterranean world, where each rock had been smoothed by an eternity of *drip-drip-drip*. Boulders were piled against the wall, arising from drifts of soft sand.

Human hands did this.

Suddenly Jake saw whose: a tiny crucifix was carved into the cave wall. It was the mark of Dr Livingstone in this chapel for his adjunct to the Bible. Jake touched the symbol, moved by the explorer's devotion, allowing his forehead to be pulled against the rock.

The clink of stone on stone distracted him.

Jenny was clawing at the pile. Rolling away boulders, digging into pebbles and scree with both hands. A triangle of pitch black was revealed, widening swiftly into a cavity. The beam caught upon particles meandering in the air, disturbed after a century of slumber. There was a chest inside.

The cave was flooded with light.

Jake turned to see the silhouettes of two men with torches, marching towards them like extra-terrestrials from a spaceship. He heard metal on machined metal as they released safety catches, echoing harshly in the cave. The limp and the hulking body were enough to identify one of them.

Facing the beam, shoulder to shoulder, Jake and Jenny stood to confront Frank Davis for a final time.

94

The man with the cheese-grater face regarded them with Kalashnikov primed. He looked tired and hollowed out, as if dead inside.

"Hello," said Jake.

Serval didn't respond. Only the crack and tumble of moving stone filled the cave, the canine pants of Davis at work. The gap had become a window, big enough to scramble through.

"What's your name?" Jake tried.

"Jacob."

Jake had once read that at a subconscious level, we are conditioned to prefer people with the same name as us. People are statistically more likely to move into streets with a similar name to their own.

"Me too," he said. "But I guess you already know that."

Serval did not respond.

Davis was inside the grotto. "His initials are on the chest! D.L., David Livingstone."

Serval's eyes fractionally narrowed, and it hit Jake.

They don't know why. They don't understand the Livingstone connection at all.

Which meant he'd led them to it, he reflected dismally. He leaned back against the rock and closed his eyes. Why did everything he touched turn to disaster? He had only made things worse, right from beginning to end. Davis was dragging Livingstone's chest from the grotto, lead-lined to protect the contents from water and the ravages of time.

Jake opened his eyes – and he laughed out loud.

"I really hate to piss on your parade gents," he said. "But the padlock's broken."

Davis took in the sheared-off metal, coated in rust.

"Someone got here first." Jake chuckled. "A very long time ago, by the looks of things."

"All righty, you'd best enjoy your little laugh." Davis's lips trembled with anger. "'Cos you will not be grinning in a moment, my love."

He lunged at Jake. Punched him in the temple. Punched him in the throat. Punched him in the eye so hard that he passed out. When he came around his face was in the sand and Davis's knee was pressed into his neck. The assassin was far too strong to resist; Jake was a child in his embrace. Dimly he was aware of Jenny's screams. So this was what a violent end felt like. He tried to think about something happy, and a memory of eating bread and cheese with Jenny on an Italian hillside came to him. But something else was happening. His right arm was wrenched backward – it felt as if his shoulder-blade would pop out – and his shirt sleeve was ripped open. Before he knew it there was a needle in his wrist. Davis pressed down the plunger and fire rushed up Jake's arm. He braced himself for the cave to start spinning, for his world to stop.

Nothing happened.

"That'll teach you to be a cheeky bastard," said Davis.

"What did you just put in me?"

"Oh, that little thing? Well, seeing as you ask. You just main-lined the Ebola virus, matey."

Ebola.

Ebola.

The most terrifying three syllables in the English language. Jake grabbed his elbow and tried to restrict the flow of blood into his torso.

"Don't be a mug," said Davis. "You've just had enough of the virus to infect fifteen thousand people, direct to the heart." He thumped his own ribcage. "Oh, and it's a fast acting strain. Give it a few hours, then my hunch is you'll start feeling a little bit … out of sorts."

Serval brandished a vial. "We do have this though. It's a course of experimental drugs. Proven to be quite efficacious. With decent medical care you'd probably make it. Whether you get the cure depends on how much you tell us."

"Time being of the essence, so to speak, let me set out my stall right away," said Davis. "One, how is Livingstone wrapped up in all this? Two, how did Britain lose the *Disciplina*? And three, we'll take your best guess as to where it is now."

"He won't tell you," said Jenny. "Don't you know Jake at all by now?"

"Oh yes he fucking well will," said Davis. "I'd bet my wig on it."

"That's what you think," said Jake.

"So now we play the waiting game," said Davis.

95

It was 10 pm when the first wave of fever swept Jake's body, an unearthly symbiosis of heat and cold that bulldozed through him like a gigantic rolling pin. His throat was sore and he was getting pins and needles in his hands.

Davis had quarantined himself at the end of the passage. "How's the patient?"

"You may as well put a bullet in me, because I'm telling you sod all," said Jake. "Oh – and one more thing."

"What's that then?"

"You're a twat."

Jenny's bark of laughter was as sudden as it was incongruous.

Davis stepped back in mock surprise. "Well, well, well! What have we here? It's Billy Big Bollocks. A fiver says he won't keep it up when he starts haemorrhaging out of his arse." He peered at Jake. "You do look a bit peaky, fella. Why don't you just get it off your chest, son?"

Jake's headache increased by the second and the cave walls seemed to tremble before his eyes. The most feared virus on earth was in him.

"I'm proud of you, Jake," Jenny yelled. "You'll get through this. I *know* that you will."

"Put a cake in it, you silly hag," said Davis. "Don't get all emotional, it's an embarrassment. And take those sunglasses off too, you look ridiculous."

Jake was about to retort when another wave of iciness burst through him, followed by a nausea of dizzying intensity that liquefied his stomach. He was riding the onset of the worst flu imaginable, magnified five thousand-fold.

E-bo-la.

"I'm going to make you an offer," said Serval. His arms were wrapped around his own chest, as if he was cold. "Ten million quid if you come on board – authorised by London, right from the top. That's what the British government thinks you're worth. Let's get some fresh air and some phone signal, and you can watch the funds hitting your account."

"That's the down payment," said Davis.

"You'll be on a half a million annual retainer as for long as your services are needed," said Serval.

"More than I get for doing Number 10's dirty work, I'll tell you that," said Davis.

"You can't buy him," said Jenny. "He's better than you."

"Oh why don't you shut your rat trap?" Davis snarled, swiping her across the face with the back of his hand. "Stupid tart. We don't want to hear it, *all right*?"

"I don't agree with his methods." Everyone turned to Serval and Serval turned to Davis. "I don't, Frank. To speak candidly, I think you're a brute."

Jake *sensed* something in this man. A grain of residual decency, though somewhere along the line he had evidently turned very bad indeed.

"I do agree with the goal, though," said Serval. "I agree with what the government plans to *do* with this thing once we've obtained it."

"Over my dead body," whispered Jake.

Without warning another rush of fever surged through him. He heard the rasp of cicadas in his eardrums, felt the cave closing in.

"Do you know what that plan is?" said Serval. "Have you guessed it yet?"

"I'm all ears," said Jake.

Serval coughed, a ragged noise. "Why don't you work it out

for yourself? You're supposed to be the 'great analytical prodigy' after all, the guy who'd finally lead us to the *Disciplina*. Let's see those famous grey cells in action. Exhibit A, Sierra Leone. Pacified and improved beyond measure, yes?"

Jake made no comment.

"Exhibit B, Nigeria. Even as we speak, thousands of lives are being saved by British intervention."

"If you say so. Your point?"

When Serval coughed again his hand flew to his mouth and he inspected his palm before continuing. "My point is that the Prime Minister's goal is *nothing less than total rebuilding of the British Empire*."

Total silence.

"And this is a *Good Thing*. And with the Book of Thunder to guide him, he'll be able to *actually accomplish* it."

"You're stark raving mad," said Jake. "You realise that, don't you?"

"This sort of thing is exactly why I fell out with MI6," muttered Jenny.

"Tell me this then, which was the better world?" Serval's voice sounded reedy and thin. "The British-run planet of the nineteenth century, or the madhouse of today? Think of Russian expansionism, the growth of the Islamic State. The human rights abuses going on in China would *never* have been allowed under Disraeli. You ask why I'm doing this? I'm doing it because I believe in the Anglo-Saxon way. I believe the world was a fairer place when it was run by the British."

For a heartbeat Jake was in sympathy with his namesake.

"We can make a new British golden era, a new Victorian Age. *You* can make it happen, Jake. And as an aside, you'll be filthy rich – though do I do appreciate you're not the biddable type."

Jake closed his eyes, trying to fight the revolving of his stomach, the sickness in his blood. The crack of lightning, the thunderous roar of a Napoleonic cannonade. Hot vomit surged up his throat, cascading out of him by the pail-load. It was bloody.

"You haven't got much time," said Serval.

Jake entertained the notion. He could become a figure on a par with Caesar and Jesus Christ – or he could die a wretched death in this cave and Jenny would be killed.

"Take part." Serval extended a hand. "Let's turn the map red once more."

My god. I could actually do it.

96

"Nice try," said Jake.

Serval frowned.

"And it's a nice vision, too," Jake continued. "Quite the utopia. Only there's a problem with it. A square you just can't circle."

"What's that then?" said Davis.

"It's that by definition you can never bestow liberty at the barrel of a gun," said Jake. "There's no freedom without independence. The subjects of conquerors have no emancipation. *That* was the contradiction at the heart of the British Empire. Yes, the Victorians believed they were civilising the world – that's what Livingstone thought, anyway. Some of them even did a bit of good. But they were propagating a tyranny with the trappings of justice. And if you want to bring that back – well, you'll need to find another stooge. I'll have no part in it. And neither should you, Jacob."

Serval flinched. Jake thought he saw a glimmer of self-awareness in his eyes, a realisation, perhaps. He stared into those deadened pupils, willing decency into them.

"You're talking bollocks," said Davis.

Serval glanced at Davis sidelong. As if *appraising* him.

"Because when the British Empire was alive," said Jake, "how you played the game meant more than winning. Every true

Englishman knows that. I think you do too, deep down. Don't you?"

Serval's eyes had flickered up into his skull; Jake had the curious impression that he was replaying scenes from his life. He stared at Serval and blinked three times, renewing the entreaty.

Turn back.

Serval's grip on the rifle tightened. He glanced left, sizing up Davis's position and stance. The atmosphere in the cave was electric – Jake felt it, Jenny felt it. Only Davis was unaware of the changed dynamic. He grinned like a Staffie, panting in agitation at the prospect of butchery.

Serval coughed.

He staggered.

He dropped the gun, lurched sideways onto the cave wall. Clotted blood splattered down his chin, dripping on the rock face. He leaned there panting.

"I'm sorry," he gasped.

There was movement in darkness, then gunshots. And before anyone could react, both Serval and Davis had been killed.

*

These were the scenes in Bujumbura: the city in pitch blackness; Kanisha being mobbed by curious Burundians as she bought a SIM card on the Boulevard Mwambutsa; and Eric Bafadhili, the man from the internet café, fending off the locals gamely. For Kanisha had made the most reckless decision of her life. *Someone* had the *Disciplina* – and finding it was worth risking her life for. That someone had visited her internet page once more and the IP address pinged back was in Bujumbura. She'd offered Bafadhili $1,000 to identify the men who had visited his café, and there they were. The website had been accessed from a hotel, the hotelier had described his only European customers and a taxi driver revealed where they had gone next. She would sleep for now – night driving in Burundi was a death wish – but the next morning she would follow. Like beads of water drawn by gravity to a single point, each actor was converging upon Livingstone's heart of darkness.

97

The bullet hole in Serval's forehead glistened like a glacé cherry. Davis lay sprawled upon the sand: body twisted awkwardly, legs akimbo and shot through one eye. In death his jaw still swung open with a doglike grin. Over the toppled corpses stood the Americans.

High above them Evelyn Parr had heard the gunshots, manifestly *not* the distinctive clatter of an AK47. Somehow the Americans had known where to go – and they had found another way in.

"Again," said Jenny.

At the museum in Vienna; in the backstreets of Cambridge; right across East Africa. The CIA had always been there, chasing them, waiting for them. And now Jake knew why. Deissler's eyes were blood-red: like those of Rudolf Hess, having summoned down a bolt of lightning at Mytchett Place. Jake was looking into the face of a *fulguriator*, a man who had consulted the Network that very morning and knew where they would be. At once the entire tapestry was revealed to him in all of its wicked fineness. Suddenly Jake understood what had become of Napoleon's Book of Thunder. He could detail every owner, from the time of Hannibal to the present day. He needed no black magic, had consulted no manifestation; intellect alone had revealed it.

"Henry Morton Stanley," he said.

Deissler nodded. "Very good."

"The pages of his diary, describing his first encounter with

Livingstone … they were ripped out. That's why some doubt he ever said the 'Dr Livingstone, I presume' line."

"Indeed."

"When they travelled together along Lake Tanganyika, Stanley must have observed him burying the first chest. After Livingstone's death – much later, perhaps – he returned to exhume it."

"This is also correct."

"Finally Stanley came here, following Livingstone's diaries like we did. He found the last section of the linen book and brought it to his adopted homeland. You guys discovered it worked."

"You called it," said Deissler.

Jake gritted his teeth as another pulse of fever rattled through him.

"And the British golden age was over," he said. "The American century was about to begin."

98

The United States of America. She had elbowed aside the powers of the Old World, bestridden the twentieth century like a colossus; ended it a superpower to rival ancient Rome.

"But the American century was no bad thing," said Deissler. "Wouldn't you agree?"

"The *Pax Americana* has been a good peace," said di Angelo. "Broadly, a world policed by the White House has been a good one."

Jake had to admit there was something in that.

"Unlike the Brits, we played by the rules," said Deissler.

"The rules?" said Jake. "What rules?"

"You haven't heard of the Prophecies of Vegoia?" said Deissler.

Jake heard Jenny's sharp intake of breath. He recalled Michael Beloff's notes on Napoleon's first major defeat since acquiring the Book of Fate.

1809. Austria again. During this campaign, there were the first signs of ill-health in Napoleon.

Beloff had circled *ill-health* and added: *Vegoia. Borders.*

"Let me refresh your memory," said Deissler. "Vegoia was an Etruscan prophet. She said this ..."

When he began speaking in Etruscan Jake fancied the cave had become a little darker, and he was glad of the weight of rock over his head, blocking out the sky. Jenny was on her knees beside him, trembling with each word like the pilgrim of a dark god.

"Tin is the god of boundaries," she said. "Knowing the greed of men and their lust for land, he wanted everything to be proper concerning them. Those who violate them will be damned by the gods."

"Why do you think we never built an American Empire?" Deissler chuckled.

That was why Hitler had been a shambling wreck by the end of World War Two, why similar afflictions had been visited on Napoleon – both had violated the natural borders of their realms. Here was another cruel little irony of the Network. As it toyed with men, treating rulers as its marionettes and their kingdoms as its playthings, their realms tended towards empire – just as subatomic particles arrange themselves into order. Yet this expansion would also be their downfall, and they were punished atrociously for it. An old line on Fate came to Jake, penned by the Roman scholar Boethius.

Such is a game she plays. And so she tests her strength.

"If the Victorians had obeyed Vegoia, Britannia would still rule the waves," said Deissler.

And Jake saw how indeed it was the very act of expansion that had brought the British Empire to an end. With the Scramble for Africa in the 1880s, Britain became over-extended. The Boer War began, the barbarity and concentration camps making colonialism unpopular at home for the first time. Socialism arose hand in hand with disgust at colonial excess, and the greatest empire in history disintegrated in two decades flat. Thus was the prophecy of Vegoia fulfilled.

Jake remembered something Gladstone had said of territorial acquisitions.

It ought to be understood that they are new burdens added to the old, and in augmenting space they diminish power.

Gladstone had identified the results without understanding the process.

Something else was bothering him: the parallels between Hitler and Napoleon.

History rhymes.

Why was this important?

"*We* didn't go invading a whole load of countries," Deissler was saying. "All we wanted was to do was uphold the peace – and make lots of money while we were about it. We finished off the USSR without firing a shot! Sure, we didn't always get things right. When it came to Pearl Harbor and Vietnam, the politicians just went right ahead and ignored the warnings, they wouldn't believe our own soothsayers. Just like the Romans refusing to accept Hannibal could cross the Alps, or Napoleon in Russia. Oh, the arrogance of man. But the augurs are always proved right in the end. And all our agents who've sacrificed their lives trying to stop your crazy Prime Minister finding the *Disciplina* and messing shit up? They were doing it for peace."

"They're heroes," said di Angelo quietly.

"You killed Beloff too," said Jake.

"Sure did," said Deissler. "He was getting too close."

"The perfect murder weapon," said di Angelo. "What the hell detective would suspect a lightning bolt?"

"Hey, Jennifer," said Deissler. "Why don't you take your sunglasses off?"

"I don't want to."

Deissler aimed his gun directly at her face. "Go on – you're underground. You'll be bumping into things if you're not careful."

She didn't respond.

"Take 'em off," he growled. "Or I'll shoot you in the face."

Jenny's hand rose and hesitated, rose again.

"What's the matter?" said Jake. "What is it?"

"I'm sorry," she whispered.

She removed her sunglasses, but her head was bowed and still she avoided his gaze. Finally she looked up. She turned to face him. Her eyelids were closed. Then she opened them, and at once Jake's world was destroyed and everything he had known to be good and believed in was revealed as a lie.

Her eyes were blood-red too.

99

Evelyn Parr burst into the cave and opened fire. But it was as if Deissler knew she was coming, for he wheeled on the spot and blew off her cheekbone, opening a sickening grotto right through her head. Deissler put the next one between her eyes. In the confusion Jenny snatched up a Kalashnikov and let rip with a bright yellow belch of fire, raking the cave. But Deissler had disappeared. Jake made it to cover and peered around the rock as she advanced, crosshairs sweeping the darkness.

Jenny was a *fulguriator*.

She'd had the *Disciplina Etrusca* all along.

The betrayal was monstrous. But suddenly it made sense: why she had pulled away from him, that other thing she had going on.

I've been thinking about the future. I need to do something with my life.

But how could this be? As he watched Jenny pace down the cavern to face her destiny, he had the answer. And he saw that *he* was the idiot, for all his purported brains. She had a photographic memory. When they had found Rudolf Hess's manuscript at the Tower of London, she'd leafed through the scroll, storing every symbol. Now he thought about it, she'd had a wobble even then, as the enormity of what she was holding hit her.

With this document we could do whatever we wanted. We could clean out Monte Carlo, go into politics. We could be powerful beyond our wildest dreams.

How had she learned Etruscan? That he couldn't say.

Deissler popped out from behind a rock and fired. But *before* pin hit firing cap Jenny had side-stepped the bullet's intended path. He ducked back into cover and she fired at a stalactite above him. It happened again – Deissler was moving *before* the bullet struck the needle sharp chunk of stone, sending it spiralling murderously downwards to the spot he had just been standing in. That's when Jake understood what was going on, and he felt the skin on the back of his neck turn icy with rising dread at witnessing the preternatural. There could be no lightning bolts down here. But the winner of the duel had *already been decided*. That was why both gladiators had bloodied eyes. Both had taken the auguries that morning, foreseen every move; knew what evasive action to take. As to the victor, the Network had kept that detail for its own amusement. But both of them knew this was a contest they had to fight. There could be only one *fulguriator*, one devotee alone to command the favour of the Over Power.

Another mystery was revealed to him: Jenny in Vienna, with a bottle of wine. She wasn't meeting an old flame at all, she was *making offerings*, appeasing the higher sphere like the prophets of old in the hope it might lead her to what she sought.

It's not you, it's me.

You are a good man, Jake. Sometimes I think I've been so stupid.

And the lightning they had witnessed by Big Ben was an augury too! There had been a roofing company on King Charles Street the next day – it must have struck the Foreign Office. The storm had made its point. That was how Jenny had known a Foreign Office document would be the key to the puzzle.

Agreed additional activities.

She'd worn sunglasses the next day, now he remembered it. And in Kigoma when they had watched lightning over the lake, she had *sensed* the CIA's approach. He'd put it down to intuition, gleaned from years of field work. But if Jenny could read the heavens, how did she not know that the CIA had it all along?

Such is a game she plays.

Jake heard once more that laughter: grating, guttural. Mildly amused.

Not a click, not a pop, but a *nothing*.

He was inside the Network, floating through an infinity of stars that pulsed and chattered to each other. The whole grid trembled at some mighty calculation, then the helices became ordered again, gliding silently past on all sides. A shadow was projected upon the constellations, like cancer in an X-rayed lung.

A man in a hat.

Napoleon.

The Network juddered, the image shimmered away, only to reform into a lither figure, his arm outstretched in a ramrod salute. Adolf Hitler, the second to unleash hell on earth with the Book of Fate. Still the dots of light streamed past; the structure was rotating and the stars became streaks of white, racing around him like lightning bolts.

A third figure emerged.

Sloping shoulders, diminutive height.

Jake was on the cusp of recognition ...

Not a click, not a pop, but a *nothing*.

Jake was lying on his back in the grip of high fever. The cave walls contorted with hallucination: a leering face, a set of gaping jaws. A trickle of blood escaped one eye as he let his head fall sideways – to see Deissler remove the pin from a hand grenade.

This time Jenny did not see it coming. The cave rocked with the detonation, devastatingly loud in the hard space. Part of the ceiling collapsed and Jenny was smashed to the floor by the rock-fall, her Kalashnikov buried.

"I win," said Deissler.

The Network had chosen.

100

As Jake slipped into delirium, one thought returned with crystal lucidity: that the lives of Hitler and Napoleon were lived as in a mirror.

Both adored their mothers but feared their fathers. Both were foreigners in countries they led to catastrophe.

Both had health problems, especially with digestion. Both were corporals, brave in battle. Both loved art.

And still the similarities tumbled down like tarot cards. Both admired Great Britain, and saw their dreams of world domination break upon that unprepossessing island of stubborn men and women. Trafalgar foreshadowed the Battle of Britain, just as Napoleon's march on Moscow augured Hitler's insane gamble. Both walked the same path of brilliance, adoration, hubris, overreach. Both believed in the 'triumph of the will', and more than that, in Destiny. Both would be cursed for all time. An umbilical cord linked these two men from different ages, like those invisible fronds connecting dark matter across the universe.

Why was this important?

Because there was another. That third figure came back to Jake, still shadowy and unknowable.

"The British Empire is under Providence the greatest instrument for good the world has seen," said Deissler, snapping Jake from his reverie. "Your Lord Curzon said that, at the end of the nineteenth century. Just a shame you got greedy."

Deissler's trigger finger tightened; the hammer lifted. A tiny tongue of steel was all that separated Jake from death.

Say something, quick.

"Ten saecula."

The finger relaxed; the hammer lowered. "What?"

"Ten saecula. Ten lifetimes. According to the *Disciplina*, that was the allotted period given to any civilisation before the wheel of history turns. Before a newer, brighter people take over. It's a timetable. It can't be bargained with."

"What of it?"

"Do you really want the *Disciplina* in existence when America's time's up? That freedom and liberty you think you're protecting? It'll be destroyed for certain."

Di Angelo stirred.

"Power corrupts, absolute power corrupts absolutely," said Jake. "Whoever wields that thing becomes a tyrant sooner or later. Napoleon started off enlightened. And how did he end up? Perhaps Frederick the Great put it best. *That monster choked out of hell.*"

Hell. Where Jake had just been: cruising through the Network at the speed of light.

"It's the Devil," he said with dawning wonder. "The Network is the Devil."

Deissler's eyelids flickered as he confronted the truth.

"But Faustian pacts come with a heavy price," said Jake. "Which makes Napoleon ..."

"Antichrist," croaked Jenny, who was sprawled on the bedrock. "Oh god, what have I done?"

"And Hitler ..." Jake whispered.

"The Second Coming."

There was rage in Deissler's eyes, the compulsion to end life.

"And a Third," said Jake, knowing these were his last words. "I've seen him. Foretold, like all things are. A new dark age."

Made more sinister, and perhaps more protracted, by the lights of perverted science.

Deissler closed one eye and winced. He was at point blank range. He could not possibly miss.

A final gunshot filled the cave.

101

Blood spurted from the side of Deissler's skull like a jet of struck oil. He toppled over sideways, gargled for a bit and then expired. Behind him stood Damien di Angelo, smoke rising from his Beretta.

You just carry on doing your bit for freedom and goodness, son. That's all we ask.

The rake-thin Baltimore man cast his gun aside. For a time the only sound was panting – and the far off *drip-drip-drip* that had continued all along.

"I'm sorry," whispered Jenny.

Jake did not reply.

"I'm sorry, Jake. I wanted to be somebody. I didn't realise how evil it is."

Jake fought to remain compos mentis in the gathering cytokine storm. "If you'd memorised Hess's copy, why come with me?" he said. "Why risk everything to find Napoleon's manuscript too?"

Her wordlessness spoke of great shame.

"Why?" he shouted.

"I wanted to possess it alone."

He knew then that no apology could be enough, no remorse could save her. At some level the Network had corrupted her absolutely. Like a recovering alcoholic, she could never be free.

"But you didn't know about Stanley," said Jake, confused again.

"I asked so many times – but the Network kept it from me."

Such is a game it plays.

"We've got to get rid of it," said di Angelo. "Our copy. America's copy …"

"Where's it kept?" asked Jake.

"Diego Garcia."

"The naval base?" Jake spluttered. "But that's technically part of the UK, we leased it to you! Pisstakers."

"Chosen for the remoteness and the frequency of storms. We're brewing up lightning in the middle of the Indian Ocean three times a week, man, whenever a request comes from Washington. Why do you think we forcibly removed all the inhabitants? I'm telling you, some freaky shit goes down out there." He laughed. "That island's the subject of a million YouTube conspiracy theories. Shame nobody guessed the one that just happened to be true."

Steam rose from Deissler's matt red corneas and di Angelo glanced down at him with distaste.

"Washington only keeps one *fulguriator*," he said. "A single interlocutor, to best curry the Network's favour. They'll be choosing another soon."

"Why did they send him here?" said Jake.

"To defeat the other."

Somewhere in the darkness Jenny was sobbing.

"The Third Coming," said Jake. "I think I know who it is. Our Prime Minister. At some point the US will have to stand up to him. It's like Winston Churchill said. The Americans will always do the right thing, when all other options are exhausted."

"There'll be war," whispered Jenny. "War in the English-speaking world."

"Well we can't do a goddamn thing about that," said di Angelo. "What are you gonna do, assassinate the man?"

"I don't know," Jake admitted.

Jenny struggled to her feet, hair dishevelled, face besmeared with blood and dust.

"And there's one more copy," she said.

A shockwave went through the cave.

"You're shitting me," said di Angelo.

"Where?" Jake snarled. "Where is it?"

Jenny smiled sadly, pointed to her own head. "In here."

She took a few steps back, frightened but resolute.

"What are you doing?" said Jake, voice turning to fear.

"I am going outside and may be some time."

"You don't mean …"

"I don't trust myself any more. I'm sorry, Jake."

"Stop her," Jake begged di Angelo. "I'm too weak to stand."

But the CIA man merely folded his arms and shook his head. "Woman's gotta do what a woman's gotta do."

"Don't be a *bloody idiot*, Jenny!" Jake shouted.

Jenny continued edging backwards. She was almost out of the cave. "The stuff from the *flakturm*, in Vienna. I buried it in Gibson Square – it's a park in Islington. Beneath a yew tree in the north-west corner."

"I don't want it!"

"I wish I could go back and do it differently, Jake. Oh I wish I could go back and do it differently. We were made for each other."

And with that, Jenny Frobisher departed to face her destiny.

Only then did Jake whisper to himself: "No we weren't, Jenny. No we weren't."

102

Jake didn't know how much time had passed. His body was on fire. His headache was so appalling he couldn't think and the nosebleed was unceasing. He vomited half a pint of blood, felt the clots clogging up his throat. Death could not be far off now. He could barely see.

"They gave me Ebola," he managed, though he was unsure whether di Angelo still there. "That guy's got an antidote …"

As di Angelo stood over Serval's corpse, the slain explorer was like his reflection on the surface of a lake. The upstanding and the fallen.

Di Angelo passed Jake the drugs.

"Don't touch me," hissed Jake.

The American smiled grimly. "I've already had it, dude."

He got Jake to his feet and helped him out of the cave. It was early morning, the African sky feathered with cloud turning a soft flamingo in the rising sun. They sat and Jake cried for Jenny, biting his hand, shoulders juddering, his tears cutting scarlet tracks down his face. Yet this was not the raging grief of a man who had lost the love of his life. She was a different person to the Jenny he thought he knew.

Some Livingstone came to him.

The chief is believed to possess great power of divination, even of killing unfaithful women.

What was prophecy and what wasn't? He no longer knew.

When Jake looked up he was astonished to see di Angelo weeping too. A phone was in his hand.

"What is it?" asked Jake.

The agent looked away. "Jeez, sorry man. Just had a bereavement. Someone who'd been ill, for a long time."

Freedom and goodness.

But di Angelo was no longer crying; instead he wore a look of frightening determination.

"We're going to get you fixed up," he said. "Then we're gonna do this thing."

Jake's phone buzzed. It was an email – from *Chloë* of all people, she of the beach. And she was telling him extraordinary things.

"People," hissed di Angelo. "Over there."

The woman striding towards them looked Middle Eastern; beside her Jake recognised the man from the internet café, who was pointing at them.

What the heck's going on?

Kanisha was out of breath when she reached them. "You must be David. Bloody hell, are you guys ok?"

103

Victor Milne bounced into the press conference at Number 10 with his usual ebullience. But he had aged. It happens to all Prime Ministers after they've penned their first letter to a widow, that morning's *Mail* had opined. Yet with Milne, the process seemed accelerated.

The papers were dominated by sensational news from Freetown. Sierra Leone had announced a referendum on handing government to Westminster in perpetuity. Foreign Office lawyers had coined a new status – the Enhanced Commonwealth – if it was a yes vote, the country would be something called a Democratic Dominion. Cue hysterical coverage around the world, but the protests had gained little traction with everything conditional on the ballot box. The vote was to be held in three weeks, a 'shotgun wedding', the *Times* leader had called it.

The political editor of the *Guardian* opened proceedings with a stinging salvo. "According to your white paper, Sierra Leoneans won't get the right to settle here in the UK. Are some citizens of your 'Enhanced Commonwealth' more equal than others, Prime Minister?"

The politician regarded him with pity. "The whole reason we're *considering* Sierra Leone's suggestion is because we can improve that place to the point where its citizens won't *want* to come here. I'm sure that's something the excellent journalists at King's Place would get behind?"

"What about British taxpayers?" the *Express* rejoined. "How can we invest billions building hospitals in Africa while many go without cancer drugs at home?"

Things continued in this vein, Milne fending off assaults from right and left and enjoying himself thoroughly. It was precisely this blitheness in the face of adversity that had carried public opinion with him this far.

The *Independent* went off-piste. "Can you confirm categorically that British Forces in Nigeria have not used weapons banned under the Dublin Convention on Cluster Munitions?"

Mobile phone footage had surfaced showing the outskirts of Kano cracking with thousands of explosions that danced like firecrackers across the rooftops, until all that could be seen were points of light twinkling in the smoke haze. It was a neighbourhood where British soldiers had been unable to dislodge Boko Haram.

Milne looked very serious. "For obvious reasons, I'm not in a position to disclose operational details. But we will always use technology that prevents British soldiers from losing their lives."

A YouGov poll that morning suggested the Prime Minister had public backing for this stance.

*

One hour later, three floors up, C and the Prime Minister were taking tea.

"... Serval was attacked by a farmer," C was saying. "So he was weakened when it all went down. That must have been a factor."

" 'A scrimmage in a border station, a canter down some dark defile. Two thousand pounds of education drops to a ten rupee jezail.' Kipling."

"Inappropriate," said C. "If you'll forgive my saying so. Three of my best people have laid down their lives."

"Oh, tish and pish. Now, who's next up? The hunt must go on, Dennis."

He sighed. "Alec McCabe's fully recovered from the Jerusalem incident. And I suggest we bring the lovely Chloë Smith back into the fold. She did marvellously in Freetown – that laptop was a goldmine. I've never known anyone keel over to blackmail so fast. And lord knows, we've done a few."

No mention of the other files on Conteh's hard drive.

They did not know.

104

"Jake Wolsey, as I live and breathe." The tall Aberdeen man with the aquiline noise glided across the room and shook his hand. "We thought you were dead!"

"Hello, Niall. Strange to be back."

Jake was somewhere he never thought he'd set foot again: the offices of his old newspaper in central London. Two weeks had passed; by his side was Chloë.

"Who's she?" said Niall Heston.

Jake did the introductions. "She's our source. Chloë, this is Niall Heston, the news editor. And this is Niall's boss, David Waring – the editor-in-chief."

Waring was a squat man with a paunch and a shock of rusty hair, resembling some sort of greedy bullfrog. But his smile was kindly.

"Your antics caused me some awful headaches two years ago, Jake. But you also brought in a couple of phenomenal scoops, if memory serves. Before your years in the wilderness."

"Nothing like this. It's the big one."

"Let's hear it then," said Waring. "In case you haven't noticed, we've got a rather important story about Sierra Leone breaking."

"Actually …" Chloë placed a neat folder on the table. "That's why we're here."

Jake had awoken after eight days with all manner of liquids sliding into him intravenously. On the other side of the oxygen tent sat the woman, fuzzy through the layers of diaphanous plastic.

"You're awake," said Kanisha.

"So I am."

"How do you feel?"

"Never better. Where am I?"

She laughed. "You're in a private hospital in Bujumbura. I brought you here – it was lucky we turned up when we did. Damien's paid the medical bills. The doctors say you're going to make it."

"Who's Damien?"

"The American guy."

It all came back. Henry Stanley, the Third Coming, di Angelo. Jenny. Jake's hand went to his forehead, only to be caught by the drips in his arm.

"Who are you?"

"My name's Kanisha. I work for the British Museum."

"Look, I don't mean to be rude, but I don't even know you. Could I have a few moments?"

"Of course. Damien left you a letter. It's under your pillow." She made no signs of leaving.

Jake

I've gone to Diego Garcia. The window of opportunity is now, while they're choosing his replacement. I couldn't wait. You'll know when it's done. Go to London. Sort out number Three. I used my contacts in the US Embassy here to sort you a new identity and documentation. Kanisha's got all that stuff. (She's who taught Jenny Etruscan. An academic, bit curious. Clever girl. Don't let on.) Hospital is paid for with hush money so don't let them screw you.

Your friend,
Damien

"I read the letter," said Kanisha.

"You *what*?"

"Hey, I was curious! I knew Jenny as David."

"What the hell makes you think it's ok to read private correspondence?"

"It might have been important," said Kanisha, as if that ought to have been obvious.

"How did you teach her? Did you meet in Vienna?"

"Vienna? Random. No, never, I taught her online. Her voice was disguised. I'd always just assumed she was a guy. But there was the odd feminine touch, now I think about it."

I am the unguent-bottle of the beautiful Sela.

Ha. Pretty.

"Jenny was a spy," said Kanisha triumphantly. "So is Damien, he must be. So are you. That's the only explanation."

"Jesus Christ," said Jake.

"What's number three?" she asked.

"It's rather a long story."

When the veil of the tent was raised a few days later, Jake saw her properly for the first time.

*

"Utterly sensational." Heston pored over Chloë's dossier – the photographs, the travel tickets, the associated press clippings. "It's Watergate on crystal meth. Jesus, Jake, it's historic, it's moon landings territory."

"It also has the ring of truth," said Waring carefully. "Don't you think, Niall?"

"Agreed," said Heston.

"But this isn't proof," added Waring.

Jake felt a little of the exhilaration go out of him.

"Nowhere near," said Heston. "Good god, we can't accuse a serving Prime Minister of murdering tens of thousands of people on the back of photos of people you *say* are MI6 officers and the unfortunate timing of an Ebola outbreak in Nigeria."

"Why don't you put a photographer outside Vauxhall Cross?" said Jake. "If he could get into one of those yuppie apartments overlooking Vauxhall Bridge he could shoot down with a tele-photo lens. Hopefully snap the Welsh guy going in."

"Good idea," said Heston. "We'll do that today."

"And talking of today things, we need to make some fairly

drastic changes to the paper," said Waring. "I've just signed off a leader praising the PM's shining humanitarian vision …"

"Will you go on the record?" Heston asked Chloë.

She steeled herself. "If you look after me. These people will kill."

"We've got safe houses," said Heston. "Ex-Special Forces provide our security. You'd be looked after, I promise you that."

"We need more evidence," said Waring. "This wouldn't be enough to nail a two-bit drug dealer, let alone a war criminal."

A memory of Jenny went through Jake like a stiletto.

The High Court test. You're being grilled by a QC. Can you defend this theory?

But Jenny *wasn't* Jenny – not as he'd known her.

"There's only one way we're going to get this past our lawyers," Heston said. "And that's an admission."

"I wouldn't hold my breath on that," said Waring.

"We could secretly record him?" suggested Jake.

"Secretly record a Prime Minister?" Waring chuckled. "Very droll. We'd be lucky to even sit down with him, let alone get him to spill the beans on the greatest scandal in British history."

"Actually, I'm not quite sure about that," said Chloë.

Everybody looked at her.

"You see, I've just been seconded back to MI6's Etruscan team. As its commanding officer."

"Don't tell me MI6 is *still* obsessed with all that nonsense?" Heston was aghast. "Don't these bastards have any better way to burn our taxes?"

"It's something Milne takes a close interest in," Chloë continued. "To the point of grilling MI6 field officers in person, which is pretty unheard of."

"Are you saying you could get a meeting with him?" said Heston.

"I think I could. In fact, I'm sure I could. My predecessor was in and out of Number 10 the whole time."

Waring was rubbing his cheeks with both hands. This was his call. He said nothing for three minutes. Jake and Chloë looked at each other silently.

"On one side of the scales, we put at risk all of our careers and the reputation of a two-hundred-year-old newspaper," said Waring. "On the other, we expose war crimes. It's not even a question, is it?"

"Not if we have any decency at all," said Heston.

"So let's get the bastard," Waring finished.

Jake had gone red; he couldn't help grinning.

"We'll need you back on the staff," said Waring. "If you can stand the story up, all of Fleet Street will want a piece of you. So I insist you sign a contract today. Let's say £105K a year, conditional on this story being true, of course. Choose whatever job title you like – Special Correspondent, Editor-at-Large, I really couldn't care less. But make it something grand, eh?"

A vision had appeared in front of Jake's eyes: something he never thought he'd have again.

A life.

"You'll need media training too," said Waring. "And a few new suits. You'd better brace yourself, Jake Wolsey. This time next week you might be the most famous journalist on the planet."

105

Di Angelo peered from the Path Corporation registered Learjet 35 to see Diego Garcia bumping and sliding towards him. The atoll is often described as a horseshoe, but it better resembles the coastline of Africa. The beaches were very white, most of the island given over to wild palm forest – though you would not last long uninvited. Twin runways covered one third of the island, and as di Angelo watched a B-1 bomber took off on a run to the Middle East. The Learjet passed oil silos, lines of barracks;

sinister cubed and windowless buildings fringed with radar dishes and aerials. In the centre of the island was a flat concrete disc the size of a baseball pitch, surrounded with razor wire and lookout posts. Beneath that were the archives: an inverted cone of reinforced concrete that bored down through the coral and into the earth's crust. This facility was virtually unstaffed: if defences are entirely automated they cannot be socially engineered into opening. You can spend all you like on physical security, but it's only as impenetrable as the weakest human. This is what he had to penetrate. As the plane lost height di Angelo saw off-duty sailors frolicking in the sea and jeeps buzzing about, the Stars and Stripes everywhere. They were coming in to land.

He'd flown from Bujumbura to Bahrain to await the next Diego Garcia flight – the CIA wanted him there for psychometric and cerebral tests, to judge his suitability as Deissler's successor. Commercial airlines did not fly to the island (obviously) and it was two days before the next plane from Virginia landed in the Middle East to refuel and take on passengers. That had given di Angelo time to formulate his plan.

A sign in the base's airport read *Diego Garcia, Footprint of the Free*, and on spotting it di Angelo smiled grimly. A bevvy of NBA cheerleaders were visiting to boost morale and the base was in high spirits. He went to the canteen, making sure he was seen talking to the base's commanding officer – they'd served together in Afghanistan. Then he made his excuses and went to bed.

Big day tomorrow.

He double checked his props. There was a coloured badge (orange, for a Thursday) that in combination with his CIA identity card and biometric testing should see him through the perimeter fence. He did not have permission to enter, so he intended to use an old pass that he should have returned on a previous visit. His forgery of the dates was imperfect, but humans doing a repetitive job work mainly in the subconscious. It was likely the guard would check the colour, not the words. Coloured passes are a terrible security idea. Next to it was a wad of documentation he had prepared to back up his cover story, and a classic of the blagger's kitbag: the humble clip-board.

Di Angelo rolled up his trouser legs to inspect his wounds. A crooked incision ran the length of each shin, only just beginning to scab. His calves looked distended, like over-inflated water balloons; the skin glowed angrily as his body tried to reject the objects sown inside. He had performed the operation in Bahrain with only codeine to dull the agony. Not pleasant. If they strip-searched him it was game over.

*

Six time zones away, preparations for another raid continued. Kiwi-tech Vision of Farringdon was New Zealand owned, its warehouse attic workshop an Aladdin's cave of outlandish surveillance equipment. One technician widened a hole in the top button of Chloë's blouse with a dentist's drill; a second took her through the mechanics of undercover filming. For she had been invited for tea at Number 10.

"This is cool," she said, pointing at a miniature chest of drawers.

They were labelled by objects in which a lens could be hidden: spectacles, bow ties, flowers, watches.

"Like Q's laboratory, huh?" said Jake.

Chloë nodded at the chipped tea mugs of assorted provenance, stained brown inside. "That's not very Bond."

"Welcome to real life."

Jake had a fleeting memory of that glade in Burundi; but something had changed. No longer did he implant Jenny in it. That yearning had gone along with her betrayal.

The technicians taught Chloë how to attach the recorder to her body with surgical tape, running the tiny wires to her top button, how to change the batteries on the recorder, how to insert the tiny SD cards. A blinking red light meant it was recording.

"Are you worried?" asked Jake, out of earshot of the staff.

"A little bit. I don't think anyone's done this before. Secretly filming a sitting Prime Minister, it's nuts."

"Don't be," he said. "I've run a few undercover investigations – the operative never, ever gets found out."

Once she'd disassembled and reassembled the rig three times over the engineers were satisfied.

They were ready to roll.

Did Chloë not know her new role came with extra surveillance? Did she not guess they would go through her rubbish? And it was bin collection day in Ealing. In one of her black bags: a single crumpled receipt for services rendered from a little-known company in Farringdon.

106

Jake dropped Chloë off on Birdcage Walk in one of the newspaper's pool cars.

"How do I look?" she asked.

He thought she looked pale, but he said, "Fine. Cool as a cucumber."

They watched a mother and toddler feed geese in St James's Park.

"Well – good luck," he said.

"Thanks. See you in a bit."

After an awkward moment they shook hands.

"Jake … if I get through this, I wouldn't mind getting to know you properly."

As he watched Chloë Smith walk away from him, tall and upright, her chin held high, Jake reflected that he knew her less now than ever.

Chloë accessed Downing Street via the Horse Guards Parade entrance, where armed police X-rayed her handbag and waved her through. She skipped up a flight of stairs and onto the famous road itself, a hubbub of activity as reporters performed pieces to camera. The faint *bong* of Big Ben wafted over from Parliament Square.

"The Prime Minister's been closeted up behind me for most of the morning with the Cabinet Secretary and his top civil servants," said Sky's political editor. "I'm told they've been putting the finishing touches to the resolution that will bring Sierra Leone back to British rule permanently – with the blessing of Sierra Leonean voters, of course. Sources in Buckingham Palace suggest the monarch harbours strong reservations about these sensational developments, and I understand Victor Milne will be visiting Buckingham Palace to explain his plans in person later today ..."

Chloë was searched more closely in the foyer of Number 10, every item in her handbag inspected. The policeman nodded and she stepped through a metal detector. Milne was waiting.

"You must be Chloë," he said. "Crikey, I wish all my spooks were made like you!"

She ignored the comment.

"Well, don't just stand there gawping," he said. "Come on in and have a peek around the old bachelor pad. All a bit formal down here. I don't mind admitting, upstairs is where the business of keeping Great Britain PLC on track gets done."

Something made Chloë think he had said this before. At the landing she paused. "Is that the ladies? Do you mind?"

"Of *course* not," he roared. "I'd use the disabled though, if I were you. I'll wait here, we don't let people just wander around Number 10 willy-nilly, you know. Especially not MI6's finest ... goodness knows what you might find."

Chloë leaned against the lavatory door to catch her breath. When she was calm she placed her phone on the floor and stamped on it; the two sides fell apart to reveal the recorder and the squiggle of black spaghetti that would connect it to her shirt button, which concealed a lens. Also inside were three cocktail sticks with small strips of masking tape wound around them, which she used to attach the rig to her body. She put on her blouse, dropped the broken phone into the tampon bin and emerged.

The Prime Minister raced up the stairs ahead of her and they went into his flat.

Oh, shit.

A Nace machine stood in the porch – they detected electronic circuits, making it impossible to be wired. Chloë had sat with one a hundred times at Vauxhall Cross. She braced herself for the thin warble of its alarm, for outrage and arrest, for captivity and ...

Nothing happened.

"Don't tell Dennis, but I disabled it," Milne hissed conspiratorially. "Did it myself with a spanner and brute force. Bloody thing kept interrupting *The Archers*. Massive pain in the arse."

C was sitting rather primly with his knees together, as if the mess in the flat was contagious. Amid coffee cups and cake-smeared plates, John Toland's *Adolf Hitler* lay open on a page about the Führer's upbringing. Milne had an abusive father too, it was part of his 'story'.

"Down to business," said C. "First off, David Livingstone."

Chloë held up her hand. "There's something I need to tell you both."

"Chloë, that's against protocol. You know everything comes through me before the Prime Minister ..."

"Oh pipe down, will you?" said Milne. "Let her speak."

"Thank you, Prime Minister." A serious smile. "Before I tell you this, there's something I want you to know about me."

"Go on."

"My great-great-grandfather on my mother's side was Sir Charles Napier, the Empire builder. My great-grandfather also served in India. And my grandad died in the siege of Singapore."

"What's your point?" asked C.

"I want you to know that the empire is in my blood."

C wriggled uncomfortably on the sofa.

"The files I sent you from Conteh's laptop weren't the only thing I found on there," she said.

"And you are telling us this now *why*?" said C dangerously. "You took it upon yourself to selectively edit what we received *why*?"

"Because what I discovered – I couldn't trust it to a courier, not even MI6. I couldn't be sure they wouldn't share your peccadilloes. *Our* peccadilloes."

The sofa was too low and the secret camera fired upwards in a cone, aiming for the face. It was possible she was only filming Milne's chest, so she angled her body downward.

"What did you find?" Milne's voice had turned low and deadly.

"They know," said Chloë. "They know what you've done. Spreading Ebola deliberately. Trying to rebuild the empire. They know it all."

At Thames House on Millbank, a junior MI5 officer unfurled the pellet of paper he'd found inside half an eggshell among empty packets of tofu and vegetable peelings.

He typed 'Kiwi-tech Vision' into Google and turned to his superior. "What do you make of this, boss?"

107

Di Angelo did a hundred press-ups, showered and went to the canteen. There he had a large breakfast (bacon, eggs, waffles with maple syrup) and a cup of black coffee, dwelling on every mouthful. Finally he strolled to the concrete apron beneath which the grimmest secrets of America are entombed. His CIA identity card caused consternation in the guardhouse and a list of arrivals was consulted.

"Sir," said the Ranger. "I can't let you in here without an appointment, sir."

"This is the pass you need," said di Angelo, looking him in the eye and *believing* that it was.

The soldier glanced at the orange piece of paper.

"I need to see your commanding officer," said di Angelo.

Special Agents were held in a certain awe. "Sir, yes sir."

Two minutes later a Master Sergeant Gompert stood before him: ginger-haired and barrel-chested, imposing as a column.

"He's got the right pass, sir," said the rifleman. "But we're not expecting him."

Blag had been laundered into fact.

"How can I help you, sir?" said Gompert.

"We'll talk in your guardhouse," said di Angelo – imposing authority.

The soldier weighed the minor breach of the rules against the figure who confronted him.

"Certainly, sir. It's cooler in there."

"Is that a Philly accent?" asked di Angelo.

"Sure is, sir."

"I'm from Kensington," said di Angelo in a Philly accent.

Gompert grinned. "No way! I'm from the Upper North."

Di Angelo's smile fell away.

"Sir," added Gompert. "What can I do for you today, sir?"

"I'm a CIA Special Investigator," said di Angelo. "I'm here to carry out an audit of your security."

"An audit?" Gompert frowned. "I wasn't told ..."

"It wouldn't be much of an audit if you knew I was coming, would it?"

Di Angelo watched the good sense of this statement settle in the soldier's brain. And here was the deviousness of his plan: for an unannounced visit was only logical if he was to judge the security measures in their usual state of operation. He could very reasonably demand to be taken deeper and deeper to inspect the automated gates and checkpoints, insuring everything worked as it should; penetrating the concentric barriers that separated him from the *Disciplina* like growth rings in a tree trunk.

The top page on di Angelo's clipboard had boxes to be filled out, rating the perimeter security. Gompert was gladdened to see his men had been judged ten out of ten for awareness.

"Come with me, sir," he said.

Di Angelo's left iris and the structure of the blood vessels in his hand were scanned, then he strolled through the steel fence and out across the concrete, already baking in the tropical sun. A small outhouse protruded from the centre with steel blast-doors and a card reader.

"I'm going to see whether I can override this door," di Angelo explained.

He produced a laptop, connected to a blank white card. Gompert peered with interest at the lines of code swarming across the screen as di Angelo placed the card on the reader. There was a beep and a red light came on. He ran another programme; it had the same result.

"Good," said di Angelo.

He rated the secondary gates ten out of ten too.

"Ok, let's go inside," he added.

Gompert swiped his own card and went to place his thumb on the reader.

He pulled back.

"Sir, out of interest, sir – if the programme had worked, how would you have provided a fingerprint?"

Di Angelo placed a square of jelly on the pad and the door swung open.

"What in the …"

"Jello picks up fingerprints. I got yours while we were in the guardhouse. You didn't notice."

Gompert's face reddened as di Angelo marked him down on page three.

Before di Angelo entered, he paused. He stared at the sky. He watched a little bird skitter and dive across the tarmac. He took three deep breaths of air. An onlooker would have said there was a definite reluctance to tear himself away from that very blue sky. They descended.

We are conditioned to obey authority from an early age. First by our parents; then by our teachers; then by our employers and some of us by our spouse. People love thinking of themselves as free-spirited, but in fact the compulsion to obey is encoded into human bone marrow. With soldiers, of course, this trait is even more strongly pronounced. And the predisposition to follow orders is heightened further when we feel ignorant about the situation we are in, when we think we're in the company of an expert who knows more about the matter in hand than ourselves. Di Angelo exploited these essential truths as he made Gompert lead him deeper into the facility – past voice scanners and devices that checked the bone structure of his throat; through doors opened by encrypted digital keys and floors made of twenty feet of steel. When soldiers were encountered, di Angelo's authority was magnified through Gompert's compliance, and his underlings obeyed unquestioningly. Page upon page were filled with di Angelo's stern evaluation of the most sophisticated physical defences yet devised, all of which opened for him like the Red Sea. He had penetrated half a billion dollars' worth of security features. Then he hit a wall of steel manned by men in blue overalls wearing the insignia of the Federal Government of the United States of America.

"Sir, I can't take you any further, sir. Military aren't permitted any deeper in than here."

The deputy director of the archive was summoned from the lower reaches, a snivelling, sharp-faced man called Ronaldson.

"What's going on here?" he said.

Gompert explained the situation.

"Audit?" said Ronaldson. "I wasn't told about any audit."

Di Angelo repeated the line about an audit being useless without the element of surprise and let slip that he was reporting directly to the director of the CIA.

"His documentation checks out, sir," said Gompert.

Ronaldson capitulated. He was a clever man, but intelligence only correlates slightly with lack of susceptibility to social engineering. He hadn't applied the 'What do I really know about this person?' test. His belief in di Angelo's identity outweighed his own security awareness.

This is going too smoothly, di Angelo reflected as his ears popped in a lift.

They descended to minus 74. The corridor was titanium and down here blue-suited guards were in abundance, glancing interestedly at the visitor.

"I want to inspect vault 4751," said di Angelo.

47/51 – the *Double-Roswell*, Deissler used to call it in his soft mocking tone. The year 1947, Area 51.

"You want to inspect vault 4751?" Ronaldson repeated carefully. "Did I hear that right?"

"You got it."

He pointed a Glock at di Angelo's head. "You're under arrest, pal."

108

"We don't know what you're talking about," said C.

When Chloë produced her dossier and laid photographs on the table, both men flinched.

"That's Dai Elliot," she said. "I trained with him. Everywhere he went, he was photographed. And the outbreak was documented."

"Documented?" said C sceptically. "By whom, might I ask?"

"By the Sierra Leonean Secret Service."

"Don't be ridiculous," said Milne. "That can't have. They're … they're the Sierra Leoneans."

Even under the strain of the moment, a wrinkle of annoyance traced C's brow.

"They tracked Dai all the way to Nigeria, where Ebola sprang up too. Within days."

Blood was draining from the Prime Minister's face.

Chloë slapped a photo of Serval on the coffee table. "I don't know who this guy is, but the Sierra Leoneans reckon he's MI6 too. And I wouldn't be surprised."

"But why are they keeping mum?" blurted Milne.

"Prime Minister, remember yourself," pleaded C.

"Because after the referendum the Contehs mean to blackmail you," said Chloë. "For tens of billions of pounds."

Milne's eyes flashed with malevolence. "*Kill them*," he hissed. "We have to *kill them*! In a road crash or something. Fix their cars or put a bomb in their helicopter."

"Prime Minister, *please*," C begged him. "I urge you to remember that she …"

Milne sent the coffee table flying, the contents of Chloë's dossier fluttering across the room.

"Can't you see she's on our side, Dennis?" he cried. "She's the one that brought this to us. If it wasn't for her, we'd be sunk."

C glanced at the Nace machine. Placated, he gave a little nod. Then he collapsed back into his chair like a wilting sunflower with one hand over his eyes.

At that moment the chief of MI5 was telephoning Number 10, asking to be put through to the Prime Minister urgently. He was refused: Milne had ordered that his conclave not be interrupted for anyone or anything.

Get the admission, Heston had told Chloë. *With allegations like these, nothing else will do. You need the actual words coming out of his actual mouth. Yes, I fucking well did it, I'm guilty as sin. I am a fucking war criminal.*

Chloë tracked Milne with her bosom as he sat down again.

"It was your plan, wasn't it?" she asked. "Using the Ebola virus to foment unrest. Stepping in as the hero, as a ploy to carve out a new Empire. You're a genius."

Milne dithered.

"Sir Charles Napier would have been impressed," she added.

Sir Charles Napier would have hated every sordid detail, she thought.

Milne plumped up his collar. "Yes, yes it was me, seeing as you ask. The whole thing. Though Sir Dennis here's had my back, haven't you, Dennis?"

"I, er, I saw commendable ambition in your proposals," C mumbled.

Gotcha.

The chief of MI5 had got through to Downing Street's police bureau; but convincing the junior officers of his identity was taking a few moments.

Once you've got the admission, get the hell out. Heston again. *Don't get cocky. Don't start enjoying it too much. Just vamoose, sod off out of there as soon as you decently can.*

Milne and his spy chief had launched into a dialogue about the best way to assassinate a head of state. Should they wait until the referendum, or act without delay? Bumping him off now would look fishy at best.

"Here's the pen drive," interrupted Chloë. "It's the only copy, obviously. So if it's ok with you, I'm going to get on with my job. We've got a *Disciplina* to find."

"Go, go, in the name of god, go," said Milne.

She left the two men in full crisis mode.

That crisis was about to get a damned sight worse.

A junior civil servant met Chloë outside the flat to escort her from Number 10, and she took the staircase as swiftly as she dared. She emerged onto Downing Street. Reporters pontificated away, moulding news into theatre with flourishes and sweeping arms. Soon they'd have something to *really* get excited about. With jerky strides, Chloë headed for the St James's Park exit. Five MI5 officers burst onto the street from Whitehall and sprinted for Number 10. They didn't see her vanishing through the security gates at the other end of Downing Street.

Out onto Horse Guard's Parade. Tearing through St James's Park. Kicking off her high heels, a flock of pigeons sent skittering away skyward. Jake was waiting for her in the car.

"Got him," she screamed. "Got him, got him, got him!"

"Oh you little bloody *beauty*!" Jake stamped on the accelerator and the Volvo fairly raced down Birdcage Walk.

In Downing Street a bit of a scene was taking place.

109

"I'm going to have to ask you to come with me," said Ronaldson. "We're going to the surface."

The guards levelled machine pistols at di Angelo.

"What are you playing at?" shouted di Angelo. "Point those guns at someone else, man."

"There's one vault here with special orders attached," said Ronaldson. "One room we're not permitted to open without the direct, verbal orders of the President of the United States. If asked to do so, we are to apprehend the individual. That's you. So like I said, you're under arrest, pal. Put your hands up or I'll shoot you now."

But di Angelo still had his Get out of Jail Free card to play.

"I'm going to ask you to do something," he said.

Ronaldson regarded him with infinite suspicion.

"In my jacket pocket is a letter," di Angelo continued. "Ask one of your men to pass it to you. Without reading it, that's very important."

One of Ronaldson's eyebrows twitched.

"Go on," he told the nearest guard.

He opened the letter.

Dear Patriot,
THIS IS A TEST.

*If you are being shown this letter, the Director of the
Central Intelligence Agency congratulates you on your watchfulness. The United States of America needs more citizens
of your calibre. The Special Investigator showing you this
letter has made a note of your name and your vigilance
will be included in his final report. You are now required to
enable the Special Investigator to audit the performance of
your colleagues.*

*Thank you for your devotion to duty and the American
people.*

Robert Ardrey.

A single eye swivelled from the letter to di Angelo and back to the
letter. A breath escaped Ronaldson's mouth; his eyebrow stopped
twitching and the ghost of a smile traced his countenance.

He gave a fractional nod. "You may proceed."

All along the corridor the tension went out of necks and backs.

Ronaldson had missed every warning sign. The demand
to override established process (essential for gaining access).
Urgency (no time to refer up). Strange requests (a major red
flag). Name-dropping and flattery (and this really should have
put him on guard). Di Angelo had played the man for a fool.

At the end of the corridor was door 4751, nothing unusual
to mark it out. For fifteen minutes di Angelo fed junk code into
the card, which beeped ineffectually at the door. Ronaldson
seemed gratified.

"You didn't see it," he said. "Did you?"

"What's that?"

"Up there."

There was a hole in the titanium doorframe big enough to slot
a matchstick into. From his wristwatch Ronaldson drew out a
single metal pin, a few Byzantine notches at the end.

"It's with me at every moment," he said. "The wizened-looking
guy who normally comes – you know him?"

"Deissler."

"That's him. In and out the whole time. Wakes me up in the middle of the night. Interrupts me when I'm having sex with my wife. Sends me away once he's got the key." And in a hoarse whisper: "My god, how I've wondered what's in this room."

"You're about to find out."

Ronaldson inserted the pin and there was a deep humming, like the warp drive of a spaceship. The doors rolled open.

"What in the ..."

A darkened room, the eye drawn to a central plinth illuminated by dozens of spotlights. Across it were laid strips of yellowed linen, marked with hundreds of characters that were archaic and strange. The complete and unabridged *Disciplina Etrusca*, in all of its ancient glory. This book had been wielded by Roman consuls; borne onto the field of Austerlitz by Napoleon Bonaparte; gazed upon by Queen Victoria and Prince Albert, the direst secret of the Imperial age.

"I want you and your men to leave now," said di Angelo. "Go to a different level."

Ronaldson had recovered. "I ... I can't do that, sir. Not for you."

"That's a shame." Di Angelo rolled up his left trouser-leg and plunged his pen deep into the calf. A transparent liquid pooled on the floor. It smelled faintly like hydrogen peroxide.

"What is this?" Ronaldson took a step back. "What are you doing?"

"I'm sorry, man," said di Angelo.

He stabbed himself in the other calf and a milkier liquid flowed out. The first substance was C-Stoff, the second was D-Stoff; together they make a crude and volatile jet fuel. Suddenly Ronaldson saw the danger and went for his gun, but already it was too late. The puddles were about to touch.

Di Angelo smiled. He would be in heaven soon. Perhaps he would meet Andy there. They could be friends. The liquids connected and there was a quite tremendous explosion.

110

By Jake Wolsey, Special Correspondent

THE PRIME MINISTER *has resigned after a plot he masterminded to spread the Ebola virus and enable his designs for a new British Empire in West Africa was exposed by this newspaper.*

MI6 *agents deliberately infected entire villages in Sierra Leone and Nigeria in order to destabilise both countries and facilitate a British military takeover. Irrefutable evidence of the conspiracy was obtained in the form of secretly recorded footage of Victor Milne and the Chief of MI6, Sir Dennis Amaoko, admitting to the scheme. Photographs of MI6 agents at work and other leaked documents also point to the veracity of the claims. At least 30,000 people have died in the outbreaks, while Sierra Leone is shortly due to vote in a referendum to transfer its government to Westminster in perpetuity. The revelations are already being compared to Watergate.*

Confronted with the evidence yesterday afternoon, Mr Milne tendered his resignation to fight the allegations. He was due to visit Buckingham Palace this morning to offer The Queen an account of his actions and seek permission to dissolve the government. A snap general election is expected before the end of the year and the Home Secretary has become acting Prime Minister. Her first action was to invite a UN peacekeeping force to take over in Sierra Leone. It is thought British troops will remain in Nigeria for now, as a disordered withdrawal could put frontline soldiers at risk.

The White House has released the following statement from the President of the United States: "I am shocked and appalled to hear these allegations, which, if true, cast a mark of terrible shame against our longest-standing ally.

"There can be no excuse, no justification, for such wicked deeds. I will be ensuring these matters are investigated by the War Crimes Tribunal at The Hague at the earliest opportunity.

"The British people themselves, however, remain friends and cousins of the United States. The shameful actions of one man and his handful of acolytes must not be allowed to besmirch the good name of a nation with a long and noble history of standing up for freedom and confronting tyranny. His ambitions were not their ambitions, his crime is not their crime."

In a day of fast-moving developments:

- Britain's membership of Nato and the UN Security Council has been suspended with immediate effect.
- Sir Dennis Amaoko was found dead in a car near his home in Barnet, north London. Police sources say it appears he took his own life.
- The Scottish National Party disassociated the Scottish people from the government's actions and demanded a new independence referendum immediately.
- There have been suggestions that the full-blown constitutional crisis Britain finds itself in may see the dissolving of the Commonwealth, although the Monarchy itself is not thought under threat.

There have been calls for The Queen to make a public statement. There is however no suggestion that Her Majesty was aware of the plot in any way.

Alison Tovey, leader of the Opposition, said: "Victor Milne appears to have presided over a crime of a heinousness not perpetrated by British hands since the slave trade. Now justice must take its course.

"I applaud the heroic investigative journalism that brought this to light."

A total of 48 British soldiers died during the invasion of Sierra Leone, while 17 have already lost their lives in Nigeria.

Sandra Brabham, mother of Captain James Brabham, 29, killed in Kano two days ago, said: "I am sickened to think that my eldest son may have sacrificed his life to satiate the monstrous and egotistical plans of a man …"

(Story continues pages 2 –35).

BENEATH THE STORY, by Jake Wolsey, Special Correspondent.

While exposing crimes perpetrated by the British Secret Service I was forced to live in hiding for more than two years, during which time numerous attempts on my life were made. But mine was not the only sacrifice. Two whistleblowers at MI6 were instrumental in bringing the matter to light. The name of the first is being withheld for their own safety. The second, Jennifer Frobisher, is missing and presumed dead. But for their heroism, these deeds may have gone unpunished. This newspaper pays tribute to them.

111

So it was that Waring, Heston and their new star reporter came to be standing with arms over each other's shoulders like footballers during a World Cup penalty shootout to watch the Prime Minister resign. As the door to Number 10 opened, a newsroom which had spent twenty-four hours in tumult became that rarer thing: silent. History was unfolding before them. Milne shuffled to the lectern and looked at his feet for a long time. He appeared on the verge of tears.

"I am hereby resigning this great office," he began. "Though I deny every word of these allegations, I know well enough that when the sands of politics shift and turn against a man, he can no more fight his destiny than he might Fate itself."

Milne took a step away from the lectern – then returned, as if he could not bear to be parted from it, and glared at the cameras.

"Above all, I enjoin the people of Britain to cherish their Commonwealth and uphold it, to the death."

"Just bizarre," whispered Heston. "The man's lost his mind."

With that Milne departed, sloping off along Downing Street in a blaze of flashes, his rounded shoulders suddenly those of a worn old school caretaker, not the global statesman nor the builder of Empire. Jake Wolsey, a man who had fought Fate and won, watched him go. Outside the gates Milne was read his rights, handcuffed and placed in a scuffed old police Transit van like a common criminal. The last photograph captured a morose stare through the vehicle's window up at Big Ben as Milne thought about all it stood for; all he had betrayed. Winston Churchill gave the van a flinty glare as it circled Parliament Square.

On a big screen in a corner of the newsroom, Jake spotted something. He slipped his editor's embrace and took a few steps towards it: hesitant, dazed, his heart hammering a double-beat. The plasma screen was split into twenty different feeds. All but one was fixated on Westminster, but Fox News had cut to a different story. The pictures came from a news plane, circling an atoll in the Indian Ocean. Smoke billowed upwards, as if the island was a live volcano. Jake enlarged the feed until it filled the screen, the vapours pouring towards him as the plane circled, and clenched a fist.

He did it.

Then a curious thing happened. Just as one might spot fanciful shapes in clouds on a summer's day, the smoke seemed to form the silhouette of a cloaked man in a bicorne hat. A hat that was once worth forty thousand men. But it simply faded away. Something departed Jake then, some shadow that had been with him a long time. He had a new lightness in his chest, and he felt too the eye of Fate turn from him, turn away from earth and man, as if bored with its plaything: seeking some new bauble with which to while away an infinity of time and space. And even a measure of *respect*. For what a mortal man could do, when he put his mind to it.

"Let's get cracking," said Heston. "We've got a newspaper to write."

"I have to go to Islington," said Jake. "I need to go and get something."

The news editor was about to answer back, but he merely nodded. "All right Jake-lad, I guess you've earned an afternoon off."

Before he left Jake was seized by an impulse and he took the lift to the roof, staring into the heavens. The spires of the Tower of London could be seen protruding over the rooftops a few miles away. It was a clear blue sky. He thought of Jenny and hoped she was at peace. He thought of Chloë too, what she had told him in the car. It might be interesting to get to know her; but it would be just too damn weird. Finally he thought of Kanisha, who had tracked him down in Burundi of all places: as if sent there by the whims of providence.

There was something about her.

He wasn't going to contact her yet. He needed to do nothing for a while, to digest everything that had happened. But sooner or later, he decided, he would ask Kanisha out for a coffee. And he did not need the Book of Fate to know she would say yes.